ADAM HAMDY

Red Wolves

PAN BOOKS

First published in paperback 2021 by Macmillan

This paperback edition first published 2021 by Pan Books
an imprint of Pan Macmillan
The Smithson, 6 Briset Street, London EC1M 5NR
EU representative: Macmillan Publishers Ireland Limited,
Mallard Lodge, Lansdowne Village, Dublin 4
Associated companies throughout the world
www.panmacmillan.com

ISBN 978-1-5098-9924-1

9 8 7 6 5 4 3 2 1

A CIP catalogue record for this book is available from the British Library.

Typeset in Scala by Jouve (UK), Milton Keynes
Printed and bound by CPI Group (UK) Ltd, Croydon, CR0 4YY

Visit www.panmacmillan.com to read more about all our books
and to buy them. You will also find features, author interviews and
news of any author events, and you can sign up for e-newsletters
so that you're always first to hear about our new releases.

For Amy

Part One

Part One

Chapter 1

Hell had a name.

In Arabic it was *Al Aqarab*. In English, Scorpion, one of the most notorious prisons in the Arab world. Elroy Lang had been in the sweltering hole for seven hours, during which he'd been tested for Covid-19, stripped of his clothes, given a drab grey tunic and matching trousers, plastic shoes, and an orientation that would have bewildered most people. He'd been served his evening meal in a huge cafeteria and had felt the eyes of four hundred inmates on him, all imagining ways they could exploit the new arrival. Elroy had eaten the rancid prison slop calmly, confident no one would make a move under the nose of the grim-faced, armed Egyptian prison guards who patrolled the vast hall.

After their meal, they'd been led to their cells. Elroy had been allotted a communal cell with seventy other men, all roasting in the August heat, cooled by nothing more than the faintest breath of desert air coming through three barred windows. Elroy lay on a low bunk in the darkest corner of the cell, furthest from the door. It was a place for victims, a spot easily encircled by a crowd of bodies to block the view from the door. Elroy was happy to be there because the man he was looking for was lying on the bunk next to him. The ends of their beds met in the apex of the dark corner. The bribes Elroy had paid to get into Al Aqarab on the relatively minor charge of outraging public decency, the money that had changed hands to ensure the correct cell assignment, had all been worth it. Here was the broken man he'd come to see; Ziad Malek.

Born and raised in America to Egyptian immigrant parents, Ziad had once been a confident, handsome minor-league villain who'd been arrested in Cairo on a drug smuggling charge, and was now thirteen months through a seven-year sentence. His wavy brown hair was lank and matted, his once handsome, tanned face now marred by a broken nose and scars, and his wrist and ankle bones bulged through too little flesh. His uniform hung off his emaciated six-foot frame, and was stained with filth. He oozed the sour stench of sweat and urine. But it was his sunken eyes that gave the greatest hint of his suffering in this cruel place. They were hollow and dead, and looked blankly at Elroy with all the hope of a corpse. Elroy held the man's gaze across the small patch of rough concrete that separated their bunks.

'*Homa hi igi delwati,*' Ziad said in the flat tone of the damned. *They will come now.*

'Good,' Elroy replied. 'You've suffered enough.'

Despair held Ziad too tightly – he didn't react to Elroy's words, and simply responded with the same blank stare.

Time ticked by slowly and with each passing moment the air thickened with the odours of so many bodies. The rhythmic sound of heavy breathing and loud snores almost drowned out the toots and hum of distant traffic.

Elroy sensed movement on the other side of the cell, and looked across the large space to see four shadows rise. As they stepped away from their bunks, they murmured conspiratorial words to each other. They picked their way past the beds that were haphazardly packed into the baking room. For every man that was asleep another was awake, and Elroy could see the glint of eyes watching, some with relief as the shadows passed, some with perverse anticipation of what was to come. The cell crackled with expectation and anticipation as the four figures drew near.

When they were a few paces away, they took proper form and shape, and Elroy could distinguish their features from the darkness. All four were well-nourished, muscular and had the cruel, hungry faces of predators. The man at the head of the group was the block *bey*, or boss, a triple murderer named Magdi who'd killed his wife and in-laws for an inheritance. Elroy had been warned that he was a ruthless, sadistic man who led the gang of psychopaths who ruled the block. Why they'd chosen to brutalize Ziad Malek was a mystery. Maybe he'd angered them, or perhaps they knew he wouldn't fight back. Elroy glanced at Ziad, and saw the man was frozen with terror. Tears glistened as they rolled down his face and soaked into the filthy mattress beneath him.

'*Amrekani*,' Magdi whispered to Ziad, using the Arabic word for American. '*Hertha waat al madrassa.*' *It's time for school.*

Magdi's words left little doubt as to his violent intention. Elroy didn't like the odds of a brawl. Four against one with his back to the corner left far too much to chance. Much better to send a message, one that would be felt throughout Scorpion prison.

Elroy lay still until Magdi was a couple of paces from Ziad's bunk, and then he got to his feet. He sensed hesitation from the big block boss. The man wasn't used to being challenged.

'*Na'ame, ya ghabi. Hi'etla sahala le'ek,*' Magdi said menacingly. *Sleep, you fool, it will go easier for you.*

Elroy stood his ground and saw Magdi's face twist into a sneer.

'*Tiyab. Hertha tariq helwa cammaan,*' he snarled. *OK, this way is also nice.*

He swung a heavy fist at Elroy and was surprised when the lithe, athletic American reacted like lightning. Elroy raised his elbow to block the blow and popped a jab at Magdi's nose. It wasn't designed to floor the man, just disorientate him, and it did exactly that. He stumbled back, clutching his face, and Elroy saw Magdi's three accomplices rush forward. He didn't have much time. He punched the block boss in the throat and when the man's hands went down to instinctively soothe the pain, Elroy grabbed Magdi's left wrist, twisted it and pulled the man into a choke hold. The message had to deter Magdi's accomplices and would have to be heard throughout Scorpion prison, but it had to be felt most powerfully by Ziad Malek, who was watching the fight in utter amazement.

Elroy grabbed hold of Magdi's skull and drove his index and middle fingers into the man's eye sockets. Magdi screamed and clawed at Elroy's hands, but Elroy ignored the pain and resisted his efforts. The three henchmen rushed forward as Magdi let out a soul-shredding howl. Elroy felt cloying warm blood run over his fingers and, satisfied the job was done, he pushed the screaming, blinded man towards his horrified accomplices.

'Come closer, and you all die,' Elroy said.

The three men took hold of their wailing leader, and hesitated as the cell filled with the sounds of people waking up and the shouts of approaching guards. Blood formed dark pools where Magdi's eyes should have been, and spilled down his anguished face. The horror was too much for his men, and Elroy stared them down as they dragged the mutilated man towards the door.

When they were nothing more than shadows in the darkness on the other side of the cell, Elroy looked down at Ziad and was pleased to see a broad, almost hysterical smile on the man's tearful face.

'You don't have to be afraid anymore,' Elroy assured him. 'You're with me now. The dark days are done.'

Chapter 2

Ziad woke the following morning afraid the events of the previous night had been a dream, but the bloodstains on the floor by his bunk were real enough. The American, who'd only arrived in Al Aqarab the previous day, brimming with quiet confidence, had been hauled off by prison guards after his fight with Magdi. But he must have been returned in the early hours while Ziad enjoyed his first unbroken night's sleep in months, because he was lying on his bunk now, watching Ziad with his piercing blue eyes.

Ziad had been confident and cocksure once. He experienced something approaching grief when he recalled the way he'd once swaggered through life. That man had died the day he'd come to Al Aqarab, and his body had been taken over by a pitiful wretch. To begin with, in the early hours of each night, immediately after Magdi and his men had brutally beaten him, Ziad would lie in his bunk picturing the revenge he'd take on all the people who'd sent him to this place. He'd imagined their cries of anguish as they suffered at his hand. But after a while the dreams of vengeance were swept away like wisps of smoke on a cruel wind of despair, and instead his sleepless nights were spent planning his own end. His thoughts were black with the bleak acceptance that one day, when he could no longer take the torment of the place, his life would end by his own hand.

But all that had changed, and now, for the first time in months, he'd slept untroubled by nightmares, and the man responsible for his new-found peace seemed nothing less than a shining hero.

'Thank you,' Ziad said, but before he could say anything else, the cell came alive with commotion as the guards entered with their customary shouts of, '*Yala, yala, ya hayawanaat!*'

Come on, come on, you animals.

Ziad got to his feet and joined the line of inmates shuffling towards the door. Seventy serious criminals walked silently through the cell block towards the cafeteria, while Muqtada, the head guard, explained the prison was on special measures after the violence of the previous night. The men of each cell would take their meals separately, there would be no exercise and the prison would be on lockdown until the deputy governor felt certain the incident would not be repeated. There were mutterings of discontent, and Ziad glanced back to see the American being jostled by those around him. Up ahead, Magdi's three goons, Basha, Tawfik and Riaz, eyed the American angrily.

The vast cafeteria was strangely quiet when Ziad and his cellmates entered. Normally alive with the squabbles, boasting and complaints of hundreds of men, the only other people in the room were the armed guards, who seemed particularly attentive. Ziad grabbed a plastic tray and joined the line to receive his allotted meal of *fool* and *ta'amaya*; fava bean stew and a falafel made of the same bean. Ziad went to an empty table and sat alone. He'd lost weight since his conviction, largely thanks to Magdi's theft of most of his food at every meal.

Ziad wasted no time, wolfing his food as he hunched over his tray with one hand coiled around it protectively. He scanned the cafeteria for Magdi's men and saw them three tables away, but for once he wasn't the target of their animosity. Their eyes were on the American, who was in the food line. Ziad did a double take when he saw the inmate serving the American hand over a can of Coca-Cola, a luxury unheard of in Al Aqarab. Ziad's eyes flitted back to Magdi's men, and he caught sight of a flash of steel beneath the table. Basha was armed with a shiv. Ziad flushed with shame. If he warned the American or told the guards, Magdi's men would surely punish him. So, disgusted with himself, Ziad turned his back on the line and focused on finishing his meal as quickly as possible. The brash man he'd once been was long gone, supplanted by a faint shadow who lacked courage, hope or ambition.

Ziad heard movement behind him. When he turned, his stomach lurched at the sight of the American heading straight for him. Standing a little over six feet tall with a thick tuft of wavy blond hair, the man, who must have been in his mid-thirties, had the muscular frame of a boxer, and carried himself with the same easy confidence he'd exuded the previous day. He seemed untroubled by the night's violence or the murderous looks he was getting from Magdi's men. Ziad was aghast when the American sat beside him. The man was forcing him to choose a side, but Ziad couldn't face the consequences and turned to finish his meal.

'You don't look well, Ziad,' the American said.

Ziad glanced up to see the man's piercing eyes locked on him.

'My name is Elroy Lang and I came here to find you.'

'Came here?' Ziad scoffed at the idea anyone would venture into Al Aqarab by choice.

'Yes,' Elroy replied. 'I wanted to find you because I believe we can help each other.'

Ziad couldn't suppress a bleak smile. How could this man talk of helping each other in this place? Ziad noticed Magdi's men whispering and gesturing towards Elroy.

'We don't have long,' Elroy continued. 'My intervention last night checked them, but they're mustering their courage and they'll soon come for revenge.'

'This isn't my fight,' Ziad said.

'Oh, it is. I've heard what those men have done to you. I'm offering you a chance.'

'A chance for what?' Ziad asked hesitantly.

'For revenge,' Elroy replied. 'On them. On everyone who put you here. On Deni Salamov.'

Elroy's words were like a cattle prod, and sent a jolt of life coursing through Ziad's body. He'd dreamed of such things, but to hear them voiced was almost too much to bear. Despair and misery had hollowed him out to such an extent, even the faintest hope strained the husk that remained.

'You have suffered, Ziad,' Elroy said. 'It's written all over your face. I'm offering you my friendship.'

Ziad's eyes filled with tears. This was the first time anyone had spoken to him kindly in more than a year. He glanced over his shoulder and saw Magdi's men rise from their seats. They started towards him, their intent clear. Basha's hand was curled against his side, undoubtedly holding the blade.

'What do you want me to do?' Ziad asked urgently, and a faint smile of satisfaction crossed Elroy's face.

'I was worried you'd lost all hope,' Elroy said. 'We need to leave this place.'

He took the Coca-Cola can from his tray and twisted the bottom to reveal a false compartment. Inside was a small metal canister that had a ring pull. Magdi's men were only a few feet away, and Ziad's skin crawled with anticipation of imminent violence.

'This is the key,' Elroy said, as he reached into his pocket and produced two surgical masks with air filters on either side of the nasal bridge. 'Put this on,' he instructed, thrusting one of the masks across the table.

Elroy pulled the other mask over his face.

'Hey,' a guard yelled, and the cry acted as a spur to action.

Magdi's men ran forward, and a fight broke out on the other side of the cafeteria. Ziad couldn't tell if it was genuine or staged to cover the murder attempt, but the two men slugging it out succeeded in capturing the guards' attention, and soon other inmates were getting involved in the scuffle.

'Put the mask on and pull the pin,' Elroy said. 'It's that simple.'

Ziad looked at the objects on the table in front of him, but he was robbed of the opportunity to take action by firm hands pulling him from his seat. Riaz and Tawfik had hold of him, and Basha was squaring up to Elroy.

As the familiar slaps and punches began, Ziad felt a fury he hadn't experienced since his first few days in Al Aqarab, an anger so visceral it almost frightened him. He did something he hadn't done for more than a year; he struggled, and the men holding him were surprised by his uncharacteristic resistance. He managed to lunge for the table and grabbed the canister and mask. As his two captors yanked him back,

Ziad saw Elroy break Basha's arm at the elbow, and as the big man shrieked in pain, Elroy snatched the blade and plunged it his throat. In that moment, Ziad longed for Elroy's strength and fearlessness. He brimmed with anger at the thought of what these men and this place had done to him. Fury consumed him, and for the first time in months he wasn't afraid.

Tawfik and Riaz had stopped hitting him and were watching in horror as their friend fell to the floor, clutching the bloody hilt sticking out of his neck. Ziad took advantage of their horror, put the mask to his face and pulled the trigger on the canister.

The device popped like a loud firework and filled the air with a cloud of white powder that spread throughout the cafeteria. Guards and inmates stopped struggling, and watched in puzzlement as the powder eddied and swirled its way through the room. For a moment, all violence stopped and the place fell silent.

Then Tawfik started choking. His eyes went wide and he clutched at his throat, gasping as he emitted coarse, guttural cries. It was a short, painful death, and it brought Ziad nothing but pleasure to see one of his tormentors suffer. Riaz joined him and soon almost every man in the cafeteria was choking to death. Only Ziad and Elroy were unaffected – Ziad felt nothing but warmth. All these cruel men deserved the horror and fear that blighted their final moments. In less than twenty seconds, the room was completely still.

Elroy wiped his bloody hands on his tunic as he joined Ziad. 'You've shown me what I needed to see,' he said, 'that there's still strength in there.' He tapped Ziad's chest. 'You're going to need it.'

Ziad surveyed the carnage. He'd never killed anyone before,

but he felt no remorse at crossing that line in this hateful place. The sound of the alarm startled Ziad and he looked at Elroy questioningly.

'It's time for us to leave,' the American said, heading for the door that led to the main block.

Still stunned by his change in fortune, Ziad followed Elroy. As he picked his way past the fallen bodies and saw the pained rictus faces, a dark thought flashed through his mind.

You're a murderer now. Hell has spawned a new devil.

Chapter 3

Nothing about the building opposite gave the slightest hint the men inside peddled death. Passers-by saw only the gaudy red and white sign that proclaimed 'Top Racing'. It was fixed atop a low warehouse beside Jalan Sakeh, one of the principal north to south routes that cut through Muar, one of Malaysia's oldest towns. Scott Pearce shifted on the hard office chair that had been his perch for eight days. He'd broken into an unoccupied office block opposite the motorcycle repair shop the previous week and discovered the perfect location for a long stakeout. The three-storey block was separated from Jalan Sakeh by a small car park which served the surrounding businesses. The ground floor was divided into four units – a cafe, clothes shop, convenience store, and accounting firm. In the offices above them were an import–export business, a financial adviser, a general trader and a food and beverage supplier. Pearce was in the general trader's premises, surrounded by abandoned desks, broken old computers, mouldy files and musty carpet which had been chewed by rodents. It was a miserable place, but perfect for his needs. It had a functioning toilet, which he was careful to only flush at night, and the occasional, carefully planned visit to the convenience store kept him well supplied with food and drink.

He'd come to Muar on the trail of a gang of smugglers.

After taking down the Black Thirteen group, he'd refused Huxley Blaine Carter's offer of a job and had returned to the mission that had consumed him for the past two years: proving there were other, as yet unidentified conspirators involved in the terror attack he'd thwarted in Islamabad. Pearce's conviction that some of the perpetrators had escaped justice had led to his dismissal from MI6, but he hadn't allowed that to affect his determination, and had used his own money to finance his investigation.

Once the global travel restrictions of the Covid-19 pandemic had been lifted, Pearce had returned to Thailand, but hadn't gone back to Railay, the tropical paradise where he'd spent months posing as a climbing guide while investigating potential smuggling sites in the region. The last time he'd seen the golden sands of Railay beach, a cadre of Thai police officers and their criminal associates had been on his tail. He was too well known and his departure had been far too noisy to risk returning to the dreamy tourist retreat. Instead, Pearce had gone to Krabi, the main regional town, and bought an old fisherman's boat that was just about seaworthy. The hull was almost rotten, but the fifty horsepower Yamaha engine had been well maintained. He'd taken the leaky, flaking boat to Kok Arai, a tiny uninhabited island that lay off the Thai coast. Concealing the boat in a crag on the north of the island, Pearce had slung his small waterproof backpack on his shoulders and swum round the 300-metre-wide weathered mushroom of jungle-capped rock, until he'd reached the start of the limestone scar that he'd last tried to climb a little over four months earlier.

The wounds on his forearms had long since healed, but the scars were a permanent reminder of his encounter with

Lancelot Oxnard-Clarke and his far-right associates. The ugly, newborn flesh had no impact on Pearce's climbing ability, and after pulling on his climbing shoes, he had started up the arduous route he'd failed to ascend months before. This time, he'd cleared the brutal overhang, pulled himself onto the vertical face and quickly picked his way through a sequence of pinches and crimps until he hauled himself onto the summit, a small plateau covered in lush grass. Further from the edge was thick jungle, and, as he'd suspected, Pearce had discovered a well-camouflaged hollow that contained a portable hoist and a cache of four crates. He'd prised open one of the crates to find two dozen Kalashnikovs. He'd opened the others and secreted tiny tracking devices in each of them. The bugs, which he'd carried with him in his waterproof backpack, were powered by tiny lithium batteries and contained locator beacons similar to a cell sim card, to enable satellite tracking.

Pearce's backpack had held enough supplies to last a week, so he'd found a suitable hiding place in the surrounding undergrowth and had settled in to wait. He was looking for a group of smugglers he believed were linked to a Thai man he'd killed during the terror attack he'd foiled in Islamabad. The other terrorists he'd killed were local Pakistani recruits, but the Thai man was interesting. According to Thai Intelligence, his name was Chao Fah Jan, and they had a file on him that linked him to smuggling operations between Thailand and Malaysia. Pearce had been drummed out of Six because of his obsession with possible conspirators, and he'd followed the dead man's trail from Islamabad to Bangkok, to track down the smuggling gang.

He'd sat atop Kok Arai for three days and nights, waiting to see who came for the cache of weapons. Each morning when the sun rose, he could hear the distant sputter of engines far below as little boats shipped tourists out to the island to climb its myriad routes. There didn't seem to be as many climbers as there'd been before the pandemic, but there were enough to keep the local skippers in business. Pearce wondered whether his friend Ananada and his son Lek were down there. He couldn't risk sneaking a look to satisfy his curiosity. As long as he stayed on the small plateau, he wasn't worried about anyone finding him. The route he'd climbed was graded 8B and was the only way to his little patch of jungle – a deep ravine split the landmass, his column of stone cleaved from the rest of the mushroom-shaped island by a long-forgotten earthquake or tidal erosion. He watched tanned tourists summit the easier routes on the main island. Some of them would spend a while exploring, but most of them would simply pose for selfies before stashing their phones in water-proof pouches and making the nerve-racking jump from the edge to the sea far below. He'd hear their cries of delight as they surfaced.

Finally, on the fourth night, when the moon had been little more than a tiny cuticle, Pearce had heard the rhythmic sputter of an outboard motor. Thirty minutes later he'd sensed movement, and peering through the thick jungle, he'd seen a shirtless, lithe Thai man of no more than thirty crest the summit and pad through the jungle to the smuggler's cache. The man wore 5.10 shoes and his pumped forearms spoke of considerable climbing experience. He'd used a system of ropes to secure the portable hoist and had then lowered the four crates of Kalashnikovs. Pearce had heard multiple voices calling instructions from below, perhaps four or five men.

After about forty-five minutes, when the Thai climber had finished, he'd stowed the hoist and made the dive into the sea below.

Pearce had emerged from his hiding place and watched a thirty-foot fishing vessel head south-east. He'd been able to see three men lashing canvas over the crates of weapons. The climber and another two men sat near the pilot at the tiller. Pearce had gone to the other side of the small plateau and jumped into the warm water a hundred or so feet below. He'd swum to the crag where his small boat was hidden, ferreted in a larger rucksack for a satellite-enabled tablet computer, and, after booting it up, found two clear tracking signals moving south-east. Staying just out of visual range, Pearce had trailed the fishing vessel 200 miles south to Kuala Perlis, a Malaysian town located on the border with Thailand. There, he'd come ashore to discover the smugglers loading the crates into a small truck.

The bugs had made life easy, and after recovering his belongings from his little boat, Pearce had been able to track the shipment from a distance. First thing the following day, he'd bought a twenty-year-old Honda CR250 dirt bike for $300 and had followed the van south, stopping every so often to check progress on his tablet. His pursuit had led him through Malaysia and had finally brought him to the large motorcycle garage on Jalan Sakeh.

He'd parked his bike a block away and had scouted the neighbourhood before identifying the office that was to become his home. Breaking in had been a simple affair and he'd settled into a rhythm, watching the warehouse for sixteen hours a day, before setting up a camera that would cover the building while he slept. Each morning, he'd scrub through the footage to see what he'd missed, but so far there had been very little activity. No large vehicles came or went, and apart from a couple of motorcyclists who went into the building just long enough to be told their business wasn't welcome, Pearce only saw the same gang of six men. They turned up daily, riding in on a variety of high-powered sports bikes, and stayed in the building for a few hours before dispersing. On the second night, Pearce had broken into the warehouse and installed a camera and tiny listening device in the main space. The Kalashnikovs were still in the building, concealed behind crates full of old motorcycle parts. The tiny office computer was broken and the keyboard was covered in a thick layer of dust. The filing cabinets were empty and the shelves held nothing but a couple of old motorbike maintenance manuals. There was a latent smell of grease, but no other sign that the place had been used as a working garage for years. It was nothing but a thin cover for this criminal gang.

The camera and bug had yielded little. Each day, the men came into the warehouse, played cards, traded stories of sexual conquests and financial triumphs before going their separate ways. It was as though they were waiting for something.

On the ninth night, Pearce discovered what that something was. Two men in a blue Nissan Urvan approached the building slowly. The motorcycle men hadn't dispersed that day, and even though it was past midnight, they were still inside the warehouse. The surrounding businesses were shut, and the low houses that spread either side of the warehouse were dark. The delicious scent of the locals' late-night meals still hung in the warm tropical air, but kitchens had long since fallen quiet and the inhabitants were in bed.

Two of the motorcycle men opened the corrugated steel

doors and allowed the Urvan to drive into the warehouse. Pearce switched to the interior camera and saw the Nissan roll to a halt in the centre of the large space. The motorcycle men were gathered in a semi-circle, standing in front of the four crates of Kalashnikovs.

The two men in the van climbed out, nodded greetings at the larger group and swaggered round the vehicle. Pearce got the impression these men had seniority over the others. They opened the van's rear doors, and Pearce was dismayed to see faces inside. Four women, bound and gagged and wearing nothing but their underwear, were huddled together on one side of the flatbed. Their tear-streaked faces and fearful eyes said it all.

They were to be traded for the guns.

Chapter 4

Pearce sat back and shook his head. On screen, the motorcycle men were pawing at the four women, sizing them up. They were all white. Maybe they were relief workers whose drinks had been spiked in a bar, or students who'd been lured to Malaysia with the promise of well-paid work. Whatever method had been used to trap them in that van, the women all now faced the same ugly future. They trembled, their eyes downcast. One of them had wet herself. The leader of the motorcycle men, a paunchy man with a thick mop of black hair, indicated his satisfaction with the women and signalled two subordinates to load the crates into the vehicle.

Working alone was challenging. It demanded ingenuity and dedication, but Pearce preferred the hard hours and mental pressure to the politics of MI6. There was also no risk of betrayal. The Black Thirteen investigation had unmasked his former superior, Dominic McClusky, as a traitor, and Pearce suspected the man had orchestrated his dismissal from the service in order to prevent questions being asked about his own loyalties. Running solo, Pearce didn't need to have faith in anyone but himself, but there were disadvantages, and this dark moment in the deepest hours of the night was one of them. He had to make a choice. Go with the guns, which were likely to lead him higher up the food chain, or stay with the women, who were almost certainly destined for sex work in a Muar brothel. With a Six team behind him, Pearce could have tracked the guns and left the human traffickers to be picked up by his colleagues, but he was on his own, and immediate human misery trumped his investigation. He had trackers in the crates and decided to risk losing the guns in order to follow the women. Once he'd identified the women's final destination, he'd inform local police and make sure they were rescued safely, before using the signal from the tracking devices to return to the trail of the guns.

Pearce's plan was thrown into disarray when he saw a couple of the motorcycle men frogmarch two of the women towards the small office at the back of the warehouse. The women knew what was coming, and pleaded with the cruel men, while the others jeered and egged them on. When he'd been serving in the forces or working for Six, Pearce had watched horrors unfold and resisted his urge to intervene in order to protect the broader mission, but he wasn't about to do the same now. Working alone, he only had himself to answer to, and he couldn't stand by and do nothing.

Pearce went to his sleeping area in the corner of the room and picked up the battered ZEV Core Elite assault rifle he'd bought in Krabi. He slipped three magazines into the pockets of his lightweight bomber jacket and hurried from the room. He ran down the dank stairs at the rear of the building and unbolted the back door. He checked the alley and, finding it deserted, sprinted north to the nearest corner. High palms provided the cover of shadow as he ran the width of the office block and raced through the empty car park. The humid night was still, the air undisturbed by wind or noise until he crossed the street and heard the faintest sounds coming from inside the motorcycle garage. The noises grew louder as he got closer and he made out high-pitched shrieks and approving grunts and cheers. As he neared the corrugated steel double doors, Pearce glanced around to check the neighbouring bungalows. Their windows were dark, their inhabitants doubtless sleeping, unaware of the horrors being perpetrated yards away.

Pearce flipped the ZEV's safety. It wouldn't have been his first choice. The distinctive bronze barrel was far too visible for covert operations, but it had been the most reliable gun on offer from the low-rent Krabi gun dealer. The warehouse doors had been left ajar and Pearce crept to the narrow gap. The men were more or less where he'd last seen them. The men who'd brought the women were helping two of the motorcycle men load the crates into the van, while the leader of the biker crew and one of the others forced the remaining two women into a corner and pushed them to the floor. Pearce couldn't see what was happening in the office, but faint moonlight shone from the interior windows and he could see shadows cast against the east wall, two shapes, each an indistinct mass broken by the occasional distinguishable limb, as the two women struggled to resist their assailants. Pearce had no doubt the men would be armed, but they could only be carrying pistols or knives beneath their clothes, and he had the element of surprise.

He edged one of the doors open with his foot and crept inside. One of the men near the van sensed movement and cried out when he saw the intruder. Pearce shot him in the chest and the cry turned to a wet scream of pain. The two new arrivals ran for cover round the front of their van, while the three other men produced pistols. Two opened fire as Pearce ducked behind a steel column. He sprayed bullets at the two motorcycle men who hadn't had the sense to take cover. He caught the dark-haired leader of the gang in the legs and the man went down with a wail. The other was hit in the abdomen and collapsed with a pained cry. As Pearce concealed himself behind the metal support, the third grabbed one of the terrified women and put the muzzle of his gun to her head.

'Drop your weapon!' he yelled in Thai.

A deafening volley of automatic gunfire hit the steel column, enveloping Pearce in a shower of sparks. When the bullets stopped, he peered out to see one of the men duck back behind the van. The vehicle's lights flared and the exhaust rattled as the engine rumbled to life. The van was thrown into reverse and accelerated towards the doors, both men in the cab. Pearce opened fire on the nearside rear tyre and it burst with a satisfying pop. The sudden puncture sent the van veering out of control and it missed the doorway and collided with the adjacent wall.

Pearce seized the moment of confusion and shot the driver, hitting him once in the neck and once in the temple. As the man slumped forward, Pearce got a clear view of the motorcycle man holding the woman hostage through the passenger window. Believing the van had provided him with cover, the guy had taken his gun away from the woman's head. His startled eyes met Pearce's but he didn't move quickly enough and Pearce shot him through the van window, before rolling onto his side and opening fire on the legs of the second man in the van, which were visible beneath the vehicle as he climbed out. The man screamed and dropped his assault rifle as he fell to the floor, writhing in agony.

Gunfire from close range. Pearce rolled instinctively and tried to get to his feet, but as he rose, he caught sight of the two Thai men who'd taken the women into the office bearing down on him. They'd come through the double doors and must have climbed out of a window to get round the building and behind him. The taller of the two held a black pistol, which he was reloading. The other man came at Pearce with a huge hunting knife. Pearce tried to raise the barrel of the ZEV, but the knifeman was too close and swatted the muzzle aside as Pearce pulled the trigger. The bullets went wide and clattered into the steel doors. Pearce flipped the gun and tried to drive the stock into the knifeman's face, but he ducked and swung the huge blade at Pearce's head. Pearce jerked back and the keen edge sliced the air centimetres in front of him. The gunman had reloaded, but his line of fire was blocked by his ferocious comrade.

'Get out of the way,' he yelled in Thai, striding forward.

The knifeman lashed out with his boot and the fierce kick sent the ZEV flying from Pearce's hands. He was defenceless and outnumbered. His best chance was to engage the knifeman and use the guy's body to block the shooter. But the vicious, sinewy man wasn't stupid and jolted back as Pearce lunged for him. The gunman now had a clear line of fire and raised his gun, aiming it at Pearce's face. Two gunshots echoed around the warehouse.

The first popped the gunman's head like a melon. The second tore a hole through the knifeman's chest. He looked at Pearce in dismay, dropped the knife and pawed at the bloody opening as he fell to his knees. Moments later, he was dead.

Pearce looked at the figure striding through the doorway. Wearing black tactical gear, complete with protective vest and balaclava, and holding a smoking SIG MPX Copperhead was the woman he knew as Brigitte Attali, a former operative for

DGSE – French Intelligence – he'd encountered while investigating Black Thirteen. Her brilliant blue eyes shone with pride and as she removed her balaclava, her distinctive white hair glowed in the low light.

'That's the second time I've save your life, *n'est-ce pas?*' she said in her thick French accent.

Pearce stood upright and shook his head, trying not to betray his surprise at the presence of the capable woman.

'Impressive, huh?' Brigitte went on. 'Blaine Carter had me follow you when you left San Francisco. Those tracking devices you use made it quite easy, really. I also tapped into your video feed. When I saw the mess you were making, well . . . I couldn't stand by and let you get yourself killed. Coming in here was foolish. You've blown any chance of finding what you were looking for.'

'How'd you know—' Pearce began, but she cut him off.

'The report you wrote before you left Six made it clear you thought the conspirators were connected to the Islamabad attack through the Thai man you killed. But now it will take a feat of magic to pick up the trail.' She hesitated and smiled wryly. 'Still, it was commendable, trying to save these women.' She gestured at the four kidnap victims, who had gathered near the office door. They were still afraid, but had started to regain their composure. 'You were their knight in shining armour, but it seems that even a knight needs to be saved by the more powerful queen.'

'That's you?' Pearce asked.

'Of course,' Brigitte replied, checking her watch. She indicated her earpiece. 'One of the locals has called the police. They're about three minutes out. We should go.'

Pearce leaned down and picked up the pistol that had fallen

by the dead men. He walked towards the four women, glancing round the van to see the man whose legs he'd shredded. He was clutching at the bloody mess, weeping and moaning in pain.

'Do you speak English?' Pearce asked.

One of the women nodded. 'Thank you,' she said tearfully.

'The police will be here soon. If *they* give you any trouble –' he indicated the three wounded men, who were too focused on their serious injuries to concern themselves with the women – 'shoot them. The safety is off,' he advised, handing the pistol to the woman.

'Come on,' Brigitte urged.

Pearce joined her by the doors. 'I appreciate your help, but I meant what I said. I'm not working for the American.'

'Not even if it leads you to your objective?' she replied playfully. 'I said it would take magic for you to find the elusive conspirators. Well, you really should come and speak to the wizard who can make that happen.'

She hurried outside and, after a moment's pause, an intrigued Pearce followed her into the night.

Chapter 5

Deni Salamov must pay for what he's done. The words had become a refrain that cascaded through Ziad's mind, bringing with them a storm of anger which swept away all other emotions. Sometimes the words would rise unbidden. Other times they would come from Elroy Lang. Ziad knew what his companion was doing, stoking his hatred of the man who'd sent him to Al Aqarab. But he didn't mind. In his quiet moments, often when he was on the cusp of sleep, Ziad felt cloying guilt at the lives he'd taken during their escape. Some of those men had been evil, but not all, and who was he to have become their executioner? His nightmares were plagued by visions of the men rasping and choking out their final moments, so he embraced his righteous fury at every opportunity. His anger left no place for guilt.

Ziad and Elroy had been met outside the prison by a wiry Thai man who'd been introduced as Awut. The man had driven them across Cairo in an old Fiat and taken them to a safe house where they'd stayed the night before starting their week-long journey to America. Elroy had said little about himself other than to reveal that he worked for a group that wanted to revolutionize the drugs trade on the Pacific Coast. This meant they had a mutual interest in the fall of Deni Salamov. Having abandoned all hope of vengeance inside Al Aqarab,

Ziad was surprised at how quickly and powerfully the old fire was rekindled.

It took them seven days and numerous false passports to reach Seattle. The people Elroy worked for must have been well connected because they arrived on the West Coast without incident. Elroy took them to a three-bedroom house on Kenyon Street, in South Park, a run-down neighbourhood a couple of miles south of Seattle Port. It was a tumbledown wooden house on the kind of impoverished street where people knew it was better for their health to mind their own business. Elroy had spent their first evening quizzing Ziad about Deni's operation, confirming things he already knew, probing for details he didn't.

The next day, Elroy had gone out before Ziad was up and hadn't returned until the evening. Ziad had kicked around the house, watching TV, while Awut, the silent Thai sentinel, padded around the place like a caged tiger.

When Elroy finally returned, he said, 'There's something you need to see, Ziad.'

He took Ziad across town in a dilapidated Buick. Ziad felt a flush of humiliation and panic when he realized where he was being taken. They went to Point Edwards, to the condo where Essi Salamov lived. Deni Salamov's daughter had been the love of Ziad's life and being this close to her home pained him.

'Why are we here?' Ziad asked as they rolled to a halt across the street from Essi's building.

'You need to see what they've been doing while they left you to rot in prison,' Elroy replied. 'It's important you know. It will carry you through the difficult times ahead.'

Ziad watched the building with a growing sense of dread.

He knew what was coming, and as much as the prospect horrified him, he simply couldn't look away. He had to see it, he had to take in the scale of his betrayal. He kidded himself he was prepared for anything, but when Essi finally left her building arm in arm with another man, Ziad felt as though a giant hole had been torn in his guts. The hollow pain was made worse by the fact he recognized this tall white guy; his chiselled jawline and his tight frame like that of a long-distance athlete. He flashed a bright mouthful of perfect teeth at Essi, and his short brown hair fluttered in the ocean breeze, giving him a fun, impetuous air, when in reality he was a corrupt, greedy man. His name was Jack Gray and he was Deni Salamov's lawyer, but tonight he and Essi looked like a couple of catalogue models, smiling and chatting in groomed perfection. As they crossed the parking lot towards a black Porsche 911, Ziad pictured himself smashing the man's perfect teeth with a brick and drilling a couple of holes through his skull. Why not? He was a murderer now. A mass murderer with all the bodies of Al Aqarab to his name.

'Follow them,' Ziad said.

'We can't do anything to him,' Elroy replied. 'Not yet.'

Ziad flushed crimson. The fact this relative stranger was witness to the betrayal made it even more shameful.

'Follow them,' Ziad repeated through gritted teeth. 'I have to see this.'

The first heavy raindrops burst on the road as the Porsche left the parking lot. Elroy gave Ziad a sympathetic glance before he put the car in gear and followed.

Chapter 6

Jack took Essi to Rustica, the Italian restaurant on the corner of East Pine Street and 14th Avenue. The hostess tested them for Covid-19 before they were allowed inside. Ziad, unsettled by the terrible anger that burned within him, told Elroy to leave.

'I'll make my own way back to the house,' he said.

'You sure?' Elroy asked. 'You must have seen enough.'

Like a desperate addict, Ziad needed more. This woman, this beautiful heartless woman, was who he'd planned to spend his life with, and as painful as it was to see her with another, Ziad didn't feel he could leave. Not yet.

'Don't do anything to him,' Elroy cautioned.

'I won't,' Ziad replied, before he got out of the car.

He pulled the soft fabric hood of his jersey over his head to shield himself from the rain. He crossed the slick sidewalk as Elroy drove away, and took up a position in a shadowed doorway opposite Rustica. With Elroy gone, he didn't have to keep up a pretence, but he was still grateful for the autumn storm that whipped the worst of the Seattle rain into his face. The weather masked his tears and the sharp sting of each windblown drop was a tiny penance for his failure.

He'd promised her he wouldn't get caught, that he'd be careful, but in the end it hadn't been his assurances that had earned her blessing. Her father, Deni Salamov, his name now forever synonymous with treachery, had spoken to Essi and told her how important it was for Ziad to go to Cairo to open up another supply line. Ziad sneered at the memory. The trip had been important, but not for the reasons Deni had claimed. Ziad's stomach churned as he considered the possibility Essi had been in on what her father had planned. Had they both lacked the courage to reject him in person?

No, Ziad told himself. *Essi loved me*. That's why her father had sent him to Cairo and set him up. To get rid of him. In one move Deni neutralized a potential threat to his power and brought Ziad's unwelcome relationship with his daughter to an end.

But she'd moved on pretty quickly. The man sitting opposite her, Jack Gray, was nothing more than a thief. Jack had been Ziad's only point of contact after his arrest, and the lawyer had made it clear the Salamovs wanted nothing to do with him, and had even hinted they'd set him up. With Ziad out of the way, Jack had moved in and stolen the love of Ziad's life.

Ziad was in turmoil as he watched from the darkness and saw the young couple trade gentle touches, loving glances and soft words on the other side of the brightly lit restaurant window. Even if Essi had known his fate, she'd think he was destined to spend another seven years behind bars. He'd tried to phone her from Al Aqarab, but had never been able to get through. All her phone numbers had changed. As had Deni and Rasul Salamov's. He'd managed to reach Jack Gray once after he'd been moved to Al Aqarab, and the lawyer had reiterated that the Salamovs wanted nothing to do with him.

'*They sent you to Cairo,*' Jack had said. '*It should be obvious, even to you, what they really want.*'

Ziad's anger rose as he watched Jack reach across the table and take Essi's hand. The lawyer had his own reasons to cut Ziad off. Had they all colluded to get him out of the picture? No, he couldn't believe it of Essi. Nor could he blame her for moving on. Seven years was a long time. It was unreasonable to have expected her to wait for him.

You would have, a little voice said. *You would have waited until the end of time.*

And the fury built again, because Ziad knew the voice was right. He would have waited an eternity for her. But the eyes that once lit up his world were now turned to another.

Ziad wiped away the rain and tears and shrank into the doorway as Essi and her all-American jock left the restaurant. Jack the jock kissed her and ran down the street, heroically braving the weather to retrieve his car, while Essi waited under the restaurant canopy. But she didn't wait long. Once Jack was out of sight, she skipped into the rain, navigated the passing traffic and crossed the street. Ziad's heart thundered. She was coming for him, of that there was no doubt, but his stomach churned at the thought of what she might say.

'Zee, what the hell are you doing here?' she began. 'Dad told me you'd been arrested in Cairo.' She stood on the sidewalk a few paces from the doorway, her long black hair already grouping into thick tresses in the relentless down-pour. Her tanned face glowed with vitality in the light of the corner street lamp, and her azure eyes shone as brightly as ever. She wore a light woollen three-quarter length coat and the green dress Ziad had taken off so many times. He sensed no warmth from her and was dismayed that she hadn't even given him so much as a hug.

'I got out early,' he replied.

'And you decided you'd stalk me instead of phoning like a normal person,' Essi said accusingly. 'What happened to your nose? Did you break it?'

Ziad ignored the question. 'I tried calling. From prison. I tried phoning you, but I couldn't get through.'

'Oh, Zee.' Essi softened slightly and her face flashed with realization. 'I had to change my number and email. Dad said we needed to review our security after you got arrested. He said you'd sent a message releasing me, that I shouldn't wait for you.'

She'd been sold a lie. He longed to tell her the truth; that her father had cut ties with him the moment he'd been arrested. Deni hadn't answered any of his emails or phone calls and had offered no support whatsoever. Ziad had been cut off and cast adrift. But questioning her father's actions could make him more wary, a more difficult target. Ziad couldn't give any hint he knew Deni had betrayed him. So he remained silent and fumed as the rain lashed his face.

'I told you not to go,' Essi said. 'I'm sorry. You probably didn't need to hear that. What are you doing following me? Did you really think I wouldn't notice?'

'So you're with Jack now?' Ziad responded coolly.

The look in her eyes at that moment, more than the lack of warmth, the absence of a greeting, or the way she folded her arms around herself, told him he had no chance. He studied the blue gemstones and saw their normal lustre was lost to pity. She looked so sad and sorry for him.

'We started seeing each other a few months ago. He helped me forget.' Her face was covered in rain, but Ziad was certain he could see tears in her eyes. 'He helped me move on. I'm sorry, Zee.'

Ziad longed to wrap his arms around her and take away the pain. Just as he'd done in so many sad moments, like when her uncle had died. But pride and anger kept him rooted. If the tables had been turned, he would have found her no matter what. He wouldn't have abandoned her to seven hard years in Hell. Her father might have gutted their relationship, but she'd slit its throat.

'What are you—' Essi began, but she was interrupted by the toot of a car horn.

Jack the jock leaned out of the open window of his Porsche and called out to Essi, 'Hey, honey, who are you talking to?'

Essi made a show of reaching into her pocket. She produced a crumpled mass of bills and shoved them into Ziad's hands. 'I'm sorry,' she whispered before turning away. 'Just a homeless guy,' she told Jack as she ran to the car. 'I hate seeing them out in this weather.'

She gave Ziad a final glance as she slid into the passenger seat. Jack peered at the doorway, but Ziad wasn't sure how much he could see through the shadows and rain.

And then they were gone, leaving Ziad with nothing but the cold chill of the driving rain and the cascading rush of spray from passing traffic. He looked down at the wet bills in his hands and let every single one of them fall on the flagstone steps. Essi Salamov couldn't buy her way out so cheaply. She would have to pay a much higher price.

Chapter 7

When he'd returned to the dilapidated house on Kenyon Street later that night, his body numb with ice-cold fury, Ziad had asked Elroy a simple question.

'What do you want me to do?'

In the grip of fierce anger, the answer had seemed so reasonable, but now, here in this crowded bar, Ziad's heart thundered as he prepared to make Elroy's words real. Tony's Place was a favourite with port workers and it was heaving as Ziad pushed his way through the crowd. A bouncer had tested him for the virus before granting entry; a common inconvenience of the post-pandemic world. He finally spotted the men he was looking for; Richie Cutter, Weasel, and Hot Rod. Three greedy, stupid, live-for-today dockers who'd come up with Ziad. According to Elroy Lang, Richie Cutter – ambitious, ruthless Richie Cutter – had taken Ziad's old job at the port. He needed it back if they were to implement their plan, but Cutter wouldn't surrender it willingly. Elroy had given Ziad his instructions, and, as though anticipating the misgivings he'd feel when confronted with the reality of following them, had told him that this was Ziad's initiation. He would view it as proof Ziad was truly with them – that he had a genuine desire for revenge and was willing to do whatever it took to get it.

As Ziad pressed through the crowd towards Cutter's table, he reminded himself of all he'd suffered, the pain and humiliation, the physical assaults in Al Aqarab, the heartbreak. The people responsible needed to suffer in reply, and if the price was a few incidental casualties like Cutter, so be it. Besides, this man was no angel. Tall and physically fit, Cutter would strike most casual observers as a prime specimen, but Ziad could see hints of the man's debauched lifestyle, which was funded by the illicit work he did for Deni Salamov. Cutter had the puffiness of a heavy drinker, the red raw nostrils of a habitual cokehead, and the pinprick eyes of an opiate fiend.

'Holy shit,' Weasel cried when he caught sight of Ziad. 'Ziad Malek!'

'What the . . .' Hot Rod said, staggering to his feet.

Weasel and Hot Rod embraced Ziad enthusiastically, but Cutter gave him a muted, cagey welcome.

'Ziad,' he remarked simply, without rising.

'Take a seat,' Hot Rod said. 'What the hell happened to you, man?'

Ziad sat next to Weasel, aware that Cutter was eying him coldly.

'I got pulled on a charge,' he replied. 'But I beat it.'

'Sorry to hear that, man,' Hot Rod slurred. 'We should celebrate.'

Ziad felt a wave of nausea. He wasn't in the mood to celebrate, but he played along. 'That's what I'm here for,' he lied.

'The blonde keeps looking at you,' Weasel said.

'Which one?' Place is full of blondes,' Cutter replied, casting his eyes around the heaving bar.

'The tall one by the taps,' Weasel said, nodding towards the crowded counter.

Hot Rod turned his unfocused eyes in the direction of the bar. 'She's looking at me, man.'

Weasel grabbed Hot Rod's skull and pointed it in the right direction. 'You're so wasted you can't even see straight. She's over there.'

Ziad spied out the woman Weasel was talking about and it seemed the wiry little man was right; she was eying Cutter.

'I'm going in,' Cutter declared, getting to his feet. 'I'll buy a round to celebrate the old boss's return.' He emphasized the word 'old'. 'Who wants a drink?'

Weasel nodded and Hot Rod declared, a little too loudly, 'You know it!'

Cutter pushed his way through the pressed bodies of port workers and slotted into a space beside the blonde. She was with four friends.

Ziad watched the arrogant player schmooze the swaying woman.

'When did you get back?' Weasel asked him.

'Few days ago,' Ziad replied absently. His eyes were fixed on Cutter, but he wasn't sure he had the stone-cold guts to do what Elroy expected of him. The prison escape had been one thing, his actions born of necessity. This was something else. Cold. Calculated.

'What are you going to do?' Hot Rod asked.

'I don't know,' Ziad replied automatically. He couldn't go through with it. He got to his feet. 'You know what, I've got something I need to take care of. I'll catch you guys later.'

Hot Rod and Weasel slurred entreaties to stay, but Ziad ignored them and started for the door.

He passed Cutter, on his way back to the table with the blonde and her four friends. 'Hey, loser, where are you going?'

Cutter called to him, before turning to the blonde and saying, 'This guy used to be someone.'

Ziad flushed with humiliation and felt a sudden resurgence of the anger that had become his familiar companion.

'He used to be me,' Cutter told the woman, before laughing at his own joke.

'I was coming over to help with the drinks,' Ziad replied, finding fresh resolve in Cutter's cruelty.

'I don't carry my own drinks,' Cutter said. 'Tony will bring them over.' He pushed on through the crowd, trailed by the women.

Ziad glanced past the massed bodies and saw Tony, the balding owner of the bar, at the counter, preparing a tray of drinks. Cutter was right; he had taken Ziad's life, or at least a large part of it, and Ziad wanted it back. He watched the brash bully introduce the women to Hot Rod and Weasel, then turned and pushed through the crowd. As he neared the bar, Ziad reached into his pocket for a small tube shaped like a chapstick. Somewhere beneath the rowdy hubbub, a bed of music played, but Ziad couldn't make out what the song was.

'Richie still drinking those rum and tonics?' Ziad asked the barman.

'Holy crap,' Tony remarked when he registered who'd asked the question. 'Ziad. Good to see you. Yeah, Cutter's still on that weird concoction.'

'Let me run these over,' Ziad replied, signalling the tray of drinks.

'You don't have to do that,' Tony said.

'My pleasure,' Ziad responded.

'Thanks,' Tony said, before turning his attention to another customer.

Ziad took the plastic tube from his pocket and unscrewed the lid. As he slipped the inner tube from its protective housing, the sound of the blood rushing through his veins drowned out all else. The end of the tube was tipped by foam that had been soaked in a clear liquid. Ziad swiped the foam tip around the edge of Cutter's glass, screwed the protective housing back onto the tube, and returned it to his pocket. With his heart pounding in his ears, he picked up the heavy tray and carried it carefully through the crowd.

Weasel and a couple of the women who'd joined their group cheered when Ziad set the tray on the table.

'You work here now?' Cutter asked as Ziad pulled up a chair.

'My name's Rodney, but everyone calls me Hot Rod on account of my giant rod,' Hot Rod was slurring to another of the women.

Ziad kept his eyes on Cutter, who took his glass from the tray and drank long and hard.

'Men are so insecure,' the woman countered. 'I've never met a woman who went round calling herself Big Tits.'

'She should. She'd be very popular,' Rod slurred, provoking a round of giggles.

'Please ignore my friend, ladies,' Weasel said.

It started with a cough. Ziad registered a look of discomfort cross Cutter's face. Whatever was in the tube Elroy had given him was as fast-acting as he'd promised – within moments Cutter was coughing and spluttering like the men in Al Aqarab. He was struggling to breathe, and the chuckles, giggles and bawdy talk were replaced by consternation as Cutter started to paw at his throat.

'Stop screwing around, Richie,' Weasel said. 'It ain't funny.'

But Cutter wasn't pretending. His legs kicked out, knocking over the table and sending all the drinks flying.

One of the women screamed, and panic spread through the bar as Richie Cutter choked to death.

Ziad noticed Cutter's eyes settle on him. Part of him wished he felt remorse, but he only experienced a slight rush of satisfaction at seeing the first casualty of his vengeance suffer. When Cutter's eyes bulged from his head and turned red as the blood vessels burst, Ziad wondered whether he knew who'd done this to him. Ziad held the man's horrified gaze as he made a futile effort to cling to the life that was leaving him. A moment later, Richie Cutter toppled sideways and fell to the floor, dead.

Chapter 8

Brigitte had taken Pearce overland for more than a week. They'd driven north into Thailand in an ancient red Volkswagen Polo, before heading east into Cambodia. The tiny car had no air conditioning and the autumn humidity made the journey almost unbearable. Brigitte had made it clear early on that she wouldn't answer any questions and they weren't the kind of people who did small talk, so most of the journey passed in silence, which suited Pearce. He didn't trust the Frenchwoman. He tried to ignore the oppressive heat as he watched the lush jungle landscape roll by, and reflected on a life that had put him alongside the former French agent.

Abandoned by both parents as a young child, Pearce had drifted from one foster home to another, and, during a time he'd come to refer to as the wilding, he'd become increasingly hostile and angry. He'd seemingly been destined for a life of juvenile delinquency and crime, until fate intervened and a despairing Merseyside social worker had sent him to St David's, a specialist school in Wales. The caring, insightful headmaster, Malcolm Jones, had spotted Pearce's potential and rescued him from his destructive path. Pearce had gone into the army, shown aptitude and had applied for and endured SAS selection. He'd served with a specialist unit, the Increment, which provided operational support to MI6.

After years of trying, his liaison and mentor Kyle Wollerton finally managed to convince Pearce to leave the Regiment and work for Six at Vauxhall Cross, and for a few years he was an operations specialist in the field, until the fateful day he'd found himself in Islamabad and had got caught up in a terror attack. He'd been in the city for personal reasons and it was pure chance he'd been there when the horror unfolded. Isolated and up against the odds, he'd almost single-handedly thwarted a devastating plan to subvert Pakistan's government.

Acclaim turned to criticism when it became clear to Pearce's superiors that he would not drop his investigation into what he believed was a wider conspiracy, and, after a final confrontation with his superior Dominic McClusky, the man he would later expose as a traitor, Pearce was let go. He'd been on the trail of the conspirators ever since, pausing only to avenge his old comrade Nathan Foster's death and deal with a British far-right group called Black Thirteen. It was during that investigation that he'd met Brigitte Attali, when she had been working for the DGSE. Her encounter with Pearce had blown her cover – she'd subsequently been relieved of duty and had wound up working for Huxley Blaine Carter, the man they were on their way to meet, a Silicon Valley billionaire who fancied himself as some sort of private spymaster.

They'd ditched the Polo and crossed the porous land border into Cambodia, where Brigitte had bought an old Suzuki hatchback for cash. They'd driven to a remote airstrip in the heart of the country where they'd been met by a private jet that had brought them to Geneva.

A pair of Mercedes G-Wagens had been waiting for them, driven by a duo of lean, shaven-headed hard men in dark suits who looked so alike they could have been related. Each driver had a passenger riding shotgun. Similarly hard, gaunt men, their eyes had betrayed no emotion when Brigitte led Pearce out of the terminal.

They'd been shown to the lead vehicle, and as they'd been driven through Geneva's busy streets, shielded by opaque privacy glass, Pearce had become aware of two motorcycle outriders who swept the roads around them for potential tails. Blaine Carter had upped his security since their previous encounter in San Francisco. Pearce looked at Brigitte and wondered how many of the improvements were down to her.

The traffic was so heavy it took over an hour to get out of Geneva and another forty-five minutes to reach the French border. Night had fallen by the time they started into the foothills of the Alps. They turned off the main highway and joined the Route d'Abondance, a winding two-lane road that snaked around steep, richly forested slopes, sheer cliffs and high waterfalls. The summer hiking season was over and the snow was at least a couple of months off, so they encountered very little traffic in either direction. Some fifteen miles after leaving the highway, the G-Wagen slowed for a sharp left bend, but rather than straighten up to follow the road, the driver held the turn and headed for what Pearce thought was a solid cliff. He almost yelled at the man, until he realized that what he'd mistaken for darker rock was actually shadow and that a narrow road lay between two tiers of the cliff. People probably drove past the cut in the rock every day without even realizing it was there.

The powerful Mercedes started a steep climb and sheer rock sped by inches from either side of the big car. After a couple of hundred metres, they'd risen above the cliffs and the road wound its way through forest, making a series of sharp turns to climb the steep sides of the mountain. The road became little more than a track in places and when they headed north, Pearce's window was directly over the precipice that marked the edge of the road. There was no barrier and one wrong move would send them plummeting hundreds of feet. But the driver was confident and controlled and had the skill of someone who'd been born in the mountains. When the road looped back on itself and they headed south, Pearce peered into the dark shadows between the high pines and wondered what secrets they concealed.

After a quarter of an hour, a pair of slatted metal gates barred their way. Pearce saw movement, and a suited guard stepped out from a gatehouse partially shielded by the tree-line. As the G-Wagen slowed to a stop, Pearce took in the twelve-foot-high chain-link fence disappearing into the darkness of the forest, and the dizzying precipice on the other side of the gate. The first guard stood in the middle of the road, while another remained in the gatehouse opposite the edge and held a pair of infrared field glasses to his eyes. The gates weren't opened until the driver had lowered all the windows to allow the vehicle's occupants to be identified. They were all subjected to a rapid Covid-19 test. When the G-Wagen finally rolled on, Pearce looked over his shoulder and saw the trailing vehicle park across the road in front of the closing gates. The two motorcycles pulled up beside the gatehouse. Huxley Blaine Carter really had upped his game since their last meeting.

Chapter 9

After forty-eight hours the magnificent home had started to feel like a prison to Leila Nuhman. It was a mind-boggling achievement of architecture, a fifty-metre-long, four-storey crescent-shaped structure of concrete, brushed metal and glass carved into the side of a mountain at an altitude of 6,000 feet. The house was wedged into a sheer cliff and the bend of the crescent was supported by struts that were pinned to the bottom of the face, so any rooms on the curve, including the one Leila had been given, hung in very thin air. A curved window took up an entire wall of Leila's bedroom and below it was a two-foot-wide strip of toughened glass flooring that enabled her to peer hundreds of feet down into the valley below. Leila had gathered some of the pillows from her king-size bed and spent hours lying on the floor, gazing down at the miniature tops of giant trees far beneath wisps of cloud. Every so often her stomach would flip and her toes tingle at the thought of the fall and she'd press the glass floor to reassure herself it was still there.

Leila's patience was being tested by her American host. Huxley Blaine Carter had welcomed her when she'd arrived and told her he was working hard to make good on the rumour that had enticed her to his home in the French mountains, but she hadn't seen him since. He'd told her to make herself at home and use the gym, spa and glass-bottomed pool located on the lowest level of the house. She'd limped through the house, supporting herself on her black Derby walking stick, and visited the sauna and swimming pool. She'd even made use of the gym, admiring the mountain view as she moved around the large room, using the state-of-the-art weights machines to work on her arms. She'd brought her wheelchair with her, but so far she hadn't needed it and was pleased to be moving about the huge house in little pain.

Pearce had told her about his encounter with Huxley Blaine Carter after the Black Thirteen investigation and Leila had satisfied her curiosity with some basic research on the man. He'd made his fortune in online payments and had subsequently backed a number of extremely successful tech start-ups as an early investor. He was worth billions, and could do just about anything, so Leila was puzzled why, unlike his peers who focused on space exploration, medical research and philanthropy, Blaine Carter had tried to get into the espionage business. Apart from a long-retired former NSA director who sat on the board of a couple of his companies, there was nothing in the tech mogul's history that suggested a connection to any intelligence agency.

Leila had spent two days killing time, trying to avoid dwelling on the rumour Blaine Carter had shared with her. He claimed he might be able to get information on Leila's sister Hannan, the only member of her family who wasn't known to have died in Syria's brutal civil war. Everyone else Leila cared about had been killed when ISIS had taken Raqqa or had been murdered trying to escape. Only Hannan was unaccounted for – missing presumed dead. But this man, this rich American, claimed he might be able to get news of

Hannan's whereabouts. Leila had spent years thinking she was alone, that everyone who connected her to her ancestors was long dead. She'd spent countless hours and long, restless nights trying to suppress the horrors of occupation and the memories of her time spent as a forced bride to two murderous men, vainly hoping she could find some peace. Blaine Carter had given her something she hadn't felt for a very long time: hope.

Leila was lying on the glass walkway, absently watching the valley below, when she heard a knock at the door.

'Come in,' she said, hauling herself upright.

The door opened, and a man in a dark suit leaned into the room. He had the close-cropped hair and ramrod bearing of someone who was ex-military. 'Huxley would like to see you,' he said.

Leila grabbed her Derby stick and propelled herself to her feet. She was in a pair of thick socks, jeans and a baggy T-shirt, but if the man had news of her sister, she wasn't about to waste a second trying to make herself look more presentable. And shoes? She really couldn't face the rigmarole. 'Let's go,' she told her visitor.

Leila's guide took her through the only door she hadn't been able to open. She'd had the run of the lower two levels and had spent some time exploring the opulent guest bedrooms and living spaces, but this one door, secured by a biometric palm scanner, had remained resolutely locked. As she suspected, it led to the upper levels of the property. Leila followed the suited man into a wide glass-walled atrium that overlooked the valley. He led her up a wide staircase into a huge living room that occupied the centre of the structure's curve, the floor-to-ceiling windows offering a magnificent view of the mountains. But her eyes weren't on the jagged peaks. They were drawn across the eighty-foot room to a figure seated on a large corner sofa unit. It was a man she recognized; Scott Pearce's recruiter and mentor, Kyle Wollerton. His craggy face betrayed surprise when he saw Leila and he hurried towards her.

'Leila, how long have you been here?'

'Two days. You?'

'Three.'

Leila turned to ask her guide some harsh questions, but she caught a flash of him hurrying down the stairs. 'Hey!' she yelled, limping after him, but by the time she reached the top of the stairs he'd slipped through the security door.

Had she been lured here with a lie? Was the stuff about her sister simply part of a ruse? If it was, Huxley Blaine Carter would regret ever having pulled such a stunt.

'What do you think this is about?' Wollerton asked.

'I thought it was about my sister,' Leila replied.

'Leila, I'm so sorry,' Wollerton said sympathetically.

She didn't need pity. Not now.

She heard footsteps coming up the staircase and hurried over to see her friend and former colleague, the man who'd saved her life: Scott Pearce.

Chapter 10

'Lyly,' Pearce said fondly, using her childhood nickname. 'You didn't tell me she'd be here,' he remarked to the woman who was coming up the stairs with him. Brigitte Attali, a former French DGSE agent with albinism who'd been on the other side of the Black Thirteen investigation.

'You didn't ask,' Brigitte replied with a wry smile.

Wollerton embraced Pearce. 'Good to see you, man.'

'I was—'

'He decided to be a hero,' Brigitte interrupted. 'And blew his only lead.'

'Thank you all for coming.' Blaine Carter's deep California drawl filled the room.

Leila turned to see the American emerge from a doorway that had appeared in what had previously seemed to be an unbroken interior wall. As he stepped into the room, a door slid across the opening behind him and slotted back into place. Now she knew where it was, Leila could discern the line of the opening, but it was cleverly designed to be part of a pattern that ran along every interior wall. She wondered how many other secret doors were concealed about the place.

'Good to see you again, Scott,' he said as he approached Pearce and offered his hand. 'Athena, go secure please,' he said to no one in particular.

'*Going secure, Mr Blaine Carter,*' a synthetic voice replied.

Leila looked up at what she'd assumed was a decorative grille that ran along the perimeter of every ceiling in the building and realized it could conceal any number of sensors, cameras and speakers. The massive windows started to darken and the lights came on. Soon the mountains were gone, replaced by black screens.

'Athena, bring up the photo of Hannan Nahum,' Blaine Carter said, and an eight- by six-foot section of the window displayed a photograph of a crowd of people clustered round a UN World Food Programme relief truck. Aid workers were distributing food to a desperate group of Syrian refugees whose gaunt, weary faces and dirty, tattered clothes spoke of long hardship. 'Athena, zoom in on the top right-hand corner.'

Leila gasped when that section of the image was magnified and she saw her sister. Hannan was part of a group that spilled into the photo from round the side of the truck, but her face could be clearly seen in the crowd. She was wearing a hijab, something she swore she'd never do, and Leila didn't recognize the ragged dress she was in. Her olive skin was covered in dirt and she looked as though she'd lost a lot of weight. Tears of joy sprung in Leila's eyes and she staggered back, unable to cope with the sheer weight of hope. Pearce caught her arm and offered her his support. She tried to talk, but the words choked in her throat.

'The picture was taken in the Zaatari Refugee Camp in Jordan three months ago,' Blaine Carter said. 'I didn't want to share this until I had more, because, well . . .' he tailed off. 'Hope and grief are too powerful to toy with. But if you want proof of my bona fides then here it is. My people have checked with the camp authorities and your sister left the camp six weeks after this photograph was taken. They believe she used a false name to register.'

Leila was reeling. She'd spent years searching for the one surviving member of her family. When she'd been contracting for Six, she'd used their systems to run image searches and checked the records of every refugee camp, police report and record in the countries neighbouring Syria. She'd set up a border alert on Hannan's passport and photograph. Leila knew she was very good at her job and she could not help but look at Blaine Carter in awe. How had he managed to do what she had found impossible?

'If you help me, I will use all of my resources to learn what happened to your sister,' Blaine Carter said. 'If she's alive, I can help you find her.'

Chapter 11

Pearce saw clouds of emotion sweep over Leila's face and her whole body trembled. She was reeling. The guy was clever. Pearce had refused him, and now he was back with an offer so alluring it would be almost impossible to resist. How could Leila pass up the opportunity to find her sister? How could Pearce or Wollerton say no to helping her?

'How did you get this? Why are you interested in her sister?' Pearce asked Blaine Carter.

'I told you before, I keep tabs on people with certain backgrounds. I hear things from the ether. You turned me down, Mr Pearce,' Blaine Carter replied. 'You refused to work for me. Fine. But if our interests align, perhaps we can help each other. You have spent more than two years hunting the people who are connected to the Thai man you killed in Islamabad. You don't even know his real name.'

Pearce was surprised Blaine Carter knew so much about his mission.

'You know the man you killed as Chao Fah Jan, but his real name was Chatri Angsakul,' Blaine Carter revealed. 'Athena, please show the Scorpion footage.'

Another section of the window displayed security camera footage of what looked like a prison gate. A Thai man with long hair sat in a car parked on an access road near the prison.

Two men in prison uniforms stepped through the gate and got in the car before it drove away.

'Two weeks ago, his brother Narong Angsakul, a man known to be connected to the smuggling network you've been tracking, helped two men escape Al Aqarab, Scorpion Prison, in Cairo,' Blaine Carter said. The footage switched to a shot of a cafeteria full of corpses. 'The men he helped used some kind of chemical weapon to facilitate the escape. It killed everyone in the cafeteria, but autopsies found no trace of any harmful substances in the victims' bloodstreams. Whatever it was leaves no trace. Three more guards were killed when the two men escaped. Once again there was no toxin found in their bloodstreams and no obvious cause of death.'

'And the prisoners?' Wollerton asked.

'One was serving seven years for attempted drug trafficking,' Blaine Carter replied. 'The Egyptians had identified him as Ibrahim Mahmood based on the Kuwaiti passport he had on him when he was arrested, but that identity is false and his real name is a mystery. Athena, please show the arrest photograph of Ibrahim Mahmood.'

A section of the huge screen displayed the image of a dejected man with minor injuries, looking directly at the camera. He looked Middle Eastern; the man's large round eyes, dark skin, and black hair gave away that much.

'Surely you can run an image look-up?' Wollerton suggested.

'I can and have,' Blaine Carter replied. 'All digital records of this man's true identity have been erased. There is no trace of it anywhere. Whoever he's working with doesn't want him found. The second man was an American. Arrest records show his name to be Elroy Lang, but that's a false identity. We don't even have an arrest photo of him. Someone has erased all visual records of his existence.'

'Erased?' Pearce said. 'That would mean—'

'Government involvement?' Blaine Carter interrupted. 'Did you think your old boss Dominic McClusky was the only corrupt bureaucrat in the world? You might not want to work for me, Mr Pearce, but for now it seems our interests are aligned. I'd like you to go to Cairo and learn the real identity of the men Angsakul helped escape. You will get the next link to your Thai smuggling network, and I will find out what he and these unknown men have planned.' Blaine Carter approached Leila, who was starting to regain her composure. 'If you help Mr Pearce, I promise to do everything I can to find your sister.'

'What about me?' Wollerton asked sourly. 'You've found the levers you need to manipulate these two. What's in it for me?'

'You need to feel good about yourself,' Blaine Carter replied. 'Your wife left and took your children. That's a profound loss. It can't be easy being alone. I don't need any leverage, Mr Wollerton. You need to feel part of something.'

Pearce knew his old friend and mentor well enough to see beyond his attempt to conceal his hurt.

'You'll all be paid,' Blaine Carter said. 'Just for as long as our interests coincide. Miss Attali will be your liaison and can provide you with whatever resources you need.'

Pearce glanced at the Frenchwoman. He didn't trust her. It wasn't just her allegiance to Blaine Carter; when Pearce had first met her, she'd been on the verge of killing an innocent man. She was ruthless and pragmatic. A dangerous combination.

'Why are you doing this?' Pearce asked.

'What do you know about my family?' Blaine Carter responded. 'Specifically my father?'

Pearce had researched Blaine Carter before their encounter in San Francisco. There were acres of newsprint on the man's rise to fortune, and the tragic story of his father's demise was well known. He'd died of a heart attack when Huxley was twenty-six, a newly minted PhD. He'd taken over his father's successful data-mining business and had turned it into one of the most successful digital payments platforms in the world. 'He died of a heart attack twelve years ago.'

'That's what they say,' Blaine Carter replied. 'But what if he was murdered? Would that be an honourable reason for a rich man to play the game?'

'You think his death is connected?' Pearce asked.

'All I've ever seen are wisps of smoke. I need people like you to help me find the fire.'

Pearce studied the charming, eccentric man and saw vulnerability beneath the carefully cultivated veneer. Blaine Carter must have realized he'd shown too much because his demeanour shifted and he slapped Pearce on the back. 'So what's it to be, bud, you in or out? You want to answer the question that's been keeping you awake at night? Or do you want to go back to sleep?'

'I need to go to Zaatari,' Leila said. Pearce saw she'd recovered her composure and her familiar steel had returned. 'If my sister is out there, I'm the one who needs to find her.'

'And how will you do that on your own?' Blaine Carter asked. 'Even if the three of you go, how far do you think you'll get without the intel I've gathered?'

Leila shuffled forward menacingly, and Pearce sensed Brigitte tense.

'I'll take it,' Leila said. 'And I'll make you suffer for keeping it from me.'

'You could do that,' Blaine Carter replied, 'and we both lose. Or you could spend a few weeks helping me and in return I'll give you whatever you need to find her. We both win.'

Leila took another step closer and gripped the top of her walking stick so hard her knuckles turned white. She stared at Blaine Carter with a ferocity that would have made most people wilt.

'I don't like playing hardball,' he said. 'It's not my style, but I'll do whatever it takes. Angsakul is a bad guy, but he's working for people who are worse. You saw the people killed during the prison break. I need to know what they're planning. It's important.'

Pearce could feel Leila bristling with anger and he was convinced she was going to hit Blaine Carter. He placed a hand on her forearm and squeezed gently. She looked at him with fire in her eyes and for a moment he caught a glimpse of the savage anger horror had spawned in her. Then it was gone. She looked for confirmation, and Pearce nodded. He wanted to find Narong Angsakul, and if it meant they'd get the billionaire's help locating Leila's sister, so much the better.

'Three weeks,' Leila said as the fire within her abated. She turned to Blaine Carter. 'You have three weeks. After that, I'm gone.'

Chapter 12

'I was worried it might be the corona. The last thing we need is another outbreak round here, but they say it was a heart attack. Too much coke. That's what I reckon. Keeled over like a falling cedar and died in a puddle of beer,' Harry Martin said. 'God rest his soul.'

Harry Martin was the bombastic Director of Operations for the Port of Seattle. He was a man of fleshy folds, from the rolls that clung to his wide neck to the creases at his wrists and elbows. His bulbous pot belly strained the buttons of his short-sleeved white shirt and even in the air-conditioned office his face was crimson and his bald head was beaded with sweat. The guy devoted his every waking hour to ensuring the port ran smoothly and spent most of his life trapped at his desk guzzling sweet black coffee and donuts. He rubbed a lot of people the wrong way, but Ziad had always liked his direct no-nonsense style. A person always knew where they stood.

'I was there,' Ziad revealed, and Harry's eyes widened.

'Really? Was it as bad as people say?'

Ziad had tried not to think about Cutter's ugly death. The satisfaction he'd felt on the night had given way to waves of guilt and pangs of regret, and Cutter's face now mingled with those of the men in Al Aqarab, haunting his memory, plaguing his nightmares.

'It was horrible,' Ziad replied.

'What the heck happened to you anyway?' Harry asked, leaning back in his large leather chair. 'One moment you're signed off for a two-week vacation, the next you disappear.'

'I was in a car accident,' Ziad lied. 'They put me in an induced coma.'

'Shit,' Harry sighed. 'Sorry to hear that. Are you OK?'

'I think so. Few broken bones, a bleed on the brain, but they've given me the all clear.'

Harry nodded sombrely. 'Well, like I said, your timing couldn't be better. Richie's death means I need a new shift supervisor. You were always a good worker, Ziad,' he said, and he cast his broad arms into the air and gestured expansively at the mass of papers on his desk and the schedules pinned to the walls. 'And we're busier than ever. We'll have to go through the formalities, but if you want your old job back, it's yours.'

Ziad stood and offered his hand across the cluttered desk. Harry rose and clasped it warmly.

'Thank you, Mr Martin,' Ziad said. 'It's good to be home.'

The 1988 Buick Electra rattled and spluttered at every intersection and the tan bodywork was marred by dents and rust, but Ziad didn't care. The car got him around and his image wasn't important to him anymore. When he'd first come to Seattle, he'd stretched himself to buy a used BMW M5 in an attempt to give himself cred. He'd never been able to understand Deni Salamov's low-key approach to life. The Chechen had unimaginable wealth, but the world only ever saw a pious man who ran a handful of small businesses. The passing observer would have no idea Deni controlled the supply of drugs into the western seaboard.

The Buick made a horrible crunching sound as Ziad turned into the parking lot on the corner of 140th Street. Most of the eighty or so spaces were empty and Ziad chose one near the converted mini-mall. Occupying an entire city block, the broad, low building was home to the Salam Islamic Centre, a large civic hall in the heart of the complex. There were four businesses in the building, two either side of the Islamic Centre. To the north were Sunshine Bank, a Sharia financial institution that enabled neighbourhood Muslims to invest according to scripture. Next to it was the Salamov travel agency and currency exchange. To the south of the Islamic Centre were the Haqeeq Bookstore and, on the very southern-most corner of the complex, the Al Jamaea coffee shop. The parking lot that lay to the south of the building had been closed and converted into a makeshift soccer pitch. Men sat at tables outside Al Jamaea, dragging on cigarettes and drinking coffee as they watched two teams of boys in *salwar kameezes* battle over a flat soccer ball. The men were first- and second-generation immigrants drawn from all over Asia, North Africa and the Middle East and Ziad recognized a few familiar faces. He felt a pang of nervous excitement at the prospect of stepping back into his old life. He took a deep breath and calmed himself. None of the men outside the cafe were dangerous. His biggest concern was that Deni would realize the threat he posed and have him fed to the gulls. Ziad's stomach flipped again, but he turned his attention away from the men and reminded himself why he was here; to avenge himself.

To the east of the makeshift soccer pitch was a smaller stand-alone building, the Salam Mini-mart, a convenience store that specialized in Middle Eastern produce. Few people knew that all the businesses, the community centre and most of the surrounding residential buildings belonged to Salamov.

As he got out of the car, Ziad saw a man he recognized emerging from the goods entrance of the mini-mart. Abbas Idrisov, also known as Abacus, was Deni's human calculator. The Chechen never kept a record of any of his dealings for fear of prosecution, so every transaction he'd ever made was stored in the eidetic memory of this wizened old man. No one was sure of Abacus's age, but he moved with the aching hesitancy of a septuagenarian. He had a long white beard, a craggy face with drooping eyes and a bulbous nose that had lost the battle with gravity a long time ago. Even though it was a warm autumn day, Abbas wore a thick full-length wool coat and a traditional ushanka fur hat. He carried a paper bag in one hand and muttered words under his breath as the fingers of his other hand worried a set of red *misbaha* prayer beads. His eyes lit up with surprise when he caught sight of Ziad.

'*Masha'Alla. Masha'Alla,*' Abbas exclaimed. 'Ziad Malek. I heard you'd disappeared.' The old man shuffled over and raised his palm in greeting. He was being cautious, avoiding close contact.

The encounter was a good warm-up. Ziad resisted the urge to close the gap between them, grab the man's neck and squeeze it until the breath left his body. Everyone associated with Deni was tainted. He couldn't trust any of them. Had Abacus known he'd been set up? He peered into the old eyes for any sign of guilt. Had Abbas been a party to his betrayal?

'I ran into some trouble, Abbas, but it's good to be back,' Ziad said. The old man's eyes shone with warmth and happiness, but Ziad knew a jackal like Abacus couldn't survive the criminal underworld for so long without being an expert at masking his true feelings. 'Is Deni around?'

'Of course,' Abbas replied. 'This is a great day. He will be like an excited child when he sees you have returned.'

Ziad very much doubted that.

'Come,' Abbas said as he headed towards the bookshop. 'Come, follow me. You will put a smile on your old friend's face.'

Chapter 13

Abbas took a rapid test from behind the counter and checked Ziad on the threshold of the bookshop, but when the result was negative, the old man ushered him on.

There was no smile, at least not to start with. They found Deni in a small seating area near the back of the bookshop. He was in one of four lounge armchairs that were arranged around a low coffee table laden with books and magazines. The bookshop was Deni's favourite place to do business. The high shelves packed with Islamic poetry and religious texts prevented prying eyes seeing anything that happened this far back, and the store had little custom, meaning undercover cops or FBI would be noticed.

There was a moment's hesitation as a startled Deni took in what Abbas had brought back with him. Then came the smile. It rose more quickly than the Chechen, who stumbled a little as he got to his feet. His lips curled in the most forced, false expression of joy Ziad had ever seen.

'*Marhaba*,' Deni said, as he stepped round the chairs and pulled Ziad into a tight bear hug. 'I had lost hope, brother. It's so good to see you.'

Ziad's smile never wavered. Not even when he saw Rasul, Deni's twenty-eight-year-old son, emerge from the stockroom. The vicious and vindictive true heir to the Salamov fortune,

Ziad had little doubt Rasul had been part of the plot to get rid of him. Essi's brother curled his face into a snarl when he caught sight of Ziad in Deni's embrace, but his expression quickly changed to one of fraudulent happiness as he drew near.

'Brother,' Rasul said. 'I can't believe our good fortune. *Masha'Allah. Mabrouk.*'

Ziad stepped back from Deni and shook Rasul's hand. His smile held, even when he caught father and son shooting each other sideways glances. Images of both men with bullets in their temples or knives in their hearts floated up from Ziad's vengeful subconscious, but he did not react to them. He would not indulge in the immediate gratification of a violent fantasy. These men would be taken apart piece by piece.

'Sit, sit,' Deni suggested. 'Tell us what happened.'

The four men settled into the armchairs arranged around the table.

'Can I get you a tea or coffee?' Deni asked. 'A cake?'

Unlike his son, Deni's American accent was tinged with more than a hint of his Chechen heritage. Rasul could have passed for a Caucasian-American in both sound and appearance. He and his father both stood a couple of inches taller than six feet, carried very little excess weight and had the pinched faces of mountain folk from the Eastern Caucasus. Unlike his son, whose dark hair was unblemished, Deni's was flecked with grey. Rasul dressed like a member of a nineties grunge band – skinny jeans and distressed T-shirts – while Deni wore a light suit.

'I'm OK,' Ziad replied. 'Thank you,' he added, taking great care to give no hint of the anger he felt towards these men.

'What happened to you, brother?' Rasul asked. 'We searched for any trace, but you vanished.'

'The Egyptian police raided the meeting. They killed one of the contacts your father sent me to meet,' Ziad replied. 'The other was arrested with me, but he turned and cut a deal with the prosecutor. I was sentenced to seven years.'

Deni tutted and shook his head wistfully.

'But it has not been seven years,' Abbas noted.

'By God's grace I was able to get early release,' Ziad said. The true nature of his escape could be learned by anyone who read the relevant edition of the Egyptian national newspapers and recognized his mugshot, but he wasn't about to share the information with these three. They would hear nothing but good fortune, experience nothing but good humour and consider him nothing but a good friend. 'And I could not wait to come home.'

'Do you know how the Egyptians knew about you?' Rasul asked.

Ziad shook his head. 'An informant within the contacts' organization maybe. Or just bad luck. It comes with the territory.'

'We hope you know it had nothing to do with anyone here,' Rasul said emphatically.

'Of course,' Ziad replied. 'I would hardly be sitting here if I thought otherwise.'

'That's good,' Rasul said. 'It's over now, and we're glad to have you back safe.'

Lying snake, Ziad thought as he nodded and smiled.

'Essi said she'd seen you,' Deni revealed, but even as the words cut him, Ziad kept his smile. 'I'm sorry, brother. And ashamed that she did not wait. But she could not have known.

And she is more American than Chechen now. A full-blown Yankee, like this one,' he said, tousling Rasul's hair.

'I have my old job back,' Ziad said. 'I met Harry Martin and he hired me on the spot.'

Deni's face fell for a moment, before he rallied. '*Mabrouk*. This is a great favour from God. He has blessed us all. Cutter was no good. We kept the business going with him, but he was greedy and unreliable. It will be better to go back to how things were. Working with someone we can trust.'

'Family,' Rasul said sagely.

'Family,' Ziad agreed, smiling at the snakes who'd betrayed him. They nodded and smiled right back.

Chapter 14

Huxley Blaine Carter provided a Global 8000 jet that took Pearce and the team from Geneva to Cairo, where they were met by an Egyptian contact, a reed-thin former Egyptian Army colonel called Kamal Abdel Nour. He had a kind, open face and an engaging sense of humour that was obvious from the outset.

Pearce introduced himself using the false name Ed Barton. 'Mr Barton? Hmm . . . maybe Smith would be easier to remember? And Ed isn't a very good name for an Egyptian. *Inta Musri, mish keda*?' Kamal added, astutely noting Pearce's ethnicity. Few people had ever accurately discerned his mixed heritage and he'd been mistaken for a native of just about every continent on Earth.

'Let's just stick to the job,' Pearce responded.

'Of course,' Kamal said, holding his hands up. 'As you wish.'

The private jet had taxied to a remote part of Cairo International, where Kamal had been waiting alongside a pair of old Land Rover Discoveries.

'Welcome to Egypt. Please come,' he said, gesturing at the white cars. Blacked-out windows prevented Pearce seeing who was inside, so he let Kamal lead the way.

The driver's door of the first vehicle opened and a short, stout middle-aged man with a rough stubble clambered out.

'This is Sharif, my deputy,' Kamal said. 'We've been instructed to give you whatever assistance you need. We will take you to your lodgings now. In the morning, as per the message we received, we have arranged visits to the police laboratory and the prison. We will all be tested now.'

Kamal opened the passenger door of the first vehicle and indicated a stack of rapid testing kits. Regular testing for coronavirus had become commonplace since the pandemic, particularly among groups of people working in close contact. Pearce was pleased to see Kamal and Sharif taking their safety seriously.

Their lodgings were a four-bedroom apartment on the top floor of an eight-storey block in the heart of Zamalek, a lush four-kilometre-long island in the River Nile. Zamalek was connected to the rest of Cairo by three bridges that spanned from east to west, linking the island to neighbourhoods on both banks of the Nile. Their building was east of the Gezira Club, an exclusive private estate that offered members use of its sporting facilities and extensive parkland. Pearce stood on the apartment's large roof terrace and looked west at the families gathered around the club's huge swimming pool. He could hear the squeals of children braving the pool's evening chill and saw a couple of kids pop out of the water and race to their parents. Towels were immediately flung around them, and the happy foursome huddled around their poolside table to enjoy a meal produced by a pair of waiters.

Further into the club, a handful of walkers and joggers fol-lowed the track that traced the park's perimeter. Pearce found himself wondering about his father, Adel, the man who'd abandoned him and his mother. He knew his father was part

Egyptian and part Sudanese and that he'd been raised in Cairo. Had he returned here when he'd left Pearce and his mother in London? Was he down there in the club now, making happy with another family? Was he somewhere in the overcrowded, chaotic city? Or was he long gone? Remembered only as a ghost by the son he'd never really known?

Pearce had grown up an outsider, and his isolation had given him strength, but sometimes he felt his solitude more sharply and yearned to find somewhere he could belong. He'd despised Lancelot Oxnard-Clarke, but had felt sorry for the men he'd radicalized into Black Thirteen. Like Pearce, many of them had just wanted a place to belong. *Desire that had made them vulnerable to radicalization*, Pearce reminded himself. His desire could also be a weakness if he wasn't careful.

'When was the last time you were here?' Wollerton asked, and Pearce turned to see the man step onto the balcony through the French doors that led to the large living room.

'Six years ago, on a stopover from Iraq,' Pearce replied.

'It's been longer for me. But some things never change. I don't think there's anywhere else in the world that manages to function in such chaos. Kamal has gone. Sharif is staying here.'

'To keep an eye on us?'

'Probably,' Wollerton replied. 'A private security contractor in Cairo is likely to be connected to Egyptian Intelligence, if not a fully paid-up operative.'

'Then we'd better not do anything to upset them,' Pearce suggested.

'Or we should do it now. Sharif's gone out to get dinner. Apparently he knows the best shawarma place in Cairo.'

'Everyone always knows the best places,' Pearce scoffed,

but his mouth had already started watering and he realized how hungry he was.

Wollerton smiled. 'What do you make of HBC?'

'There was a reason I turned him down,' Pearce replied. 'I don't trust him. You?'

'Huxley Blaine Carter.' Wollerton said, chewing over his thoughts. 'Even his name sounds dodgy. Like a magician or lion tamer. I don't like him or his French assistant. I think we should be careful. Very careful. I don't want to get sawn in half.'

'Or fed to the lions,' Pearce agreed.

Chapter 15

Leila rinsed her long black hair and allowed the warm water to cascade over her face. She imagined her troubles being stripped away and swirling down the waste pipe along with the day's grime. If only it was that easy. She was still troubled by the constant guilt that had burrowed deep into her mind. She shouldn't be here. She should be in Jordan tracking down her sister. But she knew an emotional response wouldn't have served her well. Pearce was right. The photo Blaine Carter had shown her was three months old. The trail wouldn't grow any colder with another three weeks' delay. Reconciled to carry the painful guilt until the job was over or the three weeks were up, Leila rubbed her eyes, turned around and tilted her head back so her hair was directly beneath the shower nozzle. She ran her fingers through her thick tresses and, satisfied any conditioner had been expunged, she shut off the shower and carefully clambered out of the cast-iron bathtub. She tottered unsteadily across the bath mat to the rail where she'd hung her soft bath sheet. She wrapped it around herself, and spun a smaller towel into a loose turban before steadying herself against the rail. Everywhere she looked, she was reminded of Syria. The colonial-era French furniture, the grand mahogany-framed mirrors, the tiny blue and white Islamic tiles, the toilet with the inbuilt bidet – it was as though she'd come home.

Except Leila could never go home. Everything she'd known in Syria had been destroyed by war, and everyone dear to her was gone.

Almost everyone, she corrected herself. Hannan might be alive. Leila had to find her sister soon. If the guilt didn't drive her mad, the hope almost certainly would.

As she gently towelled her hair, Leila became aware of a reflection in the large mirror that hung above the basin. She turned and saw Brigitte Attali watching her through a gap in the door. Leila was certain she'd shut it behind her. Had it slipped open? Or had the Frenchwoman pushed it? And exactly how long had she been standing there? Leila felt her anger rise. She hated the thought of anyone seeing the scars that marred her torso, a consequence of the emergency surgery that had saved her life in childbirth, but which had left her permanently disabled.

Brigitte realized she'd been spotted and had the good sense to look away as she put her mouth to the gap in the door. 'Dinner is ready,' she said, before backing away into shadow.

Leila didn't acknowledge her, but shuffled over and slammed the door shut as loudly as she could. She didn't like the Frenchwoman, but they'd done a deal with a devil who'd promised to give them all exactly what they wanted. Leila returned to the mirror and sighed when she saw her troubled reflection. Life had taken a heavy toll on her. What price would this mission extract? How much did she have left to give? As her mind filled with nightmares from her past and shapeless fears of the future, she became aware she'd suddenly lost her appetite.

Chapter 16

Pearce's breath felt hot against his skin. The face mask was stifling in the brutal heat. The cafeteria had no air conditioning and the block had been evacuated and quarantined as a precaution, so Pearce and Brigitte were experiencing the cumulative effects of over a fortnight of trapped air. They were being shown the sealed crime scene by Ibrahim Yousef, the deputy governor. Officious and pompous with a ponderous sense of self-regard, Yousef struck Pearce as the kind of man who'd have litter bearers if he could have got away with it. He and Kamal seemed to be old friends, and the retired Egyptian army officer played the deputy governor perfectly, laughing at his every joke, and making him feel every inch the potentate.

They'd undergone another test for Covid-19 before being admitted to the prison. When they'd arrived in Yousef's opulently furnished corner office, the deputy governor had given them a long-winded speech about the sanctity of the crime scene and the difficulty of obtaining access. Kamal had serviced the man's ego by saying that few in the country would have the power to authorize a visit by two FBI forensics specialists – Brigitte had succeeded in obtaining a couple of passable Quantico Lab IDs – and that hardly any of those who had the power would also have the wisdom to do so.

Puffed up by Kamal's flattery, Yousef had insisted on leading the expedition personally.

They were accompanied by Salah Abushady, the punctilious captain of the guards, who insisted they don particulate filters. He told Pearce and Brigitte that their colleagues from the FBI, who had visited the scene days after the incident at the request of the Egyptian government, had been unable to find any toxins, but had recommended the block remain quarantined until further analysis could be carried out at the lab in Quantico. Yousef was full of bluster and was on the verge of refusing to wear a mask, until Salah reminded him of the terrible way the inmates and guards had died.

Pearce didn't think he'd get anything useful from visiting the scene. He was interested in the human intelligence Yousef and Salah might provide. A prisoner had been able to smuggle masks and the toxic canister into the prison in contravention of the institution's established security procedures. Pearce wanted to know how he'd done it.

Trussed up in a suit that was a size too small for him, Yousef leaned on the serving counter at the edge of the room and mopped his sweaty brow with the back of his hand.

'*Ya basha,*' Salah remarked, using the colloquial term for boss. 'Our own police and the FBI said we shouldn't touch anything.'

Yousef glared at the man and didn't move. 'They have done their investigations. And my suit is clean.'

Pearce caught Kamal's eye. The former colonel was standing by the table the two escapees had been sitting at. He shook his head and smiled, and Pearce moved through the room, towards Brigitte, who was examining the area around the table.

'We need to get our hands on the Quantico lab report,' Pearce whispered.

Brigitte nodded. 'Something for Nahum?'

'Maybe,' he conceded. 'You ever hear of a compound that goes from lethal to inert in such a short space of time?'

The Frenchwoman shook her head. 'The autopsies found no toxins.'

'Which is very worrying. A poison that leaves no trace.' He turned to Salah. 'Captain, do you have any idea how the visitor was able to smuggle such a dangerous weapon into a secure facility?'

Yousef scowled at his subordinate, who studied the floor with a hangdog expression. 'Video suggests the fake Coke can was given to the prisoner by one of the chefs. The guard responsible for searching food stocks must have overlooked it, or he was an accomplice.'

'You've questioned him?'

'His name was Ismail Mahmoud,' Salah replied sadly. 'He died in here with all the others.'

'Is there video of the kitchen stores?' Pearce asked.

Salah shook his head, but it was Yousef who answered. 'The camera was broken. A replacement was scheduled to be fitted the following week.'

'There was nothing wrong with that camera,' Salah remarked angrily. 'It was sabotaged.'

'So you keep saying,' Yousef responded. 'You will have the opportunity to think about all the incidents that caused this terrible atrocity during your retirement.'

Pearce sensed the hostility between the two men.

'A commander cannot stay after something like this,' Salah said. 'So I've taken early retirement. No man of honour could remain in his job after such an atrocity.' He looked pointedly at Yousef.

'Is there a search log?' Brigitte asked.

'Of course,' Salah replied.

Chapter 17

Pearce was glad to be out of the cafeteria. They were still in their stifling masks, but were no longer surrounded by the upturned chairs and disarray that marked horrific mass murder.

'Here,' Salah said, leading Pearce and Brigitte to a booth in the austere concrete guard room.

The booth had a window that was covered by a metal grille. Access was through a locked metal door, which Salah opened. Inside was a desk, an old plastic chair and shelves stacked with papers, folders and large ledgers.

'All search reports go to the duty officer,' Salah said, opening the ledger that lay on the desk. He flipped to a page near the back of the book. 'This is a log of the most recent searches of the food stores.'

'What's that?' Pearce asked, noting an Arabic signature in an adjacent column.

'When a search is carried out, the guard who does this writes his name here,' Salah replied.

'Ismail Mahmoud,' Pearce said, sounding out the Arabic letters. 'May I?'

Salah nodded. 'Of course. Your colleagues and the Egyptian security forces have already conducted their forensics.' He stepped back and allowed Pearce to get to the desk.

Pearce leafed through the book, only partly aware of Kamal and Yousef's conversation in the corridor outside. The former colonel had asked the deputy governor what changes he'd make to the prison if he was promoted and the pompous man's voice echoed off the concrete walls as he rattled through a catalogue of failings and recriminations, most of which were aimed at his boss. Pearce focused on the ledger and felt a familiar pang of excitement as he spotted something tiny, but very significant.

'Captain, could you look at this?'

Salah peered over his shoulder and Brigitte crowded in and looked from the other side.

Pearce flipped from the page Salah had shown him to one from three days earlier. He pointed at the signature next to the most recent search log entry and then at Ismail Mahmoud's earlier scrawl.

'Do you notice anything?' Pearce asked.

Salah looked clueless, but Brigitte spotted the discrepancy immediately. 'The swirl above the line goes in different directions.'

'It's called a *hamza*,' Pearce remarked. 'Above the *alif*, it is written like a five, rather than a two.'

Salah studied the lettering of the two signatures and nodded. Alif was the first letter of the Arabic alphabet and was often written with a tiny *hamza* at the top, like the dot on an 'i'. Pearce flipped through the book and pointed out more of Ismail's signatures.

'He wrote all his *hamza* like a two, except on this one day,' he noted. 'Whoever did the forgery got it almost perfect.'

Pearce carried on leafing through the ledger until he saw what he was looking for. 'Karim Halabi,' he said. 'The only guard who writes his *hamza* like a five. Was he one of those killed?'

'No,' Salah replied, his face suddenly hardening. 'He and all the other guards who worked on this block have been signed off for health reasons.'

Yousef sensed something was up and broke off his speech to sidle over. 'What's this?'

'Someone might have forged the search records,' Pearce said. 'Possibly a guard called Karim Halabi.'

'Then we must call internal security,' Yousef responded excitedly, no doubt imagining the political advantage he'd obtain. 'He must be interrogated.'

'If it's all the same, we'd like to talk to him first,' Pearce said.

Brigitte nodded at Kamal. The former colonel pulled Yousef aside and Pearce only caught the first couple of words of their whispered conversation. '*Ya habibi . . .*' it began. *My good friend*; the words used to prime countless corrupt deals in the Middle East. Pearce wasn't interested in what grubby arrangement Kamal made to ensure Yousef didn't escalate the discovery. He was thinking about what he'd do when he met Karim Halabi.

Chapter 18

Leila was locked in a quiet windowless room, searching for inspiration. She could hear Wollerton's breathing nearby and the low hum of activity coming from elsewhere in the building, but the technical analysis laboratory was otherwise silent and the microscopes, spectrometers and computer scanners stood idle. They were inside one of the most secure buildings in Cairo, the headquarters of *Keta El Amn El Watani*, the Egyptian National Security Agency. Many Egyptians referred to it as the *Mukhabarat*, a common catch-all term across the Middle East for the state intelligence agencies, but Egypt's NSA was separate from the nation's true Mukhabarat, the General Intelligence Directorate, in that it focused purely on domestic threats. Lacking the budgets and technological sophistication of its western counterparts, the Egyptian NSA still relied heavily on human intelligence, and Leila had heard rumours that it had over 100,000 informants concealed within the general population. She could only begin to imagine the complexities of managing a network of that size, but Egypt faced serious social and political challenges and was fighting an ongoing campaign against violent Islamic militants in the Sinai and elsewhere. The very foundations of its republic were under threat, so she could understand the resources the Egyptian government was prepared to throw at its intelligence organizations. She had lived through the failure of a state and had to cope with the aftermath every single day.

However large its network, the NSA hadn't been able to identify the source of the canister lying inside the isolation tank directly in front of her. She had her hands inside the tank's inbuilt rubber gloves, but had given up manipulating the canister – there were no machining markings or evidence of calibrations of any kind. The canister had been inside a false can of Coca-Cola, but that too offered no traceable secrets.

According to Amina, the lab technician who had gone for a coffee with their Egyptian handler, Sharif, the canister was made of steel and had been cast rather than milled, no doubt to further reduce the chances of its origins being traced. The trigger was an electrical charge delivered to a tiny quantity of propellant. It worked like a large party popper.

'Anything?' Wollerton asked.

Leila shook her head slowly. She was frustrated by the puzzle, but at least it took her mind off her sister. She couldn't get over the ease with which they'd infiltrated Egypt's NSA and was more convinced than ever that Kamal, the former colonel, and his associate had ties to the Egyptian intelligence community. Sharif had been able to get them into the building with no more than a coronavirus test and a quiet conversation with a senior executive. Leila knew familial and tribal ties trumped all else in the Middle East, but Sharif's relationship and ease of access had to be based on something more. The nameless executive who was never introduced to Leila or Wollerton had instructed Amina to be their liaison and give them unrestricted access to the case files and evidence.

The young woman had the thoughtful demeanour of a priestess, but she wore a patterned floral dress and matching hijab, and stored her pens and personal tools in a large Minnie Mouse pencil case that looked out of place on the counter next to the isolation tank. Amina had told them that searches for the identities of the two men had yielded nothing; not a single photo match on any database the Egyptians had access to, or on the Internet.

Leila had been troubled by this digital invisibility ever since Blaine Carter had told them the American prisoner had no photo record of any kind. That sort of anonymity could only be achieved by one of the larger intelligence players – the CIA, America's NSA, Russia's FSB or SVR, or China's MSS. And even they would struggle. Digital invisibility was almost impossible in the era of constant surveillance, omnipresent cameras and cloud computing.

There had been no physical evidence at the scene other than the men's fingerprints, which had yielded just as much of a blank as their images.

'No marks?' Wollerton asked.

'Nothing,' Leila replied. 'Just their prints, which lead nowhere.'

'Why didn't he use a grenade?' Wollerton asked. 'It's mechanical, less to go wrong with it. Same result and you'd have the benefit of destroying the delivery device in the process.'

Leila pondered the question. People usually opted for the least troublesome, quickest solution to any problem. Wollerton was right, a grenade would have been the better option, so why use a bespoke canister? She picked it up and manipulated it with the thick rubber gloves. The lid contained a tiny lithium battery and wiring that ran to the interior charge in the base, but what if the button on the top wasn't the only way to detonate the device?

Feeling a rush of excitement, Leila turned the canister over. The base was almost certainly thick enough.

'Can you find Amina?' Leila said. 'Ask her if they've X-rayed it.'

Wollerton nodded, unlocked the door and left the lab.

Leila held the top of the canister in one glove and grabbed the base with the other. She tried to twist the base off, but it didn't budge. She put the canister down, withdrew her hands from the protective gloves and locked the lab door. As she limped back to the isolation tank, she studied the grey receptacle. She pushed her hands into the gloves and picked it up. She gripped the top again, but this time she held the very edge of the bottom of the canister. She tried to turn the base, but it didn't give. She tried the other way and a hairline appeared less than half a centimetre from the bottom. She hurriedly unscrewed the base and was gratified to see tiny wires running from the main chamber to something in the base. It was a computer chip. She took her hands out of the gloves, ignored the hazard warnings on the outer airlock and opened the isolation tank. The toxin within the canister had become a harmless carbonate, so the isolation tank was just a precaution. Or at least that's what Leila told herself as she opened the inner airlock.

She heard the door handle rattle and turned to see figures in the frosted panel window. The door caught against the lock.

'Leila?' Wollerton said from the other side.

She ignored him and reached into the tank. She snatched the chip from the base and slipped it into her pocket.

Wollerton tried the door again. 'Hello?' he said.

'I have a key,' Amina told him, and Leila saw the figures shift position.

She hurriedly reattached the base to the canister and closed the inner airlock. She kicked her cane to the floor as she shut the other hatch. When the door opened and Amina, Wollerton and Sharif entered, she was stooping to recover it. The three of them looked at her in puzzlement and there was a trace of suspicion in Amina's face.

'Sorry,' Leila said. 'I dropped my stick.'

She didn't care whether they believed her. All she cared about was the tiny silicon wafer in her pocket. Featureless metal containers couldn't be traced, but computer chips left a trail she could read.

Chapter 19

Yousef had grumbled the whole way to the City of the Dead. The deputy governor was unhappy they weren't calling the authorities, but Kamal had convinced him to give them a chance to question Karim Halabi, the guard Pearce believed had forged the search log. The man who might have been responsible for getting the canister into Al Aqarab. Yousef had produced his phone a number of times and threatened to call the agent at Egypt's NSA who was leading the investigation. As they'd travelled through Cairo in the Land Rover, Kamal had coaxed, cajoled and in the end threatened, saying Yousef wouldn't want the NSA probing around all his dealings. Whatever information the former colonel had on the deputy governor must have been damaging because the pompous man had finally put his phone away and stopped talking about his duty to the nation. Pearce wondered what secrets Kamal knew and how he'd got them.

According to Salah, the captain of the prison guards, Karim Halabi was from an extremely poor peasant family, one of many who moved from the Nile Delta to Cairo in search of a better life. What Halabi's family had found was a home among Cairo's graves, the sprawling cemetery known as the City of the Dead, which lay between the grand citadel of the Mosque of Mohammed Ali and the medieval Khan el-Khalili bazaar. Families such as Karim's built shanties in the six-kilometre-square necropolis and earned money by tending the monuments of wealthier Egyptians. Each family worked a patch and might earn the equivalent of five dollars per month for each mausoleum they tended.

A few lucky inhabitants managed to get jobs outside the cemetery and could escape the narrow walkways that zig-zagged between the haphazardly arranged stone tombs. But jobs were hard to come by, particularly when many people con-sidered these families to be social outcasts who attracted bad fortune by virtue of their association with the dead. So dozens of people of all ages were consigned to live in impoverished conditions and spent their lives tending to crypts that were often larger and better cared for than the shacks they lived in.

Kamal parked the Land Rover Discovery on El-Soultan Ahmed Street, which ran through the heart of the City of the Dead, and Salah pointed out Karim's home; a ramshackle breezeblock construction with a corrugated roof. Not much larger than the Discovery, Salah told them the tiny place was home to Karim, his mother, his sister, her husband and their three children. Pearce felt sorry for the guard. If he'd been looking for a way into Al Aqarab, Karim would have been top of his list of guards to turn. Desperation made people's morals malleable.

'How would you like to proceed?' Kamal asked.

'You, Salah and Brigitte get into position in case he tries to make a break for it, and I'll go for the collar,' Pearce said. 'If he runs, one of you takes him.'

Salah nodded and Kamal said, 'OK.'

But Yousef shook his head and leaned across Pearce, who suddenly caught a blast of overpowering cologne.

'There are families in there,' Yousef said, pointing at the shanties that stood beyond the Land Rover's opaque windows. 'What if he has another device? Or if he takes a child hostage? We should draw him out.'

Salah sighed, but Pearce didn't react.

'He will respect me,' Yousef said. 'I will tell him he's needed for questioning at the prison. A routine interview to check facts. I'll bring him to the car and you can do what you want.'

Pearce pursed his lips and studied the sprawling necropolis. If Karim made a run for it, there was no guarantee they could counter his local knowledge of the labyrinthine city. He could vanish north towards the ancient bazaar or south towards the grand old mosque.

'OK,' Pearce said. 'You bring him to the car.'

Yousef nodded and stepped out. Pearce watched him hurry across the road.

'If you'll excuse me,' Kamal said. 'I think this is a bad idea. That man is not to be trusted.'

'Why?' Pearce asked.

Kamal tilted his head and raised his eyebrows. 'He has expensive habits.' He looked sideways at Salah, who was all ears.

'Are you saying he's corrupt?' Brigitte asked.

'He supplies oxycodone into the prison,' Kamal replied.

Salah's eyes widened, and he unleashed a string of curses.

'Why didn't you say something sooner?' Pearce asked.

'Sometimes it's more useful to have a pliable asset than it is to punish corruption,' Kamal said.

'I will report him,' Salah said.

'With what proof?' Kamal responded.

'How do you know this?' Salah asked, but Kamal ignored the question.

'I don't care what you do with him,' Pearce said, 'but it's clear he's not to be trusted. Let's move.' He didn't wait for a response and stepped into the heat of an autumn day. Brigitte got out of the front passenger seat and Kamal and Salah followed.

They jogged across the dusty street, and entered the vast necropolis through a hole in the crumbling perimeter wall. They picked their way round some of the smaller family tombs on the edge of the cemetery and approached Karim's home.

Pearce knew something was wrong the moment he saw Karim emerge. The tall, thin guard cleared the low doorway and as he straightened from a stoop, he caught sight of Pearce and the others and his eyes widened. But it wasn't Karim's reaction that sent a chill down Pearce's spine, it was the sight of Yousef following him out of the tiny breezeblock structure. When the deputy governor emerged, inches behind Karim, he had his hand inside his jacket. It was the pose of amateurs, one Pearce had seen in countless movies – Yousef was reaching for a gun.

An old woman – presumably Karim's mother – appeared in the doorway, her face wizened by a life of poverty and the harsh beat of a relentless sun. Her craggy features crumpled in dismay as the horror began.

Pearce started running and cried out as Karim turned on his heels and sprinted away from them. The prison guard's sandaled feet pounded the dusty ground and the hem of his striped black and white *galabeya* whipped around his ankles. Brigitte had also reacted and was a couple of paces ahead of Pearce.

Yousef already had the gun in his hand. 'Stop!' he yelled in English, no doubt for the benefit of his audience.

Karim ignored him and kept running. He was yards from the nearest monument, a low stone structure about half the area of a tennis court. More people had emerged from the neighbouring shanties and they watched aghast as Yousef took aim.

'Don't!' Pearce yelled.

Kamal shouted something, but it was lost beneath the crack of a gunshot. The black pistol spat again and a second bullet hit Karim in the back. He toppled into the dirt and his mother started screaming.

'He was trying to escape,' Yousef said, turning to Pearce and the others as they raced towards him. 'I think he had another bomb.'

Pearce was furious at the unnecessary loss of life and the grief it would inflict on Karim's family. He was enraged by the fact Yousef thought him too stupid to see through the ruse. Most of all, Pearce was angry at himself for having brought this murderer here. But they hadn't been able to leave Yousef at the prison for fear he would have called the authorities.

Yousef's eyes widened in fear as Pearce sprinted up to him and grabbed his lapels. Brigitte ran on, heading for Karim, as Pearce snatched Yousef's pistol.

'You killed that man for nothing!' Pearce yelled.

Chapter 20

Salah followed Brigitte, and Kamal stopped by Karim's mother, who'd collapsed against her home. Her daughter and grandchildren clustered around her, weeping, as Kamal phoned for an ambulance. Recovering from their shock, the crowd, mostly made up of young men, started muttering angrily and began to close menacingly. Life was hard enough for these impoverished people without wealthy outsiders coming here to murder them. Pearce had known Middle Eastern crowds to inflict rough and instant justice and he sensed the mood turning all around them.

'What are you doing?' Yousef asked. 'I had to shoot him. I aimed to injure him. I did not want to kill the man.' His voice was high and uneven, the tone of liars throughout the ages. 'Let me go.'

Pearce ignored him and pushed him up the slope towards the large mausoleum. Brigitte was crouched beside Karim and looked up as they neared.

'He's dead,' she said.

Pearce gripped Yousef tighter and forced him on.

'Hey! Let me go!'

Pearce replied with a hard smack. 'You'll talk when I tell you to.'

Yousef whimpered and his eyes welled with tears.

'We don't have long,' Brigitte said, glancing round nervously as she fell in beside Pearce.

The crowd was gathering a sense of purpose and had started following them up the gentle incline. Salah said a quick prayer over Karim's body and hurried towards the tomb.

Pearce kicked open the rusty gate that stood across a narrow corridor which ran through the middle of the squat building. He dragged a protesting Yousef along the passageway and down a run of stone steps.

'Stop!' Yousef pleaded. 'Please. I didn't mean to kill him.'

The tomb was dark and the warm air ripe with the smell of decay. Pearce pushed Yousef roughly, bouncing him from one coarse stone wall to the other. There was another corridor at the bottom of the steps, and two crumbling wooden doors stood opposite each other. Pearce forced Yousef through the one on the right.

'No!' the deputy governor shouted. 'You can't do this.' He tried to force his way out, but Pearce clocked him with the pistol and he fell back, moaning.

Brigitte followed them in, but when Pearce saw Salah in the doorway, he blocked the captain's path.

'I want him to suffer,' Salah said as he tried to push past.

'It's better if you don't see this,' Pearce replied. 'Stop anyone coming in. They want his blood.'

Yousef whined, and Salah looked at the pathetic man who was hunched over, sobbing as he cradled his head.

'Give him something from me,' Salah said before heading out of the shadows towards the sunlight at the top of the steps.

'You can't do this,' Yousef whimpered. 'You're FBI. You have rules.'

Pearce stalked up to the man, who shuffled back towards the wall of shelves that held the shrouded corpses of the family who owned this crypt. Judging by the size of the bodies, this was the chamber for men, and the one across the corridor would have been for women.

'We don't have any rules.'

Pearce punctuated his statement by driving the pistol into Yousef's clavicle, breaking the bone. Yousef's shrill scream echoed around the crypt, and he collapsed, clawing at his shoulder and crying freely.

'You didn't want us coming here,' Pearce said. 'You knew there was a risk Karim would tell us the truth. You recruited him. You hired him to smuggle the canister into the prison, didn't you?' He crouched and forced Yousef to look at him. 'Didn't you?' he yelled.

Brigitte smacked the back of Yousef's head. 'Talk to him!'

'Please,' Yousef cried.

'Who hired you?' Pearce asked.

'I don't know his name,' Yousef sobbed. 'I think he was Czech or Polish. Maybe Russian. I don't know. He came to my house a few weeks ago. He offered me a hundred thousand dollars. I didn't know. He said if I didn't help, he would tell the governor about the bad things I was doing in the prison. Tell him about the drugs. I swear I didn't know what they would do.'

'Who was he? What did he look like?' Pearce drove the muzzle of the pistol into Yousef's collarbone and the man screamed.

'Please!' he said when Pearce removed the gun. 'I don't know. He wore a mask. He had a beard. A long one. He was as tall as her,' he indicated Brigitte. 'I don't know anything else.'

Pearce heard raised voices cascade along the corridor. Then Salah spoke rapidly in Arabic, telling people to stay back. There was the sound of a commotion. They didn't have long. 'Where did they go?'

'The prisoner, the one we knew as Ibrahim Mahmood, the man who was broken out – when he'd first come to prison, he spoke of working at a big port in America,' Yousef said. 'I think he said Seattle. Please. That's all I know.'

Pearce looked at Brigitte, who nodded. The angry cries coming from outside were growing louder and more hostile, and calls for justice bounced around the tomb.

'Help me,' Yousef pleaded, his face a dirty mess of blood, tears, dust and snot. 'Don't let them in.' He understood the severity of his situation.

Pearce stared at him coldly. 'You're on your own.'

Yousef cried out as Brigitte and Pearce left the crypt. His pained lament filled their ears as they hurried into the sunlight. They found Salah at the top of the steps, struggling to hold back the growing crowd. A young man in shorts and T-shirt was out cold in the nearby dirt.

'He wouldn't listen,' Salah explained.

'We're finished here,' Brigitte responded.

Salah nodded and turned to the crowd. '*Imshi,*' he said, clearing a path that kept the gathered souls at a safe distance. The last thing they needed was to run the risk of infection and lose fourteen days in isolation.

As the angry crowd surged forward, Salah yelled commands to ensure people kept their distance, and he, Brigitte and Pearce walked away from the sounds of violence that soon sprang from within the dark crypt.

Chapter 21

People were the problem. The massive volume of freight moving through America's eighth largest seaport posed few serious issues. The freight management systems were fully automated, and while there might be the occasional illegal shipment or a consignment that needed to be quarantined, there was a process to deal with everything to do with the millions of tons of goods that flowed through the port. Apart from exceptions that needed human intervention, the majority of incoming shipments were identified and unloaded automatically, and the cargo either stored or forwarded. The huge container storage area was also automated and if a shipment was to continue its onward journey by road, the truck driver would simply present the container ID number and it would be automatically loaded onto his vehicle by the vast crane and container management system.

It was this automation that was so prized by Deni and his associates. By virtue of his position as shift supervisor, Ziad had access to the systems management room and could move a container out of the bonded customs zone, or, thanks to a kernel of code Deni had paid a hacker to develop, make a shipment disappear entirely. Deni used this power to enrich himself, shipping contraband from ports in Asia, making

Seattle Port a Pacific gateway for a range of regional organized crime groups who paid the Chechen tribute.

But it had been almost a week since their meeting in the bookstore and Deni hadn't made contact. Ziad wondered whether he was no longer needed to run product through the port because one or more of his colleagues were now working for the Chechen. He couldn't ask, and he knew better than to arouse Deni's suspicions by suggesting he was ready to run shipments. He simply had to wait. And while he waited, he thought about Essi and wondered whether she'd been in on her father's plan to get rid of him. He turned the question in his mind as he dealt with the mundane challenges of his job. Ben Samuels had to leave early to pick up his kid from school. Julio had booked a vacation that wasn't showing on his schedule. Kenny and Luke got into a fistfight and had to be suspended. And then there were Richie Cutter's friends, who were back from compassionate leave and mourning the man's passing. Ziad was still troubled by Cutter's death and the bodies he had chalked up during the escape from Al Aqarab. He tried to tell himself that thousands of people died every day and that at least the people he'd killed had lost their lives for a purpose. Besides, Richie Cutter and the prisoners were not good men.

What about the guards? he thought every so often.

They were bad too.

All of them?

He never answered the question because it was a trick designed to make him think he wasn't a good man. He *was* good. He was just doing what was necessary.

Elroy Lang and the silent Thai, Awut, seemed pleased by what he'd done. They lurked around the house on Kenyon

Street. Some evenings the two men would vanish for a few hours, but for the most part they lingered like patient reptiles, watching TV, waiting for news from Ziad. Elroy had praised Ziad for the way he'd eliminated Cutter and every now and then he talked of the satisfaction of vengeance. According to Elroy, humans are born with an inbuilt sense of right and wrong, which is why revenge and delivery of just retribution were some of the most satisfying outcomes a person could ever achieve. Ziad knew the man was bolstering his resolve, but it wasn't necessary. Despite his misgivings about the people he'd killed, Ziad just had to picture Deni Salamov's smiling face, and imagine Essi's treachery, and an unquenchable fury would rise. They would suffer for what they had done.

Ziad had just shut down his computer when Harry Martin appeared at the door.

'How's it feel to be back?' Harry asked, gesturing at Ziad's small office.

'Good,' Ziad replied, getting to his feet. 'After what I've been through, this is heaven.'

'A few of us are going for beers,' Harry remarked. 'You thirsty?'

'I can't.' Ziad pictured himself having to make awkward smalltalk with friends of the man he'd murdered, 'I'll take a rain check,' he added enthusiastically.

They left the port authority building and talked about *Elite Voyager*, a huge ship that was due in from China the following week. They reached Ziad's Buick first, and Harry eyed the old junker with a broad smile.

'Jeez, Zee,' he said. 'Is this your bid for a raise?'

'I'm trading up soon,' Ziad replied. 'It's just while I get back on my feet.'

Harry's smile disappeared and he nodded sombrely. 'Sorry, that was insensitive.'

'No problem.'

'Have a good one,' the director of operations said, and carried on walking through the large lot.

Ziad started the old Buick and left the sprawling port complex. Instead of taking the I-5 south towards South Park, he headed north and within forty minutes he was driving up the hill to Essi's Point Edwards condo. It was a pilgrimage he'd made every day since their encounter outside the restaurant, a ritual that brought him some comfort. He liked being in her life, even if it was only by virtue of sitting outside her building for twenty minutes a day. Hate was as powerfully seductive as love, and he experienced warming anger every time he caught sight of her. She brought him back to life.

But today was different. When he drove up the hill and rounded the bend just before her building, he caught sight of Essi standing on the sidewalk right where he usually parked. She was wearing dark skinny jeans and the black floral sheer top he'd always liked. She'd pulled her hair into a ponytail, and when she heard the rattling engine and saw the rusty Buick approach, she folded her arms and gave him a cold hard look of disappointment. He thought about driving on, but that would have been churlish, so he pulled over.

'I told you I didn't want to see you, Zee,' Essi said. She walked round the car and surprised him by opening the passenger door and sliding in beside him. 'We're done. You've got to stop coming round here. It's freaking me out.'

Ziad tried to control his rising anger. He recalled all the times she'd been happy to see his BMW turn into her condo complex. All the times she'd emerged from her apartment full of smiles. All she had to do was say the word and they could go back to those days. He couldn't understand why she wouldn't.

'I've moved on,' Essi said. 'But my father hasn't. He wants to see you.'

Chapter 22

The drive south was awkward. Ziad burned with the shame of rejection. Somewhere deep down he still harboured the hope Essi would come to her senses. But if she did, what would that mean for his quest for vengeance? Could he forgive her?

You're being ridiculous, his inner voice told him. *She's a stranger to you now. Look at her, she is sickened by you. Her skin is crawling just being near you.*

Ziad burned with shame. They could never go back. She sat in the passenger seat and said nothing. Ziad responded in kind and the only noise in the car were the sounds of the city drifting through the open windows. Evening had truly set in, but it was still too warm to be sealed in a car with no air conditioning. It took a little over an hour to reach 140th Street, and when Ziad parked in the lot outside the community centre, Essi turned to him.

'This is the only place I ever want to see you, Zee. I don't want you outside my apartment, my office, or anywhere else. My father wants you. I don't.'

Ziad's heart shrivelled. 'I can't . . .' he began, but he choked up and had to start again. 'How can you be so cold?'

'How can *I*?' she interrupted him angrily. Her eyes flashed with hostility. 'You left me! I told you not to go. I said it would be dangerous. You left me!' Her voice rose in pitch and started to crack. 'You did that. All I did was pick myself up and move on.'

There was a prolonged silence.

'My father is in the coffee shop,' she said at last. 'Goodbye, Zee.' She got out of the car and didn't look back as she walked into the community centre.

Ziad sat watching her until she was swallowed by an interior door. He was startled by someone banging on his window and turned to see Rasul, Deni's son, grinning at him.

'Come on,' Rasul said. 'He's waiting.'

'We need you to handle a shipment.' Deni's soft voice was almost lost beneath the clatter of crockery and the incessant hubbub. The cafe was packed with familiar faces, many of whom had shouted words of welcome and risen to slap Ziad on the shoulder as he'd followed Rasul to Deni's table at the back, near the kitchen. Ziad knew the Chechen had his properties swept for surveillance devices every week, and the background noise of the place would make it impossible for anyone to listen in on them with a directional mic. The staff tested patrons for coronavirus on entry, so any strangers would be noticed immediately. Deni had survived at the top for so long by being paranoid about security and only doing business with people he trusted.

'What is it?' Ziad asked, taking a sip of his rich Turkish coffee.

'Something from the old country,' Deni replied.

Even though none of them came from there, the old country was code for Afghanistan, which meant they were shipping heroin.

'It's coming on the *Elite*,' Deni said. 'Rasul will give you the container number.'

Ziad nodded at the men he hated and wondered whether they had any inkling of his true intentions. It was clear his fears had been unfounded; they still trusted him. But they shouldn't have. He was set on making them pay the highest possible price for their betrayal.

Awut and Elroy were eating dinner in front of the TV by the time Ziad returned to the house on Kenyon Street.

'There's food in the pot,' Elroy said, nodding towards the dank kitchen.

'They asked me to take care of a shipment,' Ziad replied.

Elroy shot Awut a triumphant glance. He put down his bowl of Pad Thai and switched off the TV. 'Eat fast,' he said. 'There are people we need to see.'

Chapter 23

Pearce woke to the sound of the *adhan* issuing from the speakers of a nearby mosque. After the encounter in the City of the Dead the previous day, they'd returned to the apartment in Zamalek to find Leila and Wollerton already working to identify the source of a silicon chip that had been concealed in the canister used in the Al Aqarab prison break.

Brigitte and Sharif had focused their attention on Seattle Port, hoping to get a lead on the mysterious escapee. Pearce thought Yousef had been telling the truth. He wondered what had happened to the man after they'd left. Salah had stayed with Karim's mother to help her and the murdered guard's family deal with the emergency services. How would he explain his role in events? Would he admit any knowledge of what had happened to the corrupt deputy governor? Pearce hoped the captain of the guard had the good sense to play ignorant.

Kamal had driven them from the necropolis through the noisy, chaotic Cairo traffic to the lush island with its high green trees, colonial apartment blocks, and large villas. The Zamalek apartment had become a hive of intelligence analysis for everyone apart from Pearce. Leila and Wollerton were working side by side, using the laptops they'd requested from Brigitte. The Frenchwoman spent most of her time on the phone, but Pearce caught her exchanging glances with Leila, who was unequivocally hostile whenever she caught Brigitte looking at her. He shared Leila's distrust of the Frenchwoman, but her presence had been forced upon them by Huxley Blaine Carter.

Kamal was glued to his mobile, pacing the apartment as he engaged in furtive conversations in an attempt to tie the escapee to Seattle.

Pearce had left them to it and wandered onto the roof terrace, where he'd spent time listening to the ceaseless toot of horns and general cacophony of Cairo's streets. His eye had been caught by a man who had a small shop on the ground floor of a nearby building. The shop was illuminated by strip lights that made it blaze brightly in the Cairo night, and Pearce had watched the white-haired man work his way through a pile of crumpled clothes, methodically straightening each one on his board before smoothing it with a traditional cast metal iron that was heated on a hotplate. As he prepared each garment, the old man would drink from a small bottle and then spit a cloud of fine mist over the item. Running the scorching iron over the moisture created hissing clouds of steam, and, as he'd been entranced by the hypnotic rhythm of the man's work, Pearce had thought back to the prison cafeteria and all the people who'd died there. Whoever wanted the escapee had been prepared to pay a high price to get him.

Pearce had joined the others for pizza before turning in. Now, with the sound of the morning call to prayer filling his room, Pearce climbed out of bed, stretched and got dressed, opting for a pair of light cargo trousers and a black T-shirt. He found Leila alone in the large living room. The French doors were open and the call to prayer louder, carried by a gentle breeze that billowed the long curtains.

'Tell me you've been to bed,' Pearce said.

'I've been to bed,' Leila replied in a flat tone that made it very clear she was humouring him. 'And when I woke up, I found out all about this little thing.' She held up the microchip. 'It's a digital transmitter, used to carry a signal from a cellular device, so the toxin can be triggered remotely. It was manufactured using a semi-conductor foundry built in a factory in Almelo, Holland. The machine in question had originally been sold to a touch-screen manufacturer in South Korea.'

'But it's moved on,' Wollerton added as he appeared in the doorway. He was in boxer shorts and a T-shirt and carried two cups of freshly brewed coffee. 'Sorry I had to crash. Did you find out where it went?' he asked Leila, handing her one of the coffees.

'I checked the sales ledger of the South Korean firm and the semi-conductor foundry was sold to a broker who then sold it to a company in Qingdao, China.'

'How do you know the chip wasn't made in Korea?' Pearce asked.

'The foundry wasn't there long enough,' Leila replied. 'My guess is the Korean firm is a front to get round European export controls that protect against providing the Chinese with high-end technology. The first chips that foundry ever made rolled out in Qingdao.'

Wollerton studied the window open on Leila's laptop. 'Qingdao Consumer Products. Suitably bland.'

'We need to get out there,' Pearce said.

'No,' Brigitte cut in as she entered the room. She was dressed in black trousers and a red top.

Pearce thought he saw Leila stiffen at the sight of the Frenchwoman.

'I found this,' Brigitte produced her phone and showed Pearce a local news report about the sudden and unexplained death of a Seattle Port worker.

'What am I looking at?' Pearce asked.

'Read on.'

Pearce took the device and scrolled through the article, until he found what Brigitte wanted him to see.

'A witness who was with Mr Cutter at the time of his death,' Pearce read aloud, 'said the victim, who had no prior conditions, suddenly developed breathing problems and suffered a cardiac arrest. Local police chief Xavier Moro reassured residents, saying they'd found no traces of any toxins at the scene.'

Pearce saw the others register the significance of his words.

'I've let the Seattle police know what we found here, a toxin that asphyxiates without leaving a trace,' Brigitte said. 'We'll see what they do with that information.'

'If that's the same stuff used in the prison break,' Wollerton said, 'then we're on the right trail.'

'But we've got a solid lead in Qingdao,' Leila protested.

'We split up,' Brigitte said. 'I will go to China with Leila. Kyle and Scott will go to Seattle.'

Leila shook her head and shot Pearce a sharp look.

'We don't work for you, remember? Our interests just happen to coincide,' he said. 'I'll go to Seattle with Leila. You and Kyle can follow up the Qingdao lead.'

Brigitte fixed Pearce with a stare and he could sense her wrestling over whether to challenge him.

'OK,' she said finally. 'I'll make the arrangements.'

Chapter 24

It was after midnight when they arrived at the roadside bar. The dusty parking lot was packed with large motorcycles and a group of leather- and denim-clad bikers were drinking, smoking and jostling each other outside. The backs of their jackets were covered with huge patches that depicted the snarling jaws of a red wolf. The bar was the kind of anarchic place that seemed to perpetually teeter on the edge of violence. Not somewhere Ziad would ever have associated with Elroy or the quiet Thai.

Ziad parked beside a row of bikes. Their chrome fittings gleamed in the gaudy neon light of a sign which declared the name of the bar: RPM. Awut and Elroy were unfazed by the rowdy bikers who clustered near the entrance, and led Ziad through the group. A guy in a black T-shirt emblazoned with a bone-white skull tested them for coronavirus before ushering them inside.

The loud thrash metal music was almost painful. Bikers of all races, genders and ages crowded the place, dancing, drinking and acting up. Almost everyone wore a Red Wolf patch or sported a similar tattoo. The interior stank of sour mash, doubtless a consequence of years of whisky spillages on the hardwood floor. The walls were covered with black and white photos of classic motorcycles and the bar was decked out in old tin road signs.

Ziad followed Awut and Elroy across the dance floor and through a door which led to the toilets. The corridor was permeated with the stench of urine and the walls were covered with Polaroid photographs of customers in various states of undress. Thought-provoking, funny or just plain lewd messages had been scrawled beneath the photos in pen and marker. One caught Ziad's eye. It read, 'I was a sex slave for a week and it fucked my mind.' Above the messy writing was a photo of a middle-aged woman in her underwear doing a Mick Jagger pout at the camera, her haunted eyes a window into her broken mind.

Elroy and Awut passed the doors to the toilets and continued towards another marked 'private'. A huge bald-headed man leaned on a stool beside it. Elroy didn't even acknowledge the giant and marched straight through the door. Ziad followed Awut inside, and found himself in a smoky back room. A couple of skinny bikers had their shirts off and were hunched on the edge of an old sofa sharing a crack pipe. A woman of no more than twenty, wearing black leather trousers and a Napalm Death T-shirt, had passed out in the chair next to them.

Awut took up a watchful position by the door. Elroy didn't even glance at the crackheads and headed for a seating area on the other side of the room. Three sofas were arranged in a corner, beside a large window that was sealed by a corrugated shutter. On the sofas sat two men and a woman.

'Ziad,' Elroy said, 'these are my associates.' He gestured to the trio, all of whom had remained seated. 'This is Eddie Fletcher. He owns this place.'

Fletcher was a bald white man in his early forties. His white vest exposed his muscular arms, which were covered in tattoos that ran up to his neck. Every image was a variation of the 'Red Wolf' patch. He nodded at Ziad, but said nothing.

'His wife Kirsty,' Elroy continued, signalling a woman of about Ziad's age.

She wore light jeans and a black vest, sported even more tattoos than her husband and had close-cropped hair that did nothing to conceal the noticeable scar which ran from her left temple down her cheek to her chin. She glared at Ziad with the wild eyes of a dangerous animal.

'And this is Andel Novak,' Elroy said, gesturing at the final member of the group.

Novak wore a light-blue suit, a sky-blue shirt that was unbuttoned at the collar, and a pair of shiny black shoes. He looked as though he was in his early fifties, but the scraggy beard that reached halfway down his throat made his age difficult to pinpoint. Like his hair, it was black with broad streaks of grey, but unlike his hair, it was curly and unkempt, giving the man a wild air. His eyes were bright blue and were alive with intensity. He smiled at Ziad indulgently.

'It's a pleasure to meet you,' Novak said, getting to his feet. The man had a pronounced Eastern European accent, but there was a clipped English formality to his speech, which made it impossible for Ziad to guess his nationality. He shook Novak's proffered hand, and found the man's grip surprisingly strong.

'Have a seat,' Elroy suggested, and Ziad sat next to him.

'You are glad to be a free man again?' Novak asked.

Ziad nodded.

'Our friend tells us you've risen to the challenge, that you can be trusted. Is he right?' Novak asked.

'I'll do whatever it takes,' Ziad replied. 'I want Deni Salamov and his family to suffer.'

'Good,' Novak said. 'Do you know what we are?'

Ziad shook his head.

'We are the Red Wolves,' Novak continued. 'Some call us criminals, but we prefer to think of ourselves as revolutionaries who aren't prepared to accept that the way things are is the way they must always be. One day, when you have truly proven yourself, you might become a wolf.'

Fletcher sneered.

'Mr Fletcher commands this chapter,' Novak explained. 'He's a very hard man to impress. And rightly so. Becoming a Red Wolf is a great honour.'

This is it, Ziad thought. *I've finally earned their trust.*

'What do you want me to do?' he asked.

'Deni Salamov has a shipment coming in. We'd like you to tell Mr Fletcher when the product is due to be collected.'

Ziad looked at the brutish biker and his wild-eyed wife. 'Sure,' he said.

'You know what this means?' Elroy asked.

Ziad nodded. 'Yeah. You're going to steal it.'

Elroy smiled. 'More than that. We're going to start a war.'

Chapter 25

They called him the Midas Killer. By the time Leila and Pearce arrived in Seattle, Brigitte's warning to Police Chief Xavier Moro had leaked to the media and been filtered through at least one hyperactive imagination that painted a picture of a crazed killer who inflicted invisible, untraceable death. Pearce had purchased a copy of the *Seattle Star* from an airside newsstand and while they waited in the arrivals hall, he and Leila leafed through four sensational pages devoted to what was essentially a thin story of conjecture and speculation that linked the death of Richard Cutter to the mass murder of the Al Aqarab prison break.

It had taken Brigitte a couple of days to make the necessary arrangements, but, seventy-two hours after deciding to split the team, Pearce and Leila had touched down in Seattle after a gruelling journey from Cairo. Leila slept poorly at the best of times, and was usually kept awake by the pain of her old injuries and a profound fear of her nightmares, but aircraft – with their stale air, cramped seats and incessant noise – offered no hope of rest. She'd stayed awake during the flight from Cairo to Amsterdam and the onward connection to Seattle and had linked her laptop to the inflight network so she could dig up as much information as she could find on Richard Cutter, the dead port worker. She'd also taken a look at Huxley Blaine Carter's father, Tate, and had started to build a file on the Silicon Valley entrepreneur whose life had apparently been cut short by a heart attack.

'You OK?' Pearce asked.

Leila nodded. She was leaning against her small upright suitcase, trying to rest her sore legs. They were travelling light, and Pearce just had a small holdall slung over his shoulder. Brigitte had assured them the gear they'd requested would be waiting for them on arrival, but Leila wasn't filled with confidence – their driver wasn't even here and they hadn't been given his contact details or told where they were going, so all they could do was wait.

'You want to find somewhere to sit?' Pearce asked.

Leila shook her head. 'You know I'm not your child, right?'

'My kids would never be as rude as you,' he smiled.

Leila replied in kind, but her smile was tinged with sadness. The mention of children reminded her of the loss of her infant child, who'd been stillborn in Syria after she'd been savagely beaten. She tried not to think about him, but it was difficult, since her disability was a result of the complications she'd suffered during the birth. Whenever her baby came to her, Leila always wondered what he might have done with his life. She did so now and felt light-headed at the thought of her boy. A memory of trauma triggered by a simple joke. Her distress must have shown.

'Come on, let's find a seat,' Pearce said, taking her arm gently.

Leila was saved from an admission of weakness by the appearance of a heavyset middle-aged man in black trousers and a white shirt. He picked his way past other travellers and touted a placard with two names on it. Susan and Isaac

Samuels; the false identities Pearce and Leila had used to enter the United States. Leila and Wollerton had established these cover identities in Cairo, building out legends for all four of them. Leila was particularly proud of the Samuels, a husband and wife team of travel bloggers who had come to Seattle to give their readers the scoop on the city. Brigitte had provided the passports through one of Kamal's contacts and they'd held up to scrutiny when they'd gone through immigration and disease control in Amsterdam and Seattle. Their matching credit cards were equally effective. Leila had created a blog for the Samuels, populating it with reviews she'd cribbed from TripAdvisor. Wollerton had added to their authenticity by giving them a few fans on social media. Such was the beauty of the digital landscape – it could be reshaped with ease to make a truth of lies. And Leila was an excellent sculptress.

The placard waver spotted Leila and Pearce and made a beeline for them. 'Sorry I'm late, Mr and Mrs Samuels,' he said breathlessly. 'Traffic.'

Leila knew Pearce sufficiently well to recognize the look of suspicion that clouded his face.

'How did you know it was us?' he asked.

'Lucky guess,' the man said, and Leila was suddenly on edge. Was this really their contact? 'Let me help you with that.' He reached for Leila's case.

She looked at Pearce for guidance and he nodded. Something wasn't quite right, but it wasn't dangerous – at least not yet.

'My car's outside,' the man said, pulling Leila's case towards the doors.

Leila followed, leaning heavily on her cane. She kept her eyes on the man purporting to be their contact. His grey hair was perfectly styled into a neat officer's cut and his hands were nicely manicured. He'd tried to present himself as a limo driver, but was wearing expensive brogues, and when she looked more closely, Leila noticed his black trousers had a satin strip running along the outside seams. They were the bottoms from a tuxedo. This was someone playing at being a driver. Leila glanced at Pearce, who smiled in reply. He was up to something.

The heavyset man took them to the multi-storey car park opposite the terminal building, where he led them to a 7 Series BMW parked on the second floor. He put Leila's bag in the trunk, and Pearce threw his in beside it.

She and Pearce rode in the back, and no one said anything until they'd left the airport and were heading north on the Pacific Highway.

'Federal pension must be pretty bad,' Pearce observed.

Leila saw the driver glance in the rear-view mirror.

'If you've got to supplement it driving a cab,' Pearce added.

'This is an executive town car,' the driver said.

'I bet you don't see too many of these driven by former directors of the NSA,' Pearce remarked, and the driver glanced at him sharply. 'Took me a moment to place you, but I remember your file photo, Director Clifton.'

'Former Director Clifton. How'd you get your hands on my file?'

'When I was investigating the Black Thirteen group we had to figure out who was instructing the lawyer who'd hired me. Huxley Blaine Carter was using an old cipher in the classifieds of a local paper to run messages. You sit on the board of three of his companies. It didn't take much imagination to figure out who was advising him on tradecraft,' Pearce revealed. 'I guess the big question is why. The NSA doesn't let people play the game when they retire, so either you haven't really retired, or you're doing this well below the radar.'

'Huxley told me how you cracked the cipher, Mr Pearce,' Clifton said. 'It's part of the reason I wanted to meet you. To see if you're as good as they say.'

'My guess is you're flying below the radar. But I can't figure out why you'd take that kind of risk. If the NSA finds out you're playing the game privately – well, that's jail time.'

'How did you meet Huxley's father?' Leila asked. She'd been watching the two men, studying Clifton's reactions to Pearce and thought she'd seen enough.

'How'd . . . ?' Clifton tailed off in astonishment.

'You're about his father's age. You probably don't need money, so your motivation has to be personal and sufficiently important to risk everything, which means a lover or a very good friend,' Leila replied.

Clifton sighed. 'Tate Blaine Carter was my best friend. We met at college and were friends until he died.'

'If you're helping Huxley, you probably also think his father was murdered,' Leila surmised. 'So this is about revenge.'

Clifton turned his attention to the busy road.

'It's about righting a wrong,' he said flatly.

Chapter 26

Clifton took them to a sixteen-storey high-rise near Pike Place Market and drove into the parking lot under the building. He steered the car down to the fifth sub-level, which was only accessible to those who had a code for a security shutter that covered the ramp.

'This is one of Hux's buildings,' Clifton said. 'This level is yours. You each have the vehicle Ms Attali requested for you.' He pulled into a space beside a blue Yukon SUV and a silver Yamaha R1. 'There are other tenants in the building, but you have the entire fifteenth floor to yourselves.'

Clifton led them to a bank of elevators, one of which was controlled by an alphanumeric keypad.

'Only people Hux trusts have the code,' Clifton said, demonstrating it to them.

They rode up in silence. Leila was surprised when they reached the fifteenth floor and elevator doors opened to reveal an entirely open-plan space. The whole floor had been stripped of walls and fixtures and was only broken up by the concrete elevator shaft that stood in the centre of the football-pitch sized office. The only other barriers between them and the huge windows that offered panoramic views in four directions were a few pieces of furniture. There were two beds positioned behind short partitions, a long table and chairs, a couple of couches and two desks. Half a dozen large Peli cases were lined up beside the desks.

'The gear you asked for,' Clifton said.

'You staying here?' Pearce asked as he dropped his holdall onto the carpeted floor.

'No. I'm not from Seattle,' Clifton replied. 'I just wanted to meet you both.' He hesitated. 'I know you refused Hux's offer of a job, but you should have another think about it. We could do a lot of good together.' He handed Pearce a piece of paper. 'This is how you reach me.' He backed towards the elevator. 'Good luck,' he said, stepping inside.

'Thanks for the ride,' Pearce responded, and the elevator doors slid closed.

Leila walked to the nearest window, pressed her forehead against the glass and peered down at the tiny figures on the streets below. A group had gathered at the edge of a promenade that overlooked the shoreline. They were gazing out over Elliot Bay, but Leila had a better view of the large expanse of water and the bluffs of Seacrest Park beyond it, rolling hills of lush green vegetation which sprouted around magnificent waterfront homes. Movement in the crowd at the foot of the building caught Leila's attention and for a moment she thought she saw Hannan looking up at her. But the woman wasn't her sister, and hope died away as quickly as it had risen. *You'll see her everywhere, until you really see her*, Leila thought sadly.

'You OK?' Pearce asked.

'You going to keep asking me that?' Leila replied, backing away from the window. 'What did you make of him?'

'He wanted to check us out,' Pearce said. 'I think he's on the level.'

'You think we can trust him?'

'I didn't say that,' Pearce scoffed. 'I don't think we can trust anyone. Apart from each other. And even then . . .'

Leila nudged him playfully. 'So, how do you want to do this?' Her legs were screaming at her to climb into one of the comfortable-looking beds, but the bright Seattle sunshine shimmering on the calm bay said it was mid-afternoon, and no matter what her body might want, it was time to go to work.

'I'll take the port,' Pearce said. 'See if any of Richard Cutter's colleagues saw anything suspicious the day he died. You check out the detective in charge of the investigation. See what they've found out.'

Chapter 27

Echo Wu looked as far from the archetype of a spy as Wollerton could have imagined; she was struggling to get a large baby seat out of her MG6 Hybrid.

'Let me help,' Wollerton said, stepping forward, but she brushed him away.

'It's OK,' she said. 'It doesn't like strangers. I have to convince it to come out.'

Wollerton stepped back and joined Brigitte, who watched Echo from the empty space next to the MG. No more than five foot three, the diminutive thirty-something waif who'd met them in the arrivals hall at Qingdao Airport cut a comic figure, wrestling with the chair and the web of straps that held it in place.

'How do you know her?' Wollerton asked Brigitte quietly.

'She was the intelligence liaison at the Chinese embassy in Paris. We became friendly and stayed in touch when she retired,' Brigitte replied. 'Don't fall for the act. She's razor sharp.'

Echo turned to them and her pretty, delicate features twisted into a grimace. She stuck out her tongue and groaned.

'Are you sure?' Wollerton asked.

Brigitte nodded solemnly.

'Got it!' Echo exclaimed, clasping the baby seat. 'I told you.

I just needed to convince it,' she said, carrying the unwieldy seat to the boot. She placed it beside Brigitte and Wollerton's leather holdalls. 'Sorry I didn't do this earlier, but life runs away when you've got kids. Hop in.'

Wollerton climbed in the back and Brigitte took the front seat. Echo skipped round to the driver's side and slid behind the wheel. The rear footwells were full of toys, and Wollerton gently nudged some under Brigitte's seat to clear a space for his feet.

'Sorry it's such a mess,' Echo said. 'If I cleaned as much as I should, my buttocks would never rest.'

Wollerton wondered where Echo had learned English. She spoke it fluently with a Home Counties accent, but used odd idioms. She put the car in drive and reversed, but the proximity sensor sounded and a car horn blasted simultaneously, and Echo stepped on the brakes to avoid a collision. She lowered her window and unleashed a stream of angry invective in Mandarin. The startled driver of the other vehicle tutted and shook his head before driving on, and when he was clear, Echo resumed her manoeuvre.

'Bloody drunk on lager or something,' Echo remarked, as the car lurched back.

If he'd been called as a witness in a court of law, Wollerton would have said Echo was entirely at fault, but he kept quiet, and when he caught Brigitte's sardonic smile, he simply raised an eyebrow in reply.

Chapter 28

Wollerton hadn't been to China for over ten years. He'd been a family man on his last trip, married with two kids. That was before Esther had decided he was an inferior version of the man she'd married and took herself and the kids off to live in Aberdyfi, a tiny seaside town on the Welsh coast. He rarely saw them, and felt their loss every single day. Freya and Luke had been his world. Their sweet faces had always lit up even the darkest day and he missed them terribly. More so because he spent most of his time alone in Overlook, the family bolt-hole that had cost years of self-denial. No drinks with the lads, no expensive holidays, no flashy car. But the sacrifice would have been worth it if he'd been able to live the dream he'd had throughout his years in Six. The house, situated on the Moray Firth, was supposed to be where he and Esther grew old together and welcomed armies of grandchildren to be spoiled with jams and treats. Now it was just an empty cave where he drank too much and moped around feeling sorry for himself. Maybe he needed to move on, to live somewhere more vibrant? And there were few places in the world with more energy and dynamism than China.

Echo had given them a potted history of Qingdao and its recent explosive growth. Situated on the Yellow Sea, the city had long been of strategic importance and had been occupied by the Japanese twice in the twentieth century. After the Second World War, Qingdao developed as a trading and manufacturing hub, and when the Chinese government implemented an open-door policy in the mid-eighties, it became one of the largest ports in the world. But Echo's enumeration of the tons of steel, concrete, miles of cable, railtracks, roads, population and GDP growth didn't impress Wollerton. What gave him the best sense of the scale of human endeavour was the view. They'd driven south from the airport, passing through a vast residential neighbourhood made up of towering apartment blocks, until they'd reached the Qingdao Haiwan Bridge, one of the longest in the world. It straddled Jiaozhou Wan, a large bay, heading towards Hongshiyacun, another residential district on the Huangdao side of the bridge. They branched off and continued south, down the peninsula towards downtown Qingdao. When the heart of the city finally came into view, Wollerton couldn't help but be impressed. The gleaming skyline of the business district lined the shore to the south, and to the west of them lay the vast port complex. Everywhere he looked there were huge glass and steel structures that rivalled anything a western city could aspire to, and there were so many of them. Such grand symbols of prosperity had taken centuries to materialize in Europe, but this city would have been nothing but fields fewer than forty years ago. Wollerton had always had to adjust his British sense of scale when visiting the grand open spaces of America, but he now had a new benchmark: China. The Covid-19 pandemic had slowed China's relentless growth, but the country had quickly adapted to the testing and public health challenges and was on the upswing again. The speed and scale of the transformation here was a testament to the strength of human will. Whatever its politics, it was impossible to see such grand achievements and not believe the People's Republic would play a defining role in the twenty-first century.

'Of course, we never talk politics,' Echo said, veering away from her tour guide spiel. 'I'm not sure I could even tell you what our politics are anymore. But at least there's money,' she shrugged. 'For some, anyway.'

'What are you doing now?' Brigitte asked.

'Same as before. Public relations for a manufacturer. We make body armour and specialist military equipment. They like my intelligence background.'

'How many kids have you got?' Wollerton chipped in.

'Two. A boy who's four and a girl of two.'

'Any names?'

'Their English names are Alex and Bethan,' Echo said. 'I'd like them to go to school in the West.'

'And your husband?' Wollerton asked.

'Sorry about the interrogation,' Brigitte said.

'What? I'm just making conversation. Just because we're . . .' He hesitated. 'Well, whatever we are, it doesn't mean we can't be human.'

'He's a lawyer.' Echo tooted her horn at a van that veered into her lane. 'It's not the most exciting job in the world, but it's stable and the money's good. So, since you're –' she mimicked Wollerton's hesitation – 'well, whatever you are, what brings you to Qingdao?'

'The fresh air,' Brigitte replied, and Echo giggled.

One consequence of the relentless industry was the air pollution which hung low over the bay.

'Still keeping things close,' Echo remarked. 'You'll never change. Well, I've got you an apartment for whatever it is you're doing. It's owned by a friend of my aunt. He's in Hong Kong on business for a couple of months, so the place is free. It's on the seventeenth floor too, so you might be high enough to get some of that fresh air.'

'Thank you,' Brigitte replied.

'Anything for an old friend,' Echo said as she turned off the main thoroughfare through Qingdao and took them into a development of four octagonal apartment blocks that towered above them.

They were so close to the sea Wollerton could smell brine in the air. Echo drove through the complex to the building nearest the waterfront and double-parked by the entrance.

'We should have drinks one night?' she said.

'Sure. Let me know when you get a babysitter,' Brigitte replied.

'Of course,' Echo said with a broad smile. 'Well, must dash. I've got to collect the kids from their grandma.'

'I've got your number,' Brigitte said, and she and Echo embraced.

Wollerton stepped out of the car and grabbed their bags from the boot.

'Apartment one seven six. The porter is expecting you.' Echo dangled a set of keys at Brigitte, who took them and got out.

'Thanks again,' she said.

'No problem. Call me.' Echo stepped on the accelerator and the car lurched forward.

'She always like that?' Wollerton asked as they started towards the building. 'Or is this her losing her touch?'

'She's not losing anything,' Brigitte assured him.

They entered an air-conditioned lobby that was decked in

brown marble and trimmed with gold. A porter in a uniform that could have been snatched from a 1950s cinema usher sat at a counter and nodded curtly as they walked towards the elevator.

Their apartment faced the sea and had a great view of the waterfront park and wide promenade. Beyond the calm waters was a lighthouse that marked the southernmost tip of the bay. Echo's aunt's friend was a man of peculiar taste. The décor made Wollerton think of an eighties stockbroker. Everything was black, red or gold, and the walls were lined with framed prints of performance cars and scantily clad women.

'Where do we—' Wollerton began.

But Brigitte cut him off. 'That was pretty outrageous what that guy did on the plane,' she said.

Wollerton had no idea what she was talking about until he saw her pull something from her holdall. He put his bag down on an eight-place glass dining table. 'You think that was outrageous? I heard a story about a guy in LA who used to go up and down Venice Beach and—'

'I hope this isn't gross,' Brigitte cut him off. 'We should see what the beach is like.'

She crossed the room, opened the sliding doors and stepped onto the small balcony.

'I thought we were talking about the gross guy,' Wollerton remarked as he followed her out.

'We were,' Brigitte replied, manipulating a small computer tablet. The device was slightly larger than a cell phone and a red sensor strip ran along one end. 'Now we're talking about beaches.'

Wollerton looked at the seafront and saw a long wide stretch of sand to their west. He glanced down at the device Brigitte was concealing from unseen eyes, and saw the screen had come to life. She pressed a button that said 'Run Scan', and the sensor, which was pointed at Brigitte's midriff, emitted a low light in a series of pulses. A processing spiral appeared on screen.

'It's beautiful,' Brigitte said, nodding towards the bay. 'And Echo was right, you can see everything from here.'

'It's really something,' Wollerton agreed.

Whatever programme Brigitte was running came to life and the device displayed a three-dimensional representation of the living room. Emphasis was placed on any electrical items, such as the television and lights. Brigitte zoomed in on the 3D model to reveal six listening devices and three cameras concealed in walls and objects around the room. She turned the device slightly and the image updated to show a listening device directly above them – but no camera.

She took Wollerton's arm. 'What do you want to do tonight?' she said. Her fingers silently tapped Morse code. *Said Echo sharp. Need know if she is curious or threat.*

'I don't know,' Wollerton said. 'Maybe grab something to eat?' He took her hand and tapped his genuine reply. *How do we find out?*

Bugs I planted on dress and in car will help, she replied, flashing a crafty smile. 'Sounds good. Why don't you see if you can find some towels?' she suggested aloud. 'Let's check out the beach.'

Chapter 29

They rode the lift in silence and Wollerton followed Brigitte through the lobby. It might have been paranoia, but Wollerton sensed the porter watched them with more than casual interest as they left the building. They walked along the busy main road to the waterfront park. It was late afternoon and families gathered on the grass. The bay was about twenty miles long and much of it was devoted to commerce or industry. Around them loomed the hotels and offices of Qingdao's business district. Stretching into the distance in both directions were more high-rises, then a sprawl of residential blocks, and beyond them, industrial plants, factories and refineries. Wollerton and Brigitte joined the broad promenade and turned right, weaving between groups of people walking the coastline. He could smell the sea on the gentle breeze, but beneath it was a chemical taint, a hint of metal blended with a touch of crude oil.

They soon reached the wide beach they'd seen from the balcony. When her shoes touched the sand, Brigitte surprised Wollerton and the people around her by taking off her top.

'You can't wear clothes on a beach,' she said, throwing the garment to the ground. A black bra stretched across her paper-white chest.

'I think you can,' Wollerton replied, indicating the locals

who were on the beach fully clothed. A few wore shorts and T-shirts, but most looked as if they'd just finished school or work.

'But we're Europeans,' Brigitte responded. 'We see sand, we strip. It's the law.' She unbuttoned her jeans and pulled them down to reveal matching black underwear. Maybe from a distance it would look like a bikini. 'Come on,' she said.

Wollerton hesitated, but she gave him an emphatic look, and he started to get undressed. He knew what she was doing. She couldn't be certain Echo hadn't bugged their clothes during the journey. Wollerton glanced around nervously. He was used to operating beneath the radar and felt uncomfortable being this exposed. Brigitte's striking pale skin and white hair – a consequence of her albinism – were turning heads. Wollerton threw his shirt onto the sand and slipped out of his trousers. He kicked off his boots while Brigitte bent over to retrieve something from the pocket of her jeans. Wollerton couldn't help but admire her lean physique, but earned himself a severe glare when she caught him looking.

'Come on,' she said, standing up and walking towards the water. 'Let's go for a swim.'

The industrial achievements stretching as far as the eye could see took on a different complexion as he followed her down. He could taste pollution in the air and wondered just how much had leeched into the water.

He thought he could feel the waves burning his skin as he joined Brigitte in the surf. They waded up to their shins.

'It's cold,' she remarked.

'Freezing.'

'Now we know we can't be heard,' she nodded towards their distant clothes. 'We can talk freely. We don't have long.' He followed her gaze and settled on two police officers who were watching them from the promenade. 'Echo is clearly working for someone. If it's the government, they may just be curious about what we're doing here. If it's someone else, she may pose a threat.'

'I thought you said she was a friend.'

'I said we were friendly,' Brigitte replied. 'You know there are no friends in this business.'

'So what do we do?'

'We have a listen.' She opened her hand to reveal a couple of earpieces and a new version of the Ghostlink, a satellite communicator Leila had developed. Brigitte handed Wollerton an earpiece. She switched on the other one and put it in, and he did likewise.

They stood quietly for a moment, listening to the sound of the waves breaking around them. Gulls called above, and cries of children drifted across the sand, but Wollerton's earpiece was silent.

'I'm not getting anything,' Wollerton said.

'She found them,' Brigitte replied.

'It could be a faulty—'

'She found them,' Brigitte cut him off. She glanced over her shoulders at the police officers who were now on the beach, heading for the pile of discarded clothes. 'Here,' she said, handing Wollerton the Ghostlink. 'Call Scott. Tell him our situation. Let him know it may take us a while to get any useful intel because we've got to be careful.'

She started up the beach towards the police officers. '*Bonjour messieurs. Y a-t-il un problème?*' she began in the brightest, most vacuous tone Wollerton had heard from her.

He activated the Ghostlink, which looked indistinguishable from a cell phone, and his call was answered within moments.

'*Go ahead,*' Pearce said.

'We've arrived, but we've got eyes on us,' Wollerton replied.

'*Who?*'

'We're trying to work that out. It may take us a while.'

'*OK. Be careful,*' Pearce said. '*And stay in touch.*'

'Will do,' Wollerton responded. 'Over and out.' He ended the call and looked up the beach, where Brigitte was playing the part of an indignant tourist perfectly. She had an angry expression pinned to her face as she reluctantly pulled on her clothes under the close supervision of the two police officers. Wollerton couldn't help but admire the diligence and resourcefulness of this impressive woman. He put on his own game face – bewildered foreigner – and headed up the beach.

Chapter 30

Pearce hung up. The improvements Leila had made to her Ghostlink communicator meant they could use them in public with little fear of anyone realizing they weren't mobile phones. The devices permitted encrypted satellite communication almost anywhere in the world, and Pearce was certain Leila could have made a small fortune if she'd sold the technology, but she'd opted to keep its existence secret. The Ghostlinks were for their exclusive use.

'Mr Martin will see you now,' the receptionist said.

Pearce was in the lobby of the Seattle Port Authority building, waiting to see Richard Cutter's boss, Harry Martin. Pearce followed the receptionist out of the charmless corporate waiting area, through a security door into the corridor beyond.

Small offices lay either side. Most featured an administrator at a desk, surrounded by stacks of paperwork. The receptionist led Pearce through the building, up a couple of flights of stairs onto the executive floor. The Director of Operations' office was located in the north-west corner of the block.

'Mr . . . er?' Martin asked, rising from behind his large desk.

'Samuels,' Pearce replied. 'Thanks for seeing me,' he added, shaking the man's hand.

'Thanks, Ken,' Harry said to the receptionist, who shut

the door behind him when he withdrew. Harry turned his attention to Pearce. 'Have a seat. What can I do for you, Mr Samuels?'

'I'm with the *Daily Star* in London,' Pearce lied. 'I was hoping to talk to friends of Richard Cutter.'

Harry immediately became defensive and his smile dropped. 'You told Ken you were here to talk about the port.'

'Would you have agreed to see me?' Pearce countered.

'We're all saddened by what happed to Richie. Most of us just want to move on,' Harry replied.

'I understand, but this idea of a Midas Killer, well, it's captured our readers' imaginations. I'd like to talk to people who might have seen Mr Cutter that day.'

'I don't think anyone here will have anything to say to you,' Harry said flatly. 'We're all pretty grossed out by the tabloid sensation. Let me show you out, Mr Samuels.'

Pearce felt sorry for Harry Martin. He could sense the man's anger at being deceived and his disapproval of the salacious angle Pearce was taking over his colleague's death, but he was still managing to be cordial. It showed real character, and Pearce didn't want to cause a good man any more pain. He'd try the bar where Richard Cutter died and canvas the staff and patrons for anything on who might have killed him.

'Sure,' Pearce said. 'Sorry to have troubled you.'

He followed Martin downstairs into the ground-floor corridor. His heart pounded out a couple of thunderous beats and it took every ounce of discipline to control the fight or flight response provoked by what he saw ahead of him. There, coming along the corridor, was one of the men who'd escaped from Al Aqarab prison.

'Hey, Harry,' the man said as he passed.

'Hey, Zee,' Harry replied. 'You got a minute later? We need to talk about the *Elite.*'

'Drop by anytime,' the escapee said. 'I'll be at my desk.'

The man walked on and so did Harry. Pearce hesitated, his mind a jumble of questions. The most pressing was why this dangerous wanted man was working in the Seattle Port Authority.

'You OK?' Harry asked, waiting for Pearce by the lobby security door.

'Yes, sorry,' Pearce replied, hurrying on. He took a deep breath and tried to calm the rising sense of excitement.

He'd just caught a huge break.

Chapter 31

Leila shifted uncomfortably. She'd been waiting out-side Seattle South Precinct for almost two hours. Evan Hill, the detective in charge of the investigation into Richard Cutter's death, had refused to see her, and the duty sergeant had forced her to leave the building, so she'd picked a spot on Myrtle Street by the car park gate that allowed her to keep an eye on the building's entrance and the vehicles coming and going. She leaned against a sign protruding from the verge, which read 'Police Only', and tried to take the weight off her legs. It was an uncomfortably humid afternoon and she was feel-ing the full effects of her journey and her long vigil outside the station. She paced every few minutes in a vain attempt to shake the pain and fatigue from her legs, and tried to keep her mind occupied by watching the children's soccer match being played on the pitch opposite the station.

South Precinct was located in a residential neighbourhood that made Leila think of England. The pitch was a rich green and was surrounded by large trees. Through their branches, heavy with golden leaves, Leila caught glimpses of charming New England-style houses on the other side of the pitches. When she grew bored of watching the game, Leila counted birds flying overhead, kept a tally of red cars versus blue, and tried to guess the life stories of the people filing in and out mission larger than anything they'd ever been part of. He knew they all professed to be men of faith, and his words would have resonated to some degree. But the glorious vision of becoming warriors in the service of God, while making even more money, had been snatched away by their unimaginative boss and his stubborn refusal to move with the times.

'Just get me the list of people who knew when the shipment was being collected,' Deni commanded.

'Of course,' Ziad said deferentially, but he knew the seed of dissent had been sown. He'd made his boss look unimaginative and small-minded. 'Is there anything else?'

Deni shook his head and dismissed Ziad with a wave.

He hurried outside and when he was a safe distance from the bookstore, he used a disposable cell phone to make a call.

'Hunter, it's Ziad Malek,' he said when the call was answered.

'*Stop bugging me. We heard what happened and we've made other arrangements,*' Hunter Lutz said. The fearsome man was Ben Cresci's fixer and second-in-command.

'I don't care what you think you know; it isn't going to play out that way. You have to get me in to see your boss. I need a meet with Ben Cresci.'

Hunter sighed. '*I told you to stop bugging me.*'

The line went dead.

Ziad took a calming breath and hurried to his car. If they couldn't get in to see Ben Cresci, their plan would be in tatters.

Chapter 38

Pearce watched from across the street. There was a coffee shop, a bookstore, a community centre, an Islamic bank and a travel agency. At the front of the block, seperate from the main building, was a Middle Eastern supermarket and behind it a football pitch that had been created from a cordoned-off section of the car park. This was a community hub for immigrants; Pearce had seen similar complexes all over the world.

He'd picked up the signal of the tracking device on Ziad's car and followed him across town, arriving just in time to see him enter the Haqeeq Bookstore. Pearce had pulled a pair of surveillance glasses from his pocket. Fitted with plain lenses, they allowed the wearer to record audio and video surreptitiously. Pearce had pressed the touch-sensitive switch that activated the device's recording function, and he'd walked the block, capturing everything he could; the names of businesses, registrations in the large car park, faces in the coffee shop, but the one thing he couldn't see was what was happening in the bookshop. The interior was hidden by bookshelves that reached to the ceiling. He'd considered going in, but the shop was empty and he'd have risked blundering into an unknown situation.

Pearce had returned to his motorbike and watched with frustration, waiting to see who came out of the bookstore.

This was when the resources of an organization like Six would have helped. In minutes, he could have had the details of who owned the property, his support team could have started working on the intel he'd already acquired and he would have been a step closer to discovering the truth. He could have called in a full surveillance unit, complete with infrared cameras and directional mics that might have been able to pick up what was happening inside the building. But hardship bred strength, and since he didn't have the resources, he'd have to rely on the ingenuity of his team. Leila had told him about the sharp response she'd received from Evan Hill, the detective investigating Richie Cutter's death, but they needed to build a rapport with someone like him. An experienced cop would be able to provide more intel on local players than any MI6 database. Pearce also considered putting himself in play. The beautiful thing about a community centre like this was that people were usually welcoming of anyone from the Muslim diaspora, making infiltration a realistic prospect.

Ziad Malek emerged fifteen minutes after he'd entered. He made what looked like a fraught phone call, and seemed full of purpose as he got into his old Buick. He drove east along 140th Street, but Pearce didn't follow. Without a field team, he had to make choices and he opted to let the tracker do its work. He would stay and focus on learning who Ziad had gone to see.

Ten minutes later, six men emerged. The three in front looked like street thugs, clearing a safe path for their principals: an old man with a long beard who wore a full-length coat, a heavyset middle-aged man in a suit, and a younger man who bore a family resemblance and might have been the middle-aged man's son. Pearce captured their faces using the high-definition camera built into his glasses and recorded the licence plates of the four cars the men got into. The old man had a 1980s Mercedes SEL, and the middle-aged man who had the confidence of a boss drove a G-Wagen, which was followed by the three heavies in an old Ford Taurus. The youngest of the group left in a Porsche 911. Following any of them wouldn't have been productive without more information about who they were, but Pearce consoled himself with the knowledge he'd captured footage that could be used to identify them.

He pulled a small tablet computer from his pocket and saw Ziad's marker travelling through the city, away from the little green house on Kenyon Street and the port. Pearce pulled on his helmet and set off to intercept him.

Chapter 39

The camera didn't pick up the two junkies passed out on the porch of the house across the street. Leila had parked on the corner, near where she'd met Pearce the previous day, and had climbed into the back of the Yukon to fill the pockets of her army surplus jacket with the gear she needed. She hadn't noticed the two men until she was almost opposite Ziad Malek's house. They were both scrawny and their skin was filthy with the kind of ground-in dirt Leila associated with a hard life on the street. Their house was even more run-down than the small green one opposite and their yard was filled with empty cans, food wrappers and what looked like used toilet paper. A couple of blankets were spread across the porch and the two men were curled on them in the foetal position. Between them lay the detritus of a drugs binge; foil, a burned spoon, a collection of plastic lighters and a glass pipe. Leila guessed they'd been freebasing, and they looked as though they were out cold. But she couldn't afford to gamble, nor could she afford to wait. She had no way of knowing how long Angsakul would be out, so to assess whether the junkies posed a threat, she went to the start of their crooked path and stood among the ragged weeds that sprouted from the cracks. She caught the pungent stench of urine and excrement, and gagged.

'Hey!' she said when she'd got her breath back. She rapped on the rotten fencepost. 'Hey, are you guys OK?' she asked.

There was no response, so she shuffled along the path, ignoring the growing stench, and prodded the nearest man with her cane. His body was limp and heavy, and if it hadn't been for the slow but steady rise and fall of his chest, she'd have thought he was dead.

Satisfied, Leila turned and crossed the street. It was a humid autumn day and the sky brooded with the promise of a storm. She wondered how wasted a person had to be to sleep outside in shorts and a T-shirt and not care about how exposed and vulnerable they were. Never mind the weather, she could have killed them and they wouldn't have known anything about it.

But she didn't have to. Their oblivion was their good fortune, and she walked up the little green house's empty driveway towards the ramshackle fence that marked the start of the garden. She tried the gate and was relieved when it opened. It creaked loudly, and she glanced back at the house across the street, but the junkies didn't stir. Leila went through and shut the gate behind her. The garden was an overgrown mess of weeds, bushes and trees, all wild and out of control. There was the faint smell of sewage and rot, and if there had ever been a path, it was now lost to thick grasses. She pushed her way through the jungle and came to the back door. A picture window offered a view of the kitchen, a room that was one level of prosperity above the porch across the street.

She produced a set of lock-picking tools and defeated the basic tumbler in moments. When she stepped inside, she was hit with the powerful smell of lemongrass and galangal, and beneath that was the musty scent of decay. Everything in the place, from the mouldy walls to the rotting kitchen chairs, was long past its prime. The house was silent and still. All Leila could hear was her breathing, which was rapid and shallow. She hated creeping around hostile places where she was vulnerable and exposed, and wanted to be out as quickly as possible.

She fished in her breast pocket for two listening devices and placed one down the side of an ancient cupboard and the other in a small hole in the skirting board beneath the old cabinets. She was about to rig a camera on top of the door frame when she heard a noise coming from outside. She pulled her tablet computer from her pocket and switched it on to see the image broadcast by the buttonhole camera on the telegraph pole across the street. Her heart skipped as she saw the two junkies moving towards the house. One was almost at the front door and the other was slipping through the side gate. Leila felt sick. They weren't moving like addicts, they were prowling with the deliberate care of soldiers. She glanced at the back door, but she was too late. If she went that way, she'd encounter the man coming through the garden. She hurried into the shadowy hallway and went up the stairs as quickly as her pained legs could manage. She heard the front door open as she crested the last step, and moved out of sight.

Four doors led off the landing. Two were closed, and one of the open ones revealed a tiny, fetid bathroom. She went through the fourth, which took her into a bedroom. Clothes covered the floor and the bed was unmade. She picked her way through the mess, went to the window and peered at the overgrown garden. She heard movement downstairs, the shift of floorboards settling and the steps of two men creeping through the building.

'Don't make this hard on yourself,' one of the men said. He had a deep, gravelly Seattle accent. 'We just want to know who you work for.'

Leila wondered how her legs would cope with the jump and tried to convince herself the window wasn't really that high. She opened it and it creaked loudly. The sound prompted hurried footsteps up the stairs and the two men burst into the room before Leila even had the chance to haul herself onto the sill. Trapped, with the foul men closing on her, Leila realized there was to be no quiet escape. She would have to take drastic steps to protect herself and the investigation.

'Who are you?' Leila asked. 'Who are you working for?'

'You got the wrong idea, lady,' the man nearest to her said. 'We're not here to answer questions.'

He reached out a grubby hand and grabbed her left arm. Her reaction was instant and deliberate, and was tinged with a visceral anger. Too many men had treated her body as their possession, and she'd vowed to punish anyone who ever did so again. The fingers of her right hand tightened around the grip of the Glock she had in her pocket; she angled the gun up and shot the man. The bullet tore through her jacket and hit him in the gut. The fitted suppressor transformed the gunshot into the pop of a champagne cork and the startled man heard another as a second bullet sent him staggering back, hunched over, clutching his stomach. He cried out and raised his hand to fend off the third shot, which lopped off two of his fingers before it drilled a hole in his skull and silenced him. The dead man's companion watched in shock, but when the body toppled over and hit the floor, he came to his senses and tried to reach behind his back.

'That's how you end,' Leila gestured at the corpse, 'if you go for your gun.'

The survivor froze.

'What's your name?' Leila asked.

There was a moment of silent defiance.

'If you won't give me answers, you're no use to me.' She let the implication hang.

'Jared,' he said at last. He looked at the body of his fallen companion. 'You just made a huge mistake, lady.'

Leila ignored the threat. 'Well, Jared, you're going to help me move this man, and then we're going to go somewhere you can answer some questions.'

Chapter 40

Pearce followed Ziad's tracker east for a while before turning north and trailing the signal into the heart of Seattle, near the building he and Leila were staying in. He went a few blocks further north and found himself in the business district, surrounded by towers of wealth and power. Ziad's decrepit Buick was noticeably out of place parked in a line of gleaming luxury cars alongside a skyscraper on Stewart Street.

Pearce pulled into a space at the end of the line and removed his helmet as he dismounted. He went over to a falafel stand and purchased a wrap. As the vendor, a Middle-Eastern man in a surgical mask, prepared his food, Pearce watched Ziad, who remained in his car some twenty metres away. The man's attention never wavered. His eyes were locked on the entrance of the high-rise across the street, a dark-brown glass building that stretched towards brooding clouds. If Ziad was spying, he didn't have the first clue about discreet surveillance. Pearce knew to keep his presence low key, to inhabit the character of someone – in his case, a touring motorcyclist – who happened to be in the vicinity. The intensity with which Ziad was watching the building left little doubt he was there for a purpose. In contrast, once he'd got his food, Pearce leaned against a railing and watched passers-by as he ate. He didn't turn to look at Ziad; he could see the man and his car reflected in the opaque window of a building further along the street.

Pearce had been there for ten minutes and was coming to the end of his wrap when he saw Ziad stiffen. Pearce glanced over his shoulder and saw a woman coming out of the building across the street. She had a Mediterranean complexion, long black hair, and wore a tailored green dress. She looked like a professional, a banker or lawyer, and exuded confidence. It didn't take a spy to recognize Ziad's desire. He watched the woman intently as she checked her phone, while pacing and scanning the sidewalk in both directions. She was clearly waiting for something or someone.

Ziad glanced away a couple of times. He looked uncomfortable, as though he was steeling himself for something – mustering courage perhaps? He finally opened the door and was about to get out of the car when a blond-haired muscular man with a square jaw grabbed Ziad and hauled him into the street. The man wore Dockers and a short-sleeve checked shirt, and his muscles bulged as he hurled Ziad onto the tarmac. A cab screeched to a halt inches from Ziad's head, and for a moment he looked frightened and bewildered.

'You should never have come back,' his assailant said, bearing down on him. 'No one wants you here. Keep away from her, you scumbag!'

The woman in the green dress noticed the altercation and dodged traffic as she ran across the street. 'Jack, don't,' she yelled. 'He's not worth it.'

Ziad registered her words and the fear and confusion drained from his eyes to be replaced by pure hostility. Pearce recognized the look and wasn't surprised to see Ziad get to his feet and rush Jack. He threw a cross that connected and sent the bigger man staggering back, and it was Jack's turn to feel fear and bewilderment. Ziad attacked him furiously, punching and kicking like a wild animal. Pearce knew never to lay hands on a man he didn't have the measure of, and it was clear Jack had underestimated Ziad. He'd probably expected some chivalrous frat-house brawl with some loud-mouth shoving. Instead, he was fighting for his life against a man who was fuelled by rage. Ziad was landing blow after painful blow and Jack was crying in agony.

The woman finally reached Ziad and tried to restrain him, but he shrugged her off.

'Zee! No! Please!' she yelled.

But he kept hammering Jack, who was reduced to trying to fend off the most damaging punches. Ziad didn't have much technique, but he was a fast brawler, and clearly had some fighting experience.

'Leave him alone!' the woman cried.

Cars stopped on both sides of the street, and drivers got out of their vehicles to watch the fight. Some were using their phones to film the action and others were calling the police. Passers-by had gathered on the sidewalk and were doing like-wise. Jack stumbled and struggled to stay upright in the face of the onslaught.

'Please! Don't! No! Come on, man,' he cried pathetically.

'Zee, don't do this,' the woman said, grabbing him by the arm.

Ziad wheeled round and slapped her, and Pearce sensed the collective intake of breath of the onlookers. The woman fell on her backside, and Jack was further humiliated when Ziad kicked him in the face, knocking him flat. Ziad jumped on the man, and Pearce looked at the bystanders, hoping someone would intervene to stop what was in danger of becoming a murder.

No one had the courage to go near the furious creature, and Pearce heard the first sirens in the distance. He realized it would be down to him to save Jack's life and salvage the investigation, and he slipped his helmet on as he ran down the street. The light-reactive visor was opaque and protected his identity from the phones and witnesses who saw him. He grabbed Ziad by the shoulders and pulled him off Jack, who was dazed and bloody. Ziad wheeled round and unleashed a punch, but Pearce stepped into it and let it connect with his helmet. Ziad immediately doubled up, cradling his right hand in his left.

'Fuck!'

'I'm trying to help you,' Pearce told him. 'Come on, let's get out of here.'

Ziad registered the gathered crowd and the sirens and hurried towards the Buick.

'Give me your keys,' Pearce said, and Ziad ferreted in his pocket and tossed them over.

Ziad got in the passenger seat and Pearce slid behind the wheel, crouching to fit his helmet inside the vehicle. They were still being filmed and he had no intention of letting himself be identified. He started the engine, which spluttered a couple of times before coming to life. He threw the car into drive and pulled out. He ignored the half-hearted attempts of bystanders who wanted to be seen trying to stop them, drove around the stationary cars and sped north.

Chapter 41

Leila had driven north-east of Seattle for almost two hours, and was in the wild forest that lay south of Verlot. She'd tried to get hold of Pearce, but he wasn't answering his Ghostlink, so she had to improvise alone. The body needed to be disposed of somewhere secluded and off the beaten track. Her only search had yielded Mount Pilchuck, a remote peak surrounded by wilderness. She'd been on a deserted country trail for twenty minutes, winding through seemingly endless evergreen woodland. She finally came to the mouth of an overgrown track she'd just been able to make out on the satellite image, and turned down it. The car bounced and rocked as she drove along the rutted, grass-covered trail. The temperature was a few degrees cooler than the city and the branches of huge pines and redwoods met high above her, casting deep shadows. Above them, black and purple clouds promised a thunderstorm.

With every jolt and bump Leila heard curses coming from the Yukon's boot. She'd tied up Jared, the surviving junkie, and had gagged him while she'd driven her SUV up to the little green house. She'd reversed it as close to the front door as possible and had then gone inside and untied her prisoner. She'd pistol-whipped him a couple of times and forced him to carry his dead companion to the car, where she'd made him put the corpse in the boot. Jared had baulked when Leila had ordered him to get in beside the body, but she'd remarked that two kills were as easy as one, and the dirty man had finally cooperated. She'd been bluffing, of course. He was too valuable as a source to kill. When he was huddled next to the corpse, Leila had smacked him with the pistol and knocked him out.

She'd returned to the house and carried out a quick clean, wiping away all visible signs of the killing with a T-shirt she'd found on the bedroom floor. She'd gathered any items of clothing that might have been hit by blood spatter and put them in the Yukon's boot. The house would have yielded a trove of forensic evidence, but to the naked eye it looked as though she and the men had never been there. The whole process had taken little more than ten minutes, and after a final check of the scene, she'd returned to the Yukon and headed north. Jared had come round some forty minutes later and had groaned and cursed ever since.

He was moaning now, locked in the dark space with his companion's corpse, but Leila couldn't feel sorry for him. Even the most savage tiger cried like a kitten when beaten. If they'd taken her, she was in no doubt those men would have done dark things to make her talk.

After another ten minutes, Leila found what she'd seen in the satellite image. The trail ended and gave way to a small meadow that stood at the summit of a high cliff. She parked ten metres from the edge and climbed out. She could hear Jared's cries for her to let him out, but she ignored him and grabbed her cane. She walked across the spongey ground, through the long grass to the very edge of the cliff. The drop must have been at least three hundred feet and the valley floor was covered in huge boulders where part of the cliff had collapsed long ago. It was the perfect place to dispose of a vehicle that was now tainted by a killing, and she could send the corpse over with it. Her plan was to knock Jared out and wait with him until Pearce could get there. It wasn't much of a plan, but it was the best she could do in the circumstances.

Leila returned to the huge car and positioned herself a couple of metres behind it. She pressed a button on the fob and the tailgate rose slowly. A foot lashed out angrily; Jared had clearly expected her to be standing right next to the car, and she was happy to disappoint him. She drew her pistol, and when the tailgate had risen high enough for them to see each other, she gestured with it.

'Get out,' she said.

The man shuffled round, swinging his legs over the lip of the boot and away from the crumpled corpse that lay behind him. As he sat up, he shocked Leila by hurling the tyre iron at her. She ducked as the heavy length of metal whirled towards her, and felt sharp pain as it glanced off her shoulder. The force almost knocked her over, but she knew she couldn't go down, because Jared was sprinting towards her, his face twisted in anger.

'I'm gonna fucking kill you,' he yelled.

He barrelled into her at full pelt and they went flying, the impact sending shards of jagged pain up her spine. The gun fell from her hand and tumbled into the long grass, and the two of them collapsed in a jumble of limbs. He fell onto her, unleashing more agony, but Leila fought through the pain and dug her nails into his neck. He yelped and kicked and punched her before springing round and diving for the gun.

Leila saw him scrabbling through the grass, searching for the weapon. She cast around, and when she caught sight of her cane, she rolled over, ignored the electric stabs that shot up her legs, and forced herself to her feet. Jared was still in the long grass, frantically searching for the gun. Leila hobbled over to her cane and stooped to pick it up. When she turned towards Jared, she saw he'd found her pistol. She hadn't run in years, but pure survival instinct forced her forward. She was ten paces from the man as he rose and turned.

Seven paces.

His eyes focused on her.

Five paces.

His hand came round.

Four.

She looked down the wavering barrel.

Three.

The gun steadied, locking on its target.

Two.

His trigger finger tensed.

Leila swiped wildly with her cane and it connected with his arm, knocking it away from her. The gun discharged and a bullet cracked into the trees.

Jared punched Leila and brought the gun round, but before he could shoot her, she drove the metal tip of her cane into his neck. The blow puckered the flesh around his windpipe, and she saw it collapse. He dropped the gun and screeched in agony. Leila didn't want to kill the man. He was too valuable alive, but the situation was out of control and she was fighting for survival. She lashed out wildly and the second strike connected with his ear, the brass-capped cane burying itself in the canal, folding the ear in on itself. Jared's eyes rolled back and he fell to the ground. He spasmed wildly, before falling still. A stream of blood flowed from his ear.

Leila sat in the long grass and wept. Her sobs were rapid and loud, so violent they could have choked her. Her body burned with pain and she was trembling. Yet again, she'd come within touching distance of death's cruel hand, and had added another body to her tally. Her jihadi husband and Artem Vasylyk, the man she'd killed in London, had been joined by these two. Most of all she cried at the thought she might have died without ever seeing her sister again.

The minutes she spent sobbing seemed like an age, but finally the sound of the wind through the trees and the call of a bird of prey pierced the fog of anguish and she returned to reality. She took a few moments to compose herself and then got to her feet. High above her, the clouds rumbled and the first drops of heavy rain burst against her skin. She headed for the car, where she'd wait out the storm before disposing of the bodies.

Chapter 42

Pearce drove five blocks before pulling into a parking garage. He'd felt the silent hum of the Ghostlink and itched for the opportunity to answer, but whoever had been calling would have to wait. He went up to the fourth level and found a space near the stairwell.

'Thanks,' Ziad said, his head hanging with shame. 'Sorry about . . .' he winced as he turned to face Pearce.

'No problem,' Pearce replied. 'It hurt you more than me.'

'You really helped me out of a jam. Can I give you something? As a thanks.'

Pearce thought for a moment. What he was about to do went against all his training. He removed his helmet. If Ziad recognized him from the port, he didn't show it.

'It's probably too much to ask, but if you know anyone who's looking, I could really use a job,' Pearce said, as his companion studied his face.

'*Inta masry, mish keda*?' Ziad asked, quizzing Pearce on his Egyptian heritage.

Pearce nodded. 'I have a British passport, so I can't get a job in America legally, but I need money. I work hard and I'm prepared to do anything. If you know anyone who could use an extra body . . .'

Ziad cradled his injured hand. 'Let me talk to some people.

Do you know Al Jamaea? It's an *ahwa* near 140th Street.'
Ahwa was the Arabic word for cafe.

'I can find it,' Pearce replied.

'Meet me there tomorrow night at eight,' Ziad said. '*Ana masry kaman.*'

I'm also Egyptian. The brethren of migrants. It wasn't a card Pearce had played much, because his heritage was only obvious to those who knew the Middle East well, but it had worked in this instance – in combination with the debt Ziad owed him for saving him from a hazardous situation.

'Thanks,' Pearce said, and he got out of the car.

'See you tomorrow,' Ziad called out as Pearce headed for the stairwell. 'What's your name, brother?'

'Amr,' Pearce said.

'*Ahlan wa sahlan, ya Amr. Ana Ziad.*'

Welcome, Amr. I'm Ziad.

Pearce nodded and went through the stairwell door. He reached street level and was on his way back to his bike when he felt his Ghostlink vibrate again. He pulled it out of his pocket and Leila's unique ID displayed on the tiny screen.

'Go ahead,' he said.

'*You busy?*' she asked.

'Not anymore.'

'*I need a ride.*'

'Problem?' he asked.

'*Yes. But I'm OK. I'm going to give you my coordinates. If you're in the city it'll take you about two hours to reach me,*' she said.

'Any family with you?' Pearce asked, using the code phrase that would give Leila the opportunity to warn him if she was under duress.

'*I'm alone,*' she replied. If she'd been taken hostage, she would have said, 'I'm on my own.'

She gave him a string of GPS coordinates which he committed to memory.

'You sure you're OK?' he asked.

'*I'll survive,*' she replied.

Something bad had happened. 'I'll be there as quickly as I can,' he said. 'Over and out.'

He'd never forgive himself if Leila had been hurt doing a task that should have been his. Pearce broke into a run and headed for his bike.

Chapter 43

Everything felt wrong. Real but somehow not. Pearce was battered and beaten, his wrists bandaged, his face full of fear and uncertainty, lit by a flickering fire. Behind him, waves caressed the shore and stars sparkled on the swells of the firth. But when Wollerton returned his gaze to the man opposite him, he was gone, replaced by the woman who'd torn a hole in his heart, his ex-wife, Esther.

'Where are you, Kyle?' she said. 'Lift him up.' Her mouth formed the words shortly after they were spoken, but the sound came from somewhere else. 'Get him on his feet.'

Wollerton was perfectly still, seated on a log on the beach outside his house, but he felt as though he was being lifted. It was utterly surreal.

'Don't drop him,' the same voice said. The accent was familiar. French.

He suddenly felt himself falling, and collided with something.

'Oh, Kyle,' Esther said. 'It's over.'

Wollerton woke from the dream to find himself on the living-room floor of the Qingdao apartment. Everything was muffled and distant, as though life had been forced into a bottle that had been thrown far out to sea. He registered the trunks of trees – no – legs, many of them, all around his head. Then he

Chapter 44

Wollerton became aware of the rolling first, then a gentle bounce. He had a pounding headache and every milli-metre of his body felt heavy and sore. His first conscious thought was of his children, Freya and Luke, and he was gripped by the sudden fear he might never see them again. They'd been his world and he'd let them be taken away too easily. He opened his eyes, which burned at the slight-est light. Thankfully there wasn't much, but it still took a moment for them to adjust to his surroundings. He made out a shoe, which was attached to a leg. Wollerton looked up to see a Chinese man on a bench seat. The man was talk-ing to another who sat next to him. Both men wore jeans, hoodies and heavy boots, and the scars on their hands and faces told Wollerton they were fighters. He was lying in the foetal position in the cargo section of a large van. He sensed at least one other person behind him, but didn't turn for fear of alerting the men to the fact he was awake. He tested his arms and discovered they'd been bound in front of him. His feet didn't seem to have been tied, perhaps to make him easier to move. It was an elementary mistake; never choose convenience over security, particularly when dealing with a dangerous captive. But there was no reason to think these men knew how dangerous he really was, or perhaps they had was flying – not flying – being carried through the apartment. There were voices around him, but he couldn't make sense of the confusing jumble of words. The room spun with the enthusiasm of a cavorting drunk, but Wollerton didn't understand; he hadn't had a drop since they'd arrived in . . . he couldn't remember where he was, and felt rising panic as he realized he wasn't himself. He'd lost his mind. He strained against the hands that held him, but he was weak.

He heard another voice and still couldn't make any sense of the words. A face filled his vision.

Then a fist sent him back to his dreams.

simply overestimated their own capabilities. Either way, they would pay the price.

Wollerton shifted slightly and felt something hard beneath him, inside his leather jacket, pressing into his ribs. He tried to think what it might be. After another day spent wandering Qingdao, trying to deceive their pursuers about their true objective, he and Brigitte had returned to the apartment near the beach. The Frenchwoman had said her meeting with Echo Wu had proved fruitless, there had been no indication who the Chinese woman worked for, and she'd not even admitted the people following them had anything to do with her. Wollerton had suggested moving to a different location, but Brigitte had disagreed, saying they were likely to be followed, and the greatest danger would be for them to pursue the investigation under the misguided belief they were free of surveillance. Wollerton had struggled with the logic of Brigitte's position and had planned to revisit the issue after dinner, but he never got the chance.

Brigitte had collected their evening meal from a nearby restaurant and they'd eaten on the balcony. Wollerton had felt extremely tired afterwards, so tired that he'd collapsed on his bed fully clothed – he suddenly realized he hadn't been tired. The rapid onset of fatigue, the strange dreams, the hangover-like symptoms and the aching body all pointed to the fact he'd been drugged. It had to have been the food. Had Echo and the people she worked for finally decided to make a move? Or had it been someone else? Had Brigitte dosed him?

He still had no idea what he was lying on, so he shifted again and things became clearer. The object was five inches long and was shaped like a smooth spearhead, apart from two prongs that protruded from one end. It felt like a folded switchblade, and Wollerton wondered whether he'd instinctively grabbed it when he'd been taken.

How he'd come by the weapon wasn't as important as what he planned to do with it. He reached inside his jacket and moved so he could clasp the knife.

'He's awake,' one of the men said in Mandarin.

Wollerton sensed movement behind him and opened the knife as he turned to see the third of four men raise his fist to strike. He pictured himself dying in the back of the van without ever seeing his kids again and his entire being flooded with adrenalin, which combined with rage to electrify him. The blade locked into position, and Wollerton lunged forward and stabbed the man in the gut. He let out a piercing shriek, and the other three shouted. The two men at the front of the van reached for their weapons, while the other grabbed him from behind and sent him hurtling against the rear doors. Wollerton's bound hands were a minor handicap, but the man who'd thrown him wasn't a proficient fighter, and when he rushed forward, Wollerton stabbed him in the neck. The man went down clutching a gushing wound. Wollerton wasted no time in attacking the last two. The nearest abductor had a gun in his hand, but Wollerton batted it away and it clattered against the chassis. They traded blows, and it became clear this man was a skilled martial artist, but the confines of the van made it difficult for him to make full use of his talent. Wollerton might not have been as young, or as skilled, but he was experienced and he knew brute force was best in a confined space. He barrelled into the man, knocking him against the final abductor, who dropped his weapon. Wollerton slashed at the man directly in front of him; as his adversary tried to defend himself, the razor-sharp blade sliced his arms open. The abductor drew back in pain, enabling Wollerton to drive the knife deep into his stomach. He pulled it sideways, cutting the man open, and as he fell with a horrific groan, Wollerton saw the final abductor retrieve his gun. Wollerton didn't hesitate and threw the knife as the man turned to take aim. The blade spun through the air and embedded itself in the man's sternum with a palpable crunch. The abductor fired a wild shot, dropped his gun and pawed at his chest ineffectually before he toppled forwards, dead.

Wollerton felt the van slow to a halt. He grabbed the pistol from the dead man and pulled the knife from his chest. It was only now that Wollerton noticed it was a Glauca B1 tactical switchblade, issued to French counterterror units. Had he taken it from Brigitte? Had she given it to him?

Wollerton used the blade to cut the restraints from his wrists, stepped over the corpses and positioned himself against the chassis, angling his body so he had good sight-lines of the rear and side doors. He heard someone climb out of the cab.

'What's happening?' a man's voice called out in Mandarin.

The reply came from whoever had got out of the van. 'I thought I heard something.' He knocked on the door. 'What's happening?'

'He gave us some trouble,' Wollerton said in Mandarin, covering his mouth to disguise his voice. 'Help us.'

He tensed as the side door was thrown open.

'What the fuck?' a fat Chinese man asked, his eyes widening as he registered the bodies. He looked at Wollerton in shock.

If he was carrying a weapon, he didn't even get the opportunity to reach for it. Wollerton shot him twice in the head, and leaped out of the van as the man's body fell to one side. Cars and trucks roared by at speed, their headlights blazing in the darkness. Wollerton glanced to his left and saw a Lexus SUV parked on the hard shoulder of a motorway. The occupants were surprised to see him, but not as shocked as he was at the sight of Brigitte Attali sitting in the back of the car with Echo Wu. He wanted to think the best, but there were no signs of duress. Had she betrayed him?

One of the two men in front produced a pistol and made to exit the vehicle, but Wollerton shot him through the windscreen, which shattered. He fired at the front wheel of the Lexus and it burst. He rushed to the front of the van, jumped behind the wheel, started the engine and stepped on the accelerator. The van sprang forward and he swerved into the steady stream of traffic.

As he glanced in the wing mirror, Wollerton caught a glimpse of Brigitte, Echo and the unknown driver. All three were out of the Lexus and they all had guns trained in the direction of Wollerton's van, but there were too many vehicles between them and their intended target, and they lowered their weapons. Wollerton was stunned. The gun left no room for doubt. Brigitte Attali had betrayed him. As he sped from the scene, Wollerton promised himself the Frenchwoman would one day pay the price of her treachery.

Chapter 45

Brigitte watched the van become part of the dazzle of distant lights. On Wei, their driver, peered into the car and looked at the body of his dead companion. He kicked the door and cursed loudly. Echo Wu slipped her pistol into the waistband of her trousers and approached.

'You fucking amateurs,' Brigitte said angrily. 'How the fuck did he escape? There's going to be a price on my head!'

'Two bounties perhaps,' Echo observed. 'My employers have paid you two million dollars for nothing.'

'Hey!' Brigitte responded. 'I delivered. Your people fucked up. Not me. I'm out of here.'

Echo grabbed her. 'I don't think so.' She looked at the body of the van driver, which lay ahead of them, and at the bloody mess inside the Lexus. 'It isn't safe here. We need to leave, but we go together. Until we get further instructions.'

Brigitte eyed her indignantly.

'Come on,' Echo said, pulling her towards the barrier which marked the edge of the motorway. 'Let's go,' she told On Wei in Mandarin.

Brigitte didn't resist. She followed Echo, hoping she could still play the situation to her advantage.

Chapter 46

After she'd called Pearce, Leila sat in the car, waiting for the rain to pass. The foothills and mountains opposite were lost to a grey wash cascading down the windscreen, and with her surroundings obscured and nothing to distract her, Leila's thoughts turned inward. Her emotions were as wild as the storm that raged around her and she bounced from one thought to the next in a frenetic search for answers. She wondered who Jared and his companion were working for, and what kind of operation would merit such intensive and clever surveillance. Junkies looked right at home in that neighbourhood and most people, Leila included, simply wouldn't see them as a threat.

She was missing key pieces of the puzzle, and the feeling of not being able to see the complete picture rekindled memories of London, when she'd killed Artem Vasylyk and discovered the state-of-the-art communicator in his office. She still didn't know who'd been sending him orders and hadn't shared her role in the man's death with Pearce, which troubled her. She considered Pearce a friend, but couldn't bring herself to confess to what could, in the wrong eyes, be considered murder. She would have to tell him one day. She owed it to him to honour their friendship, but today was not that day. She felt bad enough at having stumbled into a situation that had resulted in the deaths of two potentially useful informants. She'd made a mess.

Leila took scant comfort from the enforced rest. Her body ached, the pain of the fight with Jared adding to the ever-present discomfort of her disability. She took the opportunity to massage her legs, which burned after her short run. Her hips and knees felt fragile and stiff, and she suspected she would suffer in the coming days. But at least she was alive.

After more than an hour, Leila saw the back of the storm. It was clearly delineated by the end of a huge cloud that travelled from west to east. Beyond the cloud-line was nothing but blue sky, and as the brooding mass moved on, sunshine followed in its wake, bringing the mountains and valleys to life with a rich glow. When the sunlight hit the Yukon and dazzled off the drenched windshield, Leila climbed out and got to work.

She used her phone to take photographs of the dead man in the boot, capturing images of his face from every possible angle. She also took his fingerprints, harvesting them on the screen of one of the small tablet computers in her surveillance pack. She searched the body, and found nothing but a small billfold of cash. She repeated the process for Jared, and after she'd photographed and printed him, she discovered he had nothing on him other than a few crumpled dollar bills – no wallet or phone. She hauled his body to the Yukon and put him in the driver's seat. Leila found moving him painful and difficult. When he was finally positioned at the wheel, Leila grabbed the small Peli case and her rucksack full of surveillance equipment.

She opened the Yukon's fuel cap, started the car, put it in gear and stepped back to watch the large vehicle crawl slowly through the long grass. She held her breath as the car approached the precipice. The front wheels lost contact with the ground, and for a moment, the Yukon teetered on the edge before gravity took hold and pulled it over. Leila limped to the edge and saw the large vehicle tumble down the cliff face, crashing and buckling before it hit a giant boulder on the valley floor and burst into flames.

Satisfied the men and any evidence linking her to them would be incinerated, Leila picked up the rucksack and Peli case and started south, heading along the forest trail towards the country road.

An hour later, she reached the intersection and found Pearce waiting for her. He immediately noticed the bruises on her face where Jared had hit her.

'What happened?' he asked.

'I ran into trouble,' she replied. 'I had to take care of two men who were watching the house.'

'Are you OK?'

'I screwed up,' Leila admitted. 'But I'm OK.'

'And the men?'

'Gone,' Leila replied simply.

Pearce studied her with a sympathetic eye. 'I brought you this,' he said, handing her a brand new silver helmet.

'Thanks.'

She forced her tired, sore legs over the motorcycle and pulled on the helmet. Within moments, they were racing along the winding road towards Seattle. As she held Pearce with one hand and the Peli case with the other, Leila breathed a sigh of relief. She was glad to be with someone she trusted and even more grateful to be putting miles between her and the two men she'd killed.

Chapter 47

Wollerton pulled over, opened the driver's door and threw up. He was dizzy, trembling and his body was raw. His mind was a mess of confusion and he burned with a sense of failure. Had Brigitte betrayed him? Had he failed to see it coming? Had he lost his edge? Or was she playing a deeper game alone? Either way, he felt a fool for trusting her. He couldn't believe he'd been stupid enough to let her meet Echo alone. Whatever her motive, he now faced a dark battle for survival; he had to get out of China and warn Pearce and Leila that Brigitte should now be considered hostile.

He wiped his mouth and tried to steady himself, but it was hopeless. His body shook and his heart raced, though he couldn't tell whether he was experiencing the legacy of an adrenalin rush or the side effects of whatever they'd used to drug him. He sat upright and when he pulled the door shut, he glanced in the wing mirror to see a grey, sunken-eyed ghost of his former self looking back at him. He needed out, and fast. He looked around the cab and saw a backpack in the passenger footwell. Inside he found all his personal effects, his fake passports, credit cards and money. The only things missing were his phone and his Ghostlink, but the contents of the bag were more than he could have hoped for. With them he had a real chance of getting out of the country. Had his abductors slipped up? Or was this Brigitte's handiwork? He said a prayer of thanks for his good fortune.

He closed the backpack and slung it over his shoulder as he stepped out of the van. He hadn't paid much attention to his surroundings when he'd turned off the motorway. He'd simply wanted to get away from the bustling late-night traffic, but as he looked around, he realized he was in an industrial district and was surrounded by factories that would be dormant until morning. The street was deserted – there weren't even any parked cars around, so the van really stood out. The thought of the four bodies inside propelled Wollerton forward. He had no desire to be anywhere near the vehicle when it was opened up. As he walked, he started to feel a little better. He hadn't entirely disgraced himself. He replayed the fight in the van. He took no joy in ending another life, but given the choice between his or theirs, he had no hesitation. Stepping back and looking at events dispassionately, he was pleased with his performance. He hadn't seen that kind of action for years. He'd played a peripheral role in the Black Thirteen investigation and most of his contribution had been made from behind a computer. Pearce had borne the brunt of the wet work.

Wollerton looked up at the sky, and his eyes fought light pollution and the hazy smog that lingered over the city. He picked out the constellations of Orion and Corvus, which enabled him to ascertain approximate compass points. He headed towards the motorway he'd just left. If he could figure out which one it was, he'd know his location in relation to the airport. There wouldn't be any flights leaving until daybreak, but Wollerton planned to be on the very first of them.

Chapter 48

On Wei had made a phone call as they'd walked away from the motorway, and a taciturn driver in a Chery SUV met them on the corner of a nearby street. Brigitte was impressed by the depth of resources on display. The death of six men and the escape of a high-value prisoner hadn't engendered panic, just a pragmatic response. The ease with which On Wei had abandoned his vehicle, now a major crime scene, and his lack of concern, suggested Echo's employers were extremely well connected.

The grim-faced driver of the Chery took them through the city, and Brigitte found herself in a neighbourhood she recognized, an industrial estate in the west of Qingdao, the location of the company they'd been targeting.

A few minutes later, they stopped at a barrier and a uniformed guard emerged from a gatehouse and studied the occupants of the Chery. He stiffened when he recognized On Wei, and quickly raised the barrier. The car drove into the walled Qingdao Consumer Products complex. Brigitte had finally infiltrated the target, but not in a way she could have ever foreseen. They passed three large warehouses and pulled into a space outside a four-storey office block which lay at the heart of the huge complex. There were five other cars in spaces outside the building. Shift workers? Or a welcoming committee?

'Come on,' On Wei said. He got out of the car and led Echo and Brigitte inside.

The block reminded Brigitte of a hospital. It was a simple, functional building with stark lines, bare painted walls, linoleum floors and harsh strip lights. On Wei took them through the block and up to the top floor. There were no obvious signs of security – no guards and no cameras. Either the occupants were supremely confident or they used other, more discreet measures.

Finally, On Wei stopped outside a set of double doors and knocked.

'Enter,' a voice said in Mandarin, and On Wei led them inside.

The meeting room was dominated by a large mahogany table that seated eighteen. Only three of the large leather chairs were occupied, the first by a man who looked about Brigitte's age. His black hair fell just over his ears, and was styled with a neat parting. He wore a dark-blue Zhongshan suit which hung loose, robbing his body of any definitive shape, but his lean face and hungry eyes suggested that beneath the traditional garb he was fit and strong.

The man next to him was older; late fifties perhaps. He wore a tailored suit and woven silk tie that could have been made in Savile Row and wouldn't have looked out of place in any corporate boardroom, but the long scar that ran from his chin to his right ear suggested he wasn't executive material. Brigitte recognized it as the echo of a knife wound, and wondered how he'd survived such a serious injury. The ragged, heavily stitched line split his chubby cheek in two and made it seem as though he had a second, ugly smile. His hair was cropped close, revealing his skull, and his hands and neck were covered in intricate tattoos, which Brigitte guessed continued beneath his immaculate clothes. The older man remained in his chair, but the younger one stood and moved slowly around the table, walking behind the third seated figure. Brigitte stopped herself from giving any hint of recognition. The third man was the older prisoner who'd escaped from Al Aqarab prison. He eyed her carefully and his expression gave nothing away.

'Chloe Duval,' the man with two smiles said. 'It seems we have paid you for something you have not delivered.'

'I delivered,' Brigitte said. 'Your people screwed up.'

The younger man scowled. Brigitte was conscious he was getting closer.

'From what I understand, they have paid the price,' Two Smiles remarked. 'Still, we are out a considerable sum.'

'Who's this *we*? Qingdao Consumer Products? The government? Who are you?' Brigitte asked.

'We are patriots,' Two Smiles replied. 'People who believe China is a sleeping giant that must be awakened to take its place at the very highest tables. It must no longer be reactive. It must shape world affairs.' He paused. 'We are the Red Wolves.'

The westerner who'd escaped from Al Aqarab leaned over to whisper something to Two Smiles, and he nodded at the younger man, who lunged at Brigitte. He was fast, and even if she'd tried to defend herself, she doubted she'd have been able to stop him. He plunged a syringe into her neck and injected a clear liquid.

The world blurred in an instant, and Brigitte stumbled against the table.

'What was . . .' she slurred.

'Something that will help us have an honest conversation,' Two Smiles replied.

His face grew in size and split in two, and the world morphed into a trippy kaleidoscope of shapes and colours.

They're going to interrogate me, Brigitte thought before she blacked out.

Chapter 49

'Do you want to tell me what happened?' Pearce asked as they stepped out of the elevator.

Leila was exhausted and deeply unsettled. She'd messed up and two men had paid the ultimate price for her carelessness. 'There's not much to tell. Two unidentified males were watching the house from the place opposite,' she replied, crossing the large room to put the rucksack and Peli case next to her desk. 'They came for me and I defended myself.'

'I'm sorry, Lyly. I should have gone.'

'Don't make me out to be a victim, Scott. I took care of myself. I'm just annoyed we missed an opportunity for intel.'

'Come on, Lyly, it's me,' Pearce said reassuringly. 'We've been through fire together. You don't have to get defensive.'

'I messed up,' she said. 'If I hadn't been so complacent . . .' She glanced away.

'You're many things, but complacent isn't one of them. Human, maybe?'

Leila sighed and reached into her pocket for her phone, which she connected to her laptop. She opened the photos folder and looked through the images she'd taken of the dead men.

'I saw them come out of the house opposite when I planted the camera,' Pearce said. 'I thought they were drunks.'

'They weren't,' Leila replied. 'I can run an image search to find out who they really were. I got prints too. That should give us something at least.'

The sound of rush-hour traffic, muffled by the huge windows, rose from the street and filled the silence.

'I'm sorry, Scott,' she offered.

'It's OK,' he said. 'I had my own run-in today. Ziad Malek went to a community centre in Riverton Heights. He met with some guys.' Pearce handed her the surveillance glasses. 'I got faces, vehicle registrations, business names. There's a group of guys who come out of a book shop at the end of the footage. They're our priority. See what you can find out.'

'Sure.' Leila sensed there was more to come, and Pearce's hesitation didn't signal anything good.

'Then I followed Malek into the city,' he said at last. 'He got into a fight. Looked like something personal. I had to step in. He almost beat a guy to death. I helped him escape and we got talking. I asked him for a job.'

Leila was stunned. Making contact with the subject of surveillance seriously reduced their options. Malek could identify Pearce now.

'I know what you're thinking,' he said. 'But we were never going to break this from the outside.'

'We don't have the support for undercover work,' Leila said. 'I can't keep you safe on my own.' She still had nightmares about Pearce's abduction during the Black Thirteen investigation.

'I know,' he conceded. 'It's a risk I'm prepared to take. I'm seeing him tomorrow night. It would be good to have some understanding of who these people are and what we're up against.'

'I'll do what I can,' Leila replied. 'I'm also going to take a listen to the two bugs I managed to plant in the house before I had to cut out.'

'Thanks,' Pearce said. He touched her shoulder gently. 'I couldn't do this without you.'

As Leila nodded, her laptop sounded a notification alert and she switched to a secure, anonymous messaging account. The address was only known to her, Pearce and Wollerton and was to be used only in case of emergency.

'It's from Kyle,' she said, studying the coded message. 'He says, "Brigitte compromised. Tried to kidnap me. On my way. Be careful."'

Chapter 50

Wollerton arrived at the airport after walking most of the night and immediately went to the men's room to wash away the filth and fatigue. He emerged looking more like a normal traveller and went to the Hainan ticket desk where he was tested for coronavirus. When he was confirmed negative, he booked a flight to London using a false passport and credit card in the name of John Tucker. Brigitte had provided the identity so he knew there was a risk it would be flagged. Even after the payment cleared and the helpful representative gave him his boarding pass, Wollerton wasn't able to shake the ominous feeling the police or people far more sinister were circling, and might seize him at any moment. He passed through security and found a pay-by-the-minute Internet terminal in the departure lounge, which he used to send a warning to Leila and Pearce.

He wandered around the airport, marvelling at the luxury goods adverts and shops that were a sign of just how much wealth now flowed through China. When his gate was announced, he made his way to border control.

Wollerton shifted uneasily as he waited in line. This was the final check before he could get to his flight. He looked at the row of stern-faced men and women, wearing surgical masks, sealed in the tiny booths, each studying the documents of early morning travellers. Most of the passengers manifested the nervous concern of the innocent and the fear of authority that came with it. Wollerton tried to emulate it. He didn't want to appear too casual, but at the same time he had to keep a lid on the corrosive anxiety that threatened to overwhelm him.

The woman in front of him was waved forward, and as she approached the booth directly opposite, the knot in Wollerton's stomach tightened. He was next in line. If Brigitte had given up his false identity this was where he'd find out. The border official's computer would be connected to police and intelligence systems and when the John Tucker passport was scanned, it would flag any problem immediately.

The border officer, a young woman with a long black pony-tail and an unforgiving face, handed the passport back to the traveller and waved her on. She looked at Wollerton and signalled him to step forward.

'Passport,' she said flatly, as he reached the booth.

'Oh, sorry,' he replied, fumbling in his pockets. He handed over his passport and boarding pass. 'There we go,' he said with a smile.

He got nothing but a stern look in reply. She took the documents and scanned them. The time she spent studying the screen seemed to last a thousand nerve-racking years. Wollerton felt sick, but he swallowed back a mouthful of bile and smiled again. Freya and Luke rose in his mind unbidden, and he fixed on the memory of his children's sweet faces and prayed they would protect him from harm.

'OK,' she said, handing him his passport and boarding pass.

'Thank you,' Wollerton said, as he walked away.

The tension melted, but he didn't truly relax until he felt the undercarriage retract as the Airbus A330 rose into the sky.

Chapter 51

The beach was magnificent. It stretched north and south in a gentle crescent that vanished into the rose-blush horizon. The sun hadn't crested the tree-covered hills, but it was well on its way, and cast a hazy light over the dewy landscape. Pearce stood near the shoreline and watched and waited.

He'd helped Leila as much as he'd been able to the previous evening, but she liked to work alone and immersed herself in the digital world to such an extent that he often felt like an unwelcome distraction. Finally, exhaustion had forced him to crash in the early hours, but Leila had kept going, chunking data, running searches and trying to piece together the puzzle that confronted them. Pearce had risen in darkness at 4 a.m., and he'd discovered Leila slumped over her desk, sleeping where she'd collapsed. It was dedication unlike any he'd ever seen, and it was dangerous. She behaved like a machine, but she wasn't one. He didn't know how long she could keep it up before something broke. She'd made it clear she didn't want to talk about the men she'd killed. She was working on identifying them. Functional, unemotional, practical, the machine kept working.

Pearce had left the building and rode south to keep an appointment he'd made the moment they'd received

Wollerton's message. Pearce had chosen this beach in the Quinault Indian Nation, a large, sparsely populated region west of Seattle, because of its clear lines of sight in every direction. The sands were a couple of hundred yards wide and there was no road access. Getting here involved a twenty-minute hike along rough tracks, and the nearest road was the one that ran from a small parking area that lay in thick forest almost a mile away.

Pearce checked his watch. It was coming up to six thirty when he saw a figure crest one of the nearby bluffs and stumble down the steep slope that led to the beach. The man was dressed in a flannel tracksuit and looked as though he was out for a dawn run. It was Robert Clifton, Huxley Blaine Carter's intelligence advisor.

'What the heck are we doing here?' Clifton asked when he finally reached Pearce. A sheen of sweat glistened in the dawn light and he was out of breath. 'My wife thought I was nuts when I said I was going for an early run. A run that involved a four-hour drive. What's so damned urgent?'

A four-hour drive would put him somewhere around Portland – potentially useful information for the future, Pearce thought.

'Brigitte Attali might be compromised,' he replied. 'She might have been involved in an attempt to abduct Kyle.'

'Shit. How reliable is this?'

'Very,' Pearce said, studying the man.

'And you dragged me all the way out here to see if we're behind it?' Clifton asked.

'Something like that.'

'If she's turned, we had nothing to do with it,' Clifton said, putting his hands on his hips and casting his eyes at the ocean. 'Shit. If, and it's a big if, you're right, this changes everything. She could give us all up. I'm going to need to confirm this independently.'

'I know how it goes,' Pearce assured him. 'And so do you. We can't trust you. Not for now. So this is going to be our last communication until we know exactly where everyone stands.'

Clifton nodded. 'Hux isn't going to like this. He prides himself on being an exceptional judge of character.'

'No such thing in this line of work. You know that.'

Pearce headed for the trail that would take him into the bluffs. His bike was parked just over the first rise. It wasn't designed for motocross but at a push he could have used it to make a quick escape. But he didn't need to. He'd come to gauge the extent of the rot and understand the threat they faced, and when he glanced over his shoulder at the former director of the NSA, Pearce didn't see danger, he saw a man suddenly burdened. Clifton was pacing in a tight circle, speaking into a phone, running a hand through his hair, oblivious to the fact Pearce was watching him. He didn't look like a man masterminding a double-cross, but as Pearce had told him, there was no such thing as a good judge of character in this game.

They'd have to be careful.

Chapter 52

The sunlight woke Leila. There were no blinds or drapes over the huge windows and no way of blocking out light. Their sleeping areas were partitioned, but the dividers were only six feet high and didn't reach the ceiling, which was probably why they'd been provided with sleep masks. But Leila had fallen asleep at her desk and wasn't wearing one, which meant she was dazzled into consciousness by the reflection of the rising sun off a nearby mirrored building.

She smacked her dry lips and tried to shake the dirty, raw feeling from behind her eyes. She knew it was hopeless. The sensation of burning fatigue was an almost constant companion and she doubted she'd live many days without it. Her dreams were a disturbing place, and she wanted to inhabit them as little as possible. Her most recent nightmare had been a kaleidoscope of her family's deaths, mixed with the last moments of the two men she'd killed the previous day.

She tried to stand, but the circulation to her legs had been cut off and she was instantly assailed by terrible pins and needles in her feet. She sucked in a deep breath and stretched her numb limbs. It took a few minutes, but she was finally able to stand without too much pain. She picked up her cane and tried to walk off the worst of the soreness. Distant ships crossed the bay as she tried to take her mind off the pain by reviewing what she'd been able to learn the previous night.

Deni Salamov was a first-generation Chechen immigrant, rumoured to be a local crime boss. He owned the community centre Pearce had filmed, along with all the businesses in it. He had a twenty-year-old conviction for tax evasion, but nothing since. The young man with him was Rasul Salamov, his son, a flashy playboy with a penchant for fast cars. He had two Porsches, a Ferrari, a Lamborghini and a Ford GTO registered in his name. He owned Jefferson National Trucking, the company that employed Jake Lowell, the trucker who'd been murdered during the hijacking. Rasul had been ripped off, that much was clear, and it was possible he suspected Ziad. In the footage Pearce had shot, Ziad certainly looked like a man who'd been summoned to answer questions. The woman Ziad had slapped was Essi Salamov, Deni's daughter. She was a successful tax attorney with a mid-sized law firm. The man Ziad had beaten in the street was Jack Gray, the Salamovs' corporate lawyer. Deni's older companion at the bookstore was Abbas Idrisov, another first-generation immigrant and a veteran of the First Chechen War. He'd moved to the United States after the 1996 ceasefire agreement. Leila's research revealed a sizeable Chechen community in Seattle, and according to news reports and police intelligence, a handful had become leading crime figures who were rumoured to play key roles in the drugs trade. Leila believed they'd found one of those leading figures in Deni Salamov. Everything about him, from his multitude of business interests to the three ex-convict heavies who walked him out of the bookshop – Osman Barayev, Ilman Kadyrov and Surkho Otarev – spoke to who he really was.

For all her success analysing the Salamovs, Leila was troubled she hadn't been able to identify the two men she'd killed. She was still running an image search, but so far it had drawn a blank. Admittedly it was running slow because of the security precautions she'd taken to ensure no one could trace the source of the photos of two dead men, but she would have expected something to have turned up by now.

She walked over to her desk and woke the dormant laptop. She switched to the image search screen, but the programme still hadn't yielded anything. Leila opened another window and switched on KOMO local television news. Something mindless to distract her while she had breakfast. A perfectly tanned, handsome anchor was interviewing a young reporter about rumours local celebrity Kitty Kingston was getting married. Kitty, a veteran of *Dancing with the Stars*, had caused a stir a few years back by endorsing Ron Sugg, an extreme right-wing politician.

Leila kept half an ear on the babble as she went to the tiny kitchenette behind the elevators to grab a yoghurt from the fridge and pour herself a cup of stale filter coffee. As she wandered back to her desk, sipping the tepid tar-water, she heard the urgent tones of a newsreader.

'*Seattle Police Department repeated its call for any member of the public who sees the pair to contact the number below.*'

Leila hurried to her desk.

'*Officers Jared Lowe and Dean Ollander are long-serving officers with distinguished records.*'

Leila looked at the screen in horror. The faces of the men she'd killed stared back at her, both in full Seattle Police Department dress uniforms, their chests covered in service medals. Her heart started thumping and her palms suddenly became wet with perspiration.

'*A police spokesperson refused to comment on whether the officers were engaged in an ongoing investigation but did confirm the department is sufficiently concerned for their welfare to make their details public.*'

Leila bent over and grabbed the bin under her desk. She retched a couple of times, but her heaves brought nothing up.

Had they been surveilling the house as part of an operation?

She'd killed two serving police officers.

Why hadn't they identified themselves?

She knew the heat that would bring and wondered how she was going to tell Pearce.

Chapter 53

Leila had seemed preoccupied when Pearce returned from his meeting with Clifton. She'd packed up their supplies and, as they'd shifted everything they needed into the boot of a Chevy Traverse, rented with her fake ID, she'd briefed Pearce on the Salamov family and the wider network of people associated with them. Knowing Brigitte had probably been compromised, they couldn't risk staying in Huxley Blaine Carter's property and had moved to the New La Hacienda Motel on Lucille Street. The accommodation was basic, but it offered easy access to the port and industrial district, and the manager accepted cash and didn't ask any questions.

They'd taken two rooms and had spent a couple of hours getting the gear set up in Leila's. As they worked, she continued briefing him on the Salamovs. She told him about Rasul Salamov's trucking company, Ziad's job at the port and Deni's various business interests, which all pointed to a smuggling operation. Later that evening, Pearce felt much more confident about the dynamics of the situation he was walking into when he parked his bike near the community centre on 140th Street. The last light of the sun was fast disappearing, and the Al Jamaea coffee shop was lit up like a beacon, packed with men who hailed from a variety of Middle Eastern, Asian and African countries.

'You getting this?' Pearce asked, adjusting his surveillance glasses.

'*Crystal clear,*' Leila replied through a concealed earpiece.

Even at a distance, Pearce could sense something was wrong. Her voice lacked its normal confidence. She might have been struggling to process the deaths of the two men she'd killed the previous day, or it might have been the situation with her sister. Whatever the cause of her distress, she didn't want to talk about it, and when Pearce had tried to probe, she'd shut him down and pointedly steered the conversation back to the Salamovs.

The smell of rich coffee and fruit-flavoured tobacco reminded Pearce of Cairo. Dozens of men sat at tables outside the coffee shop, talking animatedly, smoking cigarettes and shisha with an enthusiasm that would have given big tobacco hope for the future. Many of the men sipped potent jolts of the thickest, blackest coffee from tiny cups. They looked at ease, chatting, laughing, and Pearce envied them their camaraderie, that sense of belonging. He missed the feeling of mattering to someone. He'd known it in the army, but had experienced nothing like it since. He searched for Ziad but didn't see him, and headed inside.

'*Ahlan,*' a waiter with a craggy, friendly face said enthusiastically. He tested Pearce for coronavirus and once it had registered a negative result, the welcome in Arabic was followed by, '*Fee tarabaiza fi' warra.*' *There's a table at the back.*

Pearce nodded and scanned faces as he headed towards the rear of the large cafe. There were no women, just men. Many of them watched him as he made his way through the room. This was clearly a place for locals and he was unfamiliar, worthy of note.

'*Ah, a room full of men sorting out the world's problems,*' Leila said sarcastically. '*We need more of this sort of thing.*'

Pearce understood her ire. She was one of the most capable people he'd ever worked with, but many of the men in this place would likely have regarded her opinions and abilities as second-rate. He struggled to comprehend cultures that thought it acceptable to deprive women of the rights and freedoms accorded to men. It was oppression masked by sophistry and supposed good intentions. The lack of women in this place would be dressed up as a protection of their modesty, but he wondered what was so immodest about the men's behaviour that their wives, mothers and sisters needed to be shielded from it.

He pulled up a lightweight wooden chair with a bamboo seat and sat at the only vacant table in the place. Nearby conversation became noticeably muted, and he kept catching glances from around the room. Not quite hostile, but not far off. He was accustomed to being the outsider and didn't react to the unwelcome interest.

The waiter ignored him, pointedly avoiding his table as he weaved his way around the room. Ziad appeared a few minutes later and glad-handed a few men who expressed their joy to see him. It was clear from the glances they made in Pearce's direction and Ziad's whispered replies to their questions that the escaped prisoner was vouching for Pearce in some way. Pearce felt the mood lighten when Ziad finally took a seat at the table.

'Sorry I'm late, man,' Ziad said in a perfect American accent.

Like Pearce, he was the child of immigrants, and had been raised and schooled in the West. Pearce wondered if Ziad considered himself American, or whether, like him, he felt he didn't really fit anywhere.

'No problem. I just got here,' Pearce said.

The waiter approached and took their drinks orders. Ziad opted for a fresh mint tea, and Pearce joined him.

'So you need a job?' Ziad asked. He picked a sugar cube from a bowl and fiddled with its wrapper.

'I came here three months ago and my money's almost gone,' Pearce replied. 'I was on an ESTA, but that capped out at ninety days, so . . .'

'So you're an illegal,' Ziad remarked. 'What kind of experience have you got?'

'I was in the army for seven years,' Pearce said. He'd always found an element of truth helped make for a more convincing cover, and army experience should be of interest to Ziad and the people he worked for.

'British Army?' Ziad asked.

Pearce nodded. 'It was good money and there weren't many other choices for someone like me.'

'Like you?'

'Stupid. Rebellious. I left school with nothing,' Pearce replied. It wasn't true, but if it hadn't been for the intervention of his headteacher, Malcolm Jones, it could easily have been.

'You ever do time?' Ziad asked.

Pearce hesitated. 'What kind of job are we talking about?'

Ziad shrugged.

'No, I never did time,' Pearce said. 'But I came close.'

'So maybe you're not all that stupid,' Ziad observed. 'Either way, it sounds like you're prepared to get your hands dirty.'

'*Trouble at twelve o'clock*,' Leila said into Pearce's ear, and he looked up to see Rasul Salamov barging through the room.

Everyone in the place fell silent as Rasul bore down on their table like a storm. Ziad sensed he'd lost Pearce's attention and glanced over as the furious man closed on him.

'Rasul—' he began.

'You think you can hit my sister?' Rasul said, grabbing Ziad and hauling him out of his chair. He threw him to the ground, and Ziad collided with the neighbouring table, sending it flying. Crockery scattered and smashed on the tile floor. 'You fucking pig!'

Rasul kicked Ziad, who groaned and tried to fend off the follow-ups. If someone didn't intervene quickly, the man would die.

Chapter 54

Pearce got to his feet and put himself between the two men. He pushed Rasul back.

'Who the fuck are you?' Rasul asked. 'And what makes you think you can fucking touch me?'

He swung at Pearce, who dodged the blow and grabbed the man's left hand. He twisted Rasul's fingers into a pressure hold and Rasul yelped and held his other hand up in submission.

'I don't want to hurt you,' Pearce said. 'I saw the whole thing. He was defending himself.'

Rasul's anger dissipated and Pearce released him.

'You listen to a stranger,' Ziad remarked, getting to his feet. 'But you won't even hear me out. After all we've been through, you go straight to your fists.'

Rasul looked around sheepishly. 'Enjoying the show?' he asked, and the coffee shop patrons all looked away immediately.

Ziad picked up the fallen table and the two men sitting at it pulled it close. 'Let me buy you a drink,' he said.

'*Balash, habibi,*' one of them said. *Don't trouble yourself, friend.*

Ziad turned to face Rasul, whose face burned with angry humiliation.

'So, what happened?'

'That's how you should have started,' Ziad said.

'Don't push your luck, Ziad,' Rasul cautioned.

'I'm sorry. I'm a little shaken after being kicked half to death. Let's have a drink and I'll tell you what happened. My new friend can back me up.' Ziad indicated Pearce. 'He was there and saw the whole thing.'

Rasul glared at Pearce.

'He's a quick man, and good with his hands,' Ziad said.

'Sorry about . . .' Pearce looked pointedly at Rasul's left hand, which was cradled in his right.

'He's ready to step in,' Ziad continued, 'and he's brave and smart. Come on. Let's sit and I'll tell you everything.'

Like a tamed beast, Rasul allowed himself to be steered towards their table, and took the seat opposite Pearce.

'Where the hell is the waiter?' he asked fiercely, before Ziad started to recount the day's events.

Two hours later, Rasul was back-slapping Pearce like an old friend. He'd been impressed by Pearce's tales of military service and offered his respect when Pearce told him the reason he'd quit the army: too much time spent in the Middle East fighting his Muslim brothers. It wasn't true, but as he'd suspected, the lie bought him currency with Rasul and the handful of men nearby who were going to great lengths to pretend they weren't eavesdropping.

They were all friends now. Rasul had forgiven Ziad and cursed the ancestors of his sister's aggressive boyfriend. Ziad said he'd only gone to Essi's office to talk to her and had been the victim of an unprovoked attack. That much was true, but Pearce doubted the man had only been there to talk to his ex-girlfriend.

'Amr, my friend,' Rasul said, 'what kind of work would you be prepared to do?'

Pearce shrugged. 'I need money.'

'There are some people in Delridge who've put the word out they've come into some product. Product we believe may have been stolen from us.'

Ziad looked surprised by the revelation.

'Some of our friends are going to talk to these people and see if we can get our product back,' Rasul said.

'What product?' Pearce asked.

'Do you really want to know?' Rasul responded. 'A courier gets paid to collect packages, not find out what's inside them.'

'And if they won't give the product back?'

'What does anyone do when they catch a thief?'

Pearce nodded slowly. 'Guns?'

'Of course. That a problem?'

'No,' Pearce assured Rasul. He knew from years of undercover work that criminals and terrorists were some of the most trusting people in the world. Their confidence stemmed from the belief no one would be stupid enough to risk the retribution that would follow betrayal. Infiltrating the periphery of clandestine organizations was often surprisingly simple. Getting beyond the status of cannon fodder or foot soldier was another matter. But despite his experience, Pearce was surprised at the speed with which Rasul had accepted him and drawn him into a criminal enterprise. He suspected it was because Rasul was expecting a high body count. As an untested newcomer, Pearce had no doubt he'd be on the front line of whatever they had planned.

'No problem at all,' Pearce said.

He was on the inside.

He just had to stay alive long enough to make the most of it.

Chapter 55

The place stank of misery. It was an acrid stench, a blend of bleach, sweat and urine, and it assailed Brigitte the moment she woke. Her head throbbed and her surroundings spun violently. She was disoriented and apart from the pungent aroma, had no other purchase on reality. Her body was numb and distant and she was only dimly aware of the sweat that oozed from every pore. She tried to move and was immediately sick. An indistinct shape held something in front of her, and Brigitte heard watery vomit splatter against a hard surface.

'I'm sorry, Chloe,' the shape said. It took Brigitte a moment to recognize Echo Wu's voice. 'Try to breathe. It gets better.'

'What? What gets better?' Brigitte asked when she'd finished being sick. She felt as though she was going through the motions. It was the kind of situation in which a person should be concerned, so she'd expressed it, but she didn't feel it. She didn't feel much of anything, and her voice didn't sound like her. It was thick and throaty.

'The medicine,' another voice said. It was a man.

Brigitte looked in his direction and saw a shadow spinning in front of her.

'What medicine?' she asked. She should be puzzled. That's

how she should behave; ask questions, express interest. Find answers. But she couldn't care less about answers. She was away in another world.

'Just breathe,' Echo told her, stroking her hair.

Echo's touch was gentle and pleasant, and Brigitte smiled. Or at least that's what she thought she did. It was so hard to tell. It was as though she was in a nightmare. Maybe she was? Perhaps this was one of those vivid dreams in which she thought she'd woken, but had only stumbled into a dream within a dream. No, it felt too real, and yet somehow unreal. She had no sense of place or time. How had she got here? The meeting room at Qingdao Consumer Products was the last thing she could remember clearly. There were other moments at the edge of her memory, but she didn't reach for them. They trailed dark, terrible tendrils and she knew if she held them she'd feel only horror.

'Breathe,' Echo said.

It seemed like good advice, so Brigitte took a deep breath and held it. Her lungs burned and her mouth was sour with bile and vomit, but she felt better as the world settled and started to come into focus. She breathed out slowly and saw Echo seated next to her on the edge of a filthy, sodden mattress. The man who'd drugged her, the one in the dark blue Zhongshan suit, stood beside a trolley table in the corner of the small room. A large leather briefcase rested on the table. It looked like the kind a doctor might carry. The room itself had no windows and its bare concrete walls were lit by a single exposed bulb.

'What medicine?' Brigitte asked.

'The medicine keeping you alive,' the man said, and Brigitte noticed Echo's face cloud with sadness. He stepped closer. 'You answered our questions, Ms Duval, and your responses satisfied us you have been telling the truth. You betrayed your colleague and you don't know who you were working for.'

Brigitte knew she should be relieved, but she couldn't muster the emotion. She recalled the preparation she'd done for the interrogation she'd suspected she'd face even if Wollerton hadn't escaped. She'd used a form of self-hypnosis she'd learned in the DGSE to convince herself of the truth of certain lies, such as not knowing Huxley Blaine Carter was her employer. It had seemed so important at the time, but felt irrelevant now.

'So we have satisfied ourselves as to your honesty,' the man said. 'But we need a way to guarantee your loyalty.'

'What for?' Brigitte asked.

'So you can repay the two million dollars you owe us.'

'I don't owe—'

'You owe us so much more,' he cut in. 'You owe us your life. We're keeping you alive, Ms Duval.'

Brigitte looked at Echo, who turned away, clearly ashamed. Echo's expression pierced the numb fog that clouded Brigitte's mind and fear chilled its way down her spine.

'The symptoms you're experiencing are a side effect,' the man said, reaching into the briefcase in front of him.

'Side effect?' Brigitte asked fearfully. Her lungs were very sore.

The man produced a medical patch from the case. 'The body is such a complex organism. It's comprised of so many intricate little systems. Many of which are essential to life,' he said as he crossed the room. As he drew closer, Brigitte noticed he was wearing latex gloves. He tore the protective wrapper away from the patch, and Brigitte saw a square about the size of a playing card that looked like a black plaster. 'These patches are comprised of three ingredients. The first, fentanyl, makes a person extremely high. The second is XTX, a genetically engineered toxin that attacks and destroys your parathyroid glands in moments.'

Brigitte started trembling. 'Please. Please don't,' she pleaded. She tried to raise her hands, but they didn't respond.

'A person cannot live without their parathyroid glands,' the man said. He loomed over her, but all Brigitte could see was the patch. It had become her world.

Echo would save her, Brigitte told herself. But when she looked at Echo, all she saw was a broken woman with tears in her eyes.

'Parathyroid glands produce a hormone, PTH, that is essential for breathing. Without it, a person dies of asphyxiation almost instantly.'

'Please don't kill me,' Brigitte begged.

'Which is why we include a third ingredient in the patch. Can you guess what it is?' the man asked as he removed the plastic backing strips.

Brigitte tried to shake her head.

'It's PTH. The third ingredient is what a person needs to keep them alive,' the man said.

Brigitte struggled to understand. Why destroy the parathyroid glands, only to replace the very hormone they produced? And then the answer came, tumbling though her mind like a falling star. *To create dependency.* Without the patches, a person would die. And that person would do anything for the product that kept them alive.

'Please don't put that on me,' Brigitte implored.

The man pulled back the sweat-soaked blanket to reveal Brigitte's naked torso. She looked down in horror and saw a black patch was already clinging to her shoulder.

I already have one on me, her mind screamed. *They already have me.*

Chapter 56

'If I didn't put it on you, you'd soon die.' The man ripped off the old patch and stuck the fresh one in its place. 'You need this now, Chloe.'

The fentanyl high was instant and tremendously powerful and Brigitte's concerns were lost to an opiate fog. She fought the blissful stupor and clung to her fear, to the horror of what had happened, finally understanding the full terrible significance of what she'd just learned.

'You want to . . .' she slurred.

'Sorry,' the man said, smiling as he leaned closer. 'I didn't hear you.'

'You want to take this into America, don't you?' she remarked.

The man's face seemed to bubble and warp as he nodded. 'We know you have seen the effects of our pharmacology experiments. You told us all about it. The prison escape in Cairo was an aerosolized version of XTX. This,' he held up the old patch, 'this is a work of art. Opioids are already killing thousands of Americans every year. Those who don't die live as shadow people, costing society greatly. Imagine what our product will do. Imagine millions of people hooked on a drug that is the only thing that keeps them alive. What would they be prepared to do for their weekly fix?' He paused and stroked Brigitte's forehead. 'What will you do, Chloe?'

Brigitte struggled to take in the implications of such a thing. Even if her mind hadn't been lost to the powerful synthetic opiate, she doubted she would have been able to process what had just happened to her, and its significance for the wider world. The leverage this drug – no, this weapon – would give this man, and the people he worked for, was beyond anything Brigitte could imagine.

'What would the American government do to keep its people alive?' the man asked. 'What would any government do?'

A chemical weapon that was highly addictive and capable of delivering mass casualties over a prolonged period of time. It was the stuff of nightmares. A million addicts, and their lives could be held to ransom, changing the geopolitical landscape forever.

'I see you understand,' the man said, backing away, and Brigitte realized she was crying. 'Tell her what she is to do for us,' he instructed Echo, before he picked up the case and left the room.

'I'm sorry,' Echo said when he was gone. 'I told you certain decisions aren't ours to make.' She unbuttoned the cuff of her blouse and rolled her sleeve up to reveal a black patch on her shoulder. Her eyes glistened as she watched Brigitte register its significance. 'I was sent here to investigate intelligence we'd received that the Red Wolves were experimenting with such things. They knew why I was here,' her voice cracked, and her eyes filled to bursting. Brigitte wanted to comfort her, but still couldn't move her hands. 'Someone in Beijing is helping them. I was betrayed. They did to me what they've done to you. They told me to leave the service. They made me bring my family here.' Echo broke down entirely. 'I'm sorry, Chloe. I didn't want this for you. But I had to,' she sobbed. 'They say they will do this to my children if I don't do exactly what they ask.' She choked back loud cries and looked at the door anxiously. 'I can't escape. There is nowhere else in the world that makes these things,' she tapped her patch. 'If it isn't changed every seven days, we die.'

Brigitte smiled darkly. A long sleep sounded blissful compared to the horror she was now living.

'The effects of the fentanyl are worst for the first day or so of a new patch, then they settle down,' Echo said.

You think I'm high, Echo, Brigitte thought. *I'm not. I'm just at peace.* But no matter how hard she tried, she couldn't get her mouth to form the words.

Echo took a tissue from a box on the trolley and wiped Brigitte's mouth. Was she drooling?

'Wha . . .' Brigitte managed to say after a concerted effort.

'What do they want?' Echo guessed.

Brigitte said yes with her eyes.

'They're opening a supply line into the United States,' Echo said. 'They want you to start building one into Europe.'

As she lay with her head pressed against the damp pillow, Brigitte thought about this lethal twisted weapon hitting the streets of Europe. Sober she would have seen only the horror, but in her stupor, coddled by the powerful drug, she also saw beauty. Her opium-addled mind couldn't think of a more blissful way for a multitude of people to die.

Chapter 57

Pearce waited on the corner of Massachusetts Street and Alaskan Way, opposite the St Martin Shelter. A line of people snaked around the corner of the austere concrete building, desperate folk in dirty, ragged clothes, there for a morning meal. A small group of men and women who'd been lucky enough to have already been served sat smoking beneath a green awning near the entrance. There were no smiles and very little hope in the faces of the young and old. Most showed signs of drug or alcohol addiction; swollen hands – an early sign of oedema – flaking skin, and eyes wild and hollow as though they'd been opened too wide and could never be closed. Pearce was shocked by the number of lost souls in this largely industrial neighbourhood, but this was a story replicated the world over; growing poverty brought on by the Covid-19 pandemic.

Rasul had instructed Pearce to be on the corner at nine thirty and had offered no plan or explanation. It might have been simple for Pearce to join the periphery of the Salamov organization, but he clearly still didn't have the man's trust. After the meeting at Al Jamaea coffee shop, Pearce had returned to the New La Hacienda motel and discussed the evening's events with Leila. She'd been watching via Pearce's surveillance glasses, but seemed disengaged and distracted, and his efforts to get her to open up had failed. She'd spent the night infiltrating the Seattle Police Department's network, pulling up intelligence reports on the city's gangs. Delridge was under the control of the East Hill Mob, an unsophisticated but violent street gang that ran the neighbourhood drugs trade and had been implicated in a number of homicides. Pearce suspected these were the people Rasul had spoken of, the ones he believed had stolen his product.

Pearce watched the flow of traffic in all directions. Massachusetts Street went west for a few hundred yards before coming to an end by a port gatehouse near the waterfront. Alaskan Way was an access road that ran alongside the Highway 99 overpass. This was an ugly, functional place used to get from A to B. The only people who lived in such areas were those who were trapped; sidelined and kept away from the productive folk who hustled to and fro along the busy roads. Pearce noticed five gleaming SUVs driving south along Alaskan Way, and when they stopped at the corner, he saw Rasul in the front passenger seat of the lead vehicle.

'*Subtle*,' Leila said into Pearce's ear. She was watching everything via the surveillance glasses he wore.

'Yeah,' Pearce agreed as he walked towards the convoy.

Rasul lowered his window. 'Get in,' he said.

Pearce glanced at the trailing convoy and saw four or five men in each car. He nodded and climbed inside Rasul's car. He recognized the three other faces immediately. The driver and the two on the back seat were the men Pearce had seen coming out of the bookshop after Ziad's meeting with Deni, Rasul and Abbas. They were muscle – career criminals with long records of violence.

'This is Osman, Ilman and Surkho,' Rasul told Pearce. 'This is Amr,' he said to the others. 'Give him a tool.'

Osman, a large man with a downturned mouth and a sour face, leaned forward and produced a pistol and two clips from a holdall in the footwell. He handed them to Pearce.

'OK?' Rasul asked, as Pearce checked the weapon.

The action was a little stiff and could have used some oil, but it would do.

'Fine,' Pearce replied.

Chapter 58

They drove through Fairmont Park, which had all the trappings of a middle-class neighbourhood. Large houses stood in big plots at the side of wide, tree-lined streets, but here and there were the gnawing rust patches of poverty. Gaunt men and women with hungry eyes gathered outside apartment blocks, repossession notices were pasted to the doors of a few homes, children in filthy clothes played in yards.

'Synthetics,' Rasul said, nodding at a couple of emaciated men who couldn't have been more than thirty.

They were sitting on the porch of a large house, rubbing something on their gums, and when they looked up at the passing motorcade, Pearce saw their spaced-out eyes. Their young faces were wrinkled and covered in sores and bruises. Unemployment had rocketed around the world, and with it a desperation to escape.

'Sometimes I disagree with my father,' Rasul remarked. 'There's a lot of profit in these drugs. But then I see what they do to people, to neighbourhoods. This one is already turning. In Washington state, more people die from synthetic opioids than from car accidents. And the death toll hides the true cost, the destruction of lives. Of cities.'

Pearce thought it odd to hear a smuggler denigrating other drug dealers, but in any field of human endeavour there was a moral pecking order that made some believe they had the right to judge others. 'Supplied by the people we're going to see?' he asked.

Rasul nodded. 'The East Hill Mob manufacture and distribute synthetics. Small scale, but enough to feed the parts of the city they control. Which is why their sudden shift to a more natural product –' Pearce guessed he was talking about heroin – 'didn't go unnoticed. No one starts trying to shift that kind of volume from nowhere, unless they've ripped off someone else's stash.'

'What kind of opposition are we expecting?' Pearce asked.

'That's what we're going to find out,' Rasul replied.

Four blocks later, the convoy stopped on Fauntleroy Way beside two apartment blocks. Tucked beside them was a small tumbledown single-storey house. The yellow paint that covered the aluminium siding was chipped and flaking, and the dusty front yard was covered by scattered toys, scraps of rusty metal and garbage. A couple of women spilled out of the little house and staggered across the porch to a two-seater swing that might have once looked charming, but was now bone-white with neglect and age. The women were in their underwear, revealing skeletal frames covered in bruises and sores. One pulled her lank hair away from her face and sparked a lighter that ignited the contents of a glass pipe. She inhaled deeply and her eyes rolled back momentarily before she came to. With her mind somewhere else, she handed the pipe to her ponytailed friend, who repeated the process.

'In there,' Rasul said, pointing at the house, 'you'll find a man called Otter. He's a corner boy who shifts product for the East Hill Mob. He'll know where they've got the merchandise. Make him tell you.'

'Alone?' Pearce asked.

'Consider it your initiation,' Rasul replied.

If Pearce had been commanding these men, he too would have sent his most expendable asset into this potentially volatile location. If that asset was lost, the cost to the organization would be minimal. Pearce had assessed the situation correctly; he was cannon fodder.

He stepped out of the car, slipped the pistol into the waistband of his jeans and lifted his leather jacket over the butt to conceal it. He crossed the pavement and walked through the litter-strewn front yard towards the porch.

'Hey, friend,' the woman with the ponytail said. 'You got any dough?'

'I'm looking for Otter,' Pearce replied.

'Otter can't give you what we can,' she said, stroking her companion's arm.

Pearce guessed she was trying to be suggestive, but her companion was completely out of it; she keeled at her touch, and hung limp over the arm of the swing.

'Is he inside?' Pearce asked.

'Twenty bucks for an answer,' she slurred.

Pearce ignored her and walked inside. He had seen some hellish places, but this house ranked as one of the worst. Everything of value had been stripped; light fittings, switches, sockets, pipes, even patches of plasterboard and flooring. Rot was eating the outer structure and Pearce could see bare earth through the holes in the floor. He peered into the first room, which was in a similar state of dilapidation, and saw a figure huddled beneath a blanket, head turned towards a television that had been smashed. A breeze came through a broken window and Pearce could hear one of the women on the porch humming an unrecognizable tune. Something in the room was giving off a terrible stench, and Pearce noticed a bucket in the far corner. He didn't need to see inside to know it was a makeshift toilet. He'd had to take morphine a couple of times to deal with the pain of injury; he knew drugs didn't stop people being human, they just stopped them caring. He imagined the snatched moments of sobriety experienced by the inhabitants of this house, when they'd look around in horror at what their lives had become. What better way to escape the rotten squalor than the carefree bliss of narcotics? And so their descent became inevitable and eternal.

Pearce pressed on, navigating a section where all but one floorboard had been removed. There was a two-foot drop to the house's outer aluminium shell, which was rotten in places.

'It's to stop the kids,' a voice said, and Pearce looked up to see a man sitting on a stool in what might once have been a kitchen.

About six feet four, the man wore a WBC contender T-shirt and a pair of torn denim shorts. Pearce thought his remark was some kind of joke until he saw a toddler totter across the filthy hallway on the other side of the single-plank bridge. The boy's long blond hair was matted, and he had the blank eyes of a child who'd lost hope. He wore a pair of Spider-Man briefs, which were yellowed and foul, and his ribs stuck out like hateful question marks.

'Don't mind him,' the man said, unmoved by the child's condition. 'He knows better than to cross the bridge. Learn 'em the hard way, that's what my pops always said.'

Pearce made it across the solitary plank and peered inside

the room the toddler had entered. There were four other children, all wearing nothing but underwear, ranging from about one to about seven years old. They all had the same hollow expressions and were as filthy as the blond toddler.

'*Oh my god,*' Leila said through the concealed earpiece.

'They yours?' Pearce asked, trying to control his rising anger.

'Uh-huh.' The man nodded.

Pearce was close enough now to see his glazed eyes and smell the sour stench of cooked heroin.

'Different moms, but I sired 'em,' the man said. 'Why? Ya wanna buy one?'

Pearce fixed the man with a furious stare that must have penetrated his stupor.

'Just kidding, man. I love those younglings.'

Pearce had been abandoned by his parents, and couldn't remember the love of a family, so he found it difficult to see children so casually neglected by blood. He swallowed his anger and remembered what he was there for. 'You Otter?' he asked.

The man stiffened slightly, as Pearce entered the room. All the units were gone. The walls were cracked and bare and there were no appliances, just a paper bag on the floor, the contents of which had spilled from a split in its side. There were tins of tuna and packets of ramen noodles. Pearce couldn't see any taps or basins and when he looked at the table next to the man, he saw a half pack of noodles. They'd been eaten dry.

'You a cop?' the man asked.

'Word is some people you work for came by some horse,' Pearce said, looking pointedly at the burned spoon, foil and detritus that gave away what the man had been up to. 'Word is you're moving it for them.'

'Moving?' the man said. 'Me? I can hardly move myself. Moving?' he scoffed. 'Get the blow, smoke the blow. Sellin' don't come into it.'

'Are you Otter?' Pearce asked again.

'I'm Otter,' another voice said, and Pearce turned to see a stocky man in a Chicago Bulls vest and boxer shorts, standing in the doorway of the room the toddler had emerged from. Otter held a huge revolver – it looked like a .44 – and had it trained on Pearce.

Chapter 59

'Who the hell are you?' Otter's eyes weren't glazed. They were hostile and sharp and his scarred face was twisted into a scowl. Pearce kicked himself for letting the man get the drop on him.

'My name isn't important,' he said.

'Don't you come in my house tellin' me what's important,' Otter responded. 'Name!'

'Amr,' Pearce said. 'I've been told you're moving product.'

Otter said nothing.

'I'm in the market.'

'You ain't in the market,' Otter sneered. 'I seen who's out there. You're runnin' with the Salamovs. No one comes in my house—'

As he said the word 'house', Otter made the mistake of gesturing at their surroundings and the muzzle of the revolver veered away from Pearce for a moment. It was long enough. He drew his pistol and opened fire, catching Otter in the foot. A second slug shattered Otter's gun hand and the revolver clattered to the floor.

The man in the kitchen started shouting curses at Pearce, but stayed well back. Otter fell to the floor, crying, alternating between his foot and his hand as he tried to soothe the pain. The most disturbing reaction came from the children in the opposite room. They didn't cry or fuss, but simply gathered in the doorway and watched the wounded man with the detached disinterest common to the victims of abuse or neglect.

'Where is it?' Pearce asked, bearing down on Otter. He kicked the revolver into the hole in the floor and it clattered against the aluminium shell. He pressed the barrel of his pistol against Otter's knee. 'The secret isn't worth what it will cost you,' Pearce assured him. 'Give up the product and I leave.'

'They'll kill you,' Otter cried.

'Then you've got nothing to worry about.'

'They'll kill me,' Otter objected.

'They'll never know,' Pearce said. 'Not unless you or your friend here tell them.'

A minute later, Pearce hurried out of the house, past the two women who were now slumped on the porch. He climbed into Rasul's car and put his gun away as he settled.

'Problem?' Rasul asked.

'You got a phone?' Pearce responded.

Rasul hesitated, but then produced a cell phone. 'Who are you calling?'

'The police,' Pearce replied, and everyone in the car suddenly tensed. 'There are kids in there,' he added, 'and a man with two holes in him.'

'We heard,' Rasul said.

'But you didn't come,' Pearce observed.

'This was your initiation. Not ours.' Rasul paused. 'Did you pass it?'

Pearce fixed him with a stare. 'Head south,' he said at last.

Rasul nodded at the driver, before turning back to Pearce.

'Go ahead,' he said, as the car started moving. He indicated the phone. 'It's a burner. Make your call to the police.'

Pearce considered Rasul as he dialled 911. The man wasn't completely without sentiment, and even though he masked it well, the revelation there were children inside the house had shaken him.

Chapter 60

Brigitte woke from a nightmare, but when she looked at her shoulder she remembered reality was far more horrific than any conjured dream. The black patch clung to her, robbing her of life, only to give it back to her. The ultimate coercive control.

'I'm sorry,' Echo said, leaning out of the shadows.

She was sitting on a small chair in the corner of the room. The only light came from beneath the door, a thin bright strip that was sufficient to form shape from darkness.

'The first day is the worst,' Echo told her. 'I brought you some clothes.'

Brigitte noticed a small pile at the end of the bed, but she didn't feel like getting dressed or doing much of anything. She wanted to lie in this horrible room and drift away, move on to whatever lay beyond life. She detested her future, shackled to these people who now controlled her survival, knowing she would face death if she displeased them. It was a cruel, hopeless existence.

'You get used to it,' Echo said wistfully. 'Takes time, but you forget what life was like before.'

Brigitte hoped she never accepted the horror of what had happened to her. The idea of avenging herself on these people was the only bright feature on an otherwise bleak horizon.

'How does it work?' Brigitte asked. 'The patch is touch sensitive, but the powder used in the prison didn't affect the men who escaped.'

'The powder is an aerosol. The particles are too large to be absorbed through the skin,' Echo replied. 'They have to be inhaled. Without the replacement hormone contained in the patch, XTX destroys the parathyroid glands and the PTH hormone, and the lungs shut down within seconds.' She hesitated. 'There is another variant. A version of XTX that can be absorbed by the skin. It can be used to kill with a single touch. They use it for assassination.'

Brigitte was horrified. Weapons such as these had no business existing, let alone being in private hands. 'Who are they?' she asked.

'The Red Wolves started as a nationalist group. They were men and women loyal to Chiang Kai-shek. They established a secret network after his overthrow with the aim of infiltrating the Communist apparatus so that one day they could bring him back, but when that didn't happen, the Red Wolves morphed into a criminal entity. One with international reach. There are chapters all over the world. Only recently has it become political again. We believe its members may be behind the suppression of the Rohinga. I can't prove it, but I believe they are part of a wider network,' Echo said. 'These groups are rising all over the world. Apparently in isolation, but I don't believe in coincidences. The men who were here, Li Jun Xiao,' Echo said, 'and his master, the one you met upstairs, David Song, I believe they're taking orders from the American who was with them, Elroy Lang.'

'Who is he?' Brigitte asked.

'I don't know. But he has real power.'

It seemed the man who'd orchestrated the Al Aqarab escape was more significant than any of them had realized.

'Why haven't you gone to your government?' Brigitte asked. 'They could synthesize the hormone.'

There was just enough light for Brigitte to see Echo shake her head.

'XTX was designed by Bolin Xu. He developed the synthetic hormone that keeps us alive. The Red Wolves executed him when they took control of the formula and Li Jun and David Song are the only ones who have access to it. They personally supervise its manufacture. If the synthetic hormone is given in the wrong dosage, it triggers an allergic reaction and the body shuts down. There isn't enough time for anyone to develop a substitute, and the patches only last a week.'

'Then steal some,' Brigitte suggested.

'I have children,' Echo responded. 'I can't gamble my life or theirs. The Red Wolves have me.'

'I don't have any such baggage,' Brigitte said, slowly getting to her feet. She was clammy and trembling, and for a moment she thought she might faint, but the dizziness passed and she regained her composure. She reached for the pile of clothes and started getting dressed. 'I don't belong to the Red Wolves,' she told Echo. 'Not yet.'

Chapter 61

Echo led her out of the cell and they walked through a dark basement lined with other doors. Brigitte wondered how many people had been chemically altered in this place and whether the doors concealed others who were suffering the same fate even now.

Echo took her up a flight of stairs and Brigitte had to pause at the top to catch her breath.

'Your strength will return,' Echo assured her. 'Your body will adapt.'

Brigitte suspected she'd feel more pain were it not for the steady supply of fentanyl coming from the patch. The powerful drug smoothed the world's rough edges and made everything seem tolerable. She signalled she was OK to move on, and they walked along a short corridor and went through a door that opened into a large, brightly lit space.

Brigitte's eyes adjusted to the light and she made out a vaulted ceiling high above her, metal supports and a corrugated roof – she was in a warehouse. A glass divider separated the women from four figures who worked in a clean room. They wore white boiler suits, gloves and masks, but instead of the patch manufacturing process Brigitte had hoped to see, she spotted four semi-conductor forges; large machines capable of churning out high-end silicon chips like the one Leila had found in the canister used during the prison break. The people in boiler suits – Brigitte was unable to tell whether they were male or female – paid no attention to the women as they walked through the building. High above them was a mezzanine level of offices, accessed by a steel staircase that ran up the outer wall and ended in a wide balcony.

'You will go to Paris and connect with your underworld contacts—' Echo said.

'You're assuming I have some,' Brigitte cut in.

'We both know you do,' Echo responded. 'You will meet with them and negotiate supply of the product into France. On no account is anyone to know what it really is. You will tell them it's fentanyl, available at half market price. You are to return here within a week to receive your next dose. This is how you can contact us,' she handed Brigitte a phone. 'There's one number in its memory.'

Brigitte shook her head in disbelief.

'I'm sorry,' Echo confided. 'I'm just doing what they commanded. For my children. For me.'

Brigitte sensed movement and looked up to see the man in the Zhongshan suit, the one Echo had called Li Jun Xiao, step out of one of the offices and come to the edge of the mezzanine balcony. He was followed by the American, Elroy Lang.

'One minute,' Elroy said, and Echo pulled Brigitte to a halt.

Elroy came down the stairs and crossed the warehouse floor. The man must have been in his late thirties and carried his trim frame like a soldier. He exuded authority and confidence.

'You understand what happens if you don't do what's expected of you?' he asked.

Brigitte wanted to lash out, but she embraced the calming

effects of the fentanyl and simply nodded. She turned for the door, and Echo followed.

As they passed beneath the balcony, Brigitte looked up at Li Jun Xiao and pictured all the ways he would suffer before she killed him.

Chapter 62

'What is it?' Rasul asked, dragging on a vape. He exhaled, enveloping himself in a thick plume of smoke that swiftly dispersed over the water.

'It's a dark kitchen,' Pearce replied, looking at the huge grey warehouse beyond the high wire fence. Apart from a row of glass panels by the entrance, the building had no windows.

'Otter told me it's owned by a company called Meals Seattle,' Pearce lied. Leila had fed him information about the address on the drive over. 'It's a courier firm. They rent kitchens to take-out businesses who want to pool costs and Meals Seattle handles all the ordering and delivery.'

Pearce tried not to appear too well informed. Leila had told him there were four take-out businesses in the warehouse and all of them looked legitimate. They might have had no idea they were being used to mask a dope-dealing operation. It was a masterful cover. Couriers could move around the city freely with very little risk of a cop pulling them over. And if one did, would they see beyond the food in the heat box on the tail of the bike? If a cop found boxes of kung pao chicken or pizza, why would he or she ever think there might be opiates hidden elsewhere?

'We've been looking for this place for a long time,' Rasul said. 'We could never figure out where they were running their operation from. No wonder we couldn't find it. I'm standing here, and you've explained what it is, but I still don't understand it.'

'It's an Internet business,' Pearce responded.

'Oh well,' Rasul said mockingly, 'that makes everything clear.'

The warehouse was about the size of a football pitch and was situated at the very end of Fontanelle Street, by the west bank of Duwamish Waterway, a wide, dirty river that served the huge industrial district which stretched south of the port. The air reeked of greasy diesel and hard work, and the surrounding buildings looked like the kind of run-down places that always paid their invoices late. The Meals Seattle warehouse had been freshly painted and looked positively polished compared to its rust-covered neighbours. Pearce could hear the grinding sound of industrial machinery at work in the distance, and the rumble of a cargo tug easing its way downstream.

'Let's get the others,' Rasul said, nodding in the direction of the motorcade, which was parked around the corner.

'We can't just rush the place,' Pearce replied.

There were two uniformed guards in a gatehouse, an unknown number of innocent employees, and whatever force the East Hill Mob had stationed in the place to guard the product. Assuming Otter had been telling the truth. He might have been lying, in which case they'd storm a blameless business. Pearce counted thirty-five vehicles in the car park, which meant there could be anywhere between thirty-five and 165 people inside. Three couriers on small motorbikes had left through the high gates and sped off to make deliveries. So far, they'd only seen one inbound.

'What rush?' Rasul scoffed. 'We've already been standing here too long. Now we're just going to go in and get our stuff.'

They'd been watching the warehouse from a wharf about half a block away. Standing by some containers that were piled up at the water's edge, they had a clear view of the building and its surroundings without being too visible themselves.

'We have no idea what we're up against,' Pearce remarked. 'Let me at least get some information.'

'*This guy's a hothead*,' Leila observed quietly. She was still picking up everything that happened through the surveillance glasses.

Rasul considered Pearce's request, and then nodded. 'OK,' he said. 'You have five minutes. The time it takes me to get my men.'

Pearce wondered whether he was being treated to an extra dose of bravado or if Rasul was always this reckless and cocksure. He shook his head and started towards the gatehouse. He glanced over his shoulder and saw Rasul head west, round the corner towards the convoy of SUVs.

Pearce's mind raced as he tried to think of a way to get inside the warehouse. The pressure of time meant subtlety was out of the question. He'd have to try a more direct approach.

One of the guards stepped out; a grey-haired man with the squashed nose and hard-bitten face of a journeyman boxer.

'Can I help you, sir?' he asked.

'I'm here to see your boss,' Pearce replied. 'I've got a message for him from Deni Salamov.'

The journeyman instantly tensed and looked over Pearce's shoulder for any sign of trouble, but apart from a brown van and a couple of old cars, the street was empty. The guard's colleague was leaning out of the gatehouse and the two uniformed men exchanged concerned glances.

'Don't recognize the name, friend,' the journeyman said.

'Really? I'm pretty sure Reznor will,' Pearce said, using the name Otter had given him. According to the wounded dealer, Reznor ran this location for the East Hill Mob.

The journeyman nodded and started towards the gates, which his colleague opened. 'You'd better come with me.'

Chapter 63

Pearce was taken beyond the fence, into the car park that lay in front of the warehouse. The place had clearly been modified for the rapid deployment of food orders. A dozen motorbike bays were located by the entrance. Only two were occupied. The journeyman led Pearce inside a small lobby. One wall opened onto the warehouse and was lined with catering shelves and heat lamps. Above each shelf was a small screen that displayed order details. The room looked like the service area of a giant fast food restaurant, but without the hubbub and activity. Two motorcyclists leaned over a counter and chatted to a supervisor, who nodded at the journeyman as he took Pearce through a security door.

They stepped into a vast space that had been divided into six kitchens. Four were branded for different food businesses – Hank's Pizzeria, Hop Sing Cantonese Food, Buffalo Burgers and Ruth's Deli – and two stood empty. The four occupied kitchens were staffed by two or three people who were busy preparing for the lunchtime rush. There were common areas all around them – stainless steel fridges and freezers and huge shelving units that were piled high with ingredients and culinary equipment. No one paid Pearce and the journeyman any mind as they passed through the warehouse.

Pearce's guide punched a code into a keypad and opened

another security door. The changed atmosphere was noticeable the moment Pearce stepped into the short corridor that
lay beyond, primarily because a scruffy man in a tracksuit sat
on a stool at the other end. There was a reinforced metal door
beside him.

'Problem?' the scruffy man asked.

'He wants to see Reznor,' Journeyman replied. 'Says he's
got a message from Salamov.'

'You search him?' the scruffy man asked.

Pearce reached behind his back very slowly and produced
his pistol, holding it between his forefinger and thumb to
show he meant no harm.

Scruffy rolled his eyes at the guard.

'Sorry, I—' Journeyman said.

'That's why you're out there and I'm in here,' Scruffy cut
in testily. 'Go on. Get lost. I'll take him.'

Humbled, Journeyman went back the way they'd come.
Scruffy took Pearce's gun.

'Come on,' he said, punching another code into the pad
beside the door.

Pearce followed him into an open-plan office. At least that's
what it might once have been. Now it was little more than a
gangster's club house. A group of men gathered round a pool
table and watched one of their number attempt to make a
trick shot. There was a great deal of catcalling and jeering. A
handful of others traded insults over a game of cards. Away
from the main space were three individual offices, separated
by glass partitions. Two were empty, but Pearce saw a man
in the one in the middle. He was seated on a sofa and was
watching Heath Ledger hamming it up as a nurse before he
blew up a hospital.

Scruffy led Pearce over and knocked on the open door. 'Rez, this guy says he's got a message from Salamov.'

Reznor paused the film and faced Pearce. He had the hungry eyes of a hustler and the strained, gaunt face of someone who lost a nightly battle with his worries. He wore jeans and a T-shirt, but was barefoot. His socks had been tossed beside his boots.

'Yeah,' he said, as Scruffy took a step back.

'A couple of days ago someone stole a shipment that belongs to the Salamovs,' Pearce said. 'They want it back.'

Reznor rubbed his stubble. 'What makes you think I know anything about that?'

'Your dealers are shifting smack,' Pearce replied. 'Your normal business is synthetics.'

Reznor shook his head. 'Shit,' he said. 'That explains it.'

'What?'

'How they could sell it so cheap,' Reznor answered.

'Who?' Pearce asked.

Reznor ignored the question and got to his feet. 'We got a fuckin' problem,' he said to Scruffy. 'Lock the place down and tell the guys to—'

He stopped talking the instant he heard the rattle of automatic gunfire. Pearce felt the sharp edge of fear scrape his gut.

Rasul had arrived.

Chapter 64

'Everyone up!' Reznor yelled at his men. 'And you,' he said, turning to Pearce. 'You're coming with me. You're leverage.'

'They hardly know me,' Pearce replied. 'I'm expendable.'

'We'll see.' Reznor nodded at Scruffy, who grabbed Pearce.

It was an amateur move because it brought him within reach of Pearce's fist, which came down like a hammer on the man's clavicle. Breaking the bone required relatively little force, but generated a tremendous amount of pain. Scruffy yelped and doubled over, crying. Pearce grabbed his confiscated pistol from the man's waistband and levelled it at Reznor.

'Tell your men to stand down,' Pearce commanded. 'We can settle this peacefully.'

'That sound peaceful to you?' Reznor asked, indicating the gunfire that came from beyond the door.

Pearce scanned the hostile faces of the East Hill Mob, but kept his weapon trained on Reznor. This situation had all the signs of spiralling out of control.

'*You need to leave, Scott,*' Leila said.

'Working on it,' Pearce muttered quietly.

Ziad hung back as Rasul and the others fought their way into the warehouse. Fought was the wrong word, because the kitchen workers were civilians and it was more like a slaughter.

When Ziad had lost sight of the Salamov gang and was satisfied no one would notice his absence, he holstered his machine pistol and ran back the way he'd come, through the lobby, past the dead men by the counter, into the car park and past the now unmanned gatehouse. He jogged down the street to a brown van with blacked-out windows, and opened the side door to be greeted by Awut, his taciturn housemate. The lithe Thai man was in his customary vest and shorts but a large tray-style remote control hung from his neck. Ziad had texted the man earlier in the day, letting him know Rasul would be launching an assault on the East Hill Mob and the notice had given Awut time to get ready. Ziad had no idea whether Elroy Lang and the Red Wolves had sold the East Hill Mob the stolen heroin, but the Thai assassin certainly knew all he needed to know about the gang's operations.

'Are they inside?' Awut asked.

Ziad nodded.

'Good,' Awut said. 'Stand back.'

Ziad moved aside and Awut climbed out of the van. He flipped a switch on the remote and Ziad heard something stir within the van. It sounded like a swarm of huge, angry wasps. Awut manipulated the remote control and five drones flew from the van, all linked in a data daisy chain, the trailing four precisely tracking the leader's flightpath. Awut watched the remote's inbuilt screen, which broadcast footage from the camera on the lead drone.

Ziad couldn't take his eyes off the insectoid devices as they buzzed over the wire fence and headed for the warehouse entrance, which he'd remembered to leave open as instructed. The speeding devices would deliver the first part of his revenge against the Salamovs.

Chapter 65

'Put the gun down,' a voice said, and Pearce looked across the room to see a mountain of a man targeting him with an AR-15.

Pearce kept his pistol aimed at Reznor's face. 'No can do.'

The brief exchange was cut short when the security door flew open and the two gate guards were pushed inside by Rasul and his men, who burst into the room waving their guns and shouting wildly.

'Execute him,' Rasul shouted at Pearce when he caught sight of Reznor at the end of Pearce's gun. 'One of the others will tell us where our product is.'

'*This is turning ugly,*' Leila said into Pearce's ear. '*You want me to call the cops?*'

'No,' Pearce said. He registered Rasul's disappointment at being refused. 'We can do this without anyone getting hurt.'

Pearce heard a faint buzzing. It rapidly grew louder and he saw a flight of drones race along the corridor.

'Shut the door!' he yelled, but it was too late.

The lead drone swept into the room and the others quickly followed. Rasul, Reznor and their men were puzzled, but Pearce knew exactly what the devices were; mechanical angels of death. He recognized the metal canisters that clung to their undercarriages, replicas of the one used in Ziad's escape from

Al Aqarab. Pearce looked around, searching for the man, but he was nowhere to be seen.

'Run,' Pearce yelled, grabbing Rasul and pushing him forward.

Rasul hesitated and looked up in amazement as the canisters detonated.

'Hold your breath,' Pearce said, as white powder fell from on high.

Most of the men didn't hear him over the hubbub of panic and the sound of the drones, but Rasul and Reznor were close enough to heed the advice and took deep breaths before the dust settled on them.

'*Get out of there, Scott,*' Leila urged.

Pearce bundled Rasul and Reznor forwards as men fell all around them, choking as the white powder did its foul work. Pearce tried to shut out the awful sounds of death as he ran along the corridor, trailed by the two gangster princes. He glanced over his shoulder at the gruesome sight of men falling, clawing at their throats, unable to breathe. Rasul and Reznor also registered the horror and their eyes bulged with fear. Pearce was worried about their clothes, which were covered in the lethal powder. He didn't know how much was a fatal dose, and there was no way he could be sure he wouldn't inhale some when his burning lungs finally forced him to take a breath.

He sprinted through the warehouse, which was full of dead kitchen workers. Rasul and his men had executed them all. Pearce's lungs were on fire, and his muscles were getting heavy and tight, but he couldn't take a breath. He mustn't. He made it through the lobby, where there were more bodies, and burst out of the building. He was about to start across the car park when he had an idea, but he was distracted by a terrible sound to his rear. He looked round to see Reznor had taken a breath and was now rooted to the spot, clutching his neck, gasping for air. Rasul was gripped by fear and his eyes were almost popping from their sockets with the desperate need to breathe.

Pearce grabbed him and pulled him towards the edge of the car park. They ran to the high fence that separated them from the waterway. Pearce started climbing and Rasul followed. Every inch of Pearce's body burned with the urge to take what should have been a life-giving breath, but he had to resist. He trembled and his vision shrank to a tunnel. He mustn't pass out. He'd fall and his breathing would resume automatically, killing him before he ever regained consciousness. He was almost at the top of the fence, and Rasul was a couple of feet behind.

Pearce reached for the metal bar that capped the wire, but he didn't have the strength to pull himself over, and fumbled weakly.

'*Come on, Scott!*' Leila yelled in his ear. '*You get over there!* Yala! Ya hayawan. *Move it, soldier!*'

Pearce wanted to laugh at Leila's impression of a drill instructor, but he could only do that if he survived. With an almighty effort, he grabbed the top bar and hauled himself up and over the fence. He fell down the other side and hit the concrete bank on his way into the river. He swallowed the pain of impact, resisted the instinctive urge to cry out, bounced off the hard stone and plunged into the cold dark water below.

Chapter 66

Ziad looked over Awut's shoulder as he piloted the drones through the warehouse. The video screen displayed nothing but twisted bodies. Rasul and his men had died terrible deaths, and Ziad felt a strange combination of pride and shame. His vengeance was justified, but he had become a monster. He wondered if Awut harboured such conflicted feelings. The man's face was emotionless, focused like a concert pianist at a Steinway. Ziad had been partly avenged, and at the same time they'd removed much of the Salamov organization and most of the East Hill Mob, making the next stage of their plan a little easier.

'I'm going to bring them back,' Awut said, and Ziad produced a filtered surgical mask from his pocket and put it on.

He was paranoid about being exposed to the toxin, but Awut was unconcerned and did nothing to cover his face. According to Elroy and Awut, XTX reacted with air to become inert and undetectable in a matter of minutes.

Ziad watched the screen and saw another body outside. It was Reznor, one of the East Hill Mob's leaders.

'Did any escape?' Ziad asked. It had been a confusing, macabre scene and he'd lost track of how many had died in the cloud of powder. 'Go back and check,' he told Awut.

The pilot shook his head, and when he registered the

sound of distant sirens, Ziad understood why. Awut flew the drones back to the van. There were no visible signs of the toxin on the machines, but Ziad was still cautious as he and Awut gathered them up and put them inside. Ziad climbed behind the wheel and Awut jumped in beside him and they drove away before the first police cars arrived.

Chapter 67

Leila was trembling. She'd experienced the horror of war, but what she'd seen in that warehouse was truly grotesque. She'd burned with furious will, turning her mind to Pearce, as though lending him her spirit might have helped him survive. Watching him flee, seeing the terror on Rasul Salamov's face, the gruesome death of Reznor, Leila hadn't drawn a breath until Pearce had tumbled into the murky water. She looked at the screen which displayed the transmission from his surveillance glasses. It was blank, and there was nothing on the audio channels. Had he lost the glasses? Were they at the bottom of the river? Was he dead?

Leila couldn't let herself think such a thing. She'd been here before, when he'd been taken by Black Thirteen. Pearce was the one thing in her life she could count on. He was the closest she had to a friend, but like everyone else she'd cared about, one day he'd be gone. Perhaps today was that day? She shook the thought from her mind, got to her feet, grabbed her cane and hurried from the motel room.

By the time she arrived at Fontanelle Street, the Meals Seattle warehouse had become a major crime scene. When she'd seen the unfolding horror, Leila had ignored Pearce's instruction and had called the police. They were still arriving when she turned up, a small army of them, accompanied by news crews who'd got hold of the breaking story. Leila was waved away from the scene by a uniformed cop, who indicated she should go back. She turned left, drove a short distance up an access road and parked by a loading dock on the very edge of the Duwamish Waterway. She climbed out of the Chevy and started towards the warehouse, scanning the sage-green water, which flowed north. She studied the banks for any sign of Pearce and kept an eye out for clues he'd survived. She saw a shape near the opposite bank. It was moving with the current and looked like the shoulder and neck of a man lying face down in the water, but as it drew level, Leila realized her desperate mind was playing tricks; it was a piece of driftwood.

She carried on and was soon on Fontanelle Street. She skirted the gathering crowd and went east, keeping as close as she could to the river. She crossed the street and her path was blocked by the warehouse's wire fence. To her right was the gatehouse, which was now staffed by two police officers, who were controlling the flow of police vehicles onto the site. Another half dozen uniformed cops were maintaining a perimeter, holding reporters and local gawkers at bay. Leila heard the mutter of rumour and speculation ripple through the assembled crowd. She walked along the fence line and leaned over the low wall that marked the riverbank. Pearce had hit it on his way into the water, and she tried to suppress her fears that it had knocked him unconscious. She looked along the length of the wall, but there was no sign of Pearce anywhere. However, she did see a face she recognized. Detective Evan Hill, the policeman who'd so rudely dismissed her questions about Richie Cutter's death, stood by a mobile command unit and briefed four people in hazmat suits. By Leila's reckoning, the toxin would have become harmless by now, but the police couldn't have known that and were rightly being cautious. Leila had warned the 911 operator a chemical agent had been deployed on site.

Beyond Evan Hill's group, a pair of men in hazmat suits were erecting an isolation tent over Reznor's body. When Hill finished his briefing, he watched the four officers enter the building, before he turned and took a deep breath. Leila recognized the gesture. It was a pause, a moment of calm before the next step in managing the crisis. She felt a pang of sympathy for the man, but that dissipated when he looked up and caught Leila watching him. She registered the recognition in his eyes. *Time to go*, she thought. There was nothing useful she could do here. Pearce was either at the bottom of the river, or he was long gone. She'd check the local hospitals and police reports for any information on people recovered from the waterway.

Leila started walking back towards the car, but sensed commotion as she made her way along Fontanelle Street. She looked over her shoulder to see the officers at the perimeter listening to their radios. Her eyes darted beyond them, past the fence to Detective Hill, who was running in her direction, speaking into his handheld radio. Leila picked up the pace when she saw two of the officers spot her. They pushed their way through the crowd.

'Hey, you!' the nearest cop yelled.

Leila pretended not to hear, and hurried on, but her legs wouldn't give her the speed she longed for, and she realized her efforts were futile when she felt a strong hand on her upper arm.

'Excuse me, miss.'

The second officer took hold of her other arm. 'You're going to have to come with us.'

'Why? What for? Am I under arrest?' Leila asked, playing up her innocence.

'Only if you resist,' the first cop said.

Detective Hill jogged over. 'A good cop never ignores a hunch,' he told Leila. 'Something about you felt wrong. I called *Il Giustizia*, that magazine you said you work for. They've never heard of Maria Grattan.'

Leila was puzzled. *Il Giustizia* was a fictitious magazine she'd set up with a fake website and a virtual office. If Hill had called it, the rent-a-receptionist would have responded with a standard script and said Maria Grattan was away on assignment. Leila studied the man, wondering why he was lying.

'Take her in,' Hill said to the uniforms, and they pulled Leila towards a nearby patrol car.

Chapter 68

Wollerton tapped the lid of his coffee cup and checked the clock behind the counter. He'd been waiting for two hours. He drained his tepid flat white, exited the small Starbucks concession, and retraced his steps through the arrivals hall, weaving through crowds of travellers.

He'd regrouped in London, where his first instinct had been to go to Aberdyfi to see his children. He longed to hold them, to tell them he missed them and loved them, but his friends' lives were at stake. He had to see the mission through, but once it was over, he and Esther would have to reach a new understanding. Shock and self-pity had led him to simply accept what she'd done, but she had no right to take his children away.

While in London, he'd got rid of the false identities Brigitte Attali had provided and had picked up a new passport from an old service contact. He hoped Leila and Pearce had heeded his warning, but had received no communication from them since the briefest of acknowledgements of his original email. It wasn't unusual to go into lockdown if an asset was compromised but it was worrying that they hadn't responded to the email he'd sent when he'd arrived in Seattle two hours earlier.

He reached a row of Internet terminals outside a gift shop and sat down at one that was tucked against a wall. He fed a five-dollar bill into the machine, which came to life. He used a proxy server to access the secure email address he, Leila and Pearce used, but the inbox was empty and there was nothing in the drafts folder. He tried to stop his mind going to dark places. Pearce and Leila must be occupied. There was no reason to think anything bad had happened to them.

No reason other than Brigitte Attali's treachery, he thought darkly.

She was going to pay, no matter what, but if anything had happened to Pearce and Leila, the price would rise.

Wollerton looked around, pondering his next move. He couldn't risk making contact with Huxley Blaine Carter or anyone who worked for him, and he didn't have any connections in Seattle. He got to his feet and joined the flow of travellers heading for the exit. He'd have to figure out a way to find Leila and Pearce.

Chapter 69

Brigitte Attali was breathless and clammy by the time she reached the apartment. She shut the door and leaned against it, trying not to panic. She was dead. Her body was permanently broken and should be in the ground. The only thing keeping it going was the cursed patch that clung to her arm. But what if it stopped working? What if they'd miscalculated the dose? What if the breathlessness she was experiencing wasn't a symptom of her body adjusting to the profound change in her endocrinal system? What if it was the first sign of her lungs shutting down?

Brigitte bit back a profound sense of hysteria and forced herself to choke down the tears that threatened a deluge. She knew she was being watched. The apartment Echo had arranged for them was rife with surveillance and she would not give them the satisfaction of seeing her cry.

She went to the living room table, reached into her hold-all and slipped the CSS counter-surveillance device into her palm. She took the device onto the balcony and switched it on. A moment later, it came to life and, as it had done when she'd checked it on their arrival, it identified the location of every device giving off a cellular or radio signal. The 3D image of the apartment looked almost exactly the same as before, only this time, in addition to the cameras and bugs the device had previously located, it showed a new one implanted in her. Brigitte used the device to pinpoint the bug's location: it was in her leg. She took down her trousers and felt behind her left thigh. She touched the tiny ridges of a sewn wound. They'd implanted a tracking device to monitor her every move.

She leaned against the balcony rail and looked down at the hard pavement far below. How easy it would have been . . . Her eyes drifted up and out towards the bay. Gentle waves lapped the sandy beach where she and Wollerton had stripped to their underwear. There was nothing between her and the wide sea but clear air, but even if there had been cameras on her, Brigitte was beyond caring. She let the tears come and drowned in despair, dejected and broken.

Chapter 70

Ziad and Awut never went back to the house on Kenyon Street. Something had happened to the two cops Eddie Fletcher had on his payroll. The leader of the Seattle chapter of the Red Wolves had paid the police officers to keep watch on Ziad and Awut in case Deni Salamov tried anything, but the men had simply disappeared. Ever cautious, Awut had moved them to a warehouse on Riverside Drive, which is where they headed after the attack on the East Hill Mob. They concealed the van inside the building and traded it for an ancient sky-blue Lincoln Continental that was parked in the yard outside.

Awut drove east through the city, and as Ziad watched industrial give way to residential, his righteous fury gave way to reflection. He was assailed by memories of the men who'd died in the Meals Seattle warehouse. He'd known many of them for years and had considered some of them friends. He knew they had families, friends, hopes, dreams. They were all gone. The promise of their futures replaced by death, a horror inflicted so Ziad could satisfy his thirst for revenge. The contorted faces of Rasul's men filled his mind, spliced with memories of the people who'd died during his escape from Al Aqarab. As he recalled them clutching at their throats, unable to breathe, Ziad wondered what he'd become. He glanced at the emotionless man next to him. Was Awut ever tortured by such things? He caught Ziad's eye, and Ziad looked away immediately, feeling foolish and ashamed. Guilt was for the weak. Deni, Rasul and Essi had driven him to this, he told himself. If blame was to fall on anyone's shoulders, it must land on theirs. The shame and anger he'd felt for so long were rekindled when he pictured Essi in the arms of her lover, and Deni and Rasul laughing about the ease with which they'd framed a fool whose only mistake had been falling in love with the wrong woman. He recalled all the cruelties he'd suffered in Al Aqarab because of them. They deserved what was coming to them, and anyone who stood with them was guilty by association.

Ziad dismissed his troubling thoughts and focused on the road ahead. They were out of the city now and were on I-90, part of a ceaseless flow of traffic heading east. The six-lane highway was lined with high pines that sliced the rose-gold sunlight. Awut took Exit 34 and at the end of the slip road, he made a left on 468th Avenue and drove north. A few houses and pockets of industry kept the wilderness at bay. Many of the homes they passed proudly displayed the Stars and Stripes, and Ziad wondered whether the wholesome people who inhabited the houses knew what really happened at the huge complex a few miles up the road.

Ten minutes after leaving the interstate, the houses vanished and the old Lincoln sped through untouched forest until the trees gave way to reveal Tanner Foods – a massive processing and distribution facility – on their right. They were tested for coronavirus by a security guard who was expecting them. When the results came back negative, he waved them through the gates and they drove into a car park that was packed with vehicles. Five huge warehouses were evenly positioned around the 200-acre site, and each of the vast buildings was serviced by smaller structures and loading bays. Everything was newly painted and gleamed in the sunlight. There was real money here.

A man in a high-vis vest directed Awut to the far corner of the car park, where a group of men gathered beneath a huge redwood. Ziad recognized Ben Cresci, Deni Salamov's largest customer. Whatever the corporate filings said about Tanner Foods, it was Ben Cresci who truly called the shots. Cresci had jet-black hair pulled into a tight ponytail. He wore huge gold-framed sunglasses and sported a thick moustache. His dark-brown suit and wide-collared white shirt completed the seventies porn star vibe, but this was no seedy entertainer. He had the air of a man who knew the world was going to disappoint him, and the sharp features, hard eyes and volatility of someone who would meet such disappointment with extreme violence. Originally from somewhere in Italy, the Cresci family had controlled Seattle's heroin trade for three generations. As far as Ziad knew, Cresci's name and heritage were the only Italian things about the man; he was reputed to hate Italian food and didn't even speak the language. The men who surrounded him were a mix of nationalities and ethnicities. The only thing that united them was that same propensity for violence and an endless hunger for more. More money, more power, more of everything. These weren't the heart-of-gold mobsters of the movies. These were dangerous men.

Awut parked near the group and he and Ziad got out and walked over. Hunter, Cresci's psychopathically cold number two, the man who'd finally brokered the meeting, stopped them and waved two bodyguards forward. Ziad and Awut were searched thoroughly and when the guards were satisfied they posed no threat, they were nodded on.

'Mr Cresci,' Ziad said, offering his hand.

Cresci made no move to take it. 'We ain't friends, Malek. I'm seeing you because Hunter says you've got something to say.'

'We have a shipment—' Ziad began, but Cresci cut him off.

'This you making your move, then? Word is Deni and the East Hill Mob have almost wiped each other out over my product, which is now in the hands of the police.'

Cresci's voice rose and Ziad could see him trying to control his anger.

'I'm not making any moves,' Ziad replied. 'Just trying to fill a need. Your product is gone, but the demand isn't. We have a shipment en route from China.'

'H?' Cresci asked.

'We're getting out of that business,' Ziad said. 'The world has moved on. We're bringing in fentanyl—'

'That fucking shit!' Cresci cut in. He turned to his associates. 'Everywhere I turn, people tell me to get into that stuff, but it fucking kills people. What good is a dead customer?'

'Only if it's misused. Same as heroin,' Ziad countered. 'It's easier to transport, hard to detect and it's much more profitable.'

'So I hear.' Cresci looked pointedly at Hunter. 'Wave of the future, they say. My father always said those who don't adapt, die.'

Cresci shook his head and took a couple of frustrated paces, and that's when Ziad knew they had him.

They'd created a need, punching a hole in the man's supply

line. He had a huge beast to feed and his greed and desperation would enable Ziad and his associates to step in.

'If we switch,' Cresci said, 'it'll be the whole West Coast coming with us.'

Ziad nodded.

'You have any idea what kind of volume we do?' Cresci asked. 'Our network runs from here to San Diego, and east to Chicago.'

'We know,' Awut said.

'So, the master speaks,' Cresci observed. 'I know this one –' he nodded at Ziad – 'he's a soldier, not a player.'

Ziad ignored the slight. He wasn't here to have his ego serviced. He was here to win.

'What about you, friend?' Cresci asked Awut. 'Who are you?'

'The less we know about each other, the safer we'll all be,' Awut replied. 'We know the extent of your demand and we will guarantee to meet it.'

'We?'

'I speak on behalf of the Red Wolves,' Awut revealed, and Ziad felt a change in the atmosphere.

'I've heard of your outfit,' Cresci said. 'International. You've even got people here. Reputation for being reliable.'

'Very,' Awut replied.

'You can trust us,' Ziad said. 'I'll handle port operations. We have drivers who'll make the deliveries.'

Cresci ignored Ziad's remark and kept his eyes on Awut.

'How long before the first shipment arrives?' Cresci asked.

'Four days,' Awut replied.

Ziad was surprised at the answer. The shipment must have left China weeks ago. These guys were seriously good.

'What about Salamov?' Cresci asked.

'Rasul Salamov is dead. Killed with most of the East Hill Mob,' Awut said. 'Deni Salamov is a spent force. He'll take on what's left of the East Hill Mob to avenge his son, and they'll rip chunks out of each other until they're both finished.'

Cresci thought for a moment. He turned to Hunter. 'This is Hunter's play. He'll be your contact. Agree terms with him.'

Cresci leaned close to Awut. 'Don't ever betray me. And never let me down,' he said menacingly.

Awut didn't reply, and Ziad felt the weight of expectation in the silence that followed.

'We won't,' he assured Cresci.

Cresci glared at Ziad and Awut before walking away, followed by most of his entourage. Only Hunter and a couple of bodyguards stayed.

'We need to talk price and volume,' Hunter said, his ice-blue eyes gleaming intensely. *Was he on something?*

Ziad nodded. They'd just seized control of the most extensive drugs distribution network on the West Coast.

Part Three

Chapter 71

Neither the stagnant pools in the muddy banks nor the stench of marine fuel could do anything to diminish the sweetness of the first breath Pearce took when he finally surfaced. He gasped one lungful after another, his body tense, on edge, waiting for the first signs of choking, but each breath was followed by one more, and he gradually relaxed and realized today wasn't his last. At least not here. Not yet.

The river had washed away all traces of the toxin from his clothes, and when he glanced around he realized he'd drifted downstream. He could just about see the roof of the Meals Seattle warehouse in the distance. He heard the sound of sirens approaching and felt an urgent need to leave the area. He had no desire to be caught by the police, nor did he want to meet whoever had piloted the drones. Not with his gun somewhere at the bottom of the river.

He looked for any sign of Rasul, but saw only the whirls and eddies of current in the green water. Then he caught sight of something stuck in the bank, twenty metres upriver, towards the warehouse. The object was caught in a clump of long grass and as he swam towards it, Pearce recognized the shape as Rasul. He was face down in the shallows and wasn't moving.

Pearce grabbed him and turned him over. Rasul's face was

grey and his lips were blue, but the airborne toxin meant
Pearce couldn't risk mouth-to-mouth, so he pulled Rasul onto
the long grass and laid him down on the tiny patch of ground
that stuck out from the steep bank. Pearce sat astride Rasul
and pounded a series of chest compressions. He had no idea
how long Rasul had been dead or why he'd stopped breathing. He could have caught a breath of the toxin or might have
taken a lungful of water. Pearce pressed his palms against
the man's chest, but there was no response, so he sat up and
pounded a couple of haymakers into Rasul's solar plexus.

Rasul gasped and colour flushed his cheeks. Pearce got off
him and the man rolled onto his side and choked up river
water and vomit. Rasul's eyes were wild with fear.

'You're OK,' Pearce reassured him. 'Just take a moment.'

'What happened?' Rasul asked when he'd finished being
sick. His voice was thick and raw.

The sirens were very close now, and Pearce was growing
nervous. 'You weren't breathing,' he said.

Rasul took a moment to compose himself. 'Thank you,' he
said at last.

'Can you swim?' Pearce asked. 'We have to leave.'

Rasul sat up and rubbed his chest. 'I feel like I've been hit
by a truck.'

'It was better than the alternative,' Pearce said, sliding into
the water.

Rasul joined him and they waded out to the deeper parts
before letting the current take them. As they swam away,
Pearce saw the first flashes of blue light further upstream.

Chapter 72

It was dark by the time they reached the community centre. Pearce was driving the Ford Falcon they'd stolen after emerging from the river, and when he made a right onto 140th Street, he saw the whole neighbourhood had changed. Two men stepped off the sidewalk and blocked Pearce's path, signalling him to halt. They were part of a larger group stationed on the corner, and as Pearce scanned his surroundings, he saw similar gangs of men on every corner. There weren't many vehicles out, but any that passed were stopped and the drivers questioned. The supermarket and coffee shop were closed, and only the main entrance of the community centre was lit. Deni Salamov had put the block in lockdown, and Pearce had no doubt the men now standing in front of the car were armed.

The shorter of the two was the first to register Rasul in the passenger seat, and his eyes widened.

'Come on, Amr,' Rasul said to Pearce as he stepped out of the car. 'Leave it. These men will deal with it.'

'Allah be praised,' the shorter of the two guards exclaimed.

'Rasul, you're alive,' the other remarked in astonishment.

'Of course,' Rasul said with the bravado of a star quarterback. 'Dispose of the car. It's stolen.'

He went on without looking back, and Pearce followed

him to the community centre. Four men stood by the main entrance and Rasul's arrival prompted similar astonishment, but he ignored the words of praise and relief and took Pearce inside the building.

They stepped onto an intricately patterned Persian carpet that ran the length of a broad corridor. The walls were decorated with framed tapestries of red fabric embossed with gold Islamic scripture. There were more men here and some openly carried shotguns, pistols and assault rifles.

A figure came running out of the shadows.

'Rasul!'

It was Abbas Idrisov, the old veteran of the Chechen War. He rushed along the corridor and embraced Rasul. 'Praise be. We'd heard . . .' he left the implication hanging.

'And it would have been true,' Rasul said, 'if it hadn't been for this man.' He gestured towards Pearce.

'*Alli' er hamak*,' Abbas said, blessing Pearce in God's name. 'Your father has called everyone here. His grief is beyond anything I've seen. He wants to tear the city apart hunting every last member of the East Hill Mob.'

'This wasn't East Hill,' Rasul said, picking up pace.

The corridor led them to a large hall. The ceiling had been painted blue and was covered with white religious scripture. A divider ran down the centre of the room and on one side there were forty or so men, most of whom were over the age of fifty, and on the other side perhaps double the number of women.

Pearce saw Essi Salamov, the young woman Ziad Malek had hit during the street fight with her boyfriend. She was at the heart of a group of grieving women and they all looked stunned when they saw Rasul, but he hadn't noticed his sister and went straight to the men's side of the centre, where his father choked on his sobs with a group of elders. The other men were astonished to see Rasul and one of them nudged Deni. The old gangster looked up, and for a moment his face registered nothing but confusion. Then disbelief, and finally the years fell away as hope filled him. He got to his feet and sprang towards his son, tears flowing with every step.

They embraced each other and Deni clung to his boy like a man who planned to never let go. Pearce was touched by the moment, and almost forgot about Rasul's murderous behaviour earlier that day. Even the worst villains could be human.

'How?' Deni said, finally, almost choking on the words.

Rasul was also weeping and simply nodded at Pearce.

Deni locked eyes with Pearce and they shared a moment of profound gratitude. Deni grabbed Pearce's arm and pulled him into their hug. Pearce couldn't help but get swept into the emotion of the moment. He hadn't felt the embrace of family since childhood and had almost forgotten what it was like to be the centre of someone's world. Sharing Deni and Rasul's reunion might be as close as Pearce would ever get, and the sadness of that thought struck him like a blow. For the first time he accepted the gap in his life was real. He'd suppressed the realization, fearing it might make him vulnerable, but the need was there. He'd live a solitary existence as a perpetual outsider, but sharing in these profound emotions, he realized what he was missing.

'I owe you everything,' Deni Salamov told Pearce. 'Everything.'

These are bad men, Pearce told himself. Killers. Drug dealers. *Humans*, he caught himself thinking. *Just human beings.*

Another body joined them and Pearce saw Essi Salamov on

the other side of her father and brother. Tears streamed down her upturned face. Her smile was so broad it threatened to split her cheeks.

'Rasul,' she said, pulling her brother down so she could kiss his forehead.

Soon the four of them were joined by others, and they formed the heart of a crowd of mourners who all wanted to embrace the son who'd returned from the dead.

Chapter 73

'The people will take their time to grieve,' Deni said. He gestured towards the mourners on the other side of the room, those who'd lost sons, brothers, fathers that day.

He, Rasul and Pearce had stepped away from the group and were standing by the large windows which overlooked the football pitch.

'Then we will get to work,' Deni continued. 'We will hunt down the East Hill pigs and make them pay for what they've done.'

'This wasn't East Hill,' Rasul replied. 'They were set up. Just like us. We weren't meant to survive. You and East Hill were each supposed to believe the other was responsible for the massacre. You were supposed to destroy each other in your quest to avenge your dead. If we hadn't escaped, the truth would have died with us. East Hill didn't do this. Those men in there were as shocked as us. Someone else did this. Someone else set us up. Someone else tried to start a war.'

Deni considered the revelation. 'Is this true?' he asked Pearce.

'Yeah,' Pearce replied. He desperately wanted to make contact with Leila and let her know he was OK, but he couldn't leave now without arousing suspicion.

'It was a trap,' Rasul said.

Deni gestured to Abbas, who was hovering nearby, and the old man came over.

'Find a way to get a message to Ryan Fox. Tell him we've all been set up, his crew and ours. Tell him I want to meet to agree a truce so we can find the people responsible and repay them for this atrocity.'

Chapter 74

A dead man walking. A ghost returned to ruin them. That's all Ziad saw when he looked through the scope and watched Rasul Salamov from the roof of the building on the corner of 37th Avenue. He and Awut had come to watch the Salamovs and the East Hill Mob tear each other apart in the war they thought they'd started. Ziad shot Awut a sidelong glance and saw the man's jaw set hard, and the glint of anger in his eyes. This wasn't their plan. Their careful preparation was being ruined by Rasul Salamov, a man who should be lying in a police morgue, a man who should have perished with dozens of others, whose death was supposed to have sparked a war. Instead, Rasul was standing alongside his father and was undoubtedly telling the cunning old Chechen what had really happened in the warehouse on Fontanelle Street.

Ziad lowered the scope and turned to Awut.

'There won't be any war now, will there?'

Awut glared at him coldly. 'I will take care of it myself.'

Ziad felt a dread chill at the words. He looked into the scope again, and through the community centre windows he saw Deni and Rasul Salamov talk to Amr, the man he'd introduced to them. He felt a pang of pity for the newcomer. He'd intervened to save Ziad from himself, and had only wanted a job. He had no idea he'd soon be dead.

Chapter 75

She packed everything that might be of use, but left Wollerton's belongings in his holdall on the table in the living room. Guilt, shame and regret stirred whenever she thought of him. She'd seen betrayal as her only option in the circumstances, but now regretted the single-minded drive that was responsible for such reasoning. She wished she'd aborted the mission and that the two of them had left Qingdao as failures. She would never have encountered the Red Wolves and wouldn't have to live with a death sentence hanging over her. *Pity won't help you*, she told herself as she left the apartment to catch a taxi for the airport.

The mechanical pencil had come from the gift shop. The food concessions offered chopsticks or spoons and Brigitte could not find a blade anywhere in the airport. The sharp metal tip of the 0.7 mm pencil would have to do.

She hadn't been able to risk doing this anywhere other than the departures lounge. The apartment had been under surveillance and until she'd passed through airport security, she couldn't be sure she wasn't being watched.

But here, past Qingdao Airport's extensive security checks, locked alone in a toilet cubicle, Brigitte could be sure she wasn't being spied upon. She pulled down her trousers and felt the back of her left thigh for the stitched wound. She stuck the pencil nib in, and the pain almost made her pass out. She bit her left forearm to stop herself from screaming, and once the shock and agony of the initial incision had passed, Brigitte dragged the metal point through the stitches, reopening the wound.

She felt blood trickle down her leg, and it became a stream when she pushed her thumb and forefinger inside. She whimpered as she forced her digits deep within her flesh, searching out the tiny device the Red Wolves had implanted.

She screamed a thousand silent curses, and her pores oozed with the sweat of misery and pain. She dug deeper and felt the stream of blood run more rapidly. Had she ruptured an artery? Dizziness came over her and she thought she might faint until she felt the hard shell of a capsule that wasn't much bigger than a painkiller. She got a good purchase, pulled it out, and collapsed instantly.

She came to in the airport stall and checked her watch. The Paris flight would have been called by now. She picked up the scarf she'd bought from the gift shop and tied it around her bleeding leg. Using the rudimentary first aid kit she'd bought from the airport pharmacy, Brigitte made a bandage and dressed the wound. She searched around the stall for the bug, which she'd dropped when she'd blacked out. She found it behind the toilet, and with the device in hand, she pulled up her jeans and hurried from the cubicle.

She found the Paris gate and ignored the complaints that came when she pushed in behind an amorous couple she'd spotted at check-in. The woman had a large Hermès handbag – the kind of bag things got lost in. Brigitte lingered for a couple of minutes, waiting until the couple were stuck to each other's faces like horny limpets. When they were deep in a kiss, she dropped the bug in the woman's bag.

Then, making a play of having forgotten something in duty free, Brigitte left the queue and rushed across the airport to catch another flight. Using one of her other false IDs and credit cards, she purchased a ticket to Seattle with a short stopover in Beijing.

She sat in row twenty-six, trying to focus on the magazine. The eyes of a happy couple on the cover were visible, but the rest of their faces were obscured by the seat pocket. Large kanji announced the title of the publication, but Brigitte couldn't make them sharp enough to read. She was sweating profusely and tendrils of darkness probed the edges of her blurred vision. She sensed the man in the aisle seat giving her funny looks, but she didn't care about him. Her seat was wet and she knew she was losing too much blood.

'Excuse me,' she slurred, getting to her feet.

Everything felt disjointed, staccato, as though her passage through time was broken. Had she passed out momentarily?

The man in the aisle seat tutted, but shifted so she could pass. A flight attendant in a jump seat said something in Mandarin, but Brigitte didn't catch it as she staggered towards the nearest galley.

'Please, madam, we're taking off. You have to sit down,' the flight attendant said.

'Feeling sick,' Brigitte replied, hoping no one noticed the blood soaking the back of her jeans. She hurried aft and tried the toilet by the middle galley. It was locked, so she popped the external catch and ignored the cries of 'Madam!' and 'You have to go back to your seat.'

She locked the door behind her and leaned against it to catch her breath. The mirror reflected a ghost. Her albinism meant she was always pale, but her ordeal had made her almost translucent, as though she wasn't of this world.

Someone knocked on the door and tried to force it open, but Brigitte kept her weight against it, and the would-be intruder resorted to yelling orders. She wept. She'd never thought much about her future and had been content to take each mission as it came. She had no idea what she wanted from life, but she knew it wasn't this.

Brigitte was suddenly alert. Another blackout? She ignored the hammering and took down her jeans. The back of her left leg was soaked in blood and the bandage she'd placed over the wound was drenched. She untied the scarf she'd applied as a tourniquet and repositioned it higher up her leg, running at a diagonal from her groin to just below her hip. She pulled it tight and fought the urge to cry out. This time she was aware when the darkness took her.

She came to, and sucked down a sharp breath. Her leg was numb. The flow of blood seemed to have stopped and she no longer worried about bleeding out. Her chief concerns were infection, ischemia, neuropathy and pulmonary embolism. But these weren't immediate threats. She could address some of them during the flight. Feeling slightly better, Brigitte pulled up her trousers, washed her hands and emerged from the toilet to find two angry flight attendants, who escorted her back to her seat as the plane taxied onto the runway. Brigitte sat down as the aircraft started accelerating, and, as the nose pointed skyward, she put her head back and allowed herself to fall into sleep, safe in the knowledge she was on her way to Beijing.

From there she could reach America.

Chapter 76

Wollerton watched the coverage of the atrocity at the Meals Seattle warehouse with a growing sense of dread. The MSNBC reporter on the scene relayed a mix of speculation and rumour about a story that had become national news. Wollerton suspected the cadre of networks on the scene would be working their law enforcement contacts, so although the Seattle Police Department still hadn't issued an official statement, certain key elements had been generally accepted by the assembled media. There were multiple fatalities, some were saying up to a hundred dead. They appeared to have been killed by an unidentified chemical agent, and the victims were believed to have links to organized crime. Fox News was reporting a source in the coroner's office who said at least one body taken from the scene was covered in chalky residue, a revelation that had people asking whether there was a possible link to the Cairo prison break and the Midas Killer. Wollerton was sure there was a connection and was doubly certain the agent deployed was the same one used in the Al Aqarab escape. But his growing unease wasn't because someone had deployed a chemical agent against civilian targets on two continents; his dread stemmed from his belief Scott and Leila might have been inside that warehouse. *Why else would they have failed to respond to my many emails?*

He checked the ancient digital clock on his rickety bedside table: 10.23 p.m. He'd been in his cheap hotel room for almost five hours and apart from short breaks for the toilet or to send yet another email from the computer terminal in the lobby, he'd been glued to the developing story. The receptionist's willingness to accept a week's rent in cash with no questions had helped Wollerton choose the Regal Knights Hotel in Licton Springs, a short cab ride from the centre of Seattle, although he had no intention of spending a week holed up like a fugitive and had to find Scott and Leila, even if that meant taking risks. He slid off the heavily stained satin bedspread and left the run-down museum of battered furniture that passed for his hotel room. He avoided the tiny box elevator and went down three flights to the lobby, where he nodded at the disinterested receptionist who sat behind a Plexiglas screen.

Wollerton hurried out of the hotel and walked for fifteen minutes, zig-zagging through the city until he reached a Safeway supermarket on 85th Street. Certain he hadn't been followed, he went inside and found a pay phone near the vending machines. He dialled a number he'd committed to memory back in Huxley Blaine Carter's house in the French Alps, and prayed he wasn't making a terrible mistake.

Chapter 77

Leila shifted on the uncomfortable hard plastic chair. The police had made no allowances for her disability and had handcuffed her to an anchor point in the centre of the table, which forced her to lean forward, putting a strain on her back and hips. The pain was really starting to get to her and she'd lost track of how long she'd been left to stew in the small interview room.

She'd been booked on an immigration charge that hadn't been fully explained to her. They'd tested her for Covid-19 and taken all her belongings, including her Ghostlink, which the custody officer had logged as a cell phone. After a long spell in a holding cell, she'd been brought for interview, but she hadn't seen anyone for ages and recognized the standard police tactics, which were designed to break down a suspect's resolve by subjecting them to uncertainty and delay. Detective Evan Hill was in for a surprise if he thought standard tactics would work on her.

Leila's only real concern was that her fingerprints, which had been taken when she'd been booked, would lead to the false identity she'd used to enter the United States. If Hill ran a search with Homeland Security, her prints would name her as Susan Samuels rather than Maria Grattan, but Leila already had an answer for the detective. Maria Grattan was a pseudonym she used to protect herself from the criminal elements she wrote about as a security correspondent. She was reasonably confident she could explain away the anomaly but was still wondering why he'd lied about speaking to *Il Giustizia*.

The door opened and Detective Evan Hill entered, his face stern, a manila folder tucked under his arm. He wore a white shirt that was rolled up at the sleeves, a pair of black trousers and heavy boots that looked like they were a throwback to his days as a beat cop.

He dropped the folder on the table and sat beside it so that he towered over Leila.

'Miss Grattan,' he began, 'or should I say Mrs Samuels –' he'd run the Homeland Security search on her prints – 'we have a real problem.'

Leila said nothing.

'Because neither of those is your real name.' He paused. 'Leila Nahum.'

The words shot down Leila's pained spine like a jolt of electricity. Of all the things he could have said, those were the only words she was afraid of; the odds of him knowing her real name were so slim as to be virtually non-existent. She hadn't even countenanced the possibility and so, like a noxious spell, the two familiar words filled her with panic. How did this Seattle detective have access to information that was beyond all but the world's most sophisticated intelligence agencies?

'I see I have your attention,' Hill said. 'That's good, because your name is only the first of your problems.'

He opened the folder and revealed something that tightened the noose around Leila's panic-stricken gut. She felt as though she might be sick when she studied the photograph that lay on top of a pile of documents. The image had been taken on a camera situated inside the addicts' house on Kenyon Street. Or rather, the house of the two dead cops who'd been pretending to be addicts. The photo showed Leila holding Jared Lowe at gunpoint, forcing him to carry the body of Dean Ollander out to the Yukon.

'Two police officers, Jared Lowe and Dean Ollander, are missing,' Hill said. 'They look a lot like these men,' he pointed to Jared and Dean's body. 'Can you tell me what's happening here, Miss Nahum?'

Leila couldn't have answered even if she'd wanted to. She was nauseous and her mind was tormented by frightful thoughts. If they could tie her to the deaths of these men, she'd face a double murder charge and a lengthy prison sentence. She couldn't afford to be locked up, not with her sister out there. Not now she finally had hope for something she'd thought she'd lost forever: her family. She flushed with the heat of primal fear and if Hill had pressed at that moment she would have given him anything.

'I did some digging and found these,' he moved the first photo to reveal three others. They showed Leila going inside the Leadenhall Building with Artem Vasylyk's bodyguard, a man Pearce had referred to as Prop Forward because he looked like a rugby player. 'The Metropolitan Police issued these, appealing for information on a person of interest in the investigation into the death of Artem Vasylyk. He was killed in this building the very day these pictures were taken.'

Leila should have been terrified, but the tumult subsided and she took a couple of deep breaths to compose herself. The detective had overreached himself and had no idea he'd made a mistake. She would play his ignorance to her advantage.

'Did you get assigned the Midas Killer case? Or did you volunteer for it?' she asked.

'What the heck—' Hill began, but she cut him off.

'My guess is you asked for the case. You wanted to be assigned the Richie Cutter murder investigation,' she said, referring to the dead port supervisor.

'My case allocation isn't at issue here. If you don't want me to drop a murder charge on you, or turn you over to the British government, you'd better start telling me what I want to hear,' Hill responded.

'What do you want to hear?' Leila asked insolently.

'What you're doing in Seattle? Who you're working for?'

Leila leaned forward so she was directly beneath Hill. He recoiled slightly as she stared up at him, her eyes blazing. 'Maybe you should tell me who you're really working for,' she said. 'Because it isn't the Seattle Police Department.'

Hill hesitated.

'I see I have your attention,' Leila said. 'That's good, because that's only the first of your problems.'

'What the hell are you talking about?' Hill blustered. 'I'm a Seattle police detective and I'm giving you a chance to come clean. I don't know what you think is happening here.'

Hill couldn't have known she'd hacked the Metropolitan Police after Vasylyk's death and had a standing query for any intelligence reports featuring her name or likeness. She'd also checked the Leadenhall Building's surveillance system and found it had been erased the day of the shooting. The people Vasylyk worked with had no desire to help the police catch his killer, which meant the image in Evan Hill's folder could only have come from those same people. Leila stopped worrying about Detective Hill's empty threats and wondered what and who connected a dead Ukrainian billionaire and a Seattle police detective.

'You're out of your depth, Evan,' Leila said. 'Charge me, or let me go.'

Leila could see Hill struggling with his change of fortune. He was desperately trying to think of a way to regain command of the situation, but Leila knew he'd lost it and it was only a matter of time before he caught up. Maybe she could help him?

'Charge me, Detective. You've got me on film with your missing cops. Charge me.' Leila stared at Hill. 'I don't think you can. Now they're gone, you want them to stay gone. An investigation would get people asking questions about what they were doing at that house and who really sent them there.'

Hill flushed and Leila sensed his anger. She felt the fire of the hunt rising within her and closed for the kill.

'I think you sent them there. I think you sent them there because the people you really work for told you to make sure no harm came to the occupants of that green house, and I don't think you want people finding out you're just another dirty cop who's sold his department out for a gangster's dollar.'

The slap shocked Leila, but once its sharp sting had subsided she looked up at Hill with nothing but fury.

'Officer!' she yelled. 'Someone help!'

The door opened, and the uniformed cop who'd escorted her from the holding cell stepped into the room.

'Detective Hill just struck me,' Leila said. She could feel the heat radiating off her cheek and knew the blow had left a mark.

The cop looked at Hill awkwardly. 'Would you like to make a report?' he asked Leila.

'I don't know,' she said to Hill. 'Would I?'

Hill got to his feet, his face tight with rage. 'You could have talked to me,' he snarled. 'And life would have been so much easier for us both. Now . . .' he hesitated. 'Now it's going to get ugly.'

He stared at Leila and she held his gaze.

'Get her out of here,' Hill told the uniformed cop.

Leila watched the detective storm out of the room and wondered why she didn't feel like someone who'd just won a battle.

Chapter 78

Ziad lay at the edge of the roof and watched men he knew patrol the block. Emmett Martin, an American convert, emerged from the community centre picking his teeth. Ziad had never liked Emmett, one of four brothers and three sisters fathered by a strict Baptist minister whose zeal turned most of them into degenerates. Emmett had been a petty criminal until he'd converted to Islam in prison and he'd embraced the faith with a wholeheartedness his father would have recognized. He worked for Deni, collecting rent and other monies owed by members of the community. Ziad had seen mourners arrive at the centre with huge platters and containers. He'd been to enough wakes to know there would be a feast inside, and Emmett certainly looked like someone who'd eaten his fill.

The convert joined Adel, Ehsan and Sid on the corner of 42nd Avenue and 140th Street.

Emmett said something to Ehsan, who gave a subdued nod and headed inside. Emmett took Ehsan's place manning the checkpoint and the group scanned the street.

There was a similar squad of men on all four corners of the block and another team of four men guarded the entrance of the community centre. Ehsan was passing them now. Fearing war, Deni Salamov had summoned everyone he had left, and if the East Hill Mob had attacked, they could have finished off the Salamovs. But they weren't coming, so Awut would have to do the grisly work instead.

'Cross the road, man,' Sid yelled.

Ziad saw what looked like a homeless person approach the other side of the intersection.

The figure was cloaked in a filthy, tattered blanket that threw his face into shadow. He was pushing a cart full of cans and other garbage and had rags draped over the rim.

'Cross the road,' Sid yelled. 'This side's closed.'

'Fucking degenerates,' Adel remarked.

The figure ignored Sid's instruction and pushed the cart off the kerb. The cans rattled loudly as they headed directly for Emmett and the others.

'Shall I just shoot him?' Adel asked. 'Put the dirty bastard out of his misery.'

Ziad saw Awut's eyes blaze beneath the blanket and the Thai assassin reached out and touched Emmett's hand.

'What the . . .' Emmett asked, and Ziad saw him recoil and examine his hand. 'Eww. What the fuck is that?'

Adel and Sid ran forward and pulled Awut away from his cart.

'Get the fuck out of here!' Adel said, but rather than back away, Awut stepped forward and brushed Adel and Sid on the cheeks.

Ziad felt the thrill of excitement and anticipation and then, almost as quickly, shame. He shouldn't be enjoying this. But he was.

'You fucking . . .' Adel said, throwing a punch, but Awut sidestepped it.

'You guys OK?' Sajid yelled from the corner of 40th Avenue. He was one of another trio guarding the other side of the block.

'This fucking guy!' Adel shouted over.

Sajid, Hani and Jamal left their post and hurried over. Adel tried to kick Awut, but he stepped forward and grabbed his cart. He rolled it towards the group approaching from the other corner. Ziad's hand curled around the pistol Awut had given him. He was under strict instructions to stay hidden unless absolutely necessary.

'Get the fuck out of here!' Adel shouted after him, wiping his cheek.

Awut didn't respond. He kept walking, and Saijid, Hani and Jamal stepped aside to allow him to pass. He surprised them all by touching their hands and faces. They recoiled in disgust, much as the others had, and shouted curses at Awut.

Rather than continue up the street, Awut turned his cart right and headed along the path that led to the entrance of the community centre. The four men guarding the door watched him approach with a growing sense of bemusement. They were making the same mistake Emmett and the others had made; they were underestimating the man. Ziad watched Emmett try to yell a warning, but he couldn't get any words out, and when Ziad looked at Adel and Sid, he saw panic in their eyes. Like Emmett, they were having problems breathing. Emmett clutched his throat and fell to his knees, and Ziad watched the six men on the sidewalk struggle with the inevitable as they clawed at their throats, weeping with the realization they'd already taken their final breaths.

He saw fear in their eyes, and wondered exactly what was going through their minds. Would they be bargaining with the Almighty? Would they be lamenting their mistakes? Or mourning all the days that would never come?

Ziad's eyes shifted away from the dead and dying and settled on Awut, the Angel of Death, who was a few paces away from the men by the main entrance. He sensed the men's confusion as they looked beyond the shambling figure at their six comrades, who were well and truly done with life. Ziad produced the phone Awut had given him, and made a call.

'We're ready,' he said, before hanging up.

Chapter 79

Pearce was sitting in a dining area that lay off the main hall. There were more than forty people spread over three long tables. The food was laid out on a fourth and mourners shuttled between there and the community kitchen to top up the buffet. As in the rest of the centre, the walls were decorated with Islamic scripture embossed on coloured banners in gold thread. High windows opened onto the street and Pearce could hear only the occasional passing vehicle. It was as though the subdued, mournful atmosphere inside the centre had spread throughout the neighbourhood. Pearce wondered how many families across the city had been affected by the atrocity, and how those who'd perpetrated it could live with themselves.

The latter question was rhetorical. He already knew how such horrors happened. People of power, usually men, rarely needed to get their hands dirty. The world offered a plentiful supply of people with personality disorders who could be coaxed or cajoled into perpetrating all sorts of evil. Narcissists without empathy, borderline personality sufferers with poor impulse control; there was a long list of conditions that, with the wrong upbringing and life experiences, could yield people capable of slaughtering others without losing a wink of sleep. Then there were others who weren't defective in mind, but who had a defect of the spirit, motivated by anger, lust or vengeance, who could be radicalized into violence. Three men had fled Al Aqarab. Ziad, an unidentified American, and Narong Angsakul, the getaway driver and brother of the man Pearce had killed in Islamabad. Pearce suspected one of them was behind the Meals Seattle attack.

Was it Ziad? Pearce wondered. *Or had he died in the warehouse?*

Ziad had been in one of the trailing SUVs, but Pearce didn't remember him being part of the crew that came into the building with Rasul, and he couldn't recall seeing him in all the horror and confusion. He would have to check the footage taken by his surveillance glasses to be sure.

He looked through the folding glass doors that separated the dining area from the main hall and Essi Salamov caught his eye. She was in the female mourners' section, comforting a handful of women. Pearce wondered what could have happened between her and Ziad. They'd been lovers at some point, that much was obvious. How involved was she in her father's operation?

Deni and Rasul were sitting further along the table, talking to one another in hushed tones. Everyone else in the dining room either sat in stunned silence or sobbed quietly, their grief coming and going in overpowering waves. The subdued air of tragedy that hung over the gathering had a profound effect on Pearce. This was a community bound together by grief, taking comfort from each other. Sitting there watching them draw strength from their shared suffering, Pearce once again felt the need to belong.

Something distracted him from his thoughts. A noise. At first Pearce thought the sound was another mourner swept on a rising tide of misery, their wail echoing through the centre, but when one voice was joined by another, and then another, and the wails turned to screams, he knew something was very wrong. He ran from the dining room into the main hall. Mourners rose from their seats and turned with shocked concern towards the source of the screams: the entrance corridor beyond the double doors. Pearce sprinted towards them and pushed one open. His stomach rose and fell when he saw the man he'd been hunting, Narong Angsakul, moving along the corridor in silence, his face expressionless, his hands whipping out to touch everyone he could reach. In his wake he left a trail of death. Mourners who'd stepped into the corridor, Deni's men who were supposed to be guarding the building, all had been afflicted by Angsakul's touch and were choking to death.

Two members of Deni's crew emerged from a side room and drew their weapons, but Angsakul rushed forward and disarmed them with a combination of punches that left them reeling. Within each flurry of blows, Pearce noticed the assassin graze the men's faces with his fingertips, and by the time he stepped back, the toxin had started to do its work. The assassin reached inside his jacket and produced a metal canister, a replica of the one he'd used in Al Aqarab. Angsakul's touch meant death, and it would come quickly, but Pearce knew what would happen if Angsakul succeeded in getting into the main hall and detonating that device.

If he got through the doors, everyone in the community centre would die.

Chapter 80

'Get out!' Pearce yelled at Deni and Rasul. 'Get everyone out!'

Pearce stepped through the door and calmly pulled it closed behind him. He heard Deni, Rasul and the others mustering people and directing them towards the emergency exits. Pearce turned to face Angsakul and adopted the 'Thinker's Stance', folding his left arm across his body, raising his right fist so it touched the bottom of his chin. It was a favourite of experienced street fighters and Angsakul gave a smile of recognition. He tucked the canister into his jacket pocket and raised his fists in a classic Muay Thai stance. Pearce kept his eyes on the man's gloved hands. One touch meant death.

Angsakul darted forward and swung an open palm at Pearce. He blocked with his left elbow – his skin protected by his jacket –stepped inside the swing and brought his right fist down like a hammer, smashing it into the bridge of Angsakul's nose. The smaller man leaned back and robbed the blow of its full effect. He snapped out his left hand and Pearce lurched back just in time. Angsakul's gloved hand whipped the air in front of his face, and Pearce went low and lashed out with a sweeping right kick, which connected with Angsakul's left shin. Angsakul responded in kind, and they traded vicious, sharp kicks. The assassin kept swiping at Pearce with his hands, forcing him back towards the double doors. No matter what happened, Pearce couldn't let him through.

Pearce blocked a kick with his knee and moved forward, dodging Angsakul's lightning-fast hands. He pushed the assassin's arms away and delivered a lateral hammer punch to Angsakul's left jaw, at the point where the upper and lower bones connect. Pearce felt the satisfying crack of bone and as Angsakul recoiled, Pearce followed up with a cupped slap that drove a pocket of air into the man's left ear. Angsakul yelped and jolted back with the energy of someone stung by a cattle prod, and Pearce thought he'd burst an ear drum. The man's hands flew to his injuries and Pearce experienced a rush of satisfaction when he saw a white substance smeared across Angsakul's face. Pearce stepped back and waited for the toxin to do its work.

Angsakul took a moment to get through the pain. His jaw was hanging wrong and his face was already starting to swell, but he still managed a dark grin.

He had no reaction to the toxin. He stepped forward and swung at Pearce. He ducked and stepped back, and the blow failed to land. Pearce was horrified. The man seemed immune to the poison that should have killed him.

Automatic gunfire erupted outside the building and was met by a volley of small arms fire. Then came screams and cries, and Pearce heard movement inside the hall. He guessed Angsakul had accomplices who were trying to prevent people escaping.

Angsakul sprang forward and unleashed a flurry of kicks and punches. Like a wounded animal, the assassin fought with renewed ferocity and Pearce worked hard to avoid his darting hands. The two men moved back towards the door, and

Angsakul surprised Pearce by tackling him. Together they fell through the double doors into the hall and landed on the floor with a heavy thud. Pearce felt Angsakul pulling at his clothes, trying to reach his skin. Pearce kneed the assassin in the groin and he rolled off. Pearce got to his feet. The mourners were clustered away from the fire doors, where Deni, Rasul and their men were trading gunfire with unseen associates.

Pearce watched in horror as Angsakul rolled to his feet with the canister in his hand. He started sprinting as the assassin's fingers searched for the pull. He raced towards the fire door on the female mourners' side of the hall, where Deni and Rasul were positioned.

'Gun!' Pearce yelled, getting Rasul's attention.

Pearce glanced over his shoulder and saw Angsakul yank the pull and lob the canister into the air. It floated up towards the high ceiling as one of Rasul's men tossed Pearce a pistol.

'Get out!' he shouted without breaking his stride. He barged past the men shooting through the doorway and caught sight of a skinhead and a woman with short black hair leaning out of a van, firing machine guns. Ziad was with them, blasting a pistol at the building. The man and woman were covered with tattoos, including many variations of a large red wolf. Pearce burst out of the building as the canister popped behind him. He turned to see the hall, and everyone in it shrouded in white powder. Through the cloud he saw Narong Angsakul escape though the double doors.

Pearce's sudden emergence startled the shooters and he opened fire as he ran towards the vehicle. He could see the skinhead register the cloud of white death. The man yelled something at the driver, and the van sped away. Pearce locked eyes with Ziad the instant before the van's side door slid shut. Unless he was much mistaken, Ziad's face betrayed his shame. His murderous treachery was now public.

Pearce turned to see the interior of the community centre shrouded in white. He'd failed.

But then there was movement and he saw Rasul usher the panicked people from the hall. They were covered in the deadly toxin but had held their breath. Rasul must have recalled his experience at the Meals Seattle warehouse and instructed them before the canister burst. But they could only hold their breath for so long and their clothes were now covered in death.

Pearce cast around for a solution and saw it on the corner of 42nd Avenue and 140th Street.

'Get everyone over here,' he commanded Rasul.

Pearce ran to the street and smashed the window of the nearest car. He didn't have time to hotwire the vehicle, so he leaned in and flipped the gearshift to neutral. When Rasul and the others realized what he had in mind, they joined him, and together they pushed the car towards the corner. Pearce was surrounded by men covered in white powder, and held his breath. He was dead if he caught any of the dust that covered them. The car gathered speed and together the gang of men pushed it onto the kerb and into the fire hydrant that protruded from the sidewalk. There was a crack and a grinding of metal on metal, and then the high-pressure pipe burst and jets of water sprayed from beneath the car. They kept pushing and the car cleared the hydrant, water shooting high into the sky. Pearce banked on water being a neutralizing agent, offering the same salvation as the river.

The young and old were first. Deni, Rasul and the others helped them into the water and their clothes were jet washed, leaving them spotless in moments. The confusion provided Pearce with his opportunity.

'Tell them I'm going to find who did this,' Pearce said to the old man, Abbas, who had been one of the first through the wash. 'I'll be in touch.'

Pearce didn't wait for a response and sprinted along 42nd Avenue to the sound of oncoming sirens.

Chapter 81

Ziad had felt fear when he'd seen Amr's fierce eyes. The man had said he'd served in the military, but those eyes hadn't just seen action, they'd stared death in the face, and Ziad couldn't help shake the feeling they'd been judging him. Deni, Rasul, any of those who survived the attack would know he had betrayed them. He'd helped kill people who'd once been his friends.

They betrayed you, he told himself, but he couldn't get rid of the filth that seemed to cling to his insides.

Murder.

Friends.

Two words that should never go together. Their proximity a simple verdict on what he'd become.

As Eddie Fletcher's van sped through the city and the adrenalin of the attack subsided, Ziad looked around the cabin with a sense of shame. These were his friends now. Psychopaths and murderers. What had become of him?

'What the fuck are you looking like that for?' Fletcher asked angrily.

One of the Red Wolves was driving, taking side roads that kept them away from the approaching cops.

Ziad was about to respond when his eyes fell on Awut, who didn't look well. He stumbled against the side of the van and slumped to the floor. Ziad went to his side and kneeled beside him.

'He needs a hospital,' he told Eddie.

'No hospitals,' Kirsty said emphatically.

'Warehouse,' Awut moaned. 'Medicine.'

Eddie turned to the driver. 'Step on it, Frank,' he urged. 'We got a man down back here.'

The drive to the warehouse took a heart-pounding twenty minutes, and Awut's condition worsened. By the time the van screeched to a halt outside the isolated old building, the fearsome Thai was barely conscious. Beads of sweat pricked his grey skin and his breathing was thick, rasping and erratic. Every now and then he would choke and splutter.

Ziad and the Fletchers bundled him out of the van into the warehouse. They set him down with his back against one of the old machining benches and Eddie slapped his face.

'Where's the medicine?' the gang leader asked.

Awut slurred deliriously and for a moment his eyes regained focus and clarity. He pulled up his shirt to reveal a rectangle of black fabric stuck to his back, above his right kidney. It wasn't much bigger than a playing card and looked like a nicotine patch.

'Bag,' Awut managed to choke out the solitary word.

The needful look in Awut's eyes suggested the patch was some form of medication, and while Kirsty and Eddie helped him onto the floor, Ziad ran towards the offices at the rear of the warehouse. He could have sworn he heard Awut say something else, but when Ziad glanced over his shoulder, all he saw was a lolling head and eyes that fluttered in the grip of delirium as the tattooed husband and wife tended to him.

Ziad and Awut had converted two of the offices into bedrooms and Ziad ran into Awut's, where he found the sick man's canvas holdall at the foot of his army surplus cot. Ziad searched the pockets of the bag and found a small plastic medical case at the bottom of a side compartment. He opened the case and saw three patches in translucent wax-paper wrappers. There were some latex gloves and a pair of medical scissors, but Ziad ignored the other contents, grabbed a patch and tore the wrapping as he raced into the warehouse.

Awut teetered on the edge of consciousness, but Ziad thought he saw a flash of fear when the assassin caught sight of him pulling the patch from its wrapper. Eddie and Kirsty backed off and he kneeled beside the ailing man and ripped off the old patch. He pulled the backing from the new one and stuck it to Awut's back, pressing it firmly against the man's clammy skin.

Awut fell silent and for a moment Ziad feared the worst, but he soon realized Awut's breathing had eased and he was no longer making the horrific choking noise. Ziad coughed, surprised the condition of his companion had brought a lump to his throat. But the lump wouldn't go. It grew larger and Ziad realized he was struggling to breathe. It felt as though a band had materialized around his chest and was being pulled terribly tight. His lungs caught fire and, as he fell to the floor, Ziad saw Awut's eyes open.

'Gloves,' the man said, and Ziad realized he was repeating the word he'd said moments earlier as Ziad had run towards the office.

Ziad saw horror in the eyes of Eddie and Kirsty Fletcher, and they backed even further away. The unbearable pain started to melt, and even though he couldn't breathe, Ziad found himself unable to care. The fire in his chest seemed to grow distant, like a tiny blaze on a far horizon. All he felt was a gentle warmth, as though his body had been swaddled in an electric blanket. The last thing he saw was Awut getting to his feet and running across the warehouse.

Why the rush? Ziad thought before he blacked out.

Chapter 82

Leila sat on the edge of the thin mattress on the hard melamine bunk which ran along one wall of the tiny cell. She'd lost track of time. Earlier in the evening the cells had been full of the sounds of people moving – prisoners complaining, doors slamming, footsteps, shouts, the cacophony of law breakers and enforcers colliding – but now all was silent, and the peace suggested it must have been well past midnight. Even the villainous had to sleep, and it seemed that everyone other than her was out for the night. Her mind was racing and she tried to wrestle her whirling thoughts and find some calm. But they bounced wildly, each coming into focus for a moment before colliding with another, fuelled by the latent adrenalin coursing through her exhausted body. She recalled the feeling of terror when she'd thought she'd be locked up for life, prevented from beginning the search for her sister, and that ugly fear made Leila question the risks she was taking for Huxley Blaine Carter.

She puzzled over Detective Hill and who he was really working for, and she wondered why they'd made the mistake of overreaching themselves. Why had they tried to tie her to something from her past? To the events of the Black Thirteen investigation? She could only think they weren't sure what had happened in the green house on Kenyon Street and wanted the additional leverage in case she hadn't done anything wrong to the missing cops.

Then there was Hill's desire to know who she was working for. Would that be the prime concern of an honest cop worried about his fellow officers, or the most pressing issue for a corrupt policeman gathering intel for his clandestine masters? Leila knew she'd put him in a bind. He couldn't charge her without risking exposure, but he wasn't going to let her walk either. She thought the most likely outcomes were a tragic death in custody, or her release into the hands of the people he really worked for, who would torture and kill her. Leila tried to prepare herself for what she suspected was coming, but the constantly whirring kaleidoscope of thoughts prevented her from finding any balance.

She tensed when she heard movement outside the cell, and readied herself for a fight. She wasn't going to let Hill take her easily, but the door opened and she saw a uniformed cop standing in the brightly lit corridor. He had the bored expression of a man who'd spent too many nights behind a desk.

'Samuels,' he said. 'You're free to go.'

So they're going to take me, Leila thought. *They'll be waiting for me outside.*

'You got the time,' she asked the cop.

'Quarter after two,' he said.

Leila got to her feet and left the cell, her mind now turning to how she'd escape the predators lying in wait for her.

Chapter 83

Leila felt herself sag with relief when she saw Wollerton leaning against the booking desk. He was talking to the custody officer. She had no idea where he'd come from or how he'd done it, but she could have kissed the man for securing her release. The uniformed cop led Leila through a security door and stood aside.

'You can get your things from the desk,' he said.

Leila shuffled over and when Wollerton turned to face her, his expression changed from annoyance to surprise. She must have looked a mess. He didn't seem in great shape either. His skin was pale and his eyes had the deep shadows of a man who'd seen a lifetime's trouble.

'Susan,' he said. 'I was just . . .' he glanced at the custody officer. 'Why didn't you tell me you were letting her out?'

She wasn't big on emotional displays, but she hugged Wollerton. He patted her awkwardly.

'Come on,' he said. 'I've got a car waiting outside.'

'Let me just get my stuff,' Leila replied.

Minutes later, cane in hand, Ghostlink in her pocket, Leila joined Wollerton outside the precinct. It was a warm night and stars peeked out from behind patchy cloud.

'How did you find me?' Leila asked.

'I phoned our employer's point man,' Wollerton replied, referring to Robert Clifton, 'and asked him to use his NSA contacts to check recent hospital admissions and arrests. I thought there'd only be three reasons you and Pearce wouldn't respond to comms – arrest, capture or incapacity.'

'So you haven't heard from Scott?'

Wollerton shook his head. 'What happened?'

'He was at the warehouse,' Leila said.

'I saw it on the news. Was he inside?'

'Yeah, but he got out and made it to the river,' Leila explained. 'That's when I lost contact with him.'

'We need to find out what happened.'

'We set up at a motel. We can start there,' Leila suggested.

'Car's this way.' Wollerton indicated the public car park that lay beyond the police parking.

Leila's cane tapped against the tarmac and she leaned on it hard, eager for whatever support it could provide. Her legs were heavy and devoid of energy. 'Thanks for getting me out.'

Wollerton scoffed. 'I didn't do anything. I'd just arrived and was trying to convince the guy to tell me whether I'd got the right precinct.'

'Then you're a lucky charm,' Leila said as they walked past rows of stationary police cars. 'What happened in Qingdao?'

'Someone tried to kidnap me. I think Brigitte was involved . . .' Wollerton began, but he stopped talking. Leila followed his eye line, and saw four uniformed cops emerge from a pair of patrol vehicles that were double-parked in the service road that split the police and public parking areas.

Leila's stomach went into a violent spin as she realized she'd been right. The sight of the former MI6 operative had lulled her into a false sense of security. Those men were coming for her.

'Kyle,' she said, suddenly on edge. 'We need to—'

'I know,' he said, and they both started to back away.

Tyres screeched nearby and Leila turned to see two police officers hanging from the open side door of an unmarked van. Before she or Wollerton could react, the men jumped out and shocked them with stun guns. Fifty thousand volts shot up Leila's spine, and as she collapsed, she registered strong arms around her, propelling her into the gaping mouth of the waiting van.

Chapter 84

The compartment was completely dark, but Leila had seen the men who'd stunned them jump inside before the door had been closed and the van had been driven away. She'd been hog-tied, her hands bound behind her back and connected to her ankles by a knot that tightened every time she moved. She was lying face down on the flatbed, next to Wollerton, who'd been bound the same way before the van door had been shut. She hadn't noticed it at first, but as they bumped along, Wollerton's breathing had become erratic and she started to worry he was struggling. It wasn't until she focused on the rhythm that she realized he was communicating using Morse code.

Will untie to move us, he breathed. *We go then.*

Leila gave a long breath followed by a short one and repeated the pairing to indicate 'C', the Morse prosign for affirmative. From then on, they rode in silence that was only broken by the clatter of the van's axles over potholes and the occasional movement of the men who shared the compartment with them.

After a while, the van made a series of turns and eventually came to a halt. A door slammed and was followed by crunching footsteps. The side panel was pulled open, lighting the interior. Leila was inches away from Wollerton. He faced her and she could see anticipation in his eyes. One of the police officers jumped out and joined his colleague by the door. The other stooped over Leila.

'Don't move,' he said. 'Or you'll get cut.'

Leila stayed perfectly still and looked beyond the driver and the other captor towards a tumbledown warehouse with broken windows. A faded sign identified the place as Lenny's Bike Repairs. The sight was final confirmation these men intended to kill her and Wollerton. They had made no effort to disguise their faces and had now revealed a location.

Leila felt a release of pressure as the rope linking her arms and legs was cut. Moments later, the one binding her ankles was also severed, allowing her feet to move freely. She stretched her legs, and they were immediately engulfed by the painful crackle of pins and needles. The knifeman stepped over her and used a box cutter to slice through the ropes restraining Wollerton's legs. Their hands were still bound behind their backs, so the knifeman hauled them roughly to their feet.

Wollerton went first. He was pushed from the vehicle and stumbled onto the dirt yard. Leila winced as she was manhandled outside, but she kept her eyes fixed on the warehouse. She knew it contained nothing but an ugly end, and she resolved not to go inside at any cost. She and Wollerton were pushed towards it by the driver, and the other two took up flanking positions.

'Come on,' the driver said. 'Move it.'

Wollerton's reputation was well deserved. Leila didn't see any build-up, just the impact, a crippling headbutt that made the driver double over and cry out in pain. Leila barged the nearest cop, the knifeman, while Wollerton attacked the third with a flurry of vicious kicks to the legs, groin and midriff.

He moved like a born predator, rather than a trained man, and even though he must have had fifteen or twenty years on his adversary, it was like watching an old tiger fighting a young goat. The cop wasn't in Wollerton's league and when he buckled, Wollerton finished him with a whipping round-house to the head. Not bad for a veteran, Leila thought, but their moment of triumph was short-lived. A cold circle of metal pressed against her temple and an arm wrapped itself around her neck and yanked her back, pulling her against the knifeman's body. She was now a hostage.

She glanced round to see Knifeman glaring at Wollerton.

'Back the fuck up, hotshot,' her captor said. 'Or I kill the cripple.'

The word sparked fury. This violent, corrupt man, like so many before him, saw only her weakness. She trembled with anger and noticed the other two officers coming to their senses.

'Back the fuck up, I said,' Knifeman yelled.

She whipped her head back and cracked his nose with her skull. The gun went off, blinding her with a flash of fire against the black sky, and deafening her with a thunderous crack. Knifeman lashed out, striking her with the pistol, and she went down in excruciating pain.

'Look at me,' Knifeman commanded. Leila could hardly hear him above the ringing in her ears. 'Look at me, bitch.'

Her vision returned and she saw him standing over her, blood streaming from his nose, his gun inches from her face, the muzzle shaking.

'You fuck!' he yelled. Rage had turned his face red. 'Make sure you get one, they said. Doesn't matter if one dies, they said. You earned this,' he told Leila.

Wollerton lunged, but he couldn't reach the man before the gunshot, which made Leila jump. She looked up at the former Six operative and saw he was unscathed. Then came two more shots and Leila realized Knifeman hadn't fired at Wollerton. He hadn't fired at anyone. Knifeman dropped his weapon and fell to the ground with three bloody holes in his chest.

The other two cops were on their feet, fumbling for their weapons, peering into the darkness for a target. Another brace of shots and both men went down with bullets in their guts.

'We've got to move,' a voice said from the darkness. 'The others aren't far behind.'

Robert Clifton, former director of the NSA, now advisor to Huxley Blaine Carter, emerged from the shadows, clasping a small assault rifle. Leila noticed he was careful not to look at the men he'd shot. He used a pocket knife to cut her bonds, and she immediately snatched a gun from one of the wounded cops, who lay groaning nearby. Clifton cut Wollerton loose, and he also grabbed a weapon.

Leila heard movement and she turned to see a familiar face in the warehouse doorway; Narong Angsakul, the man who'd broken Ziad Malek out of Al Aqarab. She opened fire on him instinctively, but her shots went wide and the pitiless killer stepped back. The door slammed shut as she corrected her aim, and the second volley thudded into it.

'Come on,' Clifton said, grabbing Leila. He nodded towards approaching headlights.

Leila followed him and Wollerton across the yard into the darkness of an abandoned industrial estate. She glanced behind her to see two cop cars stop next to the van. The four officers who'd rushed them at the precinct emerged from the vehicles and hurried to their fallen colleagues. One of the new arrivals scanned the area, but Leila, Wollerton and Clifton were lost to the shadows.

'Thanks,' Wollerton said to the old NSA spy.

'When you asked me to give you a ride . . .' Clifton tailed off. 'I haven't shot anyone for years. I'm shaking.'

'You did what you had to,' Leila observed. 'And you saved our lives.'

Clifton nodded. 'My car's behind that building.' He indicated a warehouse to their right. 'Let's get out of here.'

Leila struggled with the pace set by the two men, but there was no way she was going to let them see weakness, so she pushed through every agonizing step. Pain was an old friend and she knew it ebbed and flowed. Even as her eyes watered and each jarring impact of foot against ground threatened to take her breath away, she told herself pain was the most powerful reminder she was alive. And that was all that mattered.

Chapter 85

Essi embraced him. He pulled her tight and inhaled the sweet vanilla of her soft hair. She was all the warmth he ever wanted, and when she looked up at him he saw the same desire reflected in her eyes. They were destined to be together, the map of their lives marked by marriage, children, happiness, joy, experiences that were wondrous to behold. He saw all the milestones in her glittering eyes and felt profound happiness at what lay ahead. But there was fear also, and doubt.

None of it is real.

The moment that thought flashed through his head, she was gone. And then came darkness. And the fall. A drop without end, spinning, tumbling, a terrible sense of imminent impact. He felt the chill of old sweat against his skin and the thunder of a panicked heart, and looked around but saw only black.

Then there was burning light and an ugly world came into being. He could hear distant voices, and even though they were muffled, their anger was clear. Above him, cracked grey paint flaked from the ceiling, drawing hard, unmoving veins that loomed over him. His mouth was full of bitterness, as though he'd eaten a thousand wasp stings, and every swallow burned his throat. But he didn't mind any of it, and that was perhaps the strangest thing. It was as though his life belonged to someone else and he really couldn't get that upset about any of it.

There was movement nearby and he saw a familiar face. Awut. The killer who'd rescued him from prison. The man with the black patch. The black patch.

Ziad looked down and saw one clinging to his shoulder. He remembered choking, struggling to breathe, and wondered whether the patch had somehow saved him. He was almost certain it was responsible for the dreamy detachment he was experiencing.

Awut walked to the doorway and leaned out of the dank old office that had been Ziad's bedroom for the past few days, and the angry voices stopped. Ziad tracked a shadow that moved across the dirty frosted-glass panels that separated the office from the rest of the warehouse. The shape shifted and danced across the irregular panes until it became a person in the doorway. Elroy Lang, the only friend he'd had inside Al Aqarab.

Awut stepped outside the room and leaned against one of the glass panels, while Elroy approached Ziad and sat on the low army surplus cot.

'How do you feel?' he asked.

'Out of it,' Ziad rasped.

'You saved your friend's life,' Elroy nodded towards Awut's shadow. 'He encountered a high dose of toxin that consumed the synthetic hormone far more rapidly than usual. If you hadn't given him a new patch, he would have died.'

'Toxin?' Ziad asked. 'Like in the prison? What does that have to do with these?' He gestured at his own patch.

Elroy smiled, but it wasn't a joyous expression. It was the look of a doctor about to break bad news. He stood and closed the office door, before returning to sit at the end of Ziad's bed.

'I never wanted this for you,' Elroy said. 'There was no need. We knew you'd be motivated to take revenge against the Salamovs. There was no call for any additional incentive.'

He hesitated.

'If only you'd worn the gloves,' he sighed. 'But what's done is done. You're wearing the patch now, and that means you need to know what it does, and how it keeps you alive.'

Ziad listened, and each word was like a painful hammer blow. By the time Elroy was done, Ziad's old life had been smashed and he'd been introduced to his new hellish existence and the terrible succubus that gripped his shoulder. He looked down at the patch and howled with anguish.

Chapter 86

Elroy Lang sighed. He felt sorry for the Egyptian-American boy lying on the tiny bunk, drenched in his own sweat and tears. Elroy had returned from Quingdao once the French spy had been dispatched to Paris and he was assured that Li Jun Xiao and David Song would be able to meet the demand he now had for their product. He'd arrived in Seattle to find their plan in disarray. According to the extensive media coverage of the attack on the Salam Islamic Centre, Deni Salamov's base of operations, casualties were limited to fewer than twenty. Police were working on the theory the community centre had been the target of a racially motived terror attack, which threw a different complexion on what had happened at the Meals Seattle warehouse. Their friends in the police department were spreading misinformation to ensure the authorities and media stayed well away from the truth. But Deni Salamov would know, and according to their information, he and his son had survived the attack. He was alive and would undoubtedly be planning his revenge.

Elroy looked down at Ziad. He'd never heard of anyone taking the patch in these circumstances. Not by accident. They'd used the boy, and their manipulation of him was supposed to be suffering enough, but now he was dependent and tied to them for his survival, just like Narong Angsakul.

The formidable Thai warrior had explained what had happened. He'd been exposed to a contact dose of XTX, which had rapidly depleted the parathyroid level of his patch, and when he and the others had returned to the warehouse, he'd been delirious and unable to warn Ziad against touching the replacement patch with his bare skin. The patch that had saved Awut's life had cursed Ziad. The Thai, who didn't often show his emotions, clearly felt some guilt.

Narong had been recruited into the Mujahedeen Patani to fight for the global caliphate and it should have been him chosen for the operation Pearce foiled in Islamabad, but his baby brother had persuaded the sheikhs to select him instead. Chatri Angsakul had gone and been killed by Scott Pearce, a man who'd initially been dismissed as a lucky adventurer, but who was now proving to be a serious irritation. He'd foiled their plans in Britain, and he and his associates were now doing their best to interfere in Seattle.

The camera in the house on Kenyon Street had caught Pearce planting a bug on Ziad's car, and Narong had identified him and recounted their fight in the community centre. Pearce would have to be eliminated before he did any more harm, and Elroy knew just the man to do it.

Enraged and maddened by grief at the death of his brother, Narong had persuaded the sheikhs to let him talk to the man who bankrolled Mujahedeen Patani, which is when he'd been introduced to Elroy. Mujahedeen Patani was one of many groups Elroy was responsible for. Seeing the opportunity a dedicated warrior like Narong offered, Elroy had promised to help him track down his brother's killer, and set him to work smuggling weapons through Thailand into Malaysia. As a sign of his commitment and loyalty, Elroy had demanded

Narong take the patch, and the man hadn't hesitated. He was loyal, driven by a single purpose and had proven himself in combat repeatedly. Every so often Elroy felt a pang of guilt at the deception he was perpetrating. He'd known the identity of Chatri Angsakul's killer within hours of the attack, but whenever he was assailed by conscience, Elroy reminded himself of their higher purpose. Mujahedeen Patani, Black Thirteen, Red Wolves; all part of the great objective. The struggle would only be won through great suffering. And here at Elroy's feet was the latest victim of their ambition.

Elroy stroked Ziad's hair and the young man stirred. He looked up and for a moment his eyes were wild and unfocused. Then, gradually, he came round.

'What happened?' Ziad asked. His voice was feeble and croaky.

'It's OK,' Elroy lied.

Three police officers had been shot outside the warehouse, and four of their colleagues had taken them to a friendly, discreet medical centre for treatment. Awut was standing watch beyond the frosted-glass doors, eager to leave in case Pearce or any of his people returned to finish the job. But Ziad hadn't been in a fit state to move until now.

Ziad took a couple of deep breaths and wiped the tears from his eyes. He looked down at his shoulder and saw the black patch clinging to it.

Elroy registered the boy's dismay. 'It's OK,' he reiterated. 'You'll forget about it soon. As long as you're careful, you'll live to an old age.'

Ziad looked up at Elroy with anger in his eyes. 'Is this what you're bringing here?' he asked.

Elroy didn't respond.

'This is the fentanyl,' Ziad continued. 'This is what we're supplying Cresci with, isn't it? This is what it's all been about. Spreading death.'

His eyes were wild and his pupils were as large as poppy bulbs.

Elroy smiled reassuringly. 'Don't think about that now. We need you to get on your feet. We have to leave.'

Ziad carried on as though Elroy hadn't spoken. 'I want them to have it.' Tears started flooding down his cheeks. 'Every single one of them. I want every American to feel this.' His voice trembled with the force of his fury. 'I want them all to share my joy.'

Chapter 87

Pearce was in his room at the New La Hacienda Motel, where he was using a cell phone he'd purchased from a twenty-four-hour convenience store on Lucille Street to call Seattle hospitals to see whether they'd admitted anyone matching Leila's description. He was part way through a call when he heard movement outside and hung up. He grabbed a Glock G19 from an open flight case and moved to the door. He crept behind it as it opened, the street lamp in the car park casting the intruder's shadow into the room. Pearce recognized it immediately.

'Lyly,' he said, startling Leila as he stepped out from behind the door.

Kyle Wollerton and Robert Clifton were with her.

'Come in,' Pearce told them, and once they were inside, he greeted Wollerton warmly. 'Glad you made it out. What happened?'

Wollerton gave Clifton a cagey glance.

'Really?' Clifton challenged. 'You think you can't trust me after what I just did?'

'What did he just do?' Pearce asked.

'Got us out of a jam,' Wollerton replied.

Leila looked exhausted as she hobbled over to the desk and

sat in the chair. 'We need a proper debrief,' she said, picking up a pad and pen. 'We've each got pieces of this. Let's see if we can put the puzzle together.'

Chapter 88

Brigitte Attali flinched when she woke to find a flight attendant leaning over her.

'I'm sorry,' the man said. 'I was trying to check your belt without waking you.'

Brigitte lifted her blanket and showed him the buckle.

'Thanks. You'd better put your seat back up,' he said before moving along the aisle.

Brigitte brought her seat up and squinted as blinds were raised throughout the cabin, flooding it with dazzling sunlight. The plane was diving and banking and she could see swollen grey clouds gathered over the city. She stretched and sat up straight. The elderly couple who'd been her neighbours all the way from Beijing caught her eye and smiled. She'd been an antisocial companion and had slept the entire flight. She'd missed her original connection and had been terrified the Red Wolves had discovered her subterfuge when Chinese border control had taken her aside for questioning. But it had been a routine spot check for coronavirus – maybe because she looked unwell? After two negative tests, they'd let her go. However, she'd missed her flight and had to wait another twenty-four hours for the next one, which had cut into the precious time the patch would keep her alive.

Echo had been right. Apart from a mild sensation that she

was swaddled in a feel-good blanket, the effects of the fentanyl were now muted. Her heart skipped with momentary panic.

What if the synthetic hormone has also stopped working?

You'd already be dead, she told herself.

The plane touched down and Brigitte went through immigration, but her nerves didn't really start playing up until the Homeland Security officer checked her declaration and waved her through customs. There was nothing stopping her now. She had no excuse not to make the call, but she was afraid they wouldn't take it. She had to assume they knew what she'd done to Wollerton by now, and that they'd consider her a traitor.

She swallowed heavily and went through the sliding doors into the arrivals hall, which was packed with early morning travellers meeting their drivers and loved ones. She found a quiet spot beneath a high staircase, took her Ghostlink out of her holdall, and made the call.

Chapter 89

Pearce woke to the sound of the tri-tone coming from his Ghostlink. Wollerton stirred as Pearce reached for the device. Clifton was out cold, lying on the roll-away bed. Pearce grabbed the Ghostlink from the bedside table, slid out of bed and stepped over Wollerton, who had slept on the floor by the bathroom. No matter how much Pearce had insisted, the stubborn mule had refused to take the bed.

Wollerton had told them about what Brigitte had done in China and how angry he was not only at the betrayal, but at the ease with which he'd allowed himself to be tricked. Best case, she was working a con without telling him. Worst case, she'd sold him out.

Leila had filled them in on the corrupt Seattle police detective, Evan Hill, and the other uniforms that seemed to be on the payroll of whoever was pulling Hill's strings.

Pearce had told them about Ziad Malek, Rasul, Essi and Deni Salamov and the two chemical attacks he'd survived, at least one of which had been carried out by Narong Angsakul. Leila had seen Narong at the disused bike repair shop where Clifton had rescued her and Wollerton, and they'd started working on other links between the players. Pearce had given Clifton a description of the gunman and woman he'd seen in the van outside the community centre, complete with a rundown of all the distinctive tattoos he could remember. Clifton had relayed the information to an NSA contact and was waiting to hear the results of their search.

Pearce shut the bathroom door, and answered the Ghostlink. There were only three other people in the world who had access to the communication system. One was asleep outside the bathroom and the second was in the neighbouring room.

'Go ahead,' he said.

'*It's me*,' Brigitte responded, her distinctive voice unmistakeable.

'Yeah.'

'*I'm at the airport,*' she replied. '*I need help, Scott. I need to talk to you alone.*'

'Why should I trust you?'

'*Because I can tell you exactly what this is all about.*'

Chapter 90

Leila Nahum sat at her desk, which was covered in equipment and scraps of paper. She had been staring at her laptop for the past two minutes, wondering what to do with the secrets it had revealed.

She'd slept for a little over an hour before inspiration had struck and she'd accessed the Seattle Police Department network to run a search of the arrest records of the two police officers she'd killed.

Her hunch had been rewarded with a five-year-old arrest report for Eddie and Kirsty Fletcher, the leaders of a motorcycle gang that had once been known as the Reapers, but which had become part of an outfit called the Red Wolves a few years ago. The husband and wife duo had been arrested on suspicion of supplying opiates. Jared Lowe and Dean Ollander had assisted on the arrest, which had been led by Detective Evan Hill. Eddie and Kirsty's mugshots and distinguishing marks matched the description of the people Pearce had seen in the van outside the community centre. Leila had checked the other officers Hill had worked with and had identified the three men Clifton had shot, and the four cops who'd turned up as she and Wollerton had followed the former NSA director to freedom.

She had been staring at the information, trying to figure

out what to do. Detective Evan Hill appeared to be running a crew of corrupt cops, but that wasn't what was fazing her. It was the photos he'd shown her of the day Artem Vasylyk had died. How could she tell Pearce there might be a link between the Red Wolves and Black Thirteen without confessing her role in the Ukrainian billionaire's death?

A knock at the door robbed Leila of any further opportunity to procrastinate. She closed her laptop and got to her feet, leaning on the cheap motel furniture as she shuffled across the room. She picked up the pistol she'd placed on the windowsill and opened the door to find Pearce fully dressed.

'Did I wake you?' he asked.

She shook her head.

'I'm going to the airport. Brigitte Attali's here.'

Leila was surprised. 'It could be a trap.'

'At an airport? Not a good place for guns. You know that.'

'What about an airborne toxin?' Leila asked.

Pearce hesitated. 'She says she knows why they're doing this. I've got to take the risk.'

'OK,' Leila nodded. 'But if you're going to be dumb enough to walk into a trap, I'm dumb enough to come with you.'

'She said I should come alone.'

'I'll stay out of your way,' Leila said.

Pearce smiled wryly. 'And if I refuse?'

'I'll get Wollerton,' Leila replied. 'I'm sure he'd want to come.'

Pearce pursed his lips.

'It'll give us a chance to talk,' Leila said, reaching for her collapsible cane. 'There's something I need to tell you.'

Chapter 91

Pearce glanced at Leila, but she wouldn't meet his gaze, and had her eyes fixed on the early morning traffic that was building up on the 405 Highway. The road was slick with rainwater, and heavy drops hammered the roof. Up ahead, vehicles were filtering to one lane to avoid an accident that involved half a dozen cars. Officers and paramedics were on the scene, and a couple of uniformed cops were directing traffic in their ponchos.

'Why didn't you tell me?' Pearce asked. 'I could have . . . you should have said something.'

Leila didn't respond and Pearce tried to work through the implications of what he'd just learned. A group of corrupt Seattle police detectives was working with the leaders of a notorious biker gang to take over the Salamovs' drug business, and a Thai assassin was killing people to ensure they succeeded. And then there was the death of Artem Vasylyk. How was a Seattle police detective even in a position to exploit something that had been kept secret from the Metropolitan Police? Leila had confessed to shooting Artem Vasylyk in London after discovering a sophisticated communications system in his office, and the two men she'd killed in self-defence seemed to be corrupt cops who worked for Evan Hill. The crooked detective had tried to use these things to intimidate her into revealing who she was working for. Why was he so interested in the identity of their employer? It had been a feature of the Black Thirteen investigation too. Robert Kemp and his unit had gone to great lengths to try to learn their client's true identity. The connections across three continents suggested a conspiracy that went beyond the smuggling of fentanyl into America.

And as troubling as all the revelations were, Pearce was also worried about what they meant for his relationship with Leila. She hadn't felt able to trust him with her role in Artem Vasylyk's death, and had kept vital information from him because she'd been worried about how it might have been used against her. But if she didn't trust him, how could he trust her? How could he be certain she wasn't holding something else back?

'I couldn't, Scott,' she said at last. 'I just couldn't.'

Pearce tried to separate the personal from the professional. Yes, he was hurt by her lack of trust, but the professional implications were far more serious. She'd withheld vital intelligence. The fact Artem Vasylyk was receiving communications from someone else pointed to a larger conspiracy, and if they'd had a chance to examine the comms machine Leila found in his office, they might have been able to discover the sender's identity. According to Leila, the machine was now in GCHQ, being picked over by their analysts.

'I don't know what to say,' Pearce replied.

So they drove on with nothing but the heavy rain breaking the silence. They passed a handful of twisted, buckled vehicles that blocked two lanes of the highway. Rain-soaked drivers gathered on the shoulder and gave statements to the police, while a few of those involved in the pile-up were checked by paramedics. Other drivers slowed to stare at the miserable scene, but Pearce wasn't interested. He was trying to figure out how he could ever trust Leila again.

Chapter 92

Brigitte looked up at the biplane that hung from the high ceiling. She was sitting in a row of seats that were tucked under a large staircase which rose through the huge arrivals hall. People gathered in the vast space, waiting to greet travellers. The man next to her was on his phone, and scrolled through Facebook, pausing only to play inane viral videos. The woman to Brigitte's left was reading an Anthony Horowitz novel. The blue and grey biplane was supposed to be some kind of inspirational link to the early days of flight, but it just made Brigitte maudlin. Those earliest planes had been used to drop chemical weapons on troops in the First World War, and here she was more than a hundred years later dealing with the consequences of the same evil. Would men ever stop developing foul ways to kill each other in their quest for power?

Brigitte leaned forward and rubbed her face. Her skin wasn't as sensitive as it used to be and it felt as though someone else was touching her. She guessed she was experiencing the numbing effects of the fentanyl.

'You OK?' a voice asked, and she looked up to see Scott Pearce standing over her.

'Not really,' Brigitte said. She glanced round, scanning for danger, and spotted Leila Nahum leaning against the metal rail of the mezzanine balcony above them. 'What I've got to say is for your ears only.' She looked pointedly at Leila.

'OK,' Pearce said, leading her to a vacant table in a nearby coffee concession. They were directly below the balcony and out of Leila's sight. 'Kyle says you betrayed him.'

'I did it to get inside,' Brigitte replied as she sat down. 'They had us under surveillance. It was the only way I could make progress. And I couldn't tell him about it, because I needed his reaction to be believable. And mine too. I knew they'd interrogate me, so I used self-hypnosis and neurolinguistics to convince myself of the betrayal, but I didn't turn, Scott, not for real. I slipped the knife in his pocket and made sure they took his false papers, credit cards and money in the van with him, so he could use them to escape the country. You know me well enough to know he'd never have got out if I'd really turned.'

Pearce considered her words, but she wasn't interested in his approval.

'It's not important whether you believe me or not,' Brigitte continued. 'This is what matters.' She checked they weren't being watched and pulled up her sleeve to reveal a black patch on her shoulder.

'What is it?' Pearce asked.

'This is what it's all about,' Brigitte answered. 'Life. Death. This thing controls both.'

Chapter 93

Twenty-five minutes after she'd shown him the patch, Pearce sat back and looked at the Frenchwoman. Her eyes glistened and for a moment she looked as though her spirit had been broken. He reached across the table and touched her arm reassuringly. She recoiled instantly, as though she'd been stung. She sat upright and drew a mask over her emotions. A couple of breaths later and she'd returned to her icy self and looked at him with fierce indignation.

'This is why I don't want the others to know,' she said. 'They'd treat me like I'm sick. Pity.' She spat the word. 'Sympathy. They're not my style. I told you because you're like me. You're a pragmatist.'

Pearce wasn't sure he'd have her strength. How could she even think of being pragmatic in the face of such horror? If he reached across the table and removed that patch, she'd be dead within moments. What a curse to live with.

He'd been right to suspect there was more to the plot than fentanyl. Pearce had never heard of the Red Wolves before, but there was no doubt this was a geopolitical play. This thing they'd created, this weapon, could be used to enslave hundreds of thousands of people, millions perhaps. It was a tool they could use to blackmail governments, holding their victims hostage to the supply of the patches, or they could simply commit mass murder on a terrifying scale, by refusing to provide new product.

There was no way this stuff could ever be allowed to reach America.

'How long do you have before the dose runs out?' Pearce asked.

'Three or four days,' Brigitte said. 'At least that's what they told me.'

'Then we'd better get moving.' Pearce stood, and they walked into the main arrivals hall. He looked up at Leila – another problem, but one that could wait. He nodded at her to signal the all clear, and she started towards the stairs.

'We're going to need a piece of your patch,' Pearce said to Brigitte. 'I want to give it to Clifton. See if we can put Huxley Blaine Carter's resources to good use. They might be able to replicate the synthetic hormone.'

Brigitte nodded, but Pearce sensed little hope in her.

They waited for Leila to join them, and as she limped across the hall, leaning on her collapsible cane, she eyed Brigitte with hostility.

'Well?' Leila asked.

'She's good,' Pearce said. 'We're up against a clock.'

Leila nodded, but her expression didn't change. It was clear she didn't trust Brigitte, and she was right to be suspicious. The Frenchwoman's tale might have been a ruse to get her back inside the team. As they left the airport, Pearce wondered just how much he could trust either of his companions.

Chapter 94

Pearce went into the motel room first. Wollerton was lying on the bed, watching TV. The bathroom door was closed and the shower was running. Wollerton looked round as Pearce entered.

'Where did you . . .' he cut himself off when he saw Brigitte, and after taking a moment to digest the situation, he leaped to his feet.

'Start talking,' he said sternly.

'I'm sorry,' Brigitte replied.

'She set you up to get inside,' Pearce explained.

'You had no right,' Wollerton said to Brigitte. 'How can we trust her?'

'We don't have to trust her,' Pearce replied. 'We just have to listen.'

The shower stopped.

'Even if she's telling the truth, she gambled with my life,' Wollerton said. 'If I hadn't—'

'If you hadn't what?' Brigitte cut in. 'Had a knife? Had your false identities? Your credit cards? Money? I helped you escape.'

Wollerton hesitated.

The bathroom door opened and Robert Clifton stepped

out, wrapped in a towel. He did a double take when he saw the stand-off.

Brigitte surprised them all by barging past Pearce and jumping over the bed. She grabbed Clifton and hurled him against the wall.

'You son of a bitch,' she yelled. 'What have you got us into?'

'I . . . I don't . . .' Clifton stammered.

Wollerton looked perplexed, and Pearce crossed the room and tried to pull Brigitte off the man, but she resisted. Leila entered and shut the door behind her.

'You sent us over there totally unprepared,' Brigitte said. 'You knew what we were up against, and you sent us there alone.'

'I didn't,' Clifton protested. 'You know what I know.'

'Really?' Brigitte challenged. 'Why was Huxley's father killed? What was Tate Blaine Carter doing? How did Huxley know about Black Thirteen? About Narong Angsakul and the Egyptian prison break?'

'Systems,' Clifton responded fearfully. 'Algorithms. He watches the world for this sort of thing.'

'Why?' Brigitte asked.

There was a moment of silence. Brigitte had asked all the right questions and had shifted attention from herself to the former NSA director and his paymaster. If she was playing Pearce and the others, she was doing it masterfully. Pearce believed her, but he couldn't rule out the possibility the Red Wolves were using the patch as leverage to force her to betray them.

'They did things to me over there,' Brigitte said. 'Things . . .' she tailed off. 'I wasn't prepared. None of us were.'

She looked at Wollerton, who nodded sympathetically.

'I'm sorry,' Clifton replied. 'I don't know anything else. I swear. We're trying our best to figure out what's going on.'

'But you know it's bigger than who controls the drugs coming through the Port of Seattle,' Pearce suggested.

Clifton nodded. 'We all know that.'

'There's a geopolitical angle,' Pearce said, finally managing to pull Brigitte away.

The fight had left her and she looked as though she might cry. No one else would understand her emotional turmoil. They might think she'd been tortured, but they'd have no idea she was living with a death sentence.

'Brigitte discovered an organization called the Red Wolves. Chinese ultranationalists who've developed a chemical weapon that's delivered via fentanyl patches. It attacks the endocrinal system and shuts down the production of PTH, which leads to death through suffocation in seconds. It's the toxin used in the prison break and the Meals Seattle and community centre attacks. The patch delivers a synthetic hormone that replaces PTH, but the moment the dose runs out or the patch is removed . . .' Pearce left the implication hanging. 'The Red Wolves have sought control of the West Coast drugs business so they can get this stuff out to hundreds of thousands of addicts across America.'

There was a moment of stunned silence.

'This information came at great personal cost,' Pearce said, as Brigitte stepped into the bathroom and shut the door.

'They could hold entire nations hostage,' Clifton remarked.

Pearce nodded. 'Or kill thousands by cutting off the supply.'

Wollerton whistled. 'We need to take this in. FBI. NSA.'

'Brigitte said they'd compromised Chinese Intelligence,'

Pearce replied. He saw Clifton agreeing with him. 'And Black Thirteen proved MI6 has been infiltrated.'

'Yeah, but this is different. We're not talking about a few hundred lives; we're talking about thousands. Hundreds of thousands maybe,' Wollerton protested.

Pearce glanced at Leila darkly, and she looked away. 'We think there's a link between the two operations; Black Thirteen and the Red Wolves.'

'You're kidding,' Wollerton said.

'I wish I was,' Pearce replied. 'So we've got to assume there's a chance US Intelligence has been infiltrated.'

'By who?' Wollerton asked. 'You're talking about state-level intervention. There's only a handful of organizations in the world that could pull off operations like this.'

Pearce shrugged.

'That's what we need to find out,' Clifton said.

The bathroom door opened, and Brigitte entered, carrying a glass. There was a tiny cutting from the patch in the bottom. 'I was able to get this. It's a piece of one of the fentanyl patches,' she said. She took it to Clifton, who shrank back. 'Huxley has labs. Get his people to analyse this. Find out how it works. If we can't stop the Red Wolves, the world is going to need a way to cure people who've been exposed to the patch.'

Clifton hesitated.

'The powder is airborne. The patches work by touch,' Brigitte told him. 'As long as you don't touch it, it can't hurt you.'

Clifton nodded and took the glass. 'I can get this to one of Hux's facilities in San Francisco. He's going to need to know about what's happened.'

'And since it seems we can all trust each other again,'

Pearce remarked, 'we should move back to the building on Union Street. It'll make a better base of operations than this place. And we're going to need every advantage we can get if we're going to work out a way to stop the Red Wolves.'

Chapter 95

Two hours later, they were gathered around Leila's desk in the large open-plan space on the fifteenth floor of Huxley Blaine Carter's building on Union Street. Clifton had arranged a chopper and was en route to San Francisco with the piece of Brigitte's patch.

Leila sat in the chair by her laptop, and Wollerton leaned against her desk. Brigitte was cross-legged on the floor, looking utterly fatigued. Pearce could only imagine the stress of living with a ticking clock. She had three days in which to replace the patch or find another way to keep herself alive.

'The formula is controlled by two men,' Brigitte said. 'Li Jun Xiao and David Song. No one else knows it. They murdered the scientist who developed the XTX toxin and the synthetic hormone.'

'So we kill them and destroy the production plant and this stuff dies with them,' Wollerton remarked.

'What about the shipment?' Leila asked. 'We can't let it reach the streets. If we destroy the supply, anyone who's been exposed to it will die.'

Pearce stopped pacing and looked at Brigitte, who blanched.

'We find out what ship it's coming in on,' Wollerton said. 'And we sink it.'

Pearce's old mentor didn't know it, but he'd just suggested

Brigitte agree to a death sentence. She got to her feet and walked over to the other desk, which was covered with gear. She leaned against it, and Pearce caught Wollerton and Leila exchanging puzzled glances.

'He's right,' Brigitte said at last. 'We've got no way of identifying which container the shipment might be in, or even how many containers they're using. If we miss just one . . .' She hesitated. 'Sinking the ship is the only way to be sure.'

Leila checked her laptop. 'There are fifteen container ships on their way to Seattle from China, all scheduled to dock this week. There's nothing in Ziad Malek's port system that gives any clue to the vessel's identity. We're going to need human intelligence.'

Pearce had been thinking about the problem ever since he'd learned about the nature of the shipment. 'I know someone who might be able to help us,' he said. 'I want you to work up an ops plan for taking out a container ship,' he told Wollerton and Brigitte. 'Get Robert involved. See what resources Blaine Carter can offer us.'

'And me?' Leila asked.

'Pull together everything you can on Evan Hill and his associates,' Pearce replied. 'See if you can link him to the Red Wolves.'

'*Tayib*,' Leila responded reluctantly, using the Arabic word for OK.

'And you?' Wollerton asked.

'I'm going to see an old king,' Pearce replied.

Chapter 96

Pearce caught a cab to Massachusetts Street and collected his bike, which was where he'd left it the day he'd met Rasul and his men. There was no queue outside St Martin's Shelter, but a few men and women gathered in the seating area beside the building, smoking and talking. Most of their faces were prematurely aged and their clothes were ragged and dirty. These were the people who'd be on the front line of the Red Wolves' plot to strike at America, but Pearce wondered how the US government would react. If the plan involved blackmail and the Red Wolves tried to extort money or geopolitical influence, would the government save people many already considered to be lost? Would those in power value the lives of addicts? Or would they let them die?

Pearce was determined the question would never be asked, let alone answered. He pulled on his helmet, kicked his bike into gear and sped across the city to Webster Point, an upmarket neighbourhood where mansions nestled in tree-covered, waterfront plots. High hedges offered the residents a degree of privacy, but as he rode along Laurelhurst Drive, Pearce caught glimpses of Lake Washington and the rich green mountains that towered in the distance.

Pearce found the gate for 3022 Laurelhurst and stopped beside the video intercom. He removed his helmet and pressed the buzzer. Less than a minute later, the high black metal gates swung open.

Pearce rode along a short drive that was lined with evergreens. After a hundred metres, the wood gave way to a large lawn and the drive widened as it came to an end in front of a huge waterfront house. The property stood at the edge of Lake Washington, facing Kirkland and Hunts Point. Down beyond the small back garden, Pearce saw a speedboat bobbing roughly against a jetty – the rain continued unabated, and the chop of the water told of an approaching storm. The Mediterranean-style mansion must have had a footprint of at least five thousand feet, and was two storeys high. Deni and Rasul Salamov were waiting in the driveway with two of their bodyguards. Abbas Idrisov, their wizened financial advisor, hovered by the front door. When the bike stopped, father and son approached, and after Pearce had removed his helmet and dismounted, Deni embraced him.

'You saved my family,' Deni said. 'You saved my people. I owe you everything.'

'I don't know what we would have done without you,' Rasul agreed, shaking Pearce's hand.

'Come inside,' Deni said, ushering Pearce towards the house.

As they crossed the driveway, Pearce saw Essi Salamov at one of the upstairs windows. She was standing beside her lover; the man Ziad had beaten up.

Chapter 97

'Who's the guy?' Jack asked, looking down at the men heading into the house.

'I don't know,' Essi said. Her brother had introduced him as Amr, but somehow she suspected that wasn't the man's real name. He'd intervened to save them at the community centre, and when she looked at her boyfriend of the past few months and recalled how he'd been beaten in the street at the hands of Ziad Malek, she wondered whether he'd have been brave enough to stand up to the man who'd tried to kill them. 'I think he's a friend of my brother. He was the one who saved us at the centre.'

She glanced at Jack and caught him frowning. 'Don't worry, you're still my hero,' she said, but she wasn't sure she meant it.

Jack seemed puzzled for a moment, as though his mind was somewhere else. Then he broke into a smile.

'Do I look worried?' he asked, stepping away from the window. 'How long are we going to be stuck here?'

Essi joined him on the double bed that dominated her room. She hadn't lived at home for years, but her father had kept everything the same, and she was surrounded by posters of Eminem and Pink and programmes for climate-change events. She'd been a dedicated environmentalist as a teen, but her zealotry had worn off when she'd realized how hard it was to get from the coast to the city without a car.

'I don't know,' Essi replied. 'Dad says we should stay here until it's safe.'

'So is this place a fortress or a prison?' Jack joked.

She lay with her back to him and looked out of the rear windows of her dual-aspect room. Dark clouds hung low above the water, which heaved and rolled as though it was drawing in a storm from some distant place.

'You know one of the best ways to amuse yourself when you're bored?' Jack said suggestively. He pulled Essi round to face him and lifted the hem of her dress. He ran his hand up her leg and she leaned forward and kissed him.

Chapter 98

Pearce, Deni and Rasul were in a study that overlooked the lake. French doors, closed against the weather, looked onto a terraced garden that was abundant and beautiful. The room was lined with packed bookshelves and at its heart were two Chesterfield leather couches that faced each other. There were no signs of Deni's heritage anywhere. The room could have belonged to any moneyed American. Pearce sat next to Abbas, opposite the Chechen gang boss and his son, and told them what he knew about the Red Wolves. He didn't mention that the fentanyl they were smuggling was actually a chemical weapon.

'So this has been about taking our business?' Abbas asked.

Pearce nodded.

'I know these bikers you speak of. They used to be called the Reapers,' Deni said. 'They're fucking amateurs. Village pushers. And that cop, Hill, he's a nickel and dimer. He came to me years ago, offering protection. I have his fucking bosses in my pocket. They're gonna put the hurt on him.'

'This is being run by the Red Wolves,' Pearce said. 'They're well-financed and highly organized.'

'And Ziad?' Rasul asked. 'I saw him with them at the community centre. He betrayed us.'

'Looks like it,' Pearce replied.

'Why?' Deni said. 'I treated him like a son. He was dating my daughter. It broke my heart when he was arrested in Cairo.'

'Maybe he blames you for the arrest,' Pearce suggested.

'Bullshit!' Deni exclaimed. 'Why would we do that? We sent him to Egypt to open a new supply route. It was supposed to cut our costs if we could bring product through Suez and Panama.'

'Why would we betray him?' Rasul asked. 'It broke my sister.'

'We treated Ziad Malek like family,' Abbas confirmed.

'Who arranged the trip?' Pearce asked, studying the two men.

Were they telling the truth?

'We did,' Deni responded.

'True,' Rasul said. 'But Jack Gray suggested it.'

'Jack Gray?' Pearce asked.

'Our attorney. My sister's new boyfriend. He said we could save a lot of money using the Suez route. He and Essi started dating after Ziad . . .' Rasul tailed off. He and his father shared a look of disbelief. 'He was the one who suggested we send Ziad.'

Pearce followed the two men upstairs. He could feel their fury radiating in hot pulses that seemed to grow more intense with each hurried step. They raced through the house and Rasul tried a closed door, which was locked. He stepped back and barged it open, and he and Deni spilled into what looked like a teenager's bedroom. Pearce followed and saw Essi naked. She was straddling Jack Gray. She screamed and grabbed the bedspread.

'Get out!' she yelled as she wrapped herself in the cover.

But Deni and Rasul ignored Essi and bore down on Jack, who scrabbled for his clothes.

'What the hell is going on?' he demanded.

'You're coming with us,' Rasul snarled, before punching the man and knocking him cold.

Chapter 99

The dazed, naked man moaned as they propped him up on a chair. Rasul used a thick cord to bind him, and Deni loomed over their captive. Pearce stood a few paces back, near a gym that took up much of Deni Salamov's basement. Light coming through the high windows cast long shadows everywhere, and Essi hugged the darkness by the door. Unlike her boyfriend, she was now dressed, and Pearce could see conflicting emotions playing out on her face.

'Dad, please don't do this,' she said.

'You can go,' Deni responded calmly. 'But this man is staying. He will tell us the truth.'

'If he didn't betray us, he has nothing to fear,' Rasul added.

Essi bit her lip and Pearce thought she would cry, but there were no tears.

Deni slapped Jack, and he came to his senses.

'What the fuck are you doing?' he asked, pulling against the cord.

Deni crouched down and looked him in the eye. 'You have one chance to tell me the truth, before my son goes to work.'

Essi blanched.

'I don't know what you're talking about,' Jack replied.

Deni nodded at Rasul, who drove a fist into Jack's face. The man's head snapped back before falling limp. A few more of those and they'd kill him.

Pearce noticed Essi had started weeping.

'Let me try,' he said, crossing the room. 'I'm not sure how much more of that he'll take. I have some experience of interrogation from the army.'

Rasul glanced at Deni, who nodded.

Pearce lifted Jack's head. The man stank of sweat and fear. 'You got a blade?' Pearce asked Rasul, who nodded and produced a butterfly knife.

Pearce opened it and checked the edge. It was sharp. He turned to Jack and pressed the point against the man's thigh. Not hard enough to break the skin, but sufficient to bring the man round.

'Please let me go,' Jack whined.

'You tell these men what they want to know and I won't cut you,' Pearce replied, brandishing the knife.

'I didn't sign up for this,' Jack said, his voice trembling. 'I'm a lawyer, not a fucking gangster.'

Rasul scoffed.

'You can leave any time,' Pearce said. 'All you have to do is tell the truth.'

Jack fell silent. He looked across the basement at Essi, who couldn't hold his gaze. 'Ess, please,' he implored her. 'Please don't let them do this.'

'Don't look at her,' Pearce said, turning Jack's head to face him. 'Look at this.' He signalled the blade. 'Think about how it will feel when I cut you open.'

Jack whimpered. 'They said they'd kill me.'

'They're not here,' Pearce countered. 'I am.'

'You fucking bitch,' Jack yelled at Essi. 'You're supposed

to love me. You just gonna stand there? Once a fucking dirty—'

Pearce drove the knife into Jack's leg, near where the thigh and knee met. It wasn't a deep incision, but it didn't need to be, the area was packed with nerves. Jack shrieked, jerked back, and almost toppled over.

'I told you not to look at her,' Pearce said.

Jack's face was the colour of snow, and tears rolled down his cheeks, which were inflating and deflating rapidly with each hurried breath. 'I don't know how they knew I'm your lawyer,' he said to Deni, his voice teetering on the verge of breaking. 'But they did. They started small, offering me cash for little bits of information.'

Deni grimaced and Rasul started towards the captive, but Pearce held him back.

'It wasn't anything important. The names of your businesses. Where you hung out. They gave me a lot of money. It didn't seem so bad. Nothing a half-decent private investigator couldn't have found out.' Jack took a deep breath. 'Get me a bandage!' he said, looking down at his leg.

Pearce shook his head. 'Things get better when you've talked.'

Jack sighed and brought his breathing under control. 'Then they wanted more. And they threatened to expose me. They said they'd tell you I'd been working for them. They forced me to tell them everything I knew about your operation.'

Pearce glanced over and saw Essi sobbing.

'Ziad,' she lamented softly.

'Everything we had,' Jack shouted at her. 'It was all real. Everything.'

Pearce gripped the man's cheeks hard, and looked him in the eye. 'Me. You're talking to me.'

'They told me about Egypt,' Jack revealed. 'They said I should convince you to send Ziad out there.'

'Did you know they were planning to have him arrested?' Essi asked, moving across the room.

Jack looked at Pearce pleadingly. 'They had me by then. If they'd exposed me . . .' He glanced at Deni and Rasul, who were watching him murderously. 'They told me to get you to change your phone numbers and email addresses. To say they'd been compromised by Ziad's arrest. That way he couldn't reach you. And when he tried to make contact with me, I was to tell him you'd disowned him. They made me do it,' he whined.

Pearce marvelled at the simplicity of the set-up. Using Jack as the go-between meant he could control what Ziad was told. Whoever was behind this operation truly understood human nature. Send Ziad to prison and make him believe the Salamovs had set him up and he'd do almost anything to avenge himself against them.

'Did they tell you to start seeing me?' Essi asked. Her voice had taken on a cold edge.

Jack didn't reply. 'They . . .' he sighed. 'It was real. However it started, it became real.'

'Who's behind this?' Pearce asked. 'Eddie Fletcher? Elroy Lang?'

'Fletcher is just muscle,' Jack replied. 'Elroy is higher up, but there's someone else.'

'Who?' Pearce asked.

Essi paced the area directly behind Pearce. He glanced at her and saw she was no longer weeping. Her face was a mask of pure anger.

'Ziad,' she said. 'You took him from me. You—'

'But we were happy,' Jack protested. 'He's a street thug. I'm a good guy.'

'Talk to *me*,' Pearce said, slapping Jack's face. 'Who is the other guy? Who's calling the shots?'

'Some guy from Ukraine or somewhere like that. Some Eastern European.'

'Name?' Pearce pressed.

'I don't know,' Jack confessed. 'Please. That's all I know.'

'What about the shipment?' Pearce asked.

'What shipment? I don't know anything about any shipment,' Jack said. 'Don't you get it? They used me. They fucking used me. That's all. I'm not part of whatever it is they're doing. Ess,' he looked beyond Pearce at Essi, who glared back. 'Ess, please. You've got to believe me. They used me.'

Essi looked away, and walked over to her father. She collapsed against him and he drew her into a tight embrace.

'Zee,' she sobbed. 'I'm so sorry, Zee. I didn't know.'

'It's OK,' Deni said, stroking her hair.

'Please let me go,' Jack begged. 'You'll never see me again. Please. Don't hurt me.'

'I need to know about the shipment,' Pearce said. 'I need the vessel.'

'I don't know anything about any vessel,' Jack moaned. 'Why can't you people get it through your heads? They used me.'

Pearce sensed movement behind him and turned to see Essi step away from her father. She moved towards Jack, and Pearce saw the gun too late to react. She raised the pistol she'd pilfered from her father's holster and fired two shots into Jack's head.

Chapter 100

Rasul brooded by the French doors. The other side of the lake was lost to heavy rain, which shrouded everything in sheets of grey. Pearce sat on one of the Chesterfields watching the man who'd just seen his sister murder her lover. How did people rationalize this kind of horror? How did they cope with lives that took them so far from mainstream society? Pearce smiled wryly and looked away, suddenly questioning how he rationalized his own life. Taken in isolation, few events in his life made sense, but people's lives weren't snapshots; they were stories, coherent only as a chain of causation. This afternoon's snapshot of Essi's life, her murder of Jack, could have been seen as a brutal execution by a mobster's daughter. But within the context of her story, his death was revenge for betrayal. She'd lost the man she'd loved and been manipulated by the man who'd supplanted him. Her brother and father had been falsely implicated in the betrayal and the damage to their business and all the friends and associates they'd lost had been as a result of Jack Gray's treachery. In that context, his death made perfect sense.

The study door opened, and Deni and Abbas entered, looking grave.

'She's resting,' Deni said. 'Tarek and Waheed have disposed of the body.'

'She killed him before he could tell us the name of the ship,' Rasul responded.

'I don't think he knew,' Pearce remarked. 'He wasn't holding anything back. Not by the end. He would have given up the vessel if he'd known.'

'I've been thinking about that,' Deni said. 'They stole the shipment of my biggest customer. My guess is they did it to create a shortage so he'd do a deal with them. It's what I would have done in my younger days.'

'Cresci?' Rasul asked.

Deni nodded. 'Ben Cresci, the head of the Cresci crime family. He threatened us if we didn't replace his product. Then he went quiet, like we don't matter to him anymore. If he's done a deal with the Red Wolves, he'll know when the ship is arriving. And if we know when it's coming in, it won't be difficult to figure out which ship is carrying their product.'

'How do we reach this Cresci?' Pearce asked.

'We go see him,' Deni replied. 'Tell the men to get the cars ready,' he instructed Rasul.

The Chechen's son nodded and left the room.

Deni turned to Abbas. 'I want you to stay with Essi. Look after her.'

Abbas nodded and left, and Deni took his son's place at the window. Moments later, Pearce's Ghostlink sounded its familiar tri-tone and he answered.

'Go ahead,' he said, aware Deni was watching him.

'*Sure. Uncle NSA is back,*' Leila said, referring to Clifton. '*He and our French friend are working on the operation. They want to know when you'll be home.*'

'Soon,' Pearce said.

'*Kyle and I want to check out the bike repair place where I saw*

368 ADAM HAMDY

Angsakul,' Leila revealed. '*Check if Malek and Elroy are there. Uncle NSA brought some new toys. It'll give me a chance to field-test them.*'

'Eyes only,' Pearce said. 'No engagement.' He hoped she'd have the sense to follow his instruction.

'*Copy that. Stay safe,*' Leila replied, before she hung up.

Pearce pocketed the Ghostlink and looked up to see Deni studying him.

'Cop?' the Chechen asked.

Pearce didn't answer.

'I worked counter-intelligence during the Chechen War,' Deni revealed. 'It looks enough like one to fool most people, but whatever that thing is, it's not a cell phone. And the way you talk, the way you move, the way you handled the interrogation.' He shifted slightly and opened his jacket to reveal his holster, which was now home to a new pistol. 'So I ask again, are you a cop?'

Pearce shook his head.

'Spy?' Deni asked.

'No,' Pearce said. 'I have no interest in you or your organization. I'm here for the people who've tried to destroy you.'

Deni frowned. 'Does Rasul know?'

'No.'

'My family and friends owe you their lives, but if I see you make one move against us, I will kill you,' Deni said. 'I won't even hesitate.'

Pearce stared at the man, who held his gaze, and they stayed locked like that until Rasul entered.

'The cars are ready,' he said. 'Let's go.'

Chapter 101

Pearce followed Deni and Rasul as the old Chechen and his son hurried through the grand hallway towards the front door. A convoy of cars waited outside, but Pearce sensed movement and hesitated. He looked up to see Essi Salamov standing on the landing. She leaned against the balustrade, her eyes distant and unfocused, her body sagging like a drunk's. The effect of a sedative?

'You,' she murmured as her unfocused eyes settled on Pearce.

She tried to move towards the stairs, but stumbled and fell heavily.

Pearce bounded up the wide staircase and hurried over to her. She was disorientated and made ineffective attempts to get up. Pearce crouched to help her.

'Ziad,' she said, and for a moment Pearce thought she'd confused him with her ex, but she pressed something into his hands. 'Give this to him.'

Pearce looked down to see a crumpled envelope.

'*Ya* Essi,' Abbas called out, and Pearce turned to see the old man coming up the stairs. He slipped the envelope into his pocket and helped Essi to her feet.

'She fell,' Pearce told Abbas.

'Are you coming, Amr?' Rasul yelled from the front door.

Pearce handed Essi to Abbas and hurried downstairs.

'Tell him I'm sorry,' Essi called out, as he left the building. 'I'm sorry.'

Chapter 102

Pearce was in the second vehicle in a convoy of three. There were four men in the lead car and three more in the trailing SUV. Pearce was travelling with Deni, Rasul and Tarek, who was driving them through the treacherous storm. The wipers were working furiously, but they did little to mitigate the effects of the downpour. The road ahead was a glittering starfield of red and white lights, all inching along in the slow traffic. Heavy clouds had brought night early to Seattle, and the streets were devoid of pedestrians. The rain was too heavy and the winds too strong for all but the foolhardiest.

Rasul had briefed Pearce on Ben Cresci, the head of a massive narcotics business, who used a food distribution front to smuggle product throughout the West Coast and Midwest. Deni and Cresci had been in business for six years, ever since the Chechen had established a connection to Afghanistan. Deni couldn't give an accurate estimate of the number of people Cresci supplied, but guessed it was hundreds of thousands. Rasul said Cresci moved enough product to supply the population of a large city. He could be selling to millions throughout his territory. The Cresci operation was the perfect way for the Red Wolves to distribute their toxin.

The journey from Laurelhurst to Roosevelt took over an hour. Their destination wasn't more than four miles away, but the storm had caused mayhem. There couldn't have been many gyms in the world that had bouncers, but when the convoy stopped outside the three-storey building on 65th Street, Pearce saw this was one of them. Four men in black satin bomber jackets huddled under an awning that proudly announced this was Roosevelt Boxing, the home of Seattle's own welterweight champion, Bobby Ivan. Tarek stopped the car directly opposite the entrance, and Pearce saw the bouncers fan out a little. The two closest the door reached inside their jackets.

'Cresci's kid is a contender,' Rasul explained. 'His dad comes here almost every night to watch him train.'

Deni and Rasul stepped into the rain, and Pearce followed them. Three men from the lead and two from the trailing vehicle stepped onto the sidewalk and eyed the bouncers menacingly. Deni and Rasul hurried forward and as they reached the awning, two of the bouncers stopped them and patted them down. Pearce was thoroughly frisked by a third. They took Deni's gun and a pistol and knife from Rasul. Pearce had nothing but his Ghostlink.

'You two are OK,' the nearest bouncer said. 'But him we don't know.'

All eyes fell on Pearce.

'Your boss is going to want to hear what I've got to say,' he replied. 'Even *they* don't know the whole story.'

One of the bouncers stepped away and spoke into a lapel mic, and Deni watched Pearce suspiciously as they waited beneath the awning. The bouncer returned and nodded.

'You can go up,' he said.

One of the men held the door open and as they went inside

Pearce noticed it was three inches thick and reinforced with steel. These people were ready for serious trouble.

'What don't we know?' Deni asked as they climbed the stairs. Pearce didn't answer, and the Chechen grabbed him and pinned him to the wall. 'I told you what would happen. One move. Just one move.'

Pearce held the man's gaze. 'We can waste time here, or we can go inside and you can find out exactly what I know.' There was no way he was risking being locked out of the room by sharing the secret too soon.

'Dad?' Rasul asked. 'What the hell's going on?'

Deni didn't reply, but he released Pearce and led them up the stairs to a reception area. The guy behind the counter had the lean, hard look of an ex-military man, and he gestured at a set of double doors, which he unlocked with a remote control. Pearce pulled one of the doors open and stepped inside a huge, state-of-the-art boxing gym.

Strong, fit, ambitious men trained in a free-weights area. Others worked maize balls and heavy punchbags. Some did rope or pad work, and half a dozen were sparring in three full-sized rings in the heart of the space. The gym was alive with the sounds of exertion, and beneath the grunts and cries was an up-tempo dance track. Freshly laundered towels were piled next to a water cooler, and beside them was a stack of coronavirus tests, ubiquitous in any public setting since the pandemic.

Pearce didn't need Cresci pointed out to him. A trim man in his early forties, Cresci wore a light suit with wide lapels. He had a ponytail, a thick moustache and large tinted sunglasses that made him look like a throwback to the seventies. He sat in one of two worn armchairs on a raised platform beside the centre ring. The platform was surrounded by six men in tailored suits, whose shark-like eyes swept the room in every direction. One of the men noticed Deni, hurried up to Cresci and whispered in his ear. Cresci gave an unmistakeable look of irritation when he glanced in their direction.

'Keep your gloves up!' he yelled at a young guy in the ring.

Pearce assumed the kid was Cresci's son. He had the same eyes, but was even leaner than his father. From the brief exchange he saw, Pearce could tell Cresci junior was light on his feet and could throw a solid punch. He looked as though he was making his opponent suffer.

Cresci walked down a run of steps and came over. 'You clean?' he asked before he got too close.

Deni nodded. 'Tested yesterday,' he replied.

Cresci looked at Pearce and Rasul, who both nodded.

'I'm sorry to hear about your troubles,' he said, drawing near. 'These things are bad for business.'

'Thank you, Ben,' Deni replied. 'We need to talk. It seems we've all been made fools of.'

Cresci studied Deni for a moment. 'OK,' he said. 'I can give you five.'

Chapter 103

The locker room had been emptied and there were two of Cresci's men stationed by the door to prevent any interruptions. Every now and again, they cast suspicious glances at Pearce, Deni and Rasul.

'So?' Cresci prompted.

'Can we talk freely here?' Deni asked, signalling their surroundings.

'Sure. We sweep the place once a week.'

'Remember you said we had to replace your product?' Deni began.

'Yeah. About that,' Cresci said, 'I might be able to give you more time.'

'Because you found another supplier?'

'You think I'm going to sit on my hands? You should be glad I did,' Cresci remarked. 'Otherwise we'd be having a serious problem. I can't sit by just because you got ripped off by East Hill.'

Deni shook his head and Rasul smiled darkly.

'It was the Red Wolves,' Deni corrected. 'We think they sold the product to East Hill to frame them.'

'The Red Wolves?' Cresci said incredulously.

'We think they're planning to use you and your distribution network,' Pearce said.

'Use me to do what?' Cresci asked.

'I believe they're going to attack America.'

'With blow?' Cresci scoffed. 'Who the fuck are you?'

Pearce sensed the men by the door shift in his direction.

'I don't know who this nutcase is, but the world keeps turning,' Cresci said to Deni. 'We had a good run, but I can't wait for you to get control of your business.'

'Did Ziad Malek approach you?' Pearce asked. 'Is he your resupply?'

Cresci's eyes narrowed and he studied Pearce closely.

'Did he offer you fentanyl?'

'You brought some kind of mind-reader into your outfit?' he asked Deni, before turning to Pearce. 'Look, I don't like synthetics, but my people have been trying to persuade me of the benefits for a while, and junkies don't give a shit. They just want to get high. They don't care whether the gear came out of the ground or a lab. So I cut a deal that keeps my business in operation.'

'What ship is it coming in on?' Pearce asked.

'Why? Are you going to rip them off?' Cresci scoffed.

'We're going to sink it,' Pearce replied earnestly, surprising Deni and Rasul almost as much as Cresci.

'You're what? Who the fuck is this clown?' Cresci asked the Chechen.

Deni was about to answer, but Pearce cut him off. 'You know the Midas Killer? You know the attacks on the Meals Seattle warehouse and Mr Salamov's community centre?'

'I was sorry to hear about that,' Cresci said.

'The toxin used in those attacks knocks out the parathyroid glands and causes people to suffocate. Every single dose of fentanyl you've bought is laced with the stuff. You've ordered a shipment of poison, Mr Cresci. These people are using you to hurt America.'

'What the . . .'

'I've been on the trail of a Thai national,' Pearce said, producing a photograph of Narong Angsakul. 'This is the Midas Killer. This is the man who attacked the community centre. I believe he was behind the Meals Seattle deaths.' Pearce showed Cresci a photo of Ziad Malek and Elroy Lang getting into the car outside Al Aqarab Prison. 'And this man, Elroy Lang, helped Ziad Malek escape from prison. They killed more than seventy people that day. They're planning to distribute the same toxin throughout America.'

Cresci's confusion and disbelief hardened into anger. 'That motherfu—'

'We believe they're using you,' Pearce said.

'We?' Cresci asked, suddenly suspicious.

'I'm not a cop, Mr Cresci. Beyond this shipment, I have no interest in what you do.'

Cresci studied the photos of Narong. 'He came to see me with Malek. Claimed to represent the Chinese manufacturers.' He turned to Deni. 'I thought Malek was an opportunist. You know how these things are. A young buck sees an opening and an empire is born.'

'We just need to know when the shipment is coming in,' Pearce said.

Cresci smiled. 'You're going to sink it?'

Pearce nodded.

'And the Red Wolves? You have any issue with them meeting with a hundred fucking ugly accidents?'

'I'd like to talk to the leaders, Eddie and Kirsty Fletcher,'

Pearce said. 'What happens to the rest of them isn't my concern.'

'OK, then,' Cresci said. 'I can do better than a date. I can give you a name. They're bringing it in on the *Elite Voyager*. It's due to dock tomorrow.'

'It will never arrive,' Pearce assured them.

Chapter 104

Leila watched the image on the monitor. It showed a bird's-eye view of the bike repair shop, its roof pockmarked by rust and decay, as though a giant had taken huge bites out of it. Heavy rain ran down corrugated valleys and poured through the holes.

She and Wollerton were sitting in the back of a modified Ford Transit cargo van, a block away from the building. Clifton had returned with the vehicle from whatever Huxley Blaine Carter facility he'd delivered the fentanyl patch to. The van was a sophisticated surveillance centre with equipment Leila had never encountered before. Clifton had explained that most innovation was taking place in the private sector. Governments had ceased to be at the vanguard of progress. The Hyperloop, space exploration, medical breakthroughs were all privately funded, and one of the most sophisticated intelligence agencies in the world, Mossad, relied on Israel's innovative technology sector to keep it at the forefront of the espionage business. Leila was aware of the role of private industry in the spy business, but some of the gear in the van smacked of nation-state levels of investment. The drone she was piloting, for example, was a tiny craft designed to look like a bumble bee. According to Clifton, research had shown they were the least likely of all flying bugs to get swatted. It was only close up that the device's tiny mechanical legs and synthetic wings became apparent.

Once this investigation was over and she'd found her sister, Leila planned to look into Huxley Blaine Carter's ties to the US intelligence community. Was he really a private citizen motivated by the death of his father? Or a CIA or NSA operative? His connection to Robert Clifton seemed to suggest the latter.

Leila used the intuitive joystick controls to pilot the tiny drone through a hole in the roof. It flew into a large, disused repair shop. There were benches, a few old tools, piles of rubbish, a TV and a couple of tatty chairs. There was a filthy kitchen off to one side and at the back of the warehouse a row of offices separated from the rest of the space by a long panel of frosted glass windows and doors. There were a couple of army surplus cots in two of the offices, but nothing else, and the drone confirmed what the infrared sensor had shown: the warehouse was deserted.

'They'll have cleared out as soon as we escaped,' Wollerton said.

Leila nodded. Her background on the Red Wolves showed the warehouse had once belonged to Lenny Fletcher, Eddie Fletcher's father; a mechanic and founding member of the notorious Reaper gang that had been subsumed by the Red Wolves. The place had passed to Eddie after his father's death, and as she piloted the drone out of the building, Leila considered whether the gang leader knew the horror he was bringing to America.

Chapter 105

Essi Salamov woke suddenly. It was dark and she could hear rain outside. A flash of lightning illuminated the room for a split second, and revealed a figure by her bed. Terror rendered her speechless and the silence was filled by a crack of thunder. She reached a trembling hand towards her beside light, praying the intruder couldn't see her moving. There was a gun in her top drawer, and she pictured herself rolling over and shooting the figure the moment the light came on.

She flipped the switch, yanked open the drawer, grabbed the pistol, turned, and brought the weapon round to shoot the intruder. She stopped suddenly and cried with relief when she saw a familiar face.

'Ziad!' she said. 'You scared me.'

He looked terrible. Tired and drained and soaking wet. He stood watching her, saying nothing.

'I'm so glad you're here, Zee. I wrote you a letter,' Essi said. 'Did you get it? It doesn't matter. I can tell you everything. Come closer.'

She patted the bed, and, after a moment's hesitation, he approached. *Was he crying?*

'It's OK,' Essi said. 'It's OK.'

Tears sprang to her eyes at the thought of Jack's betrayal,

at all the time she and Ziad had lost, at the way she'd treated him. She should have waited. She should have . . . The moment of Jack's death flashed through her mind, and no matter how much she told herself her actions had been justified, she felt sick as she pictured the bloody holes she'd made in his head. She'd taken another life. The life of a man who, only a short while before, had been inside her. A man she'd thought of as a lover and friend. She didn't want to cry about another man at her first reunion with Ziad, but she couldn't fight back the heavy tears.

'I'm sorry,' she said, touching Ziad gently on the arm. 'I'm so sorry.'

He was definitely crying now; his eyes were deep pools of sadness and his whole body shook. He leaned forward and Essi thought he was going to embrace her, but he simply reached out and touched her neck. His hand was cold and clammy. *Rainwater, perhaps?* But when she rubbed her neck and examined her fingertips, she saw what looked like toothpaste. It was then she noticed Ziad was wearing flesh-coloured latex gloves.

'Zee,' she said. 'Zee, what . . .' A terrible burning in her lungs cut her off.

The love of her life got to his feet and backed away from the bed as she started to choke. He wept and shook, and Essi tried to find the strength to fight the vice that tightened around her chest. Finally, Ziad turned his back on her.

No, please, no, she screamed inwardly. She just wanted to get three words out. Three simple words. But they wouldn't come.

I love you.

*

Ziad Malek looked at a poster of Eminem while Essi Salamov died. He could hear her rasping and thrashing on the bed, and each horrific sound tore part of his soul, rending chunks out until, when she finally fell still, he was no longer crying. He was numb.

When there was nothing but the sound of rain lashing the window and the crack of distant thunder, Ziad wiped the remnants of his tears and turned to look at the woman he'd loved. The woman who'd conspired with her brother and father to betray him. She was still beautiful, even in death.

Awut had come to the house to kill Deni and Rasul, and Ziad had insisted on joining him so that his revenge against the family would be complete. It was their fault he'd been imprisoned in Al Aqarab, their fault he'd joined forces with the Red Wolves, and their fault he was now burdened with the black mark of death. They'd forced him to become a monster. All because Deni hadn't thought him good enough for his daughter, and Rasul was fearful of a rival within the organization. Jack Gray hadn't said so expressly, but he'd insinuated enough to make it clear the one time Ziad had managed to reach him from Al Aqarab.

He hoped the Salamovs suffered a million agonies as they died, but when he looked at Essi's beautiful face, he felt a pang of regret. Maybe he should have been kinder and just shot her?

Ziad was startled when the bedroom door opened, and he turned to see Abbas Idrisov, the Abacus, hurry into the room fearfully. The terrible sounds of choked screams came through the open doorway. Awut was at work.

'*Masha Allah*,' Abbas said.

The old man properly took in the scene and realized

Essi was dead. He froze in horror and looked at Ziad with
contempt.

'Why?' Abacus asked.

Ziad didn't answer. Whatever good had once resided
within him had died with his love. He simply reached out
and touched the old man's cheek.

As Abbas fell to his knees choking, Awut appeared in
the doorway. The Thai gestured at the choking man and the
corpse on the bed.

'Done here? The guards are taken care of but there's no
sign of the bosses. They'll have to wait; we need to move.'

Ziad followed Awut downstairs without a word, his own
ugly task complete.

Chapter 106

My Darling Zee,

I hope you'll find it in your heart to forgive me. I've done too many terrible things to get through this on my own. I need you. Now, more than ever, I need you.

I had my eyes opened today. It's like they closed when you left and my world became darkness, but they're open now and I see more clearly than ever. The man I thought I loved was a liar and a fraud. Everything that was between us was built on lies and suffering. He told me how he manipulated me and you. He confessed to his role in separating us. I didn't know. I swear. Neither did my father or my brother. We've all been betrayed by someone who wormed his way into our family. And when he had our trust, he struck. I realize I'm not making much sense, but I'm shaking as I write this, and my mind is a mess.

I've done terrible things, Ziad. I can't even bring myself to write about the most recent, and it doesn't matter because it was deserved. But the thing that hurts me most is that I didn't come to find you. I should have gone to Cairo. I should have been with you for your trial. But I was lied to. I was told you didn't want me. I should have known that wasn't true. When you found me at that restaurant, I knew you still loved me. The look in your eyes hadn't changed. I should have known what we have will last forever. And I treated you so poorly. I'm ashamed that I said you were a homeless stranger. I should have gone with you, but I didn't know. I didn't know the truth and for that I'm sorry, but I hope there's still a chance for us to fix things. I hope you can forgive me, because the only thing I want is for us to be together.

Jack confessed to having set you up. He was the one who sent you to Cairo knowing you'd be arrested. He says he was instructed by a man called Elroy Lang. I don't know him, and neither do my father or brother, and I can't understand why a total stranger would want to hurt us, but this is the name of the man who tore us apart, who betrayed us. He told Jack to tell you we'd abandoned you. He told Jack to tell us you'd cut yourself off from us.

I hope everything that's passed since we were parted can be laid at this man's feet and we can shed the burdens of blame and guilt. I hope and pray you still love me and that we can pick up our old lives as though none of this happened.

I miss you. I miss all the laughs. I miss your loving touch. Come back to me.

With all my love,
Essi

Pearce folded the letter Essi had given him and put it back in the envelope. Ziad had been set up and manipulated by the very people he was now working with, people who didn't care about the suffering they inflicted in pursuit of their goals. Pearce felt his anger rise as he pocketed the envelope and left the quiet galley area to join the others.

Chapter 107

'The *Elite Voyager* is a two-hundred-and-eighty-metre Panamax cargo vessel registered in Hong Kong. She runs between Qingdao and Seattle six times a year and is owned by Yellow Rose Shipping,' Leila said. 'The owners look clean from what I can see and there's no connection to Qingdao Consumer Products, so the cargo could be on the ship without the captain or crew knowing.' She indicated a satellite image that displayed a beacon off the Washington State Coastline. 'Her current GPS position shows her approximately two hundred and forty miles out, in the Cascadia Basin.'

Wollerton leaned against Leila's desk and peered at the screen. 'Deep water,' he said.

Pearce turned to Clifton and Brigitte, who sat alongside him. They were clustered around Leila's desk in the large fifteenth-floor space that had become their base of operations.

'Yes,' Leila agreed. 'It is deep out there.'

'The ship is double hulled,' Brigitte said. 'Without access to a torpedo, our best hope of sinking her is to plant bombs in these compartments.'

Leila brought up a schematic of the ship.

'Our calculations are that thirty kilograms of CL-20 will be more than sufficient to breach the hull and cause irreparable damage.'

'We sound the alarm and evacuate the ship before we blow it though,' Clifton confirmed.

Pearce nodded. 'How do we get out there? Boat? Chopper?'

'We were concerned about a boat being spotted,' Clifton said. 'And if the crew are hostile there would be pilot risk with a chopper. We don't know how long it's going to take you to set the charges and if a bird needed to circle, the range could test the fuel supply, so we have another method.'

Pearce waited expectantly.

'What I'm about to show you doesn't leave this room,' Clifton said, and he was greeted with nods of reassurance. He reached into a satchel beside his chair and produced a tablet computer. 'These are modelled on the drone UAV's being developed for city transit.' He brought the computer to life and showed them an image of a single-person aircraft. A central egg-shaped pod was joined to six rotors. Attached to the underside of the pod was an M61 Vulcan cannon. 'We've been adapting the basic design for the Defence Department. Each aircraft is equipped with an M61 with a three-sixty-degree field of fire. The drones are currently going through proofing, but we have two prototypes that were supposed to have been destroyed in early flight testing.'

'I'm not a pilot,' Pearce remarked.

'Who needs to know anything nowadays?' Clifton scoffed. 'They operate point and click flight systems, or they can be piloted manually or by remote operators. Their size means you can land them in a parking space, so you can put these down on the ship, do whatever you need to do and they'll be waiting to bring you home. No need to worry about a chopper running out of fuel as it circles.'

'And the armament?' Brigitte asked.

'Fully automated,' Clifton replied. 'Select your targets and the drone's artificial intelligence system will track and destroy. Everything in the aircraft is intuitive. Like a video game. Just point and click.'

Pearce was impressed. A drone like this would have been a dream when he'd been in the service. It would have made incursions into enemy territory much less risky. 'Noise?' he asked.

'We've invested a lot of money in making it run silent,' Clifton replied. 'You get some noise coming off the rotors, but nothing that will be heard above a ship's engine.'

'Or an ocean storm,' Wollerton observed. 'How do they handle bad weather?' He signalled the torrential rain that was still lashing the windows. The storm hung low over Seattle.

'Better than a kite,' Clifton joked. 'The drone's servos and gyros will take pretty much anything the sky can throw at them.'

'And you have two of them?' Wollerton asked. 'One for me and one for the boss?'

'I'm going,' Brigitte said flatly.

'Now hold on—' Wollerton began.

'I'm going,' Brigitte cut him off.

Pearce knew what was at stake for her. That ship was full of patches that could keep her alive, and when Wollerton shot him a questioning look, Pearce shrugged. 'Sorry, Kyle,' he said. 'She's coming. Leila's going to be running support.'

'And me?' Wollerton asked. 'Should I just twiddle my thumbs?'

'I need you to keep eyes on a couple of targets,' Pearce replied. 'Eddie and Kirsty Fletcher. Ben Cresci said he's going to make sure the Red Wolves pay for what they've done. He promised he'll keep the leaders alive for us to question, but we all know how it is in the heat of action. We need whatever they can tell us about this Elroy Lang and the people he works for. So I want you to head out to RPM, the Red Wolves hangout, and see if you can get to Eddie and Kirsty. If there's a safe way to bring in one or both of them, I want you to take it, otherwise just keep eyes on them and try to stop Cresci from killing them if he makes a move.'

Wollerton nodded.

'You only engage if it's safe,' Pearce pressed. 'You hear me?'

'Yes, sir, roger that, sir,' Wollerton replied sarcastically.

One of the burner phones on Leila's desk rang, and she picked it up and identified it by the sticker on the back. 'This is yours,' she said to Pearce. 'Or Amr's, more accurately.'

'I gave the number to the Salamovs,' Pearce said. He'd left Deni and Rasul shortly after their meeting with Ben Cresci.

Leila tossed Pearce the phone and he answered. 'Hello.'

There was nothing but silence, then the sound of a heavy choking breath.

'*She's dead,*' Deni Salamov said finally. '*Essi. My little girl,*' he sobbed. '*They killed her. They killed everyone.*'

Chapter 108

Pearce didn't know what to say to the man, so he simply listened to Deni Salamov pour out his heart. The old gangster lamented every dollar he'd ever made, every deal he'd ever done, every luxury he'd ever purchased. He would have traded his whole life for his daughter, he said between increasingly violent sobs. Pearce had expressed his condolences and heard Rasul enter the room at the other end of the call, raging. Pearce pleaded with Deni not to do anything rash, but the Chechen hung up and hadn't responded to Pearce's attempts to call him back.

One question loomed above all: had Ziad been involved in Essi's death? Had he been part of whatever had happened? If he'd seen Essi's letter, if he'd known the truth . . .

Pearce shook such thoughts from his mind. They weren't helpful, particularly given his lack of resources. A bigger team would have meant he had the slack to deal with the unexpected, and Essi's death wasn't just a terrible tragedy for the Salamov family, it was almost certain to provoke a reaction, and there was no telling how the men would lash out. If Pearce had more resources, he might have been able to prevent Essi's death. At the very least, he could have tried to steer the Salamovs away from doing anything stupid in retaliation, but as it was, he had to make a choice, and the shipment had to be his priority. The *Elite Voyager* had to be sunk somewhere deep to minimize the chance of the patches being salvaged before they were neutralized by seawater.

Pearce and Brigitte changed into tactical battle gear, complete with body armour, and loaded equipment bags. They each took an HK416 assault rifle, a Glock 19, stun and flash grenades and night-vision scopes. When they were ready, Wollerton sidled over.

'Be careful,' he said.

Pearce nodded and grabbed his bike keys from Leila's desk. 'Here,' he said, handing them to Wollerton. 'Look after her until I get back.'

'Nice timing,' Wollerton said, indicating the violent storm outside. 'Perfect weather for two wheels.'

'You'll manage,' Pearce said, heaving his gear bag onto his shoulder. 'I have faith in you.'

'Be careful out there,' Wollerton replied.

Pearce joined Leila, Clifton and Brigitte in the elevator and they rode down to the parking lot. The former NSA director drove them south in the surveillance van he'd brought back with him.

The storm showed no signs of abating, and the rain obscured everything as they made slow progress through the city. Pearce had the familiar pre-mission nerves and would have been grateful for some banter to distract him from what was to come, but he sensed similar anxiety in everyone else, and they drove in silence. After a while, Clifton put on the radio, but the music and inane chatter felt out of place and he soon switched it off. They'd been on the road forty minutes when Clifton made a call and said, 'ETA twenty', before hanging up.

Ten minutes later, they turned off Ambaum Boulevard and followed a winding service road through a dense forest. After another ten minutes, Pearce saw open water and they cleared the treeline and came to a parking lot that lay in front of a large cabin. The lights of distant houses twinkled high in the surrounding hills, but there were no other signs of civilization nearby and the storm meant they were unlikely to be disturbed by hikers. Clifton's call had been made to give a couple of technicians the chance to make final preparations, and Pearce saw them now; a man and a woman, both in their early thirties, both wearing raincoats. They were shepherding a robot transporter out of a huge eighteen-wheel truck. The robot moved on caterpillar tracks and was supporting a drone. A second drone was already beside the truck, its rotors extended, its cabin lights on. The aircraft was protected from the weather by an awning that extended from the side of the truck.

The robot followed a device held by the woman, and needed no further control. It automatically tailed her to the desired spot.

'Pretty slick, huh?' Clifton remarked as he pulled up behind the truck.

Inside the trailer, beyond the space where the two drones had been stored, was a command centre, complete with screens and a bank of computers.

'Hux has access to toys I could only have dreamed of at the NSA,' Clifton observed.

They got out and ducked in the heavy rain as they headed over to the two roadies, who were getting the second drone off the robot.

'Marty, Ellen – this is the ops team,' Clifton said.

'We're kind of busy right now,' Marty replied angrily, before breaking into a broad smile. 'Just kidding. The machine does it all.'

He indicated the robot transporter, which tilted slightly and lowered the drone onto the ground using a conveyor belt.

An ergonomic chair took up most of the drone's egg-shaped carbon fibre cabin. Trimmed in matt-black leather, it looked more like the interior of a luxury car than a military transport. Four retractable legs held the cabin off the ground, and provided clearance for the M61 Vulcan mounted to the bottom of the chassis. The drone's six rotors were folded in a vertical position to reduce the craft's footprint.

'Sorry, we're running behind,' Marty said. 'It's usually twenty minutes from truck to air, but this one,' he indicated Ellen, 'wanted to run full diagnostics, since this is our first live mission.'

'Better to be safe,' Ellen remarked.

'How long before they can fly?' Clifton asked.

'We need to get her air ready. Gonna take a while,' Ellen said. She pressed a touch-sensitive panel on the hull and the cockpit opened. As the canopy rose, Ellen leaned inside and pressed something. There was a quiet hum when a power supply came on, and the cockpit illuminated. The rotors started dropping into a horizontal position. 'She's good to go.'

'So this is all hush-hush, no names,' Marty observed, 'but we're going to need a destination.'

'I've got that,' Leila said, patting her rain-covered laptop case.

'And the payload?' Brigitte asked.

'Three sets of demolition charges in the cargo holds,' Ellen replied, indicating compartments at the rear of the drones.

'If you get in, I'll set the aircraft to respond only to your biometrics.'

'Which one do you want?' Pearce asked.

Brigitte shrugged. 'One's as good as another.' She pointed to the one Ellen had just opened. 'You have it.'

Brigitte moved to the other drone and opened the cargo hold. She checked a rectangular case that held the explosive payload and detonator. Satisfied with what she saw, she put her gear bag beside it and closed the cargo hold.

Pearce did likewise and saw two rectangular cases inside his cargo hold. He stowed his gear back, closed the cargo hold and climbed into the cockpit. It looked like the interior of a Tesla. There was a single screen and black leather trim, but no obvious controls.

Ellen leaned in and tapped a pocket computer she held in her hand. The screen in the cockpit came to life and displayed a digital palm.

'Put your hand on it,' Ellen said.

Pearce complied and his print was scanned by the machine. He looked over at Brigitte and saw Marty was guiding her through the same process.

'Scan complete,' a synthetic voice said. 'Please count back from ten.'

Pearce started from ten and counted down. When he got to six, the synthetic voice said, 'Voice identification complete.'

'We'll be piloting the aircraft remotely,' Ellen said, 'but if for any reason you need to take control, just say "manual pilot".' She nodded at Pearce.

'Manual pilot,' he said.

The cockpit sprang to life. A projected heads-up display materialized on the open canopy, a joystick rose from a concealed compartment on Pearce's right and a lever came up from one on his left.

'You ever play any flying computer games?' Ellen asked.

Pearce nodded.

'This is just like them,' she said. 'Throttle –' she tapped the lever forward – 'brake –' she pulled it back. 'Dive –' she pushed the joystick – 'climb –' she pulled it back – 'and left and right. The drone's AI will compensate for anything stupid or dangerous and it is equipped with anti-stall, anti-collision programming, so if you want to fly into a cliff, you're in the wrong bird.'

'What about landing?' Pearce asked.

'We'll take care of that,' Ellen replied. 'But if anything goes wrong, in manual mode, you can lock onto a position. Doesn't matter if it's moving or not. You can select the roof of a train, a boat or whatever and the AI will model and lock that target through whatever aspect changes you experience and put you down on that point.'

Pearce was bewildered.

Ellen rolled her eyes. 'Just touch the place you want to land on the canopy. It will give you two options, "open fire" and "land". Just press "land" and the drone will do the rest.'

'And if I press fire?'

'There won't be much of anything left for you to land on.' Ellen smiled. 'Got it?'

'Am I a pilot now?' Pearce asked.

'Top gun,' she laughed. 'He's good to go,' she said to Clifton.

'Same here,' Marty announced.

'Then let's get them airborne,' Clifton replied.

Chapter 109

Wollerton hadn't ridden a motorbike for years. Esther had always considered them a shortcut to the grave and, in her usual passive-aggressive way, had done everything possible to discourage him from replacing his Ducati Monster. But she was gone now, and the kids too, and there was no longer anyone he'd selfishly be leaving behind if he got squashed by a truck. He was free to indulge his teenage self, and even though he was riding through some of the most treacherous conditions he'd ever experienced, his journey east on Pearce's bike had reawakened his love of two wheels. There was nothing like the roar of the engine filling his helmet. The propulsive acceleration that almost took his breath away, the widescreen perspective, and freedom of being on a vehicle rather than in one. As exhilarating as it was, it didn't compare to the briefest moment spent with his kids, and the joy he felt being on a bike was lost to a maudlin cloud of self-pity. He missed his family.

Once out of the city, he rode cautiously, crawling along flooded, slick roads, and after two hours he finally saw the RPM bar on the horizon. Situated in the woods just beyond Fall City, local police intelligence reports identified the place as the Red Wolves hangout.

There were hardly any vehicles out here and the roads were

awash with run-off. He slowed to take a bend and when he straightened up, he saw the RPM bar directly ahead. The lights were blazing brightly in the storm, and the parking lot was packed with bikes and trucks.

Wollerton slowed as he approached, and cruised past the bar to see it crowded with people. He pulled over a short distance further on, killed the engine and wheeled his bike into the trees. Once it was safely concealed, he walked back through the forest until he found a vantage point directly opposite the bar. Sheltered from the worst of the weather by the densely packed needles of a tall pine, Wollerton settled in to watch and wait.

Chapter 110

'What's the range?' Leila asked.

'Six hundred and fifty miles,' Ellen replied.

Leila and Clifton sat behind the two engineers, who were each piloting one of the drones over the Pacific. Two dozen LCD screens were ranged in front of Ellen and Marty. About a third of them displayed footage from on-board cameras, and the others showed telemetry data and satellite positioning. One screen gave the position of the aircraft relative to the GPS signal of the *Elite Voyager*. Pearce and Brigitte were six miles from the ship.

'Top speed?' Leila asked.

'Two hundred and eighty miles per hour,' Marty responded.

'Flight ceiling?'

'Twelve thousand feet,' Ellen replied.

'Payload?'

'*Will you let them concentrate?*' Pearce said, his voice broadcast by speakers built into the command console.

'Oh, it's no problem,' Ellen remarked. 'Everything's pretty much automated. The AI is keeping you on course and if we lose satellite uplink, the drones are programmed to hover until it's re-established or you take manual control.'

'We're ninety seconds out,' Marty informed them all. 'You might want to cut the chatter.'

'Copy that,' Pearce replied.

He was reclining in the cockpit of his drone, which was speeding above the waves at an altitude of no more than fifty feet. Brigitte was twenty feet away from him and the aircraft kept perfect formation, the AI making them rise, fall and turn together. The heads-up display projected a holographic overlay of the *Elite Voyager*, which was now some four miles distant, along with telemetry data. The cockpit lights were set low, and when Pearce looked at Brigitte, he saw little more than a shadow against the roiling clouds. The rain whipped the canopy, but the foul weather didn't seem to affect the ride. The cockpit moved independently of the hull, and Pearce could feel the rapid adjustments of the servos, working hard to keep him level.

The *Elite Voyager* loomed on the horizon; Pearce made out bridge, cabin and running lights through the storm. The vast ship was rising and falling on the huge waves, and Pearce hoped the drone was as good as the two mouthy engineers had indicated.

'*We're bringing you in on the aft deck,*' Marty said through a speaker concealed somewhere in the cockpit.

The noise of the elements was muted by extensive sound-proofing. Pearce had been right to liken the craft to a luxury car. It certainly felt more like a Bentley than a chopper. He wondered how soldiers would react to the craft, and had little doubt the Department of Defence would strip out all refinement as a cost-cutting measure if these drones ever saw front-line service.

The drone climbed as it approached the *Elite Voyager* and a marker materialized on the heads-up display's 3D rendition of the vessel. As they rose high enough to see the aft deck, Pearce caught sight of something that set his heart racing. A large motorboat was tied to the far side of the *Elite Voyager*. A group of armed men in fatigues were marshalling crew members, who'd formed a human chain and were transferring packing crates to the motorboat.

One of the men looked up, and Pearce recognized him as Elroy Lang, the man who'd broken Ziad out of Al Aqarab. He saw Elroy bark a command, and three of his comrades raised their assault rifles and opened fire.

Chapter 111

Sparks flared and danced around the sky as bullets hit the drone's rotors. Pearce heard a fearsome roar and turned to see Brigitte's Vulcan cannon rattle off a hundred rounds per second. The tracer line cut across the aft deck like a laser and shredded four of Elroy's men. Everyone else scattered.

'*Scott*,' Leila said urgently. '*Seven o'clock*.'

Pearce looked to his seven and saw a man on the aft deck of the large motorboat with what looked like a PSRL-1 shoulder-mounted rocket launcher. Pearce used the heads-up display to target him and opened fire, but the rocket blazed and took to the sky an instant before Pearce's Vulcan tore through the man and much of the deck.

'Manual control,' Pearce yelled, and the display signalled he now had command.

He pushed the joystick down and banked right into a stomach-lurching descent, as counter-measures burst all around him. He felt the rotors cut out and the craft plummeted towards the *Elite Voyager*. As the aft deck rushed to meet him, Pearce pulled back on the stick, and the rotors kicked in, stabilizing the craft.

He heard an explosion and glanced up to see one of Brigitte's rotors on fire. Her drone spun wildly out of control and dropped rapidly.

'*I'm hit! I'm hit!*' Brigitte's voice came over the radio.

Pearce watched in horror as her drone fell towards the churning waves, one of its rotors burning, the two either side of it broken and misshapen like the gnarly branches of a rotten tree.

'*Scott, they're leaving,*' Leila said, and Pearce realized Elroy Lang was mustering his men onto the motorboat, and his crew were preparing to cast off.

Pearce was torn. If that shipment made land, thousands of lives would be put at risk.

'*Mayday,*' Brigitte said. '*Mayday. I'm going down. I'm—*'

Her distress call was cut short when her drone hit the water.

Pearce knew what he had to do. He descended towards Brigitte's drone, which was slowly sinking beneath the waves.

'Notify the coastguard,' Pearce said. 'Tell them there's a bioweapon on board the –' he read the letters on the motorboat's stern as it roared away from the *Elite Voyager* – '*Orion*, and advise it needs to be intercepted as a matter of urgency.'

'*Got it,*' Leila replied. '*Can you see Brigitte? We've lost all feeds from her craft, and your cameras must have been damaged in the firefight.*'

'I've got eyes on her,' Pearce said, looking down at the Frenchwoman, who had opened the canopy and was sliding into the icy water. 'How do I get my landing lights on?'

'We can do it from here,' Marty said, and an instant later the choppy water was illuminated.

Pearce could see a lifeboat being lowered from the *Elite Voyager*. He hovered thirty feet above Brigitte, close enough to see her signalling for him to leave. Her frustration was clear as she pointed towards the *Orion*, which was vanishing into the darkness. Pearce longed to follow it, but he knew that if he left Brigitte, there was a chance the waters would take her and without a light to guide them, the frustratingly slow rescue team might never find her.

Chapter 112

It took twenty-five minutes for the lifeboat to reach and recover Brigitte. Once she was safely on board, Pearce piloted the drone towards the last contact point and conducted a sweep of the area, but the *Orion* was nowhere to be found and could have been anywhere in hundreds of miles of dark empty ocean.

'*You're getting close to your range limit,*' Marty said. '*You need to head back, or put down now.*'

'Copy,' Pearce said. Frustrated, he turned back towards the *Elite Voyager*, and minutes later set down on the aft deck, which was abuzz with activity.

Crew members were tending wounded colleagues, while others covered the dead with tarpaulins. The crew from the lifeboat were helping a wet and bedraggled Brigitte out of the small craft, which had been returned to its position between a pair of hoists.

As the rotors of his drone slowed to a halt, Pearce opened his canopy and climbed out. He was immediately approached by the ship's commanding officer, a slim black man in a thin cotton roll neck, black trousers and a captain's cap.

'Who the hell are you?' He had a Haitian accent and spoke like a man at the end of his patience. 'And what are you doing on my ship?'

'We were trying to stop those men,' Pearce said, indicating one of the Red Wolves Brigitte had shot. 'The cargo they took is extremely dangerous.'

Brigitte joined them. 'You should have gone after the shipment,' she said angrily. 'I can take care of myself.'

'What do you want with it?' the captain asked.

'To destroy it,' Pearce replied. 'It's poison.'

The captain studied Pearce and then looked at Brigitte, whose eyes were burning.

'I know what it is,' the captain responded at last. 'I know what it does. There's something you need to see.'

The Haitian captain led them through the ship, two armed crewmen alongside him.

'That vessel hijacked us three hours ago. They boarded and forced my crew to empty a container at gunpoint,' he said, taking them down a step run of metal steps. 'We formed a chain and unloaded fifteen hundred boxes onto their craft.'

They walked a short way along a corridor before the captain stopped outside a berth. 'But we already knew something was wrong. A couple of crew were reported missing this morning. We found them in their quarters.'

The captain opened the door to reveal a four-berth room. The stench of decay filled the corridor immediately, and Pearce covered his mouth. One man lay on the bottom bunk on the right. A second crewmember was sprawled on the floor. At the end of the dead man's bunk was a three feet by three feet packing crate like the ones taken off the ship, and Pearce saw black patches like the one on Brigitte's shoulder, each wrapped in translucent wax paper. He glanced at Brigitte and saw the relief on her face. Her death had been forestalled, but the grim reaper had taken these two men, and as Pearce studied the scene, he saw why.

The man on the floor clasped a tiny piece of a patch between his thumb and forefinger. About the size of a matchbox, the piece had been cut from a patch that lay next to him. There was a pair of scissors on the bunk. Some opioid users cut fentanyl patches into small pieces and rubbed them on their gums. It was a risky way of taking the drug, but it resulted in a more potent high. When these men used the patches that way, the XTX shut down their parathyroid glands and destroyed the PTH in their bodies, but without the presence of the synthetic supplied by the patch, they would have died within moments.

'We notified the coastguard about the fatalities,' the captain said. 'I had no idea these two were junkies or they wouldn't have been on my ship. They must have found what was in that container and stolen a box.'

'So you know why we came to destroy it?' Pearce replied.

The captain nodded.

'We need to find that vessel,' Pearce said to Brigitte.

Her eyes didn't leave the box that offered her life.

'We're going to need that box,' she said.

The captain hesitated.

'If it falls into the wrong hands – a corrupt cop, a careless port official – it will kill people. We can't take that risk,' Pearce said.

The captain frowned.

'Give it to us, or we'll take it anyway,' Brigitte said.

Pearce frowned at her, and the captain scoffed, which was just about the worst reaction he could have had. Brigitte heel-kicked the shorter armed crewman, punched him as he hunched over, and grabbed his pistol from its holster before his crewmate even had the chance to draw. She pointed the gun at the captain's head, and he froze and eyed her uncertainly. A moment later, she offered him the gun.

'The authorities won't miss what they didn't know existed,' she said as the captain took the weapon. 'And if they do, you can say you were robbed.'

The captain smiled. 'OK. Whatever gets this stuff out of my hair and you people off my ship.'

Chapter 113

The captain and some of the crew braved the elements and gathered on deck to watch the drone leave. According to Marty, the aircraft would have just enough power to carry both of them back to shore, so Pearce and Brigitte sat side by side in the cramped cockpit. The contents of the crate they'd taken from the dead crewmen's berth were stowed in the drone's cargo hold, stashed in a duffle bag the captain had given them.

'We're good to go,' Pearce said, as the canopy closed.

'*Copy that,*' Ellen replied.

Once the pressure seal had formed, the rotors started and the drone rose into the sky. The crew ducked and stepped back to avoid the downdraft, and the craft cleared the deck and accelerated out to sea.

'You get all that?' Pearce asked once they were over open water.

'*Yeah,*' Leila's voice came over the radio. '*The Red Wolves must have decided it was too risky to wait for the* Elite Voyager *to make port.*'

'With the Salamovs still alive, the route is exposed,' Pearce agreed. 'They know how product is brought through the port, and one call to an honest cop could have put the whole shipment at risk.'

'*The coastguard is on alert but there's no sign of the vessel,*' Leila said. '*What now?*'

'Contact Kyle. Tell him to stay with Eddie and Kirsty Fletcher. They'll know where the product is headed. When we get back we're going to bring them in.'

'*Copy that,*' Leila replied.

Pearce watched the heavy rain trace streams over the canopy as the drone raced above the dark swells. If the coastguard couldn't intercept the *Orion*, he prayed he could find the toxin taken from the *Elite Voyager* before it hit the streets.

Chapter 114

Ziad felt sick to his stomach. He'd spent much of the journey to intercept the *Elite Voyager* hunched over a chemical toilet, vomiting. The mid-sea hijacking had been fraught and dangerous and the attack from the sky as they'd been unloading the final containers had shaken him. Elroy had seemed unconcerned and the loss of four Red Wolves hadn't stirred his calm resolve. In contrast, Eddie and Kirsty Fletcher were furious. The appearance of such heavily armed state-of-the-art aircraft pointed to government intervention, and as well as the loss of their friends, they railed against the risks Elroy had exposed them to.

'What the fuck just happened?' Eddie Fletcher had asked when they were safely out of range of the *Elite Voyager* and the remaining aircraft. 'That was some military-grade shit.'

Elroy ignored the remark and headed to the bridge. Ziad, Fletcher and Kirsty followed, while the rest of the Red Wolves transferred the last of the cargo crates below deck.

Elroy order the captain to take a circuitous route back to Seattle, and checked on Awut, who manned what looked like a military surface-radar system. Elroy told him to make sure they kept well clear of any contacts.

'I asked you a question,' Fletcher pressed angrily.

'And I would have answered it, if I'd been able,' Elroy

replied calmly. 'I have no idea what those aircraft were or who sent them. But they are no longer a problem.'

'Tell that to the four men we left behind,' Kirsty snapped. 'The cops will be able to link them to us.'

Elroy sighed and left the bridge, and once he was gone Ziad saw Kirsty and Fletcher share an angry glance.

Ziad followed Elroy outside and was grateful for the fresh air. The ceaseless buck and roll of the ocean wasn't the only thing making him feel sick. Whenever he was idle, he saw Essi's face in those last moments, red and ugly with horror, tormenting him like a spectre. He'd done everything he could to keep the memory at bay, but even when his mind turned to other things, she was always there, like a shadow in the background.

Ziad found Elroy on deck. He was leaning over the guard rail, peering into the darkness. Wind whipped around them and waves crashed into the hull, hurling refreshing spray at them. Ziad wiped his face and settled beside Elroy.

'They seem worried,' he said.

'They are small people with small minds,' Elroy replied. 'They don't see the big picture. Few can.'

'Do they know?' Ziad asked. 'What these things do?' He indicated the crates being hauled below deck.

Elroy shook his head. 'Small minds.'

'So you're using them?' Ziad pressed.

Elroy turned to face him with something approaching sympathy. 'Awut told me what you did at the Salamovs' house.'

Ziad looked down, ashamed at the thought others were talking about the hideous death he'd inflicted on the woman he'd once loved.

'That took courage,' Elroy continued. 'The kind of courage we look for.'

Tears threatened, but Ziad held them back. Why was this man praising him for such horror? How would he ever know right from wrong with these people?

'When we return to Seattle and store the narcotics, there are some things that need to be done,' Elroy said. 'There is a man called Scott Pearce. He will likely use the Fletchers and their gang to try to find us. And if not them, Ben Cresci.'

'Cresci?' Ziad asked in dismay.

'I believe he's been told the truth about our plans,' Elroy revealed.

Ziad felt sick again. It made sense. Cresci was the only one outside their circle who knew the vessel the shipment was coming in on.

'The Fletchers were right. The police will link those four dead men to them, but I am concerned that Pearce or Cresci might try to force them to betray us.'

'What are you going to do?'

Elroy sighed. 'Can you see the big picture, Ziad?'

Ziad felt his mouth fill with saliva and fought the urge to be sick. He nodded.

'Then look to me,' Elroy said. 'I'll let you know when the time comes.'

Chapter 115

The nausea stayed with Ziad when they finally made land. The Red Wolves worked tirelessly to unload the crates into a waterside warehouse. Elroy posted two men Ziad hadn't seen before to guard the stockpile and the crew of twenty-two Red Wolves split between five vehicles, which headed east. Eddie and Kirsty Fletcher rode with Ziad and Elroy in a black Toyota Landcruiser. Awut drove them, and Ziad would occasionally catch the Thai assassin glancing at Elroy, who sat in the front passenger seat.

There was an atmosphere of hostility and distrust and for much of the journey no one spoke. Ziad struggled to cope with the tension and silence. His mind filled the void with memories of Essi. She laughed, held his hand, whispered her love for him. Then she died, over and over again, each time reborn as a happy moment before suffering choking agony. Ziad tried to mask the turmoil, but his emotions must have showed.

'You OK?' Fletcher asked.

'I'm . . .' Ziad began, but his voice caught, so he cleared his throat. 'Just feeling a little sick from the boat. I'm fine.'

No one said anything until they reached the RPM bar around dawn. The convoy pulled into the parking lot, which was almost empty. Red Wolves spilled from the vehicles and headed into the bar.

Eddie and Kirsty stepped out and Ziad followed. He was about to go into the bar when Elroy said, 'Ziad, a word.'

Ziad hung back to wait for Elroy, who was taking his time. Awut jumped out of the Landcruiser and followed Eddie into the building.

'Yeah?' Ziad said.

Elroy didn't reply. He simply gave an almost imperceptible nod towards the bar, and Ziad turned with a growing sense of dread. He knew what was about to happen. Awut was going to tie up this loose end.

Chapter 116

Wollerton had seen the convoy pull into the RPM car park. His legs were stiff and his back was sore, but his eyes were sharp and his mind alert, despite hours spent watching the crowd in the raucous bar dwindle through the night. The rain had finally stopped a couple of hours ago, making his tedious task slightly less unpleasant.

As people got out of the vehicles, Wollerton spotted five of their principal targets – Eddie and Kirsty Fletcher, Narong Angsakul, Ziad Malek and Elroy Lang. Wollerton produced his Ghostlink and called Pearce.

'*Go ahead,*' Pearce said.

'I've got eyes on the whole gang,' Wollerton replied.

'*Any sign of Cresci?*' Pearce asked.

'None.'

'*Stay put,*' Pearce said. '*We hit trouble, but I'm on my way to you now.*'

'You OK?'

'*We're fine,*' Pearce replied.

'Should I—' Wollerton was cut short by the sound of gunshots coming from the bar.

He peered through the branches of the pine tree and saw Narong Angsakul spring from the building. Inside, a cloud of white powder filled the windows, and as it began to settle,

Wollerton saw the occupants choking, clawing at their throats, desperately trying to breathe.

Narong ran towards a black Landcruiser where Ziad and Elroy waited.

'Oh my god,' Wollerton said.

'*What?*' Pearce asked. '*Kyle? What's happening?*'

'Narong has detonated a device inside the bar. They're all dying,' Wollerton was horrified by the suffering inside the building and had to look away. He'd never expected Elroy and Narong to turn on their own.

'*They're cleaning up,*' Pearce observed. '*Tying up loose ends.*'

'There's three of them,' Wollerton said. 'I'm going in.'

'*No. Stand down,*' Pearce commanded.

Wollerton was going to ignore his friend, but hesitated when he saw Kirsty and Eddie Fletcher stagger through the doors. Kirsty had a pistol in her hands. Both were struggling to breathe and their legs were failing.

Wollerton saw Elroy produce a pistol and shoot Kirsty twice in the chest. He watched her fall before joining Narong and Ziad inside the SUV.

Eddie Fletcher crouched beside his fallen wife, and Wollerton could sense the dying man's grief. The Landcruiser made a U-turn in the car park, and Fletcher took Kirsty's gun and made a monumental effort to force himself to his feet. He staggered towards the SUV and tried to raise the pistol, but he was too weak. The Landcruiser didn't even slow as it hit him. Eddie Fletcher bounced off the bonnet and was tossed into the dirt beside his wife.

The Landcruiser turned onto the deserted country road and sped west towards the city.

Shocked, Wollerton realized he could hear the dawn chorus. The road was silent and the bar was still.

'*Kyle?*' Pearce asked, stirring Wollerton from the haze of shock. '*Kyle, are you OK?*'

'They're dead,' Wollerton replied. 'They're all dead.'

He ran through the trees to the R1.

'I'm going to follow them,' Wollerton said into his Ghostlink before slipping it into his pocket.

He jumped on the motorbike, started the powerful engine, and set off in pursuit of the men who'd just slaughtered their own people.

Chapter 117

Wollerton hung back and followed the Landcruiser from a safe distance. The black SUV drove west towards central Seattle, and as they approached the outskirts of the city, the rush hour traffic started to build.

Wollerton tailed them through Renton, an industrial district to the east of the city, and as he rode past large warehouse units that were interspersed with small aluminium-sided homes, he thought about the horror he'd witnessed at RPM. He'd expected a conventional assault from Cresci, but to see Elroy Lang callously kill his own people made Wollerton wonder what kind of monsters they were dealing with. Narong had used a chemical weapon for what seemed like the third time in a matter of days, and had casually murdered people he knew.

Up ahead, the Landcruiser turned left onto North 4th Street, and Wollerton followed, taking the inside of a four-lane road. The Landcruiser stopped at a red light, and Wollerton pulled up at a line of cars that formed behind it.

A plain grey van drew alongside Wollerton in the outside lane, but instead of proceeding to the intersection, it stopped beside him. Wollerton's spidey-sense tingled and he reached for the pistol concealed in his waistband as the van's side door slid open and a masked man jumped out with a syringe in his hand.

They made me, Wollerton thought, and he swung the gun towards his assailant.

The big man stepped forward and drove his elbow into Wollerton's forearm. He winced and dropped the gun, which clattered onto the road. The masked man swung the syringe towards Wollerton's shoulder but he quickly dismounted and pushed the motorbike towards his assailant. The guy jumped back as the R1 toppled over and hit the road.

A shot rang out, and Wollerton turned to see Narong, Elroy and Ziad by the Landcruiser. Narong was targeting him with an assault rifle. Cars started veering away from danger, their tyres screeching as they sought to get clear as quickly as possible.

Wollerton skipped backwards and crouched behind an old Jeep Cherokee that hadn't moved. Ahead of him, the masked man with the syringe was running around the fallen motorbike. His companion, the masked driver of the van, was out of the vehicle and sprinting towards Wollerton. To his left, Wollerton saw Ziad, Narong and Elroy running in his direction. There was no way he was going to allow himself to be taken. He tried to move round to the driver's side of the Jeep, but the van driver and Narong opened fire, pinning him down.

He heard the Jeep's engine roar as the driver tried to escape, but nothing happened. The car must have been in neutral. As he heard the crunch of a gearbox wrestling with an over-revved engine, Wollerton realized he only had moments.

The revs died down as Wollerton removed his helmet. He heard the thud of the Jeep locking in gear and swung his helmet in an arc, burying his face in the crook of his elbow. The helmet smashed the Jeep's rear window, sending glass flying everywhere.

The syringe-wielding man was a few feet away when Wollerton jumped through the shattered window. The driver, a middle-aged brunette, screamed as she stepped on the accelerator and the car lurched forward. There was a scrape of metal as the Jeep hit the car in front, but the driver swung the wheel, sending Wollerton tumbling into the bags of groceries lined up in the boot. He heard the sound of gunshots and the thud of bullets hitting metal as the vehicle gathered speed.

When he finally pulled himself upright, Wollerton saw Elroy, Ziad, Narong and their two masked accomplices receding as the terrified driver sped away.

Chapter 118

'*Police have asked anyone who saw anything to come forward,*' the reporter said earnestly. She was standing by a barricade some distance from the RPM bar, now another major crime scene. '*There has been no official statement, but sources are linking this terrible attack to the atrocities at the Meals Seattle warehouse and the Salam Islamic Centre. There is speculation that this is the work of the so-called Midas Killer.*'

'Thanks, Jennifer,' the anchor said, as the screen split between the scene at RPM and the studio. '*I also understand police are concerned about the whereabouts of Detective Evan Hill, the officer who was leading the Meals Seattle investigation?*'

'*That's right, Dan,*' Jennifer replied. '*Coming so soon after the disappearances of officers Jared Lowe and Dean Ollander, there is growing concern that someone might be targeting the police.*'

Pearce leaned forward and switched off the television. He looked round the room. Leila was at her computer, looking half dead. The grey light cast by the cloudy sky robbed her skin of colour, making her look even more drained. Clifton was slumped in a chair, struggling to stay awake. He kept catching himself nodding off. Brigitte sat nearby, utterly exhausted.

He and Brigitte had made it back to shore and had ignored the complaints of Marty and Ellen, who were annoyed by the loss of one of the drones. Clifton had driven them back to Huxley Blaine Carter's building, and Brigitte had taken the duffle bag into the bathroom, where she'd undoubtedly changed her patch. When she'd emerged from the bathroom, she'd shot Pearce a knowing look and stowed the duffle bag with the rest of the gear.

'Detective Hill is either in the wind, or someone's got to him. The Red Wolves are gone,' Pearce said, 'at least the Seattle chapter. And there's a huge shipment of tainted fentanyl somewhere on the West Coast. And we've got no idea where Kyle is. Every lead we had is dead or gone and I'm out of moves.'

'The Salamovs,' Leila suggested. 'They might know where the Red Wolves would stash their shipments.'

'They've gone to ground,' Pearce replied. 'They're not answering their phones, and I think it's a long shot. Whoever is behind this doesn't want any connection to RPM. After what happened there, the cops are going to be all over anything to do with the gang. You get anything on Elroy Lang?'

'Nothing here,' Leila replied, turning her laptop screen for Pearce to see.

'So it's dead ends in every direction?' Wollerton asked.

Pearce looked round to see his old mentor standing by the elevators.

'Kyle,' he said. 'What happened?'

'I lost them,' Wollerton replied with more than a hint of frustration. 'They tried to grab me.'

'Are you OK?' Clifton asked.

Wollerton nodded. 'Nothing more than wounded pride. What's been happening here?'

'We're running out of options,' Pearce replied. 'Elroy Lang, the people he's working for; they're good. The fact you saw them at the bar means the shipment made landfall, but with the Salamovs in hiding and the Fletchers gone . . .' He trailed off and started pacing in frustration. His mind felt fuzzy and he knew he needed sleep, but they were against a clock. The toxin would start hitting the streets soon, if it wasn't already out there.

'What about the crooked cop?' Wollerton asked. 'If he's still alive, he's a link to Elroy Lang. If we find Hill, maybe we can get a lead on Lang.'

'The NSA has a back door into most hotel reservation systems,' Clifton said. 'If he's gone to ground we could piggy-back the NSA network and search for any hotel rooms taken in the Seattle area tonight.'

'He'd pay cash,' Pearce remarked. 'And stay somewhere low-rent, off the grid. At least that's what I'd do. Assuming he isn't crashing with a friend. Or dead.'

'Telemetry data from his car,' Wollerton suggested.

'It's parked outside the South Precinct,' Leila said. 'It's on camera.' She switched windows to the precinct's CCTV system, which showed the police car park, and pointed out Hill's dark-blue SUV. 'I've run his cards and phone and they all come up blank.'

'The NSA has a gait identification programme,' Clifton revealed. 'It can identify a person by how they walk. If we could get a clip of Hill, we could run a search on the city's traffic cameras.'

'That would take weeks,' Leila replied.

'We're reaching,' Pearce said. 'We need to find this stuff before it hits the streets. If Hill can help us and if he's still alive, we need to bring him in today.' He stopped pacing and turned to Leila. 'You still have access to the Box social media accounts?' he asked, referring to MI5's propaganda and disinformation network.

Leila nodded.

'How would you feel about some fake news?' Pearce asked.

Chapter 119

Ziad stood outside the loading bay, trembling as he wept. He saw Essi everywhere. He'd seen her in the windows and doorways of the city, in the brooding sky, in the puddles, in the cars and buses they'd passed on their way back to the warehouse.

What have I become? Ziad thought, but he knew it was a question that didn't really need an answer. He had too many bodies to his name to ever have a hope of living a good life. And one more than any other troubled him. She was in the raindrops and even in the flesh of his eyelids when he shut them. It had seemed so just, so necessary, but after all the carnage and death it didn't feel like justice now. It felt more like a nightmare made even more horrendous by the knowledge he could never wake up. This was his life and there was no way out.

Take off the patch.

The words came unbidden, but even though they were heard only in his mind, the voice wasn't his, it was Essi's.

Take it off. It's quick.

He gazed out at the lights of the port, the place where it had all started; where he'd become enmeshed with the Salamovs, where he'd slipped their heroin beneath the radar, where he'd spent countless days dreaming of his life with Essi. He wished he'd never set eyes on the place. She'd still be alive and he'd be someone else with another life. Not this miserable, rotten creature. He sobbed, the tears mingling with rain blown beneath the loading bay's high canopy by the vicious wind lashing Seattle. He hated himself and everything he'd become.

Take it off, Essi's voice told him. *End this life. Start again.*

He lifted his collar and looked at the patch clinging to his shoulder. There were over a million of them stacked in boxes inside the warehouse. He imagined them as foul parasites released from Hell, biding their time until they could inflict their twisted suffering. But they weren't his problem. Elroy had explained things simply and clearly. If people were prepared to dabble in synthetic opiates, they were willingly gambling with their own lives. They had already forfeited their right to that which was most precious, and one form of death was much like another. What did it matter if an addict suffered an overdose, or if they were poisoned?

Ziad had lost his zeal to spread his pain so others could share it. But how could he tell anyone about his change of heart? The nausea was still with him. He felt a little sick that he couldn't object to Elroy's plan, and part of him was even more disgusted that he didn't really care. He was empty.

'Ziad,' Awut said, appearing in the doorway that led into the storage unit. 'He wants us.'

Ziad nodded, wiped the rain from his face and followed the mass murderer inside.

'It is from such humble beginnings that revolutions are born,' Elroy Lang said.

He wasn't the same man that had saved Ziad from prison.

That man had been a hero. This one most certainly was not. He was distant, authoritarian, and untrustworthy. Ziad found himself imagining a life without Elroy Lang, one in which he'd simply endured his suffering and served his time in Al Aqarab, before being released to a quiet, anonymous existence. It would have been better than this.

He glanced round the large warehouse at the other men in the room. There was Awut, the dead-eyed killer, Elroy, and Andel Novak, the quiet, thoughtful man Ziad had met in RPM. Novak was in his customary light-blue suit, and stroked his long beard as he cast his indulgent smile at Ziad. Then there were two newcomers; the duo who'd been in the van and had fumbled the attempt to abduct the man who'd been tailing them on the motorbike. Elroy had simply referred to them as friends. One was a huge man in his mid-twenties with tree trunk legs, chiselled arms and a muscular neck. He had short brown hair and a deep tan and had been introduced as Buck. The second man stood a little under six feet and had long straight hair. He was slimmer than Buck, but was by no means scrawny and his sinewy muscles stood out whenever he moved. Elroy introduced this man as Snake, and from the way the newcomers behaved, it was clear they knew each other well. They used a lot of military slang when they spoke and Ziad suspected they might have served together. Both had deep Texan drawls and carried themselves with the confidence of men who considered themselves superior to anyone around them.

These five men were now the only people in his life. Unless he counted Deni and Rasul, who hadn't been in the house at Laurelhurst and who had cheated death once again. Ziad knew both men would very much like to see him, but only so they could kill him. *Maybe mum and dad*—? *No*, Ziad cut himself off. He'd been dead to them for years.

Take off the patch.

He ignored the voice in his head and focused on Elroy, who was still talking.

'The Cresci Family seem to have been tipped off to the nature of our product. Our friend here,' Elroy indicated Awut, 'was told by his contact within the organization that he has a price on his head. So we are working to find another distributor.'

Ziad smiled bleakly. Elroy made it sound as though they were selling Pepsi.

'In the meantime, we need to start getting the product into the world,' Elroy said. 'Tomorrow night there's an event at the Lightstar Arena. An all-night music festival with over eight thousand people attending. We've arranged access to the venue and would like each of you to offer free product to anyone who's interested in trying it. We should be able to introduce at least five or six hundred people to their new lives.'

Even though he knew the horror Elroy would be inflicting on these people, Ziad didn't demur. He was a foul, rotten creature and deserved nothing more than a foul, rotten existence living in the shadows with these evil men. He'd killed the one good thing he'd ever had, and some dark part of him didn't want anyone else to be happy if he couldn't be.

Take it off, Essi's voice said.

Not yet, he told her inwardly.

Had he lost his mind? Was he talking to a ghost? Or to himself? Neither was something a sane man would do. How would he know if he'd lost his grip on reality?

Not yet.

He replayed the words in his mind.

Not yet.

Did that mean he'd reached a decision?

Yes, Essi's voice said. *You have. Come be with me.*

Ziad nodded. In time, he would remove the patch. And everything would be better.

Chapter 120

The room smelled of rot. The furniture was from the seventies and looked as though it had seen hard nights. The veneer sideboard was chipped, the chairs buckled and the bed sagged. The drapes were thin and worn and every crevice in the bathroom was filled with black mould. Detective Evan Hill winced and pulled the stained bedspread off his legs to look at his ankle. He was convinced something had just bitten him, but when he examined the yellowing sheet, there was nothing there. He rubbed his leg, got to his feet and crossed the rough carpet to turn on the ancient television. The tube took a moment to come to life, but when it did, Hill was shocked to see his own face staring back at him.

'*Social media sources have identified Detective Evan Hill as a possible suspect in the Midas killings,*' the anchor said over Hill's photo. '*The information seems to have come from a number of reliable accounts who have a track record of breaking controversial stories. Authorities are eager to locate Detective Hill, who is believed to be armed and extremely dangerous.*'

Hill cursed inwardly. Someone was setting him up. Maybe Lang? The attack on the biker bar was a clear sign the guy was tying up loose ends. Or maybe it was Salamov, out for revenge. Or the woman he'd arrested, Leila Nahum. Whoever was behind the fake news story was smart. A missing cop didn't stick in people's minds, but the Midas Killer was sensational. Hill thought about all the people he'd interacted with since arriving at the High Mountain Motel just north of Mitchell Hill. The manager had got a good look at him, as had the two guests he'd bumped into as he'd left reception. Then there was the convenience store clerk who'd sold him a week's worth of supplies, and the chambermaid who'd taken offence when he'd told her he didn't want his room cleaned because nothing she could do would make the slightest difference to the ground-in filth. Each and every one of them would probably instantly forget a missing cop, but a notorious killer . . .

He pulled on his jeans and threw his T-shirt over his head, before sitting on the end of the bed to tie his shoes. He'd just started on the second lace when he heard a noise outside. It was faint, like a rodent scratching at his door. He stood and backed away from it hesitantly.

He jumped when the door burst open and a squad of Seattle police officers in full tactical gear stormed the room. They threw him to the floor, knocking the wind from his lungs, and each cop restrained a limb, rendering him completely immobile. It was standard procedure for dealing with violent suspects and terrorists.

They think I'm one of the bad guys, Hill realized as one of the cops started reading him his rights. Urgent radio chatter drew Hill's attention to the car park outside his room, which was full of uniformed cops and plainclothes detectives. They'd sent an army to bring him in.

Defeated and despondent, a single thought went through his mind before they took him away.

Maybe I am *the bad guy.*

Chapter 121

Pearce waited in the booking hall. Leila had been monitoring police communications and had been able to ascertain that Hill was being taken to Seattle Police Headquarters. She and Wollerton had managed to forge credentials from the public defender's office that identified Pearce as Seth Allen, a court-appointed lawyer. The plan was simple; once Hill had been booked, Pearce would request five minutes with his client and would quiz the corrupt officer on possible locations Elroy Lang might use to store a large quantity of product.

After he'd been tested for coronavirus by the duty sergeant, Pearce had taken a seat and watched the comings and goings of central booking, grateful for the two hours' sleep he'd managed to snatch once they'd put the plan in motion. Leila had discovered that many of the accounts they'd used to break the Black Thirteen story had been shut down, so she'd been forced to hack into a new batch of MI5 social media puppets to spread the allegations about Hill. The story had soon gone viral, before being picked up by a few fringe and alternative news sites, which had become sources for local Seattle media. The volume of coverage gave the claims credence and before long, news outlets were forced to choose whether to run the story or be one of the few networks that remained silent.

Once the allegations had got traction, Pearce had instructed the team to get some rest. Everyone had managed to find a spot in their base of operations to grab some shut-eye. Everyone apart from Leila, who was pushing herself beyond the limit. Pearce didn't know how she did it, but he was learning not to try to stop her. She didn't react well to being told what to do, especially if the instruction implied she might be weak in any way. And they still weren't talking much. Their easy rapport had been strained by the revelation she'd concealed her role in Artem Vasylyk's death.

Pearce saw a commotion outside the booking hall. A couple of police cars had pulled up in the loading bay directly opposite the entrance. They were soon followed by a police van that stopped and discharged its occupants. Four officers in tactical gear, and their suspect, Evan Hill.

It took a moment for Pearce to realize why the uniformed cop heading out of the building seemed out of place. It was the man's face. He wasn't a police officer; he was a criminal. It was Rasul Salamov, and his eyes were fixed on Evan Hill. Pearce could only guess that someone on the Salamovs' payroll had let Rasul know where they were bringing Hill and had helped the mobster infiltrate the building.

'No!' Pearce yelled, getting to his feet.

But he was too late. As the tactical squad entered the building, Rasul Salamov drew his sidearm and shot Evan Hill in the stomach three times.

An alarm sounded and two of the tactical officers tended to Hill, who fell to the floor, shuddering violently as he bled out. The other two officers wrestled Rasul to the floor, but he didn't put up any resistance and surrendered his weapon with the willingness of someone who had no other ambitions in life. Pearce felt sick. Hill was their last hope of reaching the mysterious Elroy Lang.

Pearce watched the two officers with Hill perform frantic CPR, but he was unresponsive and soon fell still.

The booking hall filled with cops who took statements from anyone who might have seen anything. Giving his name as Seth Allen, Pearce told the detective who questioned him that he hadn't seen the shooting because he'd been checking his emails. While Pearce was being interviewed, Rasul was taken to the booking desk and charged with murder. He caught Pearce's eye, but there was no recognition, just a dead stare as though he'd lost all reason. Once Rasul was processed, he was taken through a security door, and Pearce felt certain they would never see each other again.

Forty-five minutes after the shooting, Pearce was released from the building, and he stepped into a battleship-grey day. Standing in the relentless drizzle, with his best chance dead, Pearce wondered where he went from here.

Chapter 122

Pearce left the building feeling something close to desperation. Hill was dead, Rasul Salamov was under heavy guard, Deni Salamov had vanished, and somewhere in the city was a shipment of one of the deadliest substances he had ever encountered. He walked a block to Columbia Street, where Clifton's surveillance van was parked. He knocked on the side door and a moment later it slid open to reveal Leila in the back, surrounded by computers and surveillance equipment.

Pearce hopped inside and sat in one of a pair of captain's chairs. Leila lowered herself into the other.

'Robert has shared photos of Ziad, Elroy and Narong with his old intelligence contacts,' Leila revealed. 'There's a state-wide APB on all three of them.'

'They'll have gone to ground,' Pearce said. 'They might even have skipped town already. There's no reason to assume they're involved in distributing the product. All they need is another Cresci . . .' Pearce cut himself off.

'What?' Leila asked.

'The East Hill Mob are gone. The Red Wolves too. The Salamov organization has been destroyed and Cresci knows not to touch the stuff,' Pearce remarked, suddenly animated by inspiration. 'They're going to need another distributor to shift that much product.'

He jumped into the driver's seat and started the engine.

'Where are we going?' Leila asked.

'To see Cresci,' Pearce replied.

It was shortly after 11 a.m. when they reached the three-storey gym on 65th. Pearce parked the van a short distance up the street and he and Leila walked towards the building. He noticed she was moving stiffly and wondered whether she needed her wheelchair, but it wasn't a subject he could ever raise. She hated any suggestion she might be weak or need special treatment.

There were no bodyguards outside the gym and the place looked shut. He pressed the button on the intercom and a buzzer sounded. He looked at Leila and she smiled half-heartedly. They still hadn't spoken about Artem Vasylyk and Pearce could feel the distance growing between them.

Pearce pressed the button again, and this time he got a response.

'*Yeah?*' a voice said.

'I need to speak to Ben Cresci,' Pearce said.

'*Get lost,*' the voice responded before hanging up.

Pearce held his finger on the button.

'*I said get lost,*' the voice told him.

'OK. But then you'll have to explain why you put Mr Cresci's entire business and life in danger,' Pearce said.

There was a brief pause.

'*Come in,*' the voice replied, and the latch clicked open.

Chapter 123

Pearce was brooding. He sat on a bench next to Leila, his face a mask of impatience and frustration. They'd climbed the steps to the gym and discovered the unfriendly voice belonged to Hank Rivers, a stocky guy in his fifties who looked as though he'd been in a lifetime of fights.

'Wait,' he'd said simply, pointing to the bench in the empty boxing gym. 'I'll tell Mr Cresci you're here.'

That had been more than eight hours ago. They'd sat through the gym opening at four, the arrival of the first athletes. Leila had finally succumbed to hunger and gone for sandwiches and painkillers.

When she'd returned to the gym, Pearce and Hank had been in the middle of a heated row, which had ended when Hank said, 'If you don't wanna wait, you know where the door is. Feel free to get lost.'

That had been almost two hours ago. They hadn't said much and Leila had spent the time watching the young, fit boxers training and sparring. She envied them their easy movement and lightness on their feet. She couldn't really remember what it was like to move without pain or restriction, but sometimes in her dreams she would imagine herself running freely.

Leila had always had a good relationship with Pearce, but the Vasylyk thing had soured it. She didn't report to him in any formal sense, so she was under no obligation to explain herself to him. She guarded her independence fiercely, but she could also see why Pearce was angry. They were meant to be friends, and she hadn't trusted him. More than that, she'd deprived him of information that might have been material to the investigation.

'Scott,' Leila said at last. 'I'm sorry.'

He looked at her and his expression softened. 'Thanks. I appreciate it.'

'It won't happen again,' Leila assured him.

'I don't know why you felt you couldn't trust me,' Pearce said. 'I've always got your back, Lyly.'

Before she could respond, Pearce was distracted by the arrival of a man in a sky-blue suit who was surrounded by an entourage of bodyguards.

'Cresci,' Pearce said, getting to his feet.

Leila followed and they were intercepted by two of the bodyguards, who searched them.

'With me,' Cresci said, pointing towards the men's locker room.

Pearce followed and Leila did likewise.

'Not you,' Cresci said to Leila. 'Just him.'

Leila's path was blocked by a couple of bodyguards and she could only watch in frustration as Cresci took Pearce inside and shut the door behind them.

Chapter 124

'Someone robbed me of satisfaction,' Cresci said accusingly. 'Eddie Fletcher is dead and the Red Wolves are gone.'

'The man's name is Elroy Lang,' Pearce replied. 'One of my people was watching the bar. He saw Narong Angsakul, the Thai national who was with Ziad Malek when they came to see you. Narong detonated the device that killed most of them. Elroy shot Kirsty Fletcher and they ran down her husband.'

Cresci fixed Pearce with a critical stare.

'It was nothing to do with me. I'm trying to find them,' Pearce assured him.

'To do what?'

'They're going to try to find another way to distribute their product. I have to stop them.'

Cresci paced thoughtfully.

'Who else could help them get their product onto the street?' Pearce asked.

'You were watching the bar?' Cresci asked.

Pearce nodded.

'But you're not a cop? And your accent means you're probably not FBI either.'

Pearce shook his head. He knew what Cresci was thinking. He had him pegged as a spy.

'Do you have resources? If I gave you a phone number, could you trace it?' Cresci asked.

Pearce's heart leaped. 'Yes,' he replied simply.

'Malek gave us a contact number,' Cresci explained. 'If he still has the phone with him . . .' the implication was left hanging. 'I was going to ask one of our law enforcement contacts to try to trace it,' Cresci went on. 'But your need is greater. And if there's anything left of these men . . .'

'I'll tell you where to find them,' Pearce assured him.

'Good,' Cresci replied. 'Good.'

Pearce hurried from the gym with Leila trailing.

'Why didn't he give it to you before?' she asked when he'd filled her in.

'Maybe he didn't think I could trace it,' Pearce replied. 'Or maybe he didn't trust me?'

Cresci's motivation wasn't important. What mattered was finding out whether Ziad still had the phone.

'Can you track it?' Pearce asked.

Leila nodded. 'I have what I need in the van. It shouldn't take long, provided it hasn't been disabled or destroyed.'

Pearce produced his Ghostlink and called Brigitte.

'*What happened?*' she asked.

'He gave us a number,' Pearce replied. 'If it's valid, I want you ready to deploy to the location.'

'*Copy that,*' Brigitte said. '*We're standing by.*'

Chapter 125

'I'm sorry,' Brigitte said. She didn't have the strength to face Wollerton, so she kept her eyes on the road. They were heading for an address Leila had given them. Brigitte was sitting beside Clifton, who navigated the evening traffic. 'I shouldn't have taken that decision alone.'

'No you shouldn't,' Wollerton replied from the back seat, his voice softening as he spoke. 'But I think you've already paid a high price. It's written on your face.'

Brigitte turned towards her window so Clifton couldn't see her fighting to control her emotions.

'What did they do to you?' Wollerton asked.

She didn't answer. She couldn't. Even though they'd recovered a crate of patches from the *Elite Voyager*, Brigitte's future was still uncertain. She had no idea how long the patches remained effective. Did they have an expiry date? What were the long-term consequences of her disability? Even if the patches lasted indefinitely, what had her condition done to her life expectancy? Then there were the less pressing issues, such as whether she'd always experience a prolonged fentanyl high whenever she applied a fresh patch. What would the synthetic opiate do to her operational effectiveness? She didn't feel impaired, but would she even realize if she was?

She couldn't share these questions with either of her

companions because of the risk they'd consider her weak or somehow incapable. Clifton might insist she return to base, and Huxley Blaine Carter might fire her. And the worst of it was they'd have been right to do so. She was vulnerable. An adversary simply had to remove her patch and she'd be dead within seconds. It was another reason she couldn't talk to these men. The fewer people who knew about her condition, the safer she'd be.

'I don't want to talk about it,' she said at last. 'I just want you to know I shouldn't have done what I did to you.'

'I appreciate it,' Wollerton replied.

No one said anything else until they reached Ohio Avenue ten minutes later. Warehouses lined both sides of the street, which ran almost parallel to the Duamish Waterway. Those that backed onto the river were constructed of functional grey concrete, and were featureless apart from long corrugated steel canopies that covered the loading bays. An unbroken run of huge steel silos stood on the other side of the street. The address Ziad had given them was a concrete building at the very end of Ohio Avenue, where it met the waterway. Clifton parked in a loading bay fifty yards from their target. According the plans Leila had been able to obtain, the building had two entrances; one on the street and the other on the waterfront. The street entrance was a metal door next to a much larger roll shutter that offered access to the loading bay.

The neighbouring businesses were closed and the street was otherwise deserted. Brigitte checked the time: 9.07 p.m. The working day was long over, so there was minimal risk of them being troubled by witnesses.

'What's the plan?' Wollerton asked.

'Pearce told us to wait until he gets here,' Clifton replied.

'We can spitball,' Wollerton responded.

'Frontal,' Brigitte replied. 'Go through the door. Set the charges.'

'Bold,' Wollerton remarked. 'But I don't see any other option.'

Chapter 126

Ziad Malek sat on the toilet, shaking. They'd spent the day preparing for the night's operation. He wasn't in the loop, but he got the sense Elroy was getting close to finding another distributor. And tonight they would unleash the first of the patches on Seattle's unsuspecting population. Ziad had spent much of the day trapped with his own thoughts and Essi's ghost had visited him often. He tried to reason with her, to explain why she'd deserved her end, but when she challenged him about all the deaths he was about to cause, it became harder to argue with her. The suffering at Al Aqarab had been necessary to escape. It was payback for all the cruelty he'd experienced in the rotten prison.

The Meals Seattle attack, the assault on the community centre, all part of a rational revenge. Even Essi's death, which brought him to the brink of tears every time he thought about it, had been justified. She'd betrayed him and taken another lover in his place. But this, what they were planning to do? These poor people had done nothing to deserve what was going to happen to them.

'What have you done?' Ziad asked aloud, and his voice echoed around the cubicle.

What have you done? Essi's voice asked. *What have you become?*

Not the man I wanted to be, Ziad thought. *What have I done?*

He took out his phone and thought about calling the police, the FBI, Cresci, anyone who might stop the horror, but as he held the device, he thought of the patch on his shoulder. Why shouldn't others share his fate?

You're confused, Essi's voice said. *You need help.*

No, Ziad replied inwardly. *You want me to be weak.*

He slipped the phone into his pocket and wiped the tears from his eyes. He pulled up his trousers, flushed the toilet, stepped out of the cubicle and went to the basin. He ran the taps, washed his hands and splashed water on his haunted face. He didn't recognize the man who stared back at him, nor did he much like the look of him, but they were stuck with each other.

He'd just moved to the dryer when the men's room door swung open.

'Everything OK?' Elroy asked. 'I heard you talking to someone.'

'Yeah,' Ziad replied. 'I'm good. Just couldn't get the can to flush.' It was a weak lie, but it was all he could think of.

'It's working now though?' Elroy asked.

'Yeah,' Ziad said.

'Good,' Elroy remarked. 'It's time for us to go.'

He stepped forward and put a reassuring hand on Ziad's shoulder.

'Big picture, Ziad,' he said. 'Just think about the big picture.'

Don't do it, Zee, Essi's voice said, but he knew he couldn't fight the inevitable. He was a monster and he had to stay with his own kind. Ziad nodded sadly and followed Elroy out.

Chapter 127

Pearce and Leila were approximately fifteen minutes from the target when his Ghostlink sounded.

'Go ahead,' he said.

'*A vehicle just left the location,*' Brigitte replied. '*Navy-blue Chrysler minivan, license plate nine-five-four-Alpha-Delta-X-ray. Do you want us to follow?*'

Pearce looked at Leila, who was monitoring the cell phone signal in the back of the van.

'It's on the move,' she confirmed.

'We'll take it,' Pearce told Brigitte.

'*We've got one heat signature at the location,*' she replied. '*We should take it.*'

Pearce thought for a moment. 'OK,' he conceded. 'Be careful.'

'*Copy that,*' Brigitte acknowledged. '*You too.*'

'They're heading north,' Leila said.

Pearce nodded and pulled to the side of the road. He allowed a run of cars to pass and then swung a U-turn, putting them on an intercept with the van.

Twenty minutes later, they had eyes on it. A Chrysler minivan with blacked-out windows.

'We should alert the police,' Leila suggested. 'Have them pulled.'

Pearce nodded. 'Phone it in.'

Leila used a burner to make the call. She put it on speaker. '*Nine-one-one, what's your emergency?*' the operator said.

'I'm travelling north on Second Avenue between Lenora and Blanchard, and I've just seen a man flashing a gun. It looked like an assault rifle,' Leila replied. 'He was in a navy-blue Chrysler, license plate nine-five-four-A-D-X.'

'*Ma'am, can you stay on the line please?*' the operator asked.

'Please hurry, I think he's going to hurt someone.' Leila ended the call. 'Window please.'

Pearce lowered his window, while Leila used a cloth to wipe the phone. She leaned forward and dropped it outside, and Pearce heard it shatter against the road. He closed the window and kept his eyes peeled for police, but as the minutes went on, he grew increasingly surprised by the lack of response.

'What the hell's going on, Scott?' Leila asked.

'I don't know,' Pearce mused. 'Maybe they've got another Hill on the payroll?'

The Chrysler turned right onto Broad Street, and Pearce followed. He saw the Space Needle directly ahead, its bulbous cap lit up against the night sky. The Chrysler continued north for a while and then pulled into an access road that led to the service areas behind the Lightstorm Arena, one of Seattle's largest music venues. A large crowd was gathered outside the main entrance, waiting to be let inside, and a large banner advertised 'Submission' and listed a number of DJs.

'They're going to start tonight,' Pearce said. 'They're going to put it on the street themselves.' He looked at the young faces in the gathered crowd. 'They're going to sentence those people to death,' Pearce continued. 'I have to get inside.'

Chapter 128

Lieutenant Joe Spinoza sat in his car and watched the crowds filing into the Lightstar Arena. There were still risks attached to mass gatherings, but everyone going inside the place was tested for coronavirus, and people, young people in particular, couldn't be expected to huddle in their homes while their lives ticked by. There were those who complained about the dangers of such things, but Spinoza knew from bitter experience that life was one big gamble.

The storm had finally run out of anger and the rain had stopped. Wind still whipped the grey clouds across the sky, but the people queuing outside the vast arena no longer had to worry about getting soaked. A huge billboard above the entrance advertised the event as Submission and a tagline advised people to 'submit yourself to the rhythm'. A playbill beneath the tagline featured artists such as Sub Focus, Camo and Krooked, Netsky and Keeno. The names didn't mean anything to Spinoza, who preferred old school bands like Pink Floyd and Led Zeppelin.

His radio crackled to life. '*Command watch Lima-Alpha, this is dispatch.*'

'Go ahead,' he responded.

'*We just got a report of a 10-32 near your location. Suspect vehicle is a navy-blue Chrysler minivan, license number nine-*

five-four-Alpha-Delta-X-ray,' the dispatcher said. '*Unknown caller, unidentified cell phone. Please advise.*'

As watch commander and liaison for the event, Spinoza had ultimate responsibility for safety and security at the arena.

'Let me check with venue security,' he replied.

'*Copy that,*' the dispatcher acknowledged.

Spinoza opened the glove compartment and took out the cell phone he never wanted his colleagues to know about.

Elroy Lang was in loading bay four when one of his three phones rang. The muffled sound of a thumping bassline pulsed through the building like a jackhammer heartbeat, but the frenetic music wasn't too loud in the service areas, so he could still hear the caller clearly when he answered the phone.

'*We just had a report of a gunman in your vehicle,*' Spinoza said.

After Evan Hill's sudden death, Elroy had been forced to work with the resources available to him. Of all Hill's recruits, Elroy had chosen Lieutenant Joe Spinoza because he exhibited the perfect combination of greed, cowardice and viciousness. He wasn't as cunning as Hill, but that deficiency had its advantages. He was easier to manipulate and there was little chance of him ever seeing the big picture.

'Probably a crank,' Elroy said, but he suspected otherwise and inwardly questioned how anyone could have known about the vehicle. He looked at his companions. He had no doubts about Narong and Buck, but Ziad was troubled. Elroy had assumed he was suffering the angst of a man whose old self was slowly being destroyed, but might he have had an attack of conscience? Could he have called the police? Is that what he'd been doing in the men's room?

'Ziad,' Elroy said. 'Can I see your phone?'

Ziad produced the device and unlocked it before handing it over. There was nothing in the call history.

'Thank you,' Elroy said as he returned it. 'Almost certainly a crank,' he told Spinoza.

'*I said I'd check with the venue,*' Spinoza told him.

'Well, let's do that,' Elroy said.

He turned to the security station, where Ziad, Narong and Buck were being given a cursory check by Paul Naylor, the head of venue security. As instructed, Naylor did not search the men's bags, which were packed with patches. The mini-van was parked in the loading bay and contained another six such bags to resupply Ziad, Narong and Buck when they ran out of the first batch of product.

Elroy approached Naylor and indicated his phone. 'Lieutenant Spinoza wants to know if you're happy with building security.'

Naylor looked at the two uniformed guards who staffed the security station. They had no idea of their boss's true loyalties. 'I hire the best people in the business,' Naylor said, stroking the clueless workaday guards' egos. 'I'm very happy with the security arrangements here.'

'Did you get that?' Elroy asked.

'*Yeah,*' Spinoza replied.

'Then you can report back to your headquarters,' Elroy advised before hanging up.

'You're all good,' Naylor said, waving Ziad, Narong and Buck into the arena.

'We may need to get some more gear from the van later,' Elroy remarked.

'No problem,' Naylor replied. 'These men have been cleared to come and go,' he told the two guards. He handed Elroy,

Ziad, Buck and Narong all-area access passes, and they followed him into the building.

'What happened at RPM?' Naylor asked when they were out of earshot of the guards.

In addition to being head of venue security, Paul Naylor was a paid-up member of the Red Wolves.

'We think it was the Salamovs or Cresci,' Elroy lied. 'Someone must have tipped them to what we're doing.'

'When we're finished here, we've got to go after those sons of bitches,' Naylor said.

'Of course,' Elroy responded. 'In the meantime, Eddie Fletcher's last wish was that you should help us convert some of these youngsters into customers.'

Naylor nodded. 'Let's get to it then.'

Chapter 129

Clifton, Brigitte and Wollerton congregated at the boot of the SUV. Clifton used a pair of infrared goggles to check the warehouse.

'Still only one heat signature,' he said, handing the goggles to Brigitte.

When she looked through them, she saw the figure of a man in a chair. 'We take him out before we set the charges,' she said flatly.

She shouldered two cases of CL-20 and Wollerton took the third. They inserted in-ear transceivers and Clifton did likewise.

'I'll let you know if he moves,' he told them.

Brigitte grabbed an HK416 assault rifle and put four magazines in her belt. Wollerton opted for a Glock 19 and filled two of the pockets of his tactical jacket with clips.

'Test one,' Brigitte said.

'Test two,' Wollerton responded.

'Test three,' Clifton replied. 'We're good to go.'

Brigitte and Wollerton set off for the unit, hugging the building line as they jogged along the street. When they reached the metal door, Brigitte reached into one of the pouches on her belt for a tiny quantity of explosive putty and a detonator. She pressed the putty into the lock, set the detonator, and she and Wollerton stepped back and turned away as the device went off. The tiny explosive detonated with a bang, and the door swung inwards.

'He's on the move,' Clifton advised them.

Brigitte was first through the door. Wollerton followed her into an anteroom that was separated from the rest of the unit by frosted glass. Brigitte saw the shadow of a man running across the warehouse before it disappeared behind a large solid object.

'He's at the rear,' Clifton advised.

She signalled Wollerton to move on, and he nodded. The two of them crept through the anteroom to the door that led to the warehouse.

Brigitte didn't know whether it was the fentanyl or if at some level she already considered herself dead, but her heart wasn't racing as it normally would, and instead of nervous adrenalin, she felt completely calm.

She held the door open for Wollerton and followed him into the main storage area. The warehouse was full of crates like the one she and Pearce had recovered from the *Elite Voyager*. There must have been about 1500 of them, stacked twelve high. Each one represented a twenty-year supply of patches. But it was bad enough having just one box in the world. Much as she knew she needed the stuff to live, Brigitte didn't want to run the risk of this poison hitting the streets. If Huxley Blaine Carter's people couldn't synthesize a replacement or a cure in the time one box would give her . . . well, she'd have to cope with the consequences.

Brigitte put down the explosive charges and Wollerton did likewise, and they swept the space. They split up to circle the boxes in different directions. Wollerton took the right side and Brigitte the left.

She was halfway down when she heard a couple of gunshots, followed by a scuffle. She ran round the stacks of boxes and when she turned the second corner, she saw Wollerton struggling with a lean, muscular man with long straight hair. They'd obviously disarmed each other; their weapons were on the warehouse floor a few feet away. She immediately noticed the man was wearing latex gloves and realized he was trying to touch Wollerton with the toxin.

Brigitte raced towards the pair and yanked the assailant away. Freed of the man's weight, Wollerton stumbled back and fell over. The assailant turned to face Brigitte and reached a gloved hand out and touched her neck. She felt the clamminess of the toxin and stared at her attacker, who eyed her with a look of triumph.

Victory turned to uncertainty and then dismay as he realized the toxin was having no effect. Brigitte levelled her HK416 at the man's chest and pulled the trigger. He jerked violently when a burst of bullets hit him. He staggered as blood spread from the wound, and fell backwards.

'Thanks,' Wollerton said. 'You OK?'

Brigitte nodded.

'I thought he got you,' Wollerton remarked.

Brigitte swiftly wiped her neck with her gloved hand. 'No,' she said. 'He just missed.' She pointed to the CL-20 cases. 'I'll check the rest of the building. You set the charges.'

Brigitte moved towards the large roll shutter that fronted the waterway. She could see a jetty through windows either side of the shutter, but there were no vessels at the moorings. A doorway to her left took her into a corridor that ran along the back of the building. She found a kitchen and a ladies' room, both of which were empty. There was no one in the men's room either. When Brigitte caught sight of herself in the mirror, she was dismayed by how much she'd changed. She looked gaunt and traumatized, as though all the joy of life had been drained from her.

'*We're set,*' Wollerton's voice sounded in her earpiece.

Brigitte turned away from her troubling reflection and hurried towards the exit.

Six minutes later, they were sitting in Clifton's BMW watching the former NSA director use the infrared field goggles to survey the surrounding buildings for people.

'They're empty,' he said.

'Let's go then,' Wollerton told him.

He started the car and pulled a U-turn. As they drove away, Brigitte produced a remote detonator. She glanced over her shoulder at Wollerton, who nodded. He looked satisfied with a successful mission, but he couldn't have known she was about to destroy a huge cache of the only thing keeping her alive. Feeling conflicted and afraid, Brigitte flipped the safety and turned the detonator key. A huge explosion rocked the neighbourhood and a shockwave buffeted the car. When she looked through the rear windscreen, she saw a fireball rise into the sky.

Chapter 130

Thousands of people threw their hands in the air and screamed when a British MC told them to 'make some noise for Sub Focus.'

A blond DJ in his mid-thirties took to a raised platform at the centre of a huge stage, and started playing a thumping drum and bass track that sent the crowd wild. They started dancing to 180 beats per minute, and the MC whipped up their energy with a freestyle rap over the tune. Huge LED screens displayed a rapidly changing set of psychedelic patterns and a pulsating laser show shot colours over the vast auditorium.

'They won't be on the dance floor. Too hard to do business,' Pearce said. 'Check the access corridors.'

He watched the image on screen change as the tiny drone banked left and flew towards an open doorway. He and Leila had parked a block from the venue and had deployed a tiny bumble bee drone to infiltrate the arena.

The device was the type of equipment he expected to see at Six. It had crawled along the computer console in the back of the van like a real insect before Leila had piloted it into the air and sent it through the van's open windows.

Rather than the evacuated crowd they'd hoped to see following their warning to the police, the drone had showed them almost-empty streets around the arena. A handful of cops and security guards milled around First Avenue, as the last few latecomers had hurried to join the line of stragglers snaking into the venue. Leila's call to the police had been futile.

'Looks like the cops didn't take you seriously,' Pearce had observed. 'Or they've got others on their payroll.'

Leila had piloted the drone into the building and flown it into the huge, vaulted space where thousands danced to the pounding beat.

Now, the tiny craft swept along the south access corridor, which ran parallel to the bottom end of the dance floor and was home to food and drink concessions and the toilets. With most dancing, the corridor was quiet, but there were still a few dozen people in every section, chatting, drinking, and milling around. Pearce saw a couple of guys surreptitiously slip pills into their mouths before heading into the arena.

'There.' Leila indicated a group of men coming towards the drone.

Pearce recognized Ziad, Elroy and Narong Angsakul, but the other two men were unfamiliar. Narong, Ziad and one of the others, a large man with the face of a fighter, had messenger bags slung over their shoulders, and Pearce had no doubt about the poison they contained.

'Stay on them,' he said. 'I'm going in.'

'Test the new eyes before you go,' Leila suggested.

Pearce nodded and produced the tiny contact lens case she'd given him after they'd parked. He opened it and prodded one of the lenses until it stuck to his fingertip. He pressed it into his eye and one of the screens in the back of the van sprang to life and displayed what Pearce was seeing. It was unnerving to watch the screen showing him watching the screen, so he looked away from the infinity pattern and focused on Leila.

'Looking good. You'll need an earpiece too,' Leila said, handing him a tiny device which he slipped inside his ear.

He opened the side door and jumped into the street. The rain might have stopped, but the sky was still dark with thick cloud, and a fresh wind hinted the storm might not be over.

'Be careful, Scott,' Leila said.

He nodded. Unlike the men he was going to face, he didn't have the time or connections to circumvent building security, and was going in unarmed.

'Always,' he assured Leila, before sliding the door shut.

Chapter 131

'*They've split up,*' Leila said, as Pearce was tested for coronavirus and then patted down by a security guard.

The man waved him forward and he showed his ticket to a venue steward, who allowed him into the arena.

'Just tell me where,' Pearce said as he hurried along the south access corridor.

The place smelled of sweat and cheap beer, but the volume of the music almost drowned out the other senses.

'*Third set of men's toilets on the west corridor,*' Leila replied.

Pearce broke into a jog and wove between groups of teenagers and twenty-somethings who'd gathered around the concessions or were queuing for the toilets. He turned right and ran along the west corridor until he found the third set of toilets.

'*The two bigger guys are in there,*' Leila said.

Pearce looked up, but couldn't see the drone that gave her eyes on him. Ignoring the complaints of the guys in the short queue, Pearce pushed his way into the busy men's room. The grim stench of urine hit him the moment he entered, and he saw an unbroken line of men at the urinals. A couple of guys hung around the occupied stalls, waiting their turn, and a few men washed their hands at a line of basins. One of the men who'd been walking with Ziad and Elroy was standing in the corner, behind the door. He wore a badge that identified him as Paul Naylor, the head of venue security.

'Can I help you?' he asked.

'Where is he?' Pearce responded, as he ran along the line of cubicles, ducking down to peer beneath each door. He heard movement behind him, and turned to see Naylor bearing down on him with an extendable baton in his hand.

Pearce dodged the metal tip as it whipped out and sliced the air where his head had been, and he ran at Naylor, coming inside his reach and throwing a combination of slaps and punches that disorientated and dazed the man. Using an Aikido *morote dori*, Pearce grabbed Naylor's wrist, twisted it back and forced him to release the baton. Pearce caught the weapon as it fell and hammered it into Naylor's face, knocking him cold.

Pearce didn't pause for breath. As the other patrons started edging their way out of the men's room, he continued along the stalls and found what he was looking for in the penultimate cubicle; three pairs of shoes. When he moved closer to the door, he heard a voice say, 'Probably just a scuffle. Are you interested or what?'

'How much?' another voice asked.

'No charge. If you like what I've got, my number's on the pack. Just call for more.'

Pearce stepped back and kicked the door in. It clattered open and hit three men. Pearce recognized the closest as the guy who'd been with Ziad and Elroy. He was a huge, muscular man with eyes devoid of any humanity. The other two occupants were teenagers and they both held patches wrapped in wax paper.

The huge man pulled a gun from the messenger bag slung

over his shoulder, but Pearce was too fast and barged into the cubicle. He sent the big man hurtling into the divider, which collapsed, and they tumbled into the next cubicle and onto the unsuspecting occupant, who cried out.

Pearce hit the huge man with the baton, and the guy stumbled out of the cubicle swinging his gun round. Pearce lashed out with the baton, struck his opponent's arm, and the gun flew clear and clattered across the tiles into another cubicle. Men scattered, running from the room fearfully as Pearce and the huge man traded blows.

Pearce feinted with his left, and the man ducked, bringing him within range of the baton. Pearce hit him and he staggered back, dazed, but quickly came to his senses and lashed out with a kick that connected with Pearce's right fist and sent the baton flying.

'You've got company,' Leila said. 'Security joining in about twenty.'

'You can't stop us,' the big man said. 'We're inevitable.'

He lunged forward with a combination of punches that Pearce dodged and deflected. The guy was a proficient street brawler, nothing more.

Pearce ducked a wild punch and drove his fist into the man's ribs, before striking his chin with a left that almost knocked him off his feet. As the man staggered back, Pearce pressed his advantage and kicked him in the gut. When he crumpled, Pearce drove a fist into the bridge of his nose and the giant collapsed.

Pearce heard a commotion and heavy footsteps outside the men's room. He pulled the messenger bag from the man's shoulder and cast around for the baton or the fallen pistol, but he couldn't see either.

'Move, move,' a voice outside said urgently. Pearce guessed it was one of the approaching security guards and knew he was out of time.

He ran from the men's room and pushed his way through the crowd that had gathered in the corridor outside.

'Thank god you're here,' he said to the lead security guard. 'They're going to kill each other.'

As the security guards rushed into the men's room, Pearce broke through the edge of the crowd and saw the two teenagers who'd been in the cubicle. They were hurrying from the scene and Pearce ran to catch them.

'Give it up,' he said, confronting them.

'What?' one of them ventured.

'I don't have time. You think it's fentanyl, but that man gave you a poison that will kill you. He wasn't a drug dealer. He was a terrorist and unless you want to die, you'll give me those patches now.'

The teenagers exchanged fearful looks.

'Not worth the aggro, bro,' one said to the other, before they both ferreted in their pockets for the patches and handed them over.

'What have you got?' Pearce asked, as the two frightened teens hurried away.

'*I'm working on it,*' Leila replied. '*I can't find the others.*'

The security guards emerged from the men's room and scanned the corridor. Pearce saw members of the crowd gesture at him, and he set off as the guards started in his direction. He went through one of the large access doors into the main arena.

'I'm catching heat here,' Pearce remarked.

'*I said I'm working on it,*' Leila replied. '*You've got a big enough crowd. Lose yourself.*'

Chapter 132

Pearce ran into the huge arena. The pounding music was almost painfully loud and the vast space was packed with thousands of people dancing wildly. The smell of sweat and lust filled the ripe air. Pearce skirted the edge of the crowd and scanned the gallery of faces that were lit by the intermittent lasers and staccato lights.

'What have you got?' he asked.

'*To your right. Two o'clock,*' Leila said, and Pearce pushed into the crowd.

After a few steps he saw a familiar face in the thronging mass. Ziad Malek was watching the people around him. Pearce recognized the expression on the man's face; doubt. He was having second thoughts. Pearce had no such trouble. He saw the satchel hanging over Ziad's shoulder and headed straight for him.

Ziad registered Pearce when he was a few paces away, and tried to back off, but the crowd hemmed him in.

'I don't want to hurt you,' Pearce shouted over the thumping bassline. 'And I don't think you really want to be here.'

It was true. Ziad's eyes were brimming and his face came alive with anguish.

'Elroy Lang has used you,' Pearce said. He produced the

letter he'd been carrying with him ever since he'd left Deni Salamov's house. 'Essi Salamov wanted you to have this.'

Ziad looked at the envelope and registered the handwriting. He wiped away a tear as Pearce stepped forward and placed the envelope in his left hand. Ziad stood frozen for a moment while the world danced around him. He looked at the letter as though it might be tainted.

'She wouldn't want you to do this,' Pearce told him, and he gently reached for the strap of the satchel. 'It's OK,' he assured Ziad as he slipped the bag off the man's shoulder and slung it over his own, beside the one he'd taken off the man in the bathroom.

'Where's the last bag?' Pearce asked as he backed away.

'*I've got it,*' Leila replied. '*To your nine, at the heart of the crowd.*'

As Pearce pushed through the mass of dancers, he glanced over his shoulder and saw that Ziad Malek had opened the letter and started to read.

Chapter 133

Elroy Lang heard everything go wrong. Buck's in-ear transceiver broadcast the sounds of him being attacked in the men's room. Ziad had crumbled like a simpering wretch. Everything they'd worked for was at risk. All their careful plans to use the boy Ziad to take over the Salamovs' distribution connections, all the work that had gone into developing and manufacturing the product in sufficient quantity, years of effort to perpetrate an attack that would have global resonance and now he and Narong were wandering around a concert trying to persuade American youths to willingly take poison. Despite his talk of revolutions coming from small beginnings, this felt like a failure, and it seemed to have been caused by one man.

Elroy and Narong were trying to push their way across the huge arena. Elroy stopped suddenly when he caught sight of Scott Pearce, and Narong followed his gaze.

Elroy stepped towards his companion, and drew as close as a lover as he spoke into Narong's ear. 'That man's name is Scott Pearce. He worked for MI6. When you joined us, we made a promise to help you find your brother's killer. There he is.'

Narong looked at Elroy in disbelief.

'That's him. I swear a blood oath of honour,' Elroy assured him. 'He followed you from Thailand.'

Elroy saw anger flare in Narong's eyes. His whole being seemed to come alive with hatred.

'He was in Islamabad. He was the one who killed Chatri, your brother,' Elroy said.

Narong didn't wait to hear any more, and as Elroy pushed through the crowd, he saw Narong reaching into his messenger bag for his gloves.

'*Be careful,*' Leila said, her voice reaching Pearce through his in-ear transceiver. '*Elroy is moving on. Narong is at your eleven o'clock.*'

Pearce turned, and through the crowd he saw Narong Angsakul eyeing him over the heads of the frenetic dancers.

'*You've got another problem,*' Leila said. '*Your six.*'

Pearce glanced behind him to see venue security guards fanning across the dance floor, heading towards him. They passed Ziad Malek, who was rooted to the spot, letter in hand, tears streaming down his face. Pearce knew the contents of the letter gave the man no room to doubt the nature of his betrayal of Essi and her family. Ziad wept freely. He caught Pearce's eye and hurried away, shamefaced. He didn't look back as he pushed his way towards the exit.

'Scott Pearce,' a voice said.

Pearce turned to Elroy Lang. He wore a suit, but the neck of his shirt was wide open and Pearce saw tattoos and scars on his chest. His eyes had the haunted emptiness of a man who'd seen too much.

'You were an irritation,' Elroy said. 'But now it seems you've become a threat.'

'Elroy Lang,' Pearce said above the music. 'Is that your real name?'

The man broke into a broad smile. 'A threat indeed.'

'I've been looking for your friend for years.' Pearce nodded at Narong.

'And he has been looking for you. You killed his brother,' Elroy said. 'But we declined to tell him who you were. Until now.'

'When it was useful,' Pearce remarked. 'Who the hell do you work for? SVR?'

Elroy scoffed. 'You have no idea what you're dealing with.'

'Hasn't stopped me winning though.'

'Winning?' Elroy replied. 'You don't even know what game you're playing.' He hesitated. 'Goodbye, Mr Pearce,' he said, walking away.

Pearce reached out to grab him, but found himself being pulled back. He looked round to see two security guards had hold of him. He elbowed one and heel-kicked the other. Pearce broke free, but Elroy had vanished into the crowd. He spotted Narong, who kept glancing over his shoulder as he pressed through the mass of dancers. Pearce gave chase and barged through the arena, earning himself curses and abuse from the people he knocked over. The security guards followed, but Pearce was moving more quickly and closed the gap on Narong.

The assassin looked back, his murderous eyes blazing, and when he saw how close Pearce was, he grabbed a young reveller and pulled her in front of him with one arm. She protested but he tightened his grip, and the people immediately around them backed away, creating space for Narong and his hostage.

Narong raised his other hand, and Pearce saw the single latex glove move towards the fearful woman's face. The Thai said something, inaudible over the music, but Pearce didn't need to hear the man's words to understand their meaning.

One more step and she dies.

Chapter 134

Pearce glanced round to see four security guards closing. He couldn't risk the woman's life, and raised his hands in surrender. Narong Angsakul would have to wait for another day.

'*What are you doing?*' Leila asked.

'It's too dangerous,' Pearce replied.

Rather than flee, Narong stood rooted to the spot and eyed Pearce, clearly conflicted. This was the man whose brother he'd killed, and Pearce realized Narong was trying to choose between escape and this opportunity for revenge. Pearce could only imagine what Elroy had told Narong about how his brother had died, and what evil he'd made the man do on the promise he'd help him identify Chatri's killer. It made Pearce think of everything Leila had done in the belief Huxley Blaine Carter would help her find her sister. Pearce recalled the Buddhist truth from his study of philosophy; *trishna*, craving, is the root of suffering. People often misquoted it as 'desire', but *trishna* was more than that. It was obsession. Find out what someone craves and you can make them do almost anything. What things had Narong done on the promise his craving would one day be sated?

Pearce felt strong arms grab him, and when the security guards started to pull him away, he saw Narong reach a decision. Maybe it was the fear of never having another opportunity, or perhaps his hatred was too powerful to let him leave. Whatever the motivation, Narong touched his glove to the woman's cheek, and discarded her like a used sweet wrapper.

As she fell away, one of the men she'd been dancing with made a move for Narong, but the assassin blocked the lunge, punched the man in the face and touched his bare arm with the glove.

'Hey!' Pearce yelled to the guards who were pulling him away. 'He's killing them!'

They looked at Narong, who was fighting his way through the crowd, touching one person after another with his deadly glove. The first woman was already flailing on the ground, gasping for air.

'*The patches,*' Leila said. '*Use the patches.*'

Pearce glanced at the messenger bags he'd taken from Ziad and the huge guy in the men's room. These things were a curse, but for people who were going to die anyway, they were a blessing.

'We can save them,' he shouted at the security guards, who were transfixed by the unfolding horror.

Over a dozen people were on the floor, choking, and the surrounding crowd had started to panic. Pearce recognized the beginnings of a stampede as people fought to get away from Narong.

'Give them these,' Pearce said, grabbing a handful of patches and some latex gloves from inside one of the bags. 'Don't touch them without their wrappers. Use these gloves. These things will save those people's lives.'

The guards released their grip, and Pearce handed out the patches and gloves. He pulled on a pair himself.

'And stay away from him,' Pearce said, pointing at Narong. 'He's the Midas Killer. If he touches you, put one of these patches on.'

Each guard took some of the patches. They all put on a pair of gloves, and gave Narong a wide berth as they crossed the arena to help the fallen. Narong didn't pay them any attention; his eyes were fixed on Pearce.

The music was building to a crescendo, which masked the clamour of panic in their little pocket of the arena. Realizing what he was capable of doing, people had cleared out of Narong's path, and he ran at Pearce.

He threw a punch, which Pearce dodged, but the glove came up fast and swept the air inches from Pearce's face. Pearce kicked Narong in the shin and then leaped up and drove his knee into the man's jaw, still swollen from their encounter at the Islamic centre. The bone crunched, and as Narong fell, Pearce drove a fist into the same spot and felt a mess of bone and flesh. Narong's jaw was broken and presented Pearce with a point of weakness, which he targeted even as the assassin fell back in terrible pain. Pearce kicked Narong in the side, catching him in the ribs, and as he bent to absorb the impact, Pearce smashed another fist into the assassin's face. Something gave, and the left side of Narong's jaw hung loose, held on only by sinew and skin. But the assassin still didn't fall. Instead he took a few steps back and reached into his bag. As Narong turned, Pearce caught sight of the edge of a black patch beneath his T-shirt. It clung to Narong's back just above his kidneys. Narong showed Pearce what he had in his hand; a canister like the one he'd used in the Al Aqarab prison break. If it was detonated in here, it could kill hundreds, if not thousands. There was no way Pearce had enough patches to save them all.

He sprang at Narong and threw a combination of punches, forcing the assassin back. But hatred gave Narong strength and he replied with a flurry of punches and kicks that left Pearce reeling.

'For Chatri,' Narong yelled. He held the canister aloft and was about to pull the pin when he was sideswiped by a fire extinguisher. Pearce looked round to see Ziad Malek wielding the bright-red heavy cylinder. Pearce rushed forward as Narong regrouped and kicked the canister from the assassin's hands. It clattered across the arena floor and Narong turned to chase it, but Pearce reached out a gloved hand and tore the patch from Narong's back. When Narong looked back in horror, Pearce grabbed the man's messenger bag and ripped it away from him.

Narong lunged, but Pearce stepped away, and the assassin fell to his knees, choking. He turned and crawled towards the canister, but he was running out of oxygen. Pearce walked over to him, and as his shadow fell on the man, Narong rolled onto his back and stared up. He was crying, but he held Pearce's gaze until the last tears left his eyes and his body fell still.

Pearce looked at the men and women who'd been touched by the Midas Killer, and saw they were recovering. All of them, including the very first woman Narong had touched, were wearing patches given to them by the security guards. Pearce picked up the discarded canister and put it in one of the three messenger bags he carried.

The music stopped and the house lights came on as a voice spoke through the public address system. '*Ladies and gentlemen, the Lightstar Arena regrets to inform you there has been a* security incident at tonight's event. The threat has been contained, but we need you to evacuate the building in an orderly fashion.'

Pearce glanced round and locked eyes with Ziad, who was looking at Narong's fallen body. Pearce moved towards him, but Ziad registered his approach and took a step back. Pearce could see his intent written all over his face, which was awash with tears. Ziad reached under his shirt and ripped off his patch. Almost immediately, he began to splutter and choke.

Pearce raced towards him as he collapsed and did the only thing he could think of. He punched Ziad, knocking him out, and pulled a patch from one of the messenger bags. He peeled off the wrapper and stuck it between Ziad's shoulder blades. He wasn't going to let the man take the easy way out.

'Make sure the cops take this one in cuffed,' Pearce said to the nearest security guard.

The man looked up from tending one of Narong's victims, clocked Ziad, and nodded.

Pearce got to his feet and joined the crowd of people heading for the exits.

'*How are you feeling?*' Leila asked.

'He didn't touch me,' Pearce replied. He drew some puzzled looks from people who'd seen him fighting, but he soon pushed past them into the main throng, where he was just another face among thousands.

'*You're a hero, you know that?*' Leila remarked.

'Don't go getting soppy on me,' he replied.

'*Just this once,*' Leila said. '*And if you ever tell anyone, I'll deny it.*'

Pearce smiled and joined a line of people heading towards a fire exit.

Epilogue

The events in Seattle had created an international scandal. The United States had accused the Chinese government of trying to smuggle a chemical weapon into US territory to target American citizens. To prove it was not complicit, Beijing had purged the Red Wolves. Anyone associated with the group had been arrested and the Qingdao Consumer Products factory had been destroyed. Only Li Jun Xiao and David Song, the two ringleaders, had escaped capture, but Brigitte Attali had been on their tail for three weeks. The patches she'd taken from the *Elite Voyager* kept her alive, but there was a huge government initiative, spearheaded by Redpoint Labs, one of Huxley Blaine Carter's companies, to develop a substitute synthetic PTH. A total of eighteen people been affected at the Lightstar Arena. Clifton had arranged for the Centre for Disease Control to receive the contents of the bags Pearce had recovered from the arena, and Seattle police had found six more messenger bags in a minivan parked in an arena loading bay. Almost a full box – it was sufficient supply to keep the eighteen victims alive for fifty-five weeks, which would hopefully be long enough for Blaine Carter's researchers to develop an alternative.

Brigitte looked across the room at Echo Wu, the brilliant woman who'd helped her track her targets. When Brigitte had found her, Echo had been down to her last patch, and with the Chinese authorities having destroyed all manufacturing and stockpiles, she'd had no way to replace it. Echo had already resigned herself to death and had said her farewells to her husband and children. She'd broken down when Brigitte had presented her with three hundred patches from the *Elite Voyager* supply. Once the reality of a second lease of life had sunk in, Echo had sworn her everlasting gratitude and had joined Brigitte's quest for vengeance.

Echo smiled and stroked the QSZ-92 pistol on her lap. They were in the living room of a mansion in Shashubay on the shores of Lake Balkash in the east of Kazakhstan. The six-bedroom house was full of marble, gilt and smoked glass. It was the kind of showy decoration Brigitte despised, but she expected nothing less from the men who lived here.

She heard a car pull up outside, and checked her weapon one last time. She flipped the Glock's safety and tightened the suppressor. The front door opened and Li Jun Xiao and David Song entered the open-plan hallway, accompanied by two bodyguards. Their faces widened in surprise when they recognized Echo and Brigitte.

The bodyguards reached for their guns, but Echo shot the one on the left, and Brigitte killed the man on the right.

'Very good. We should have known the extent of your abilities by the way you deceived us into thinking you'd gone to Paris,' David Song said. 'We would—'

Brigitte shot David Song before he could say another word. She wasn't interested in anything the man had to say. Pearce had tried to persuade her to bring them in for interrogation, but he'd soon realized it wasn't an argument he could win. These men had done a terrible thing to her.

Li Jun tried to run as his companion pawed at the bloody wound in his gut, but Echo shot him in the back of the head.

Brigitte got to her feet and walked into the hallway. David Song fell to his knees, moaning and clutching at his chest. Brigitte said nothing. The man wasn't worth her precious breath. She took a black patch from her pocket and stuck it to his cheek for a moment. She looked him in the eye and tore it off his face.

'Please,' he said, but he managed nothing else, and began choking as the toxin took hold.

A few moments later, his face turned blue and he toppled forward, dead.

Satisfied with their work, Brigitte and Echo left the house.

Leila sat in the dusty tent and waited. As painful as it had been to postpone the search for her sister, it had been the right choice. Huxley Blaine Carter had kept his word and had thrown his vast resources at the hunt. His investigators had tracked down an aid worker who remembered Hannan, and Leila was now waiting to meet the doctor in a medical tent in the vast Zaatari Refugee Camp.

Gohar, the local liaison, entered, followed by Dr Miriam Abboud, a thin, harried woman.

'Dr Abboud, this is Leila Nahum,' Gohar said.

Dr Abboud shook Leila's hand.

'Dr Abboud, I believe you met my sister.'

Leila's heart filled with joy and she choked back tears of relief as Dr Abboud nodded and started talking about Hannan.

*

Unblemished sky rushed by, giving no sense of speed or distance. It was only when Wollerton sat up that he saw the rugged Snowdonia landscape rolling and folding its way down to the sea. The little two-carriage train rattled along the line that connected Machynlleth with Aberdyfi, following the curves of the coast where the valleys met the waves.

A few minutes later, Wollerton joined a handful of travellers who alighted at Aberdyfi Station. The small station house was closed, but there was a basket out front offering second-hand books in exchange for donations. Wollerton paid it no mind and hurried along the quiet street towards the main road. He pulled his coat tight against the winter chill and strode through the picturesque seaside town.

The butterflies in his stomach made him feel like a first-time lover, but this was no romantic trip. He navigated the back streets, passing grey-stone terraces, and headed up a steep single-track lane towards the high edges of town. Two hundred yards along the lane was a terrace of four Victorian houses. Each stood four storeys high and backed right into a granite cliff that loomed above them. Their elevation, halfway up the cliff face, gave them a grand view of the town, the dunes and the sandy beach, which was being lost to a choppy incoming tide.

Wollerton went to the last house and knocked on the double-width front door. He heard a rush of footsteps and the door swung open to reveal Freya, his eleven-year-old daughter. She was all smiles, and rushed out to embrace him. Luke, his thirteen-year-old son, came out hesitantly, but Wollerton pulled him into a bear hug and tousled his mop of brown hair. The boy had shot up since he'd last seen him.

'You're a giant now, Luke,' Wollerton said, and his son smiled bashfully. 'What's your mother been feeding you?'

Wollerton felt tears threaten as he held his children close to him. He'd kept a promise he'd made to himself in Qingdao, and never intended to go without his kids again. They were his joy.

Wollerton looked up to see Esther emerge from a doorway. She looked softer somehow, as though all the anger and frustration that had blighted their last few months together had dissipated.

'Hello, Kyle,' she said. 'Why don't you come in?'

Pearce stood in Huxley Blaine Carter's huge living room, admiring the majestic view of the Alps. Early snow had capped the nearby peaks in thick powder and gave the scene a picture postcard quality. It was a sight Rasul Salamov would never see. He was facing life in prison for the murder of Detective Evan Hill. As for his father, Deni Salamov, no one had seen or heard of him since the night Essi had been killed. Despite reminding himself of their long history of villainy, Pearce often found himself feeling sorry for the suffering the Salamovs had endured. Ziad Malek had been arrested, and, following multiple suicide attempts, had been hospitalized pending an evaluation to establish whether he was fit to face trial for his crimes.

Pearce heard a door open behind him, and Robert Clifton entered with Huxley Blaine Carter. The billionaire smiled, but Pearce sensed worry and unease.

'Mr Pearce,' Blaine Carter said. 'You did well.'

'How did your father die?' Pearce asked.

Blaine Carter's smile faltered. 'They say it was a heart attack, but I don't think so.'

'And you believe the people who killed him were behind Seattle?'

Blaine Carter nodded.

'And we found links between them and London,' Pearce said. 'And the Midas Killer's brother was one of the Islamabad attackers.'

Blaine Carter's strained expression relaxed and Pearce couldn't help feeling as though he was in the presence of a proud parent. 'You're starting to see it, aren't you, Scott?'

'The MO is the same. Islamabad was an attack on the city, and Black Thirteen targeted kids. The Red Wolves were trying to poison American drug users. This is street espionage. They're targeting civilians.'

'Street espionage,' Blaine Carter said. 'That's a good term for it. In the old days, malevolent actors would attack governments because it was only through the instruments of the state that they could reach people. But the world has changed. Imagine the pressure the American people would have brought to bear on the government if a million people's lives had depended on the steady supply of those patches. It could have thrown the whole country into chaos. Who needs a far-flung war, when you can put civilians on the front line in their own towns and cities?'

'Who's behind this?' Pearce asked. 'The man in the arena, Elroy Lang, laughed when I suggested Russia.'

'You're still thinking in the old way,' Blaine Carter replied. 'Nation states aren't what they once were. The world has moved on.'

'If it's not a country, how do we know who to trust? Or what they want?'

'Both excellent questions,' Blaine Carter said. 'The last time I offered you a job, you turned me down. What do you say now? Will you find the answers to those questions? Will you find out what really happened in Islamabad? In London? In Seattle?'

Pearce reached into his pocket and produced a folded photograph. He crossed the room and laid the picture flat on the top of Blaine Carter's grand piano. It showed Elroy Lang getting into a towncar near the Lightstar Arena. After Pearce's encounter with the man, Leila had used the drone to follow Elroy out of the venue. Before the tiny craft's batteries had died, she'd managed to snap the image of Elroy climbing into his getaway vehicle. But it wasn't Elroy or the car that interested Pearce. It was the man who was already inside the vehicle, whose face was just visible in the back. He wore a light-blue suit and had a long, unkempt salt-and-pepper beard and keen blue eyes.

'When I visited Lieutenant Joe Spinoza in custody, I showed him this picture. He identified the man as Andel Novak and said he worked with Eddie and Kirsty Fletcher and the Red Wolves,' Pearce revealed. 'The trouble is, I've seen this man before, at a Progress Britain meeting in Blackbird Leys. His name then was Markus Kral, Emeritus Professor of Geostrategy at Charles University in Prague.'

Pearce paused and looked Blaine Carter in the eye. 'Minutes after I saw this man at that meeting, two members of Black Thirteen kidnapped me. They tortured me and tried to kill me. So I'll take your job, Mr Carter. And the first thing I'm going to do is find out exactly who this man really is and who he works for. And once I've done that, I'm going to kill him.'

Author's Note

I started planning *Red Wolves* in December 2018, long before the world had ever heard of Covid-19. Writing this note in May 2020, we're in the grip of pandemic and the future is uncertain. It seems likely we'll experience a global economic downturn, and if previous recessions are any guide, we're likely to see an increase in drug abuse, which means the suffering caused by synthetic opioids is likely to spread. If you or anyone you know has been affected by drug abuse, please don't suffer alone. Reach out to one of the many organizations established to help people cope with drug addiction. Wikipedia has a useful international list of such organizations: https://en.wikipedia.org/wiki/Category:Addiction_and_substance_abuse_organizations

We don't know how healthcare systems are going to respond to the challenge posed by Covid-19, whether a vaccine will lead to the eradication of the SARS-CoV-2 virus and the disease it causes, or whether we'll be living with this threat for the foreseeable future. As a contemporary thriller writer, I've taken the decision to assume society will continue to function largely as normal through the use of mass and regular testing. This is the approach that has worked best in countries such as South Korea and Germany, and it seems reasonable to believe these countries will act as models for the rest of the world. If the future proves me wrong, I hope readers will forgive any divergence from reality.

Acknowledgements

I'd like to thank my wife Amy and our three children, Maya, Elliot and Thomas, for being amazing.

I'd also like to thank my editor, Vicki Mellor, my literary agent, Hannah Sheppard, and my screen agent, Christine Glover. I'm extremely grateful for all the hard work and support from Gillian Green, Kate Tolley, Hannah Corbett, Sarah Arratoon, Matthew Cole, Jeremy Trevathan and the whole team at Pan Macmillan. I'd also like to express my gratitude to Andrew Belshaw for looking after me at events, Jot Davies for the wonderful work he did on the *Black 13* audiobook, and Fraser Crichton for his attention to detail copy-editing the Scott Pearce books.

I'm also extremely grateful for all the kind words and support I've had from friends and family, and for the help I've had from so many writers who've generously shared their advice and experiences. I'd also like to thank all the reviewers, booksellers, journalists and readers who have helped spread the word about my books.

As always, I'd like to thank you, the reader, for giving Scott Pearce, Leila Nahum and the team your attention. I hope you enjoyed the book and that you'll join us for another thrilling adventure.